Born and raised just outside Toronto, Ontario,
Amy Ruttan fled the big city to settle down with
the country boy of her dreams. After the birth of her
second child Amy was lucky enough to realise her
lifelong dream of becoming a romance author. When
she's not furiously typing away at her computer she's
mum to three wonderful children, who use her as a
personal taxi and chef.

THE NURSE'S REUNION WISH

CAROL MARINELLI

BABY BOMBSHELL FOR THE DOCTOR PRINCE

AMY RUTTAN

MILLS & BOON

First Published in Great Britain 2020
by Mills & Boon, an imprint of HarperCollins*Publishers*
1 London Bridge Street, London, SE1 9GF

The Nurse's Reunion Wish © 2020 by Carol Marinelli

Baby Bombshell for the Doctor Prince © 2020 by Amy Ruttan

ISBN: 978-0-263-27968-9

MIX
Paper from
responsible sources
FSC
www.fsc.org   FSC® C007454

This book is produced from independently certified FSC™ paper
to ensure responsible forest management.
For more information visit www.harpercollins.co.uk/green.

Printed and bound in Spain
by CPI, Barcelona

THE NURSE'S REUNION WISH

CAROL MARINELLI

MILLS & BOON

For Hannah and Ben
Love you guys
Carol xxxx

CHAPTER ONE

SOME WOULD SAY that Rachel Walker had a superpower.

She was an emergency nurse, slight of build, and looked younger than her thirty-two years, which wasn't much of an advantage. With her fiery red hair and porcelain skin it might be expected that she would blush easily. But Rachel's pale skin rarely flushed. As well as that, her huge green eyes revealed little of her thoughts even as she held someone's gaze.

And while that might not sound like much of a superpower, when a patient was critically ill and terrified, or revealing his innermost troubles, it rather helped that the emergency nurse remained outwardly calm and seemingly unfazed.

Rachel had long ago learnt to hide her deepest feelings.

Growing up in Sheffield, in a loud, happy family, with gregarious parents and four older brothers, she had found it necessary, from an early age, to retain a neutral expression and not let anyone reap the effects of their persistent, albeit good-natured, teasing.

But then, aged six, Rachel had come home from school to a house full of aunts and uncles, neighbours and family friends and found out that her mother had suddenly died. The teasing had stopped and the laughter had faded from the Walker home, and the little girl had quickly discovered that her dad and her brothers could not deal with her grief and tears.

'Take her to the park,' Dad would say when she cried for her mum.

Rachel had duly been taken to the park and pushed on a swing, or spun on a roundabout, or bumped up and down on a seesaw until her brothers had been satisfied that she'd return home smiling, at least for a little while.

The tears would soon start again, of course.

Especially at night, when she'd missed her mum tucking her up in bed and reading her bedtime stories, or when she would wake from a dream calling out for her.

'Come on now, Rachel,' her dad would tell her. 'You're upsetting our Phil with your carry-on.'

When she'd cried one day at school, and they'd had to call her dad to come from work to pick her up *again*, she'd known her tears were causing real problems. Her dad owned his own removal company and, as he'd explained that afternoon, people relied on him to get the job done.

'It's their moving day, Rachel,' he said as she sat in the front of his lorry. 'If I have to be called away, who's going to move them into their new house? And what about the family that are waiting to move in to theirs? You've got them thinking they'll have nowhere to sleep tonight. Now, stop with them tears and be a good girl.'

Then one day it had been 'our Phil' himself who had warned her. 'Enough now, Rachel! Dad doesn't need to hear it. He's upset enough and missing Mum too. You're just making things worse.'

Finally Rachel had stopped with the tears and the questions about her mum. Her emotions hadn't stopped, of course—she'd just learnt to hide them.

This superpower she now possessed hadn't done much

for her relationships, but on this cold February morning, in the Emergency Department of London's Primary Hospital, even though Rachel had only worked there for a week, her particular skill had been recognised.

She had been assigned to the minor injuries unit and was helping a young man with crutches when the intercom buzzed and she heard her name being called by May, the unit manager.

'Excuse me a moment,' Rachel said. But, reluctant to leave the man wobbling, she just went and stood by the curtains, so she could keep an eye on him as she answered the call.

'Yes?'

'Can I ask you to come down to Resus?'

'Sure,' Rachel said. 'I'll just—'

'Immediately.'

As May summoned her, the chimes went off and the request for an anaesthetist to go to the ED went out.

Rachel called over her shoulder to a colleague to come and take over with the young man. Then she made her way through the department, via Reception and the central waiting room, which was particularly full, and through to the main section of the unit, where she could see May standing outside the resuscitation area looking in.

Rachel liked her new unit manager. She was caring in the way of a mother hen, but also wise and sharp.

May gestured for Rachel to stand with her and observe as she told her about the patient. 'Thomas Jennings, eighteen-month-old with query epiglottitis, just arrived in the department. Mother drove him here…thought he had croup.'

Even from this distance Rachel could see that Thomas was a very sick little boy indeed. He sat on his mother's knee, leaning forward and drooling, his breathing noisy and laboured. She could hear the stridor—a high-pitched wheezing—from outside the room.

'Where is everyone?' Rachel asked, because she could only see Tara, a fellow RN, in there.

'Jordan the paediatrician is here,' May explained. 'He's on the phone, out of earshot of Mum, trying to get hold of an anaesthetist. But the on-call team are up on ITU and the second team is in Theatre.'

Sure enough, as soon as May said that the chimes went off again, summoning an anaesthetist to the resuscitation area of the ED.

Epiglottitis could quickly turn life-threatening. It was an inflammation of the flap of cartilage and mucous membrane at the back of the throat that guarded the windpipe. Thanks to immunisation, it was now rarely seen. Still, at any moment little Thomas's airway could become obstructed—hence the need for an anaesthetist to be present.

'Mum's getting upset that we're not doing anything and Tara's getting a bit flustered,' May explained, and then glanced at Rachel, who stood there unruffled, taking it all in.

She must have looked so calm that May felt she had to double-check that she understood the precariousness of the situation.

'You *do* know how quickly a patient with epiglottitis can deteriorate?'

'Yes, May,' Rachel answered calmly. 'Has everything been set up for a tracheostomy?'

'That's why I called for you to come down,' May admitted. 'I'll leave you to it. I'm staying back, so as not to distress the little man with too many people around him, but I'll be hovering should you need me.'

'Thanks,' Rachel said, glad to know that May was near as she walked into the room.

'Morning.' Rachel smiled at both Tara and the mother, but she didn't fuss over the little boy.

His blond hair was dark with sweat and plastered to his head, and he buried his face in his mum's chest at the sight of a new arrival.

The monitors were all turned up and bleeping loudly. Rachel turned the volume down—given all the staff who were close by—doing what she could to make the surroundings less scary.

'He's never been in hospital before,' Mrs Jennings said.

'It's very overwhelming.' Rachel nodded. 'But you're doing great. I know it looks as if we're not doing much, but the most important thing right now is to keep Thomas from getting upset.'

'Where's the anaesthetist?' Mrs Jennings asked, her voice rising in panic.

'On the way,' Rachel said, privately hoping that was the case.

Tara spoke then. 'I was just explaining to Mum that if we can get a couple of local anaesthetic patches onto Thomas it would be a great help when we cannulate him.'

'Good idea—but perhaps Mum could do it,' Rachel suggested, and then looked over to Mrs Jennings. 'I'll show you how.'

There probably wouldn't be time for the cream to take effect before he was cannulated, but hopefully it would save him a little pain and distress, which was the main goal here.

Thomas didn't flinch as his mother copied Rachel's instructions and the patches were applied, which concerned Rachel greatly.

She glanced over to Tara. 'Has everything been set up for the transfer?'

'I was just about to do that,' Tara said.

Thomas had only been in the department for ten minutes, but things had to be moved along speedily, as the situation could change at any minute. And it was starting to. He was becoming increasingly exhausted, and Rachel knew she had to get everything they might possibly need on a trolley as quickly as possible.

'I'm going to get things ready for Thomas's transfer,' Rachel said to the mum, 'but I'll be right here.'

All seemed calm.

All was not.

Outside the room there was a flurry of activity taking place. The paediatrician was alerting the operating theatre, and the anaesthetist, who had just arrived in the hospital and collected his pager, was sprinting down the long corridor towards the ED. Rachel was preparing the trolley, and outside May was calling Security to clear the corridor and hold the lifts while the transfer was made.

It was imperative that the little boy did not become distressed, so the staff were hands-off, leaving it to his mother to comfort him as they hovered discreetly and prepared for the worst.

Rachel started to collect the equipment they would need for the transfer while keeping an eye on Thomas. She glanced out and saw Jordan on the phone, running a worried hand through his hair, but he plastered on a smile when he returned from his call and gave Rachel a nod, then made small talk with Mrs Jennings about his own three children while keeping a very close eye on Thomas.

'There's Nicholas, who is Thomas's age,' Jordan said, 'and the twins are three—'

His words halted as the doors slid open.

'Ah, the anaesthetist is here, Mrs Jennings. This is Dr Hadley.'

Hadley?

Rachel glanced over towards the doors at the sound of the familiar name. And the world as she knew it changed as Dominic Hadley stepped in.

Rachel quickly turned back to the trolley she was preparing, drawing in a deep breath when she suddenly felt giddy.

Dominic Hadley worked at The Primary?

Dominic was a doctor?

An anaesthetist?

How?

When?

Though his voice was slightly breathless from running, it was a deeper and more assured voice than the one she had known. As he spoke with Jordan, Rachel screwed her eyes tightly shut, for she did not know how to face him. How to turn around and deal with this situation?

Because it really was a situation.

Dominic Hadley had hurt her badly.

So badly that it had taken her more than a decade to recover her heart enough to try to love again.

So badly that as she stood there anger, hurt and recrimination fought for first place in the order of her feelings.

But she could not think of that here, so she focused on the soft bleeps of Thomas's monitors and forced the surge of animosity within her to settle. She wondered about Dominic's reaction when he saw her.

Dominic had not a clue.

Yet.

* * *

'I'm just going to let Richard know,' Dominic told Jordan. 'Though I'm not sure if he's in ye—'

His voice halted as a flash of red hair caught his eye and he couldn't help but check the profile of the nurse who was preparing to transfer Thomas up to Theatre.

It happened every now and then—a glimpse of red hair would make him turn his head, or the sound of laughter in a bar would have him scanning the crowd—but then he would remind himself that there hadn't been much laughter at the end of their relationship.

But it couldn't be Rachel, Dominic thought, and dismissed her from his mind as Jordan continued to bring him up to speed.

'Mrs Jennings understands that we won't examine Thomas until we're safely in Theatre, and she's consented to a tracheostomy, should it be necessary.'

Dominic looked over to the anxious woman, who was doing all she could to hold it together for the sake of her son.

'Hello, I'm Dominic Hadley—the anaesthetic registrar.' He gave her a smile, but noted that the little boy whimpered at the rather imposing sight of him so halted his approach. He stood a couple of inches over six foot and, sharply dressed in a navy suit, he was aware he might look rather imposing, so he sat down on the resuscitation bed a little further away from Thomas. 'What would you like me to call you?' he asked.

'Please,' Mrs Jennings said, 'call me Haylee.'

'And do you understand what's happening, Haylee?'

She gave a helpless shrug. 'Not really. The children's doctor said he might need to be put on a breathing machine, and an airway made in his neck...'

'It's called a tracheostomy.' Dominic nodded.

Time was of the essence, but so was explanation. He drew a rudimentary picture of a throat on the pad he carried in his pocket.

'The epiglottis is a flap of tissue at the back of the throat. If that swells so much that we can't get a tube past it, then an incision would need to be made here.' He pointed to the picture he'd drawn and then to the same spot on his own throat. 'That way we can bypass the swelling.'

'But he might not have to have one?'

'We won't know till we look at Thomas's throat. I'd prefer to do that in Theatre, where we can examine him properly and get treatment underway. I'll attempt to secure his airway, though a tracheostomy might well be the only course available to us.'

Haylee looked down at the picture and then to her son, who was working very hard to breathe.

Dominic was deeply concerned and he would feel a lot better if they were in Theatre. 'Thomas really needs antibiotics and IV fluids,' he said. 'But putting in a cannula is only going to upset him, so the very best thing we can do is get him up to Theatre and take care of everything there.'

'I understand that,' said Haylee Jennings as she cuddled her son.

'Have you got anyone here with you?'

'My husband's on his way.'

'Good,' Dominic said. 'I'm just going to let my senior know what's happening and…'

He glanced up to let the nurse know they'd be heading up to Theatre imminently, and it was then that Dominic realised he hadn't been wrong at all.

The nurse was Rachel.

It helped, as an anaesthetist, to have nerves of steel.

For Dominic, it was an acquired trait. Some called him arrogant, but those nerves of steel were invaluable now that he was faced with this unlikely situation.

Dominic looked through Rachel, rather than at her.

In fact, Dominic barely blinked.

'We'll head up shortly,' he informed her. 'I'm going to make a quick call first.'

'Ready when you are,' Rachel replied, in a voice that was both measured and calm.

Yes, a superpower indeed!

As Dominic Hadley selected some drugs and syringes from the cart and stalked off, there was a moment when Rachel wondered if he'd even recognised her.

After all, she'd barely recognised *him*!

There was little about this polished, suave man who commanded the room that compared with the awkward physics geek she had fallen in love with.

Although his thick black hair was the same, still damp from his morning shower, and the soapy male scent of him was familiar. His dark eyes were the same gorgeous velvet brown as they had always been too. He had always towered above her, but he seemed taller now, if that were possible. And he had definitely broadened out, and looked immaculate in his sharp navy suit, pale blue shirt and lilac tie.

Her dad, if he were here, would probably say it was pink…

What sort of man wears a pink tie? Rachel could almost hear her father's thick Yorkshire accent.

With the phone pressed between his ear and his shoulder, Dominic pulled up the drugs he might need, should there be an emergency en route, as he let his boss know the situation.

'Any history?' asked Richard Lewis, the consultant anaesthetist.

'Unvaccinated.' Dominic clipped back his response. But his voice faltered as he glanced over to Resus, where Rachel still stood. There was a whole lot of history right there...

'Healthy little boy until this morning, nil allergies...' He went through the case, and it was agreed that Richard, who was currently on ITU, would meet him up in Theatre.

'We're heading straight up,' Dominic told May as he replaced the phone.

'They're ready for you. Rachel will come up to Theatre with you.'

Dominic felt as if his heart might pump its way up to his throat and wondered if it would be better to object to Rachel escorting him.

'She's new. I need someone who knows what they're doing.'

'Which is why I'm sending Rachel. She might be new but she's worked in Paediatric Emergency up in Sheffield and is very competent.'

'Fine.' He walked over to the cooler and filled a little plastic cup with water, drained it, filled it again, drained it again, and told himself to remove Rachel from his mind entirely. He headed back in, determined to ignore the fact that Rachel had just dropped back into his life.

For now.

'We're going to get Thomas up to Theatre now,' Dominic informed Haylee. 'We'll put you in a wheelchair, with Thomas on your knee, but if there's an emergency on the way, then we've got everything we need to deal with it.'

Rachel—or rather, he told himself, *the nurse*—helped mother and child into the wheelchair as he ran a knowing eye along the equipment she had prepared for the journey.

'Ready?' Dominic checked as Rachel wrapped a blanket around Thomas and his mum.

'Ready,' *the nurse* agreed and gave the mother a smile...

Except it was Rachel's smile, and to Dominic it felt like a punch in the guts. It was summer and spring all rolled into one. It was the memory of Saturday nights watching a movie while eating a curry in bed. It was a forgotten ten-pound note found in her jeans that she'd waved over her head before taking him for breakfast in the café across the street.

But he was determined that her smile would not be his undoing.

'Ready,' Jordan said.

There was a blast of cold air as they left the department and he tried not to notice Rachel briefly rub her bare arms.

It was a reminder for Dominic that Rachel was always cold—and not just in body temperature. He'd never been allowed inside that head of hers, so he did all he could to put her out of his now.

It was a very long walk up the corridor. Rachel's eyes never left Thomas's face as Haylee nervously chatted away. 'I thought he had croup,' she admitted. 'But he was blue when I went to him...'

'Well, he's in the right place now,' Rachel said, doing her level best to keep Haylee as calm as she could.

'Have you worked here long?' Haylee asked.

'I've only been here a week,' Rachel admitted. 'Before that I worked in a paediatric emergency department in Sheffield.'

'I thought I heard a northern accent.' Haylee nodded and looked up at Rachel. 'Do you have any children?'

'No,' Rachel said.

To her utter, aching regret, the answer *was* no, even if it wasn't strictly true. But it was much easier just to say no and deny her son's existence than to walk along a corridor with someone she didn't know and admit to the agony.

'No, I don't.'

The porters were holding the lift for them, and as the group got in, Rachel gave them a nod of thanks, relieved that attention could be diverted from her answer to Haylee's question.

The lift doors closed and Haylee looked up at Jordan. 'So, you've got three children?'

'I do,' Jordan said. 'All boys.'

Rachel held her breath as Haylee asked Dominic the same question. 'What about you, Doctor?'

How would Dominic respond?

For Rachel, worse than having him reveal their past would be hearing about his present. Was she about to learn that he was married with two little ones or one on the way?

As she awaited his response, Rachel found she was holding her breath. Was she going to have to hide her reaction to hearing about a Mrs Hadley? Or a soon-to-be Mrs Hadley? And how would she react to that?

Dominic wasn't about to enlighten anyone.

He would rather be anywhere than in this lift right now. And *this* morning, of all mornings, it was imperative that he keep his private and professional worlds firmly separated.

'I try not to bring my personal life to work, Haylee,' he said, and let out a steadying breath. 'It makes it easier for me to focus.'

Haylee nodded and gave a small smile, not offended in the least at the slight rebuff, and he saw Rachel let go of the breath she'd been holding.

The lift swished them to the second floor, and they were soon gliding along the highly polished corridor and into the controlled world of the operating theatre, where more medical staff awaited them.

'Stay with him,' Dominic ordered Rachel. 'A familiar face might help.'

But Rachel's familiar face most certainly wasn't helping Dominic, so it was Thomas Jennings he kept on his mind as he went off to change into scrubs.

As the theatre nurses checked Thomas's ID, and ran through questions with his mum, Richard Lewis came in and introduced himself.

Jordan was ordering an IV and drugs, but the efficient theatre staff were taking care of that, and Rachel again found that she felt a little giddy.

Not in an about-to-faint way. Just giddy from the heat of Theatre, she tried to convince herself. Of course she was worried about Thomas, but mostly she was overwhelmed by seeing Dominic again—but she never let it show, not even for a second. Even when Dominic returned, dressed in scrubs and a theatre cap, she gave him as banal a look as she could muster.

'Let's get a line in,' Dominic said, and then added to Rachel, 'Can you try to distract him?'

The numbing gel had only recently been applied, but she hoped it would take the edge off the cannula going in. More important, Thomas was increasingly cyanosed and becoming rather listless, so it was imperative they moved quickly.

Haylee cuddled her son while Dominic eased a cannula into his little vein.

'Good boy,' Dominic said when it was all done and hooked up.

Now that IV access had been secured, it was time for Rachel to escort Thomas's mum out of the operating theatre. But before she left, Dominic caught the tearful woman's eye. 'I won't leave his side,' he said.

'Thank you,' Haylee said.

She turned and waved as her son let out a raspy cry, but allowed Rachel to lead her out.

'They'll take the very best care of him,' Rachel said.

'That anaesthetist—he seems to know what he's doing,' Haylee said as Rachel led her to the relatives' room. 'Thomas will be safe with him.'

'Yes,' Rachel said. 'Dr Hadley will take the very best care.'

It was a difficult intubation. Thomas's throat was swollen, and the vocal cords were hard to visualise, but with Richard's quiet and reassuring presence, Dominic got the tube in and thankfully a tracheostomy wasn't necessary. Swabs and bloods were taken, and antibiotics and IV fluids were started.

Thomas was moved over to the ITU, where, sedated and ventilated, his little body could finally start to fight the infection, and it wasn't long before Haylee was allowed to return to her son's side. Only then did Dominic leave him.

'Well done,' Richard said as Dominic took a seat at the nurses' station that looked out over the whole of

ITU and pulled up Thomas's incoming blood work on the computer.

'Thanks.'

Richard turned his head at this rather muted response from Dominic. He noted the pallor on his colleague's face, and saw that his usually suave registrar was suddenly anything but.

'Is everything okay?' Richard checked.

'Not really,' he admitted, and ran a hand over his forehead now that the surprising turn of events had begun to sink in. 'There's a nurse down in Emergency...'

Richard rolled his eyes. This happened all too often where Dominic was concerned. 'You need to learn to let them down more gently,' Richard suggested.

But Dominic was silent.

He knew it would be far more sensible to say nothing. To just let it go.

After all, what had happened between him and Rachel had been more than a decade ago.

Way more than a decade.

It had been thirteen years, in fact.

Yes, better to stay silent, Dominic decided.

Except the shock of the morning had been so great—or maybe it was just that he couldn't hold it in any longer—that he told his senior the truth.

'It's not like that,' Dominic said, for it wasn't a little glitch with an ex or some disgruntled lover that was troubling him.

Rachel had been way more than that.

'I just ran into my ex-wife.'

CHAPTER TWO

'EX-WIFE?' RICHARD did a double-take, perhaps thinking he had misheard or that Dominic was joking.

'Yes.'

'Your ex-wife is working in Emergency? You never said you'd been married. I had no idea.'

How could he have? Dominic thought to himself. Apart from a fleeting conversation with Jordan and his wife, a couple of years ago, he'd never discussed his brief marriage with anyone. To Dominic's colleagues, friends—and lovers—he was the personification of an eternal playboy bachelor.

'It was a long time ago,' Dominic clipped, already regretting saying anything. 'It didn't last for long.'

'What happened?' Richard persisted.

'We were young.' Dominic shrugged and turned back to the computer. 'We got married for all the wrong reasons.'

'Such as?'

But Dominic wasn't going to answer that one.

'We both agreed it was a mistake. I haven't seen her in…' He blew out a sigh. 'Years.'

'And how does it feel to see her now?'

Dominic thought for a moment. How *did* it feel to see Rachel again?

Challenging.

It felt as if every mistake he had ever made in life was suddenly being paraded in front of him, but he played it down to his boss.

'Surprised. I never thought she'd leave Sheffield,' Dominic admitted, but he deliberately didn't offer her name, nor let on that it was Rachel. There were always staff coming and going at The Primary, and he was quietly relieved Richard hadn't picked up on the tension between them this morning. 'She's all about her family.'

'What are they like?' Richard asked.

'Her mum died, so there's just her dad—and she's ever so protective of him. Oh, and there are four hulking brothers. They're all very parochial...' His voice trailed off. He didn't mean it in a derogatory way, but as an outsider it had been impossible to break in to their clique. 'They considered me weak.'

'Weak?' Richard frowned, clearly nonplussed, because Dominic, as well as being tall and broad-shouldered, was incredibly confident and assured.

'A bit of a pansy,' Dominic elaborated. 'And I guess I was back then.'

Richard laughed, but it faded when he saw the serious expression on his colleague's face.

'What was your wife like?'

'Tricky,' Dominic said—which was the understatement of the year.

But he really didn't want to discuss it, so when his pager buzzed he pounced on it and saw that it was Maternity.

'*Your* wife is paging me,' Dominic said, and gave a wry smile. Richard's wife, Freya, was a midwife, and had just started back at work after the birth of their son William. 'I'm needed over in Maternity for an epidural.'

But Richard had more to say on the topic of Dominic's ex-wife. 'I can go and give the epidural. Why don't you go and speak with…?'

Richard was waiting, Dominic guessed, for him to offer a name, but he would not be revealing that.

'It must have been a big shock for your ex-wife too,' Richard said.

'She seemed fine with it.' Dominic shrugged.

Only, he knew that couldn't be true. Rachel buried her emotions deep, and he had been denied access to them right from the start. When they'd first got together he had asked about her mother, wondering how her loss at such an early age had affected Rachel, but she had shut him down. And then, in those final painful days when he'd tried to speak to her about their son, Rachel had made it very clear she did not want him to get close.

Well, she'd got her wish, and although it appeared they might be working together for the foreseeable future, they had never been further apart.

'*I'll* head up to Maternity,' he said.

'No, no.' Richard stood and pulled rank. 'I'm going. There's a patient with COPD down in Emergency. He needs a pre-op assessment. Could you go and take care of that, please?'

Dominic's jaw gritted.

'And while you're there perhaps you could manage a conversation with your ex-wife, to ensure that you're both okay with the situation?'

'We'll be fine.'

'Good. Then you'll have no issue heading down to Emergency.'

'Of course I won't. But as for having a conversation with my ex-wife, there's nothing left to talk about,' Dominic said. 'It was all said and done with years ago.'

Not really.

There had been an awful lot left unsaid.

Rachel had walked back down towards the Emergency Department in somewhat of a daze. She had been completely unprepared to see him and felt utterly sideswiped.

Her move to London was still so new. Of course she knew that Dominic was from here, so she'd been braced to run into him on the street, or in a shop or café, even while telling herself she was being ridiculous—after all, there were more than eight million people living in London.

Not for a second had she expected to see him at work.

A doctor?

An anaesthetist!

When?

He wasn't exactly a people person. In fact, the Dominic she'd known had been rather socially awkward. The Dominic she'd known had had one interest—physics— and had been determined that one day he'd be a research scientist. He'd been heading off to university for just that purpose.

Okay, he'd had *two* interests, Rachel amended as she opened the large double doors to Emergency: physics and sex.

She dared not allow herself to think of the latter, though!

'How's Thomas?' May pounced the second Rachel returned to the department.

'I'm not sure,' Rachel said. 'I took Mum over to the ITU relatives' room, but Thomas was still in Theatre when I left.'

'I'll call them in a little while,' May said.

Rachel looked over to May, who was writing on the

whiteboard as she chatted, and oddly found that she wanted to confide in her.

May, she wanted to say, *how long has Dominic Hadley worked here?* Or, *May, that registrar anaesthetist—well, he just happens to be my ex-husband and I don't know quite what to do.*

But Rachel said nothing.

'Are you okay to go back to work in Minor Injuries?' May asked, taking her glasses off and smiling at Rachel.

'Sure.'

'Would you mind restocking Resus first?' May directed a slight eye-roll at Tara. 'You know what you used.'

Restocking was tedious, but essential—especially in Resus. It was imperative that all the equipment was exactly where it should be when it was needed the most.

A lot of the packs had been opened, though not necessarily used, so there was a lot of replacing and reordering to do. Rachel did so methodically, glad of the chance to get better acquainted with the area.

Tara was taking care of an elderly patient who'd had a seizure. He was currently sleeping while they awaited his transfer to a ward. She joined Rachel in Resus.

'How long did you work in Emergency in Sheffield?' she asked as Rachel replaced the oxygen tubing and mask and checked the suction.

'Three years in Emergency all up. I did hairdressing before I went into nursing.'

They chatted lightly as Rachel worked, though Rachel's heart wasn't really in the conversation. She was still reeling from seeing Dominic that morning, and wondering how on earth they would be with each other when they eventually spoke.

The patient Tara was caring for was soon transferred,

so she came and gave Rachel a hand, both of them checking the intubation tray's contents before sealing it up.

'Keep an eye on Dominic,' Tara said suddenly.

'Sorry?' Rachel blinked.

'Dominic Hadley—the registrar anaesthetist. I saw him looking at you when he was on the phone.'

Rachel decided it was best to act vague. 'What do you mean?'

'I'm just trying to give you a heads-up. Dominic might best be described as "nice while it lasts"—but, believe me, it never does.'

Rachel could hear the bitterness in Tara's voice. It was clear there was history between her and Dominic, and from the sound of things, he had become a bit of a player. It was all just so at odds with the man she had once known.

She wondered what Tara's reaction would be if she told her she had once been married to him, and decided there and then that her and Dominic's past would *not* be joining them at The Primary.

There was no way she wanted the fact they'd been married to get out. And aside from that…

'I'm engaged,' Rachel said, 'and even if I weren't…'

She left it there, because it felt safer to do so than to let her imagination wander down *that* track.

No way!

Her heart had been placed under lock and key after she and Dominic had broken up. It had taken years for her to forge another relationship. There had been a couple of cursory attempts at dating, but they hadn't worked out. And then, when she'd first started working in Emergency, she'd met Gordon, a friend of her flatmate, who was kind and made her feel safe.

When the accounting firm he worked for had offered

him a promotion that had required him to move to London, Gordon had asked her to join him. It had felt like a big leap to agree to live with him, on top of moving cities and jobs for him, but the night before they'd left for London Gordon had, at the leaving party her dad had thrown for them, asked her to marry him. And now they were engaged.

Not that she wore her ring to work.

With the restock done, Rachel signed off and headed back to the minor injuries section. But an hour or so later, unable to concentrate and desperate for a moment's peace, she said she was going to find her cardigan and made her way to the changing rooms. Without even bothering to switch on the light, Rachel sat on the bench in semi-darkness, the sounds of the Emergency Department muffled behind the thick door, and put her head in her hands, trying to process things.

Dominic was a doctor.

That nerdy teenager she had known was now a sharp-suited anaesthetist with something of a reputation with women, given it had taken all of one moment in his presence to be warned of his ways.

Despite keeping her head down, the giddy feeling refused to abate—and then Rachel suddenly recognised what the feeling was: it was how she had always felt when she was with him.

Yes, Dominic Hadley made her giddy—and had done so from the very first day they had met.

It had been September, and both had been starting their last year of senior school. His father, a professor, had accepted a role at the university in Sheffield, and the family had moved up there and enrolled Dominic in a top school.

Rachel had been there on a hard-won scholarship, and

had never really fitted in, while Dominic had been sent there as a matter of course.

Not that he'd wanted to be there.

He had missed London and his old school friends.

Despite being from very different backgrounds, they had struck up a friendship. They had both been complete geeks.

She'd had braces, and Dominic had just had his ceramic ones taken off, so on the very first day of their final school year their first conversation had been about the importance of retainers.

'Get two sets made,' Dominic had advised her, 'and wear them every night.' He'd told her about a friend in London who hadn't worn his and now was having to start all over again.

'Oh, I'll wear them.' Rachel had nodded and smiled her silver-and-elastic-band NHS smile. 'I won't be able to afford them once I turn eighteen.'

They had both been very serious about their schoolwork and the conversation had turned to chemistry, which she had found impossible but he'd handled with ease.

'Do you want me to help you?' he'd offered when, halfway through the first term, she'd found herself falling behind. 'We could go through some things after school?'

He had written his address down on her exercise book and that same afternoon she had made her way to his house.

His mother's smile had been tight when she'd greeted Rachel. Professor Hadley hadn't even attempted one, and had made it clear he was less than impressed by his son's choice of friend.

'You have homework of your own to do, Dominic.'

It had been obvious to Rachel that she wasn't particularly welcome in the Hadley household, so he had started to come to her little terraced home after school.

'What time does your mum get home?' Dominic had asked that first time, as they'd made tea and found biscuits in the kitchen.

'There's just my dad and my brothers, and they usually get in around seven.'

'Where's your mum?' Dominic asked.

'She's dead.'

'Rachel!'

He sounded stunned, and waited for her to elaborate, but she knew that if she explained further she would break down, and her tears had long since been removed from this house.

'I'm so sorry.'

'It's fine,' she said, picking up her mug and heading up the stairs to her room, hoping he would leave things there.

Except he did not.

'How?' Dominic asked as he followed her up. 'When?'

But Rachel reminded him that he had come over so they could study together. There should be no more to it than that.

Except those walks to her home through the park started to stretch for longer. The same park where she'd been spun and swung as a child. Sometimes they'd take a seat on the park bench, or lie on the grass and talk as they gazed up at the sky.

About the clouds.

About other kids in their class.

About their studies and how he liked coming to her home. He told her that his parents fought *a lot*.

'Badly?' Rachel asked, and turned to look at his tense expression as he nodded.

'We moved up here so they could have a fresh start,' Dominic told her. 'He had an affair.'

'Oh.' Rachel was unused to such candour.

'But it sounds as if it's still going on,' Dominic said. 'I don't know why she stays with him when he makes her so miserable.' He looked over to her then. 'Do you think your dad will ever get a girlfriend?'

'No!' Rachel gave a soft laugh at the very thought. 'He says he's got enough going on with the five of us.'

Dominic turned and looked at her. 'How *did* your mother die?'

There was gentleness in his enquiry. He rolled from his back onto his side, and then, leaning on his elbow, he looked down at her, and she looked up into dark eyes that wanted to know her better.

And, given what he'd just shared about his parents, she told him the little she could without crying. 'Something ruptured in her brain.'

'Was it sudden?'

'Very.'

'Do you miss her?'

Every day, she wanted to say, but she was so scared at the depth of her feelings that she didn't know how to share them.

'I don't really remember her,' Rachel said instead, because that was sort of true as well.

She remembered some things—like her smile and her kiss, and lying in bed listening to a story; the soft lilt of her Irish voice and the sparkle of her ring as she turned the page, her pretty red nails as she pointed to words, how safe she had felt when wrapped in her perfumed arms.

But she knew she'd cry if she told him that.

And so she didn't.

Sometimes Rachel would turn her head just for a quiet

gaze at Dominic. The more time she spent with him, the more *aware* of him she became, all the while telling herself it could never be.

So she hid how she felt, because that was the only way she knew how to live.

'I never know what you're thinking,' Dominic said late one afternoon as he met her cool green gaze.

She was about to respond that she was thinking about the equation he'd just put in front of her, but that wouldn't be true. She could feel the warmth from his thigh next to hers, and when their heads bent forward over a book she ached with the effort of not turning her face to his.

So now she did.

His gaze was intense, with an expression she had never seen before. For once it felt as if he could see her hidden desire, and yet she did not look away.

'Perhaps I don't want you to know,' she said.

'Can I at least try and guess?'

'You can try.'

'And if I'm wrong?' Dominic checked. 'Will we still be friends?'

'We'll still be—'

Her voice had been halted by the softness of his lips against hers. Dominic's guess had been absolutely right. Because of course she'd been dreaming of his kiss since the first day they'd met.

In her bedroom, sitting at her desk, he kissed her soft and slow, and she forgot about her braces, and she forgot about her inexperience, because he was new to this too.

And they were no longer shy.

No longer awkward.

At least not when it was just the two of them.

Together they revised for their looming exams, and together they learned about themselves and each other.

And Rachel's braces came off, but thanks to Dominic, she felt beautiful way before then.

It wasn't all plain sailing, though.

His parents didn't approve of their friendship, so they worked hard to hide their blossoming romance.

And *her* father, who usually got on with everyone, took an instant dislike to the awkward, polite, private school boy who, to top it all off, was from down south.

Even her brothers chimed in with less-than-sage advice.

'Don't be letting him know you like him, Rachel.'

'You have to play hard to get, Rachel.'

'He's using you, Rachel. Just stay well back.'

But nothing—not warnings, nor dire predictions, no force on this earth—could stop them.

There was secret hand-holding under desks, and stolen kisses despite the open bedroom door her dad insisted on.

And there were forbidden touches in the times when they found themselves alone...

They always made sure, though, that when Rachel's dad or brothers dropped home unannounced to check on them they would find two nerdy teenagers really studying that science.

One day Dominic decreed that Rachel had to get ninety per cent on a practice test if she wanted a reward. Since she only managed eighty-eight per cent, even with his generous marking, he refused to allow her any prize.

'Sorry, Rachel...' He gave her a sad smile. 'You failed. Back to work!'

And back to the textbook she went—until the rattle of the removals lorry rumbling up the hilly narrow street where Rachel lived announced the arrival of her family.

'We're about to be checked on...' Dominic sighed.

'Good.' Rachel smiled in utter relief—because the

sooner they were checked on, the sooner they'd be left alone again.

The front door crashed open and Phil ran up the stairs.

'Dad forgot his...' Phil stopped at the top of the stairs and saw the two of them deep in their books. 'Oh, hi, there, Dominic. Didn't know you were coming over...'

'I told Dad he would be,' Rachel said indignantly.

'Hello.' Dominic gave his usual awkward smile. 'How are you, Phil?'

'Grand. So, what are the two of you doing?'

'Revising.' Rachel rolled her eyes.

'Oh.'

They actually were. There were books, pencils, tea and biscuits, and not a single untoward thing had taken place.

'I'll leave you to it, then.'

The removals lorry rattled its noisy way down the steep road as Dominic totted up Rachel's latest score.

Ninety-two per cent!

He'd slammed the book closed and she'd lain on her bed with her skirt up and closed her eyes in the bliss he gave.

'There...' she would moan needlessly. 'There!'

And *there* he would flick with his tongue, over and over.

And *there* he would ignore a moment later, as he buried his face deep into her.

And she would press her mouth to the inside of her elbow and try not to scream his name.

'Dominic, Dominic, Dominic!'

And then, deliciously, he had to have the same. And each kiss, each intimate touch, each climax they gave to each other, led them to want more, more, *more*.

They had both been virgins. The first time they'd tried her dad and brothers had been on a removal the other side of town—a big job that would see them there every day for a week. So, on that cold but sunny November morning, they had finally, properly, been alone.

It had been an unmitigated disaster.

Rachel had bled and felt sick because it had hurt so much, and Dominic had finished before they'd barely started.

Yes, a serious disaster.

Embarrassing and awkward didn't even begin to describe it.

Never again, they'd both fervently agreed.

Never, *ever* again.

Absolutely not.

Dominic had arrived for their usual study session the next day. It had been pouring with rain. He'd shaken off his dad's golf umbrella in the little porch, and with a lot of residual blushing and awkwardness, they'd resumed their studies...

Despite the umbrella, his damp hair had dripped on the page as the rain beat on the window, and when they'd kissed, they'd matched again. The pressure of their attempt the day before had fallen away as easily as their clothing.

She'd felt as if she were drowning in his kisses, and at his touch, as if she were floating across the sky...

Their second time had been sublime.

That had been their first winter. And as spring had inched towards summer, and they'd lain on her little single bed, naked and sated, Rachel had made an admission.

'I'm going to miss our study sessions when we're at university.'

Dominic was hoping to study physics at St Andrews

in Scotland, or at Imperial College in London, whereas Rachel wanted to do midwifery in Sheffield.

'What are you talking about?' Dominic asked. 'If we both get in, then we've got years of studying ahead of us.'

'Yes, but you'll be in Scotland or London…'

'There *are* trains, Rachel.'

And now, all these years later, sitting on a changing room bench with her head in her hands, Rachel could still recall with absolute precision the glowing feeling those words had delivered.

Who *was* that woman? Rachel thought as she recalled the ecstasy and unbridled passion that had once been the norm between them.

Who was that woman who had shed her clothes with ease, who had physically ached to be with another person?

Where had she gone?

'There you are,' May said as she peered into the changing room and saw Rachel sitting there, with her head still in her hands.

'Sorry,' Rachel said. 'I was just…' *Just what?* 'Getting my cardigan.'

'It's fine.' May smiled. 'I'm just about to go for my break—why don't you do the same?'

'Sounds great.'

They walked to the staff room together. 'Now, take a seat and I'll get us both a cuppa,' May said.

But there was to be no solace in the staff room for Rachel, because Dominic was sitting there—and not by chance.

Richard had made it very clear that he wanted this dealt with quickly, and so Dominic had sat waiting.

Wondering.

Wondering about Rachel Walker, who, for the shortest of whiles, had once been Rachel Hadley.

'Tea?' he heard May say as they came in to the staff room.

'I'll have coffee,' Rachel said, and then hurriedly added, 'But I'll get it.'

She did a quick about-turn when she saw Dominic, and May, who he knew liked to make a fuss of her staff when she could, halted her.

'Don't be daft,' May said. 'How do you have it?'

White with one sugar, Dominic was tempted to answer.

'White, no sugar,' Rachel said.

So she had given up that pleasure.

May turned to Dominic. 'How's young Thomas doing?'

'Stable,' Dominic said. 'Which is a hell of a lot better than he was a couple of hours ago.'

'Indeed,' May agreed. 'Would you like some tea?'

'Aye,' he answered in a thick northern accent. 'But none of that namby-pamby herbal stuff…'

May gave a slightly bemused smile, because of course she didn't get the private joke that had once existed between them: Rachel had been in a camomile tea phase, and Dominic, who had been strictly a coffee drinker, had unwittingly made camomile tea for her dad when he'd dropped by their flat.

'What the bloody hell is this?' Dave Walker had said as he'd spat it out.

Yes, he'd thought Dominic a pansy who drank *namby-pamby* herbal tea.

Dominic looked over at Rachel, to see if they might share a private smile, but she was staring hard at the television on the wall and continued to stare at it even as May headed to the kitchen and they were left alone.

'Aren't you going to say hello, Rachel?' Dominic asked.

'Hello.'

Rachel turned and looked at him, but couldn't help her eyes drifting from his dark eyes to his jaw, to his mouth.

His mouth had always enthralled her.

The mouth that had kissed every inch of her skin.

'How have you been?' she asked.

But it was clear Dominic wasn't going to answer that here.

'Do you want to meet for a drink? Clear the air and catch up?'

'No, thanks.' She shook her head, but then, worrying that she'd appear petty, and knowing they had to have this conversation at some point if they were going to be able to work in the same hospital, she changed her mind. 'Actually, a quick catch-up might be good.'

'There's a pub across the road from the hospital,' Dominic suggested. 'I should finish around six—'

'My lunch is at one,' Rachel interrupted. 'If you want to speak we can meet then.'

'I am *not* doing this in the canteen.'

And neither would she be going to a pub with him.

Those days were long since gone.

'It's not as if we're going to be holding hands across the table, Dominic,' Rachel said, but then she questioned her own wisdom. After all, she wanted this kept well away from work.

But Dominic was already nodding.

'I'll do my best to be there,' he replied, rather tartly.

They fell into silence as May came in with a tray of drinks and a huge coffee-and-walnut cake which she had brought from home. Dominic fell upon it immediately, and devoured his slice in a few bites.

He'd always been hungry, Rachel recalled.

'Will you have a piece, Rachel?' May offered.

'Not for me, thanks.' She was struggling to hold her mug of coffee, let alone negotiate eating cake.

'Oh, while I've got you, Dominic…' May chatted on as she cut the cake. 'The Emergency Department are having a night out for all those who worked at Christmas and couldn't make the do.'

'That would be me,' Dominic said.

'So, shall I put you down?' May asked as she handed him a second generous slice. 'We haven't finalised where just yet.'

'I'm not sure…' Dominic said, and then glanced over to Rachel, who was back to staring at the television screen. 'I'll check my roster and let you know.'

'You've already put your name down, haven't you, Rachel?' May said, taking out a list from her pocket and reading through it. 'That's right—Rachel, plus one.' May smiled. 'It will be lovely to meet your fiancé. What's his name again?'

The air seemed to have been sucked out of the room. 'Gordon,' Rachel said rather flatly.

'That's right—Gordon.' May nodded, but then frowned as Dominic abruptly stood up. 'Where are you going in such a hurry? Don't you want that second piece of cake?'

'I've got to see that COPD patient.' He clipped out the words as he stalked off.

Rachel fought not to turn her head at his rapid departure and continued to stare at the television screen.

Oh, dear…oh, dear…oh, dear…

CHAPTER THREE

IN AN EFFORT to save money for the wedding, Rachel had brought her own packed lunch to work. Sitting in the canteen, she peeled the lid off her sandwich box and stared at the slice of frittata that Gordon had made. They'd spent Sunday cooking at home, preparing for the week ahead, with Rachel telling herself that she'd soon get the swing of this new domesticity and that it was exactly what she wanted.

Her mind crept back to long-ago Sundays, lazy café breakfasts and making love in the afternoon...

The frittata didn't appeal, but perhaps that was because she was too nervous about speaking with Dominic to feel hungry. She regretted suggesting the canteen, but a cosy catch-up in the pub had felt too hard at the time. This way they'd just look like two hospital workers sitting at the same table.

That was all they were now.

She scanned the canteen and saw Dominic lining up to pay for his lunch. She put on her best poker face as he made his way over.

'Rachel,' Dominic said as he approached the table.

How odd, she thought, to hear her name from his lips. 'Dominic,' she responded politely and attempted a smile, but her mouth flat-lined like an asystole cardiac arrest and there was nothing she could do to revive it.

The huge roast beef baguette, the slice of cheesecake and mug of coffee on the tray that he plonked down on the table in front of him indicated that the prospect of lunch with his ex-wife hadn't interfered with *his* appetite.

As if to further cement that fact, he took from his pocket a bar of chocolate and put that down on the table too.

'Hungry?' Rachel commented.

'Always.' He nodded and glanced at her sandwich box. 'What are you having?'

It was easier to speak about their food than their past. 'Frittata.'

'Quiche without the best bit?' Dominic said, and briefly screwed up his nose at her choice of lunch. 'So, what brings you to The Primary?'

'I could ask the same of you,' Rachel said. 'I had no idea you wanted to be a doctor...'

'Well, you wouldn't have,' Dominic clipped. 'It's not as if you kept in touch.'

'Neither did you.'

She took a swift gulp of water to dilute the surge of venom that threatened to lace her voice, because it still galled, still burnt, still hurt that he had left without so much as a backward glance.

'So, how have you been?'

'I can't complain.' He put down the baguette he had started eating. 'Look, this is awkward, I know...'

'I don't feel awkward,' Rachel refuted. 'I'm just taken aback to find you working here.'

'Same.' He nodded. 'Especially as you always said you'd never leave Sheffield.'

Location had been a bone of contention between them.

A born-and-bred Yorkshire girl, she had said she never wanted to leave, whereas Dominic had never wanted to be there in the first place.

'I was eighteen when I said that,' she pointed out coldly.

'True,' he conceded, then took another bite of his baguette.

Rachel sneaked a closer look. His hair was more tousled than this morning, and he looked more like the Dominic she'd once known. He was different in other ways, though. She noticed the little fan of lines beside his eyes, and there was already a shadow to his jaw when there hadn't been one this morning. The Dominic she had married had only shaved once a week. She noticed, too, the arrogant edge to him that hadn't been there before.

'We all say stupid things when we're young,' Rachel added.

'We do,' Dominic agreed, and their eyes properly met and held for the very first time since their unexpected reunion. 'You didn't answer my question, Rachel,' Dominic said, still holding her gaze. 'What brings you here?'

It was Rachel who flicked her eyes away. 'My fiancé got a transfer and…well, nursing's pretty portable.'

'So when's the wedding?'

'We haven't set a date yet,' Rachel said.

'You're living together?' he asked, then retracted his question. 'Sorry, that's none of my business.'

'Yes,' she said—because, yes, it was none of his business, but also, yes, she and Gordon were living together. Well, they had been for all of ten days…

'How long have you been together?'

'Nearly three years now.'

'Oh.'

He looked as if he were about to say something else,

but then changed his mind and took a huge bite of his baguette instead. He chewed carefully and then swallowed, but it must have stuck a little in his throat because he took a slug of his drink and then offered a comment.

'You're not exactly rushing into things, then?'

'I did that once,' Rachel responded tartly, and saw a small flicker of a smile on his mouth.

His mouth.

Yes, that one.

And this time she could not haul her thoughts away. They had taken each other to bliss over and over and over and, although it scared her to admit it even to herself, she had never quite found that bliss again.

'How's the family?' Dominic asked.

'Much the same.' Rachel nodded. 'Well, bigger. There are a lot of nieces and nephews. How's yours?' she asked.

'I don't see an awful lot of them. I haven't really since...' He swallowed. 'Well, they didn't exactly help matters.'

They had cut him off at the knees when Dominic had married her. They hadn't even sent a card, let alone attended the wedding. She looked up at the man who had, despite his family's strong objections, once stood by her.

'They're back living in London,' he said, 'but we just catch up at Christmas...things like that.'

'I'm sorry you fell out because of us.'

He smiled grimly. 'Don't take all the credit—it honestly wasn't down to you.'

'I ought to get back soon,' Rachel said, packing up her sandwich box.

'But we haven't caught up.'

'What is there to say, Dominic?' She gave a helpless shrug. 'What do you want to know?'

'Are you happy?'

He asked as if it mattered. And she answered as if she were certain.

'Yes.'

Except she hadn't really paused to examine it of late. Her relationship with Gordon had progressed much more slowly than the hurtling freight train of her and Dominic.

Of course she was happy, Rachel told herself.

Okay, maybe she wasn't as deliriously happy as she had been in the early days with Dominic, but she'd been a teenager back then, and flooded with a cocktail of hormones which had ensured she'd felt everything so much more acutely.

His dark brown eyes were frowning slightly as he waited for her to elaborate on her state of happiness.

'I'm very happy,' she said finally. 'Gordon and I both want the same things.'

'What things?' Dominic asked.

'You know…a house, a family…' Rachel's voice trailed off. She was scared to ask herself if that was *all* that she wanted. 'And you?' she asked. 'Are you happy?'

'Yep,' Dominic said, but did not elaborate.

'You asked for this catch-up, Dominic,' she pointed out, because he wasn't exactly helping the conversation. 'What is it you want to talk about?'

'Okay, I'll ask. Is it going to be a problem for you— us working together?'

'Of course not.' She smiled, but he did not return it. 'Is it a problem for you?'

'Yes.'

She was taken aback by his directness. 'Are you saying you want me to resign…?'

'For God's sake!' he snapped.

It was something she'd never seen him do before. She

was starting to realise that Dominic was an entirely different beast now.

'I'm not asking you to resign. I'm just trying to have an honest conversation, Rachel—but then, you were never very good at that.'

'Meaning?' Her hackles were rising—not that she let them show. 'I never lied to you, Dominic.'

'You never told the truth, though. I practically had to be a mind-reader to work out what you were thinking.' He took in a breath—a long one—and gave it to her straight. 'Yes, it's a problem having my ex-wife working at the same hospital as me.'

Oh!

'And I don't know how you're going to react when…' He didn't finish.

It looked as if Dominic wasn't sure quite how to discuss his love life with Rachel.

Or rather, his sex life.

'Are you seeing anyone?' Rachel forced herself to ask. 'Because if it's going to be an issue for her, then I can assure you—'

'Them,' Dominic said, and took another bite of his baguette.

'Them?' Rachel frowned.

'What I mean is, I'm not seeing anyone seriously enough to bring an ex-wife into the equation.'

'I see,' Rachel said, even though she didn't. She couldn't imagine him playing the field.

'I have no intention of getting involved with anyone or making any kind of commitment. I'm not very good at relationships,' Dominic said, and gave her a slightly twisted smile. 'Though I don't have to tell *you* that.'

'I'm not so sure,' Rachel said. 'We had…'

She blew out a breath and tried to haul her mind back

from the place it was dancing towards: the good times, the great times, the best of times.

'It wasn't all bad.'

'It wasn't all *good*.'

And therein lay the difference between them.

If she laid together the years of her life on a grid, then seventeen and eighteen would be tall towers that dwarfed the rest. Those two years with Dominic had been the utter highs.

Yes, their future had sunk, and the bills had piled high, but when the light had been switched off, the door closed on the day, and it had been them…*just them*…

'I don't know how I feel about seeing you again,' Dominic admitted. 'I would really like to shrug…to say, *It's good to see you happy, Rachel*. But I wouldn't be telling the truth.'

'Oh…'

'I'm not going to lie and pretend I'm okay with this.'

'I really don't see the issue,' Rachel said. 'It was years ago. We're different people now—well, you certainly are.'

'Yes,' he said. 'I am.'

Dominic had had to reinvent himself after their failed marriage.

Freshers' Week? What a joke. He had looked around at the sea of happy faces, all excited to start the next phase of their lives, and all he had felt was wrung out.

Everyone had been introducing themselves, getting to know each other. Would anyone want to hear that he was separated, with a divorce pending? That he was a father without a son and looking for a job in order to finish paying for the funeral.

Ask about my gap year? Please don't.

He hadn't wanted to wade through that hellish time

with strangers. He hadn't wanted to get close to anyone when the one person he had wanted to get close to had completely shut him out.

But instead of being entirely antisocial, as he'd wished to, he'd fallen into bar work to support himself and discovered the art of meaningless conversation—and, even better, meaningless sex.

Apart from one maudlin night, when Dominic had lapsed and admitted the truth to Jordan and his wife, Heather, he'd let no one in—because there was nothing he wanted them to see.

After a scare with another woman, despite being hypervigilant about birth control, Dominic had gone and got the snip to ensure it could never happen again—and he *revelled* in his infertility.

As his ex-wife was probably about to find out.

No, he did not want her here.

'I could lie,' he said suddenly, and flashed a smile and his white even teeth. 'If that's what you want me to do. Rachel, *hello*! It's *brilliant* to see you!' he exclaimed, and he knew there wasn't even a trace of sarcasm to his tone—except he'd just told her that he didn't mean a word of it. 'Gordon seems *so* good for you.'

She rolled her eyes.

'It's *so* nice to catch up!' Dominic persisted with his taunt. 'I've been *dying* to know what happened to you—'

'Stop it!' she snapped, and for the first time she let him glimpse that, despite her cool façade, she was struggling too. 'You don't have to outright lie,' Rachel said. 'But at the very least I'm sure we can manage to be professional and polite.'

'*That* I can do.'

'Good.'

'But it goes both ways,' Dominic warned her. 'I mean it, Rachel. I expect the same from you.'

'You'll get it. I would never let my past interfere with my work.'

Only perhaps she didn't understand what he was saying—so Dominic made it clear. 'Please don't think that just because we were married for five minutes it gives you any licence to lecture me.'

'Why would I lecture you?'

'Maybe not lecture…' Dominic said. 'But I date, Rachel. I date a *lot*.'

'That's fine. It's none of my business.'

'Exactly.'

Except Rachel felt her nostrils tighten and pinch, for she loathed the thought of him with someone else. Lots of someone elses.

She hated herself for it, but couldn't help asking, 'When you say *a lot*…?'

'I'm single,' Dominic said, 'and I'm staying that way. But that doesn't mean I've taken a vow of celibacy.'

'That's your choice.'

'Yes, it is,' Dominic said, 'and one that I'll continue to make even if my ex-wife is working in the same building.'

'About that…' Rachel said. 'I think it would be better if we don't tell anyone we were married.' She registered his quick swallow. 'You haven't told anyone, surely?'

'I said something to Richard—my boss. I didn't say that it was you…just that I'd run into my ex-wife.'

'Why would you do that?'

He answered with a question of his own. 'Will you tell your fiancé that your ex-husband is working at The Primary?' Dominic asked.

She glanced up, a little stunned by the question. 'That's different…'

'Not really,' Dominic said. 'Aside from the fact we work together all day, Richard's a good friend. He knew something was up and he asked.'

Rachel let out a breath.

'So?' Dominic persisted. 'Will you tell your fiancé?'

'Yes,' Rachel said, though she wasn't so sure.

There was a knot in her chest—a whole matted knot of emotions that she wasn't sure she wanted to dissect. Of course the answer should be yes. After all, she and Gordon didn't keep secrets. He knew about her past.

'Rachel, there is one other thing I'd like to say.' Dominic interrupted her thoughts. 'And not just because we're going to be working together. It's something I've wanted to be able to say to you for a long time…'

He shifted in his seat and then those velvet brown eyes met hers.

He took a breath and looked right at her. 'I'm sorry that I wasn't able to adequately support you.'

She frowned, and then gave a sort of half-laugh. 'We were eighteen, Dominic. We got by. Well, barely… But—'

'I'm not talking about financially. I know I didn't handle things as well as I could have when you lost the baby…'

It had been her dad who'd alerted Rachel to the fact that her period was late. Not through conversation—they were far too awkward to talk about that type of thing. She'd taken a break from her studies to make lunch for her dad when he'd come back from doing the weekly shop. And there on the bench was a bag just for her, containing her 'bits'—pink deodorant and pink razors, tampons and pads. Enough for an entire pack of Girl Guides, because her dad got embarrassed buying them so got a job lot every couple of months.

And it was then she'd realised that she was late.

A few days of silent panic later she had taken a test and then curled up on her bed and wished, more than ever, that her mum was alive—for she would surely have known what to do.

Her exams had been awful. Everything Rachel knew, everything she had learnt, had flown out of the window as she'd panicked at the prospect of telling her dad.

And Dominic.

She'd waited outside the school, where he'd been sitting a physics exam, and he'd come out wearing a wide relieved smile—which had soon faded when she'd shared her news.

'I've got a doctor's appointment this afternoon,' Rachel had added, when Dominic had said nothing.

'So it's not definite, then?'

'The test says I am.'

'But we're *always* careful.'

And they had been. They'd used condoms every single time. But a dull flush had come to her cheeks as they'd walked.

One time.

One time they'd dozed and then started fooling around again. When he'd entered her for a second time, they'd lingered a while before putting the condom on.

But that had been ages ago.

Months…

'I think my dad's guessed,' she'd admitted as they walked through the park. 'I keep on being sick. I told him it was just exam nerves, but now the exams are over…'

'Why didn't you tell me when you first found out?' he'd demanded.

'Because I wanted at least one of us to pass the exams!'

Rachel had wanted to hide it for as long as possible, but Dominic had faced it head-on.

His parents had been appalling, and had made it clear what a disappointment their son was, and later they had even told Rachel that she was bringing their son down to her working-class level.

Her father's reaction…

Well, Rachel would never know what his initial reaction had been.

Dominic had insisted *he* would deal with it, so she had sat in a bar, nursing a grapefruit juice, while he had spoken to her father alone.

'Was he angry?' she'd asked when Dominic had joined her.

'More worried than angry,' Dominic had said. 'He asked what I intended to do about it. I told him that I'll take care of you both…that we'll get married.'

'Married?' She'd shaken her head. Because in her most private thoughts, before the pregnancy, she'd dreamt of that.

Just not like this.

Never like this.

'Your dad's offered me a job.'

'But you're going to university. That's what you've always wanted.'

'Rachel, we're having a *baby*!'

That was when, for the first time, it had started to sink in. They had sat there, staring at each other, both a little stunned as reality hit.

'I'm going to defer,' Dominic had told her. 'Assuming I get the right results…'

'You'll get them.'

'I'll work my backside off this year,' Dominic had

gone on. 'And maybe next year, once the baby's here...'
His voice had trailed off, but then he'd rallied. 'We'll
get there.'

A month later they'd been married at Sheffield Town
Hall. Her family had been there to cheer them on, dressed
in suits and wearing wide smiles, whereas his family
had refused to attend and hadn't sent so much as a card.

His family, who would have happily supported him
through his degree, had cut Dominic off at the knees in
an attempt to force him away from Rachel.

Her dad had offered them a place to live for a while—
at home with him. But Dominic had refused.

'I can't live *and* work with him, Rachel.'

'Meaning...?' She had been instantly defensive, but
Dominic had refused to elaborate.

After a little celebration in her dad's back garden they
had headed for the tiny flat they had rented.

For the first couple of months of their marriage it had
felt a little like a game. Back then, as they'd realised they
were a married couple—a *real* married couple—they'd
enjoyed the freedom and privacy of having their own
place, with no parents to check on them or tell them to
leave the bedroom door open.

'You can do your exams again,' Dominic had told her
when the results had come in.

Dominic had aced his, yet he'd deferred his studies,
as he'd promised, and taken the job with her father and
her brothers.

'Just till we get sorted,' he'd said.

But they had never got themselves sorted, no matter
how hard they'd tried.

And now here they were, face to face in a hospital canteen, looking back on their lives, with Dominic trying
to speak to her about the most difficult part: their baby.

'I really don't want to discuss it here, Dominic.' She snapped the top down on her little sandwich box and screwed the lid on her water bottle.

'You're the one who suggested the canteen.'

'Yes—and now I have to get back.'

They were all caught up. What more was there to say that could be said in a place like this? That she would ever want to say?

'But you haven't eaten your frittata.'

That made her smile.

'It's no fun without the pastry.'

It was a tiny joke, yet it smacked of *them*, of how they'd used to be, of how easy it had once been between them. And when he gave a low laugh her regret was instant.

She'd missed that laugh.

She'd missed him.

Missed *them*.

Oh, Houston, Rachel thought, *we have a problem!*

Rachel let herself into her flat and with a sigh of relief closed the door on a wretched day.

Gordon had texted to say he'd be late and it had come as a relief.

Should she tell him that Dominic was working at The Primary?

Of course she should.

It was no big deal.

She took off her coat and kicked off her shoes, but instead of putting them away, instead of flicking on the kettle or turning her mind to dinner, she padded through to the bedroom and closed the curtains. Half an hour of sleep might get rid of the headache that had been building all day.

Or rather, the heartache. The ache of the scar tissue wrapped around a heart that had had to learn to beat again.

She had deeply mourned both the end of her marriage and the death of their son, and for a long time her grief had felt insurmountable.

And now, on this particular evening, Rachel stared at the wall and watched her own private screening of the best and worst times in her life.

There she was at the start of their short marriage, standing on the gorgeous staircase in Sheffield Town Hall, so happy to be Dominic's wife.

So very, incredibly happy.

She'd worn an ochre dress, and there had been just the hint of her bump, but it was her smile that stood out, and it had been captured in a photo.

But then she'd turned to her new husband and seen his smile, and she had known he was faking it—or at the very least not as delirious with joy as she was on their wedding day.

Of course they'd made love on their wedding night. After all, they were very good at that. But despite the ring on her finger, despite the baby inside her and despite the passion between them, for Rachel there had been something missing.

She'd waited for those words as she'd lain there in the dark, needing to be told by her husband that he loved her.

Those words had never come.

It hadn't been her imagination, and it hadn't been her making a big deal of things. She'd known that Dominic didn't love her the way she loved him.

But love would grow, she had told herself.

Once the baby had arrived, once they'd got on top of things, his feelings would deepen and change.

And so, knowing that he didn't quite love her, Rachel had chosen not to tell him that she loved *him*.

Ever so, *ever so* much.

As their school pals had all headed off to university, or for a gap year trekking in Nepal or building houses in Africa, Dominic had taken the job in her father's removals business and together the two of them had attempted to make a home in a flat above a shop.

Rachel had got a job in a hairdresser's, washing hair, sweeping, tidying and making drinks, and Dominic had taken an extra job in a local bar in the evenings.

They had lived for a while in that little idyll, working hard, saving hard for the baby.

And, as Dominic had often said, sex didn't cost a thing…

Until one sleepy morning, a couple of weeks before her due date, his hand had come to rest on her stomach, waiting for a little kick before he headed to work.

Waiting…

'He's still asleep,' Dominic had said.

They'd already found out they were having a boy.

'Did he kick last night?' Rachel had turned and rolled onto her back. 'Dominic, I can't remember if he kicked.'

'Of course he did,' Dominic had soothed.

She'd moved her hand to her stomach and pushed her fingers down…waiting.

Waiting…

Forever waiting…

The labour had been horrific.

Even now, thirteen years on, Rachel was unable to relive it. So she pressed fast forward on that part—and fast forward on the funeral as well—to the time they had gone back to their little flat.

Except they hadn't known how to *be* with each other—

how to touch, how to sit, how to sleep, how to speak after all that.

To be fair, Dominic had tried.

'If you want me to stay home I can ask your dad if I can take a few more days,' he had said, when his alarm clock had gone off two weeks after their loss.

A few more days?

The little Moses basket had been returned, as well as all the baby clothes, and the bags of nappies had been donated, but she'd kept a little pair of socks.

Her dad had paid for the funeral, but Dominic had insisted it was a loan. He'd loathed—*loathed*—the fact that he hadn't had the money to bury his son, and he wanted to work to pay every penny of it back.

'Go to work,' she'd mumbled, and turned away from him.

Go to work so I can close my eyes on this nightmare, she'd been thinking.

But Dominic had wanted to talk.

'A book I was reading last night says that you'll want to speak about him...that we should talk about the baby—'

'His name's Christopher!' she'd snapped, and looked into bemused brown eyes that were looking at her as if she were a stranger.

'Talk to me,' Dominic had said. 'Tell me how you're feeling.'

As if everyone I love leaves. My mum. My baby. And soon you will leave me too, and I can't bear it. I cannot bear the thought of it all being over. I know you were only with me because of the baby. Christopher. If he'd lived... But I can't go there, because he didn't. I lost our baby and now I'm going to lose you. I'm losing you already, and we both know it...

She'd felt as if her grief were too big to traverse, and

she had not known how to share her pain nor voice her fears. She'd been told so many times that her tears and her drama only made things worse.

'Go to work,' she'd said again, and rolled away from him.

And so life had hurtled on, when she'd wished it might stop for a while and let her grieve for her terrible loss.

'Come on now, lass,' her dad had said when he'd come to visit them in their little flat and Rachel hadn't been able to face getting out of bed. 'I know it's difficult, but lying in bed and mooching around the flat is getting you nowhere. When your mum died I had to get back to work, and to tell the truth, it helped.'

Instead of sympathy cards thudding through the door, it had soon been bills, and even Dominic, with his mathematical brain, had struggled to make sense of them.

Water bills.

Gas bills.

Final reminder notices.

At the six-week follow-up appointment with her obstetrician, Rachel had been told there was nothing she could have done differently to change the outcome.

'Can we try again?' she had asked the doctor, because her arms had ached for her baby. Ached to hold her tiny boy, with his little pinched face and slender hands.

She'd turned when she'd heard Dominic's sharp intake of breath and had seen his eyes shutter in his shell-shocked face as the doctor had told them that while there was nothing to suggest it would happen again, she would be monitored very closely next time.

They had walked past the other mothers at their postnatal check-ups, with their carry slings and prams and the *wah-wah-wah* noise of newborns crying, and Rachel and Dominic had each been in separate versions of silence.

Rachel, bereft.

Dominic, stunned.

It had been Dominic who had broken the silence as they'd walked through the park. 'What did you mean, try again?'

She hadn't been able to answer, so Dominic had answered for her.

'Rachel, we are *not* trying for another baby. I'm going to university next year.'

She had heard the determination in his voice, as if there was no other option to consider.

He was already thinking of the future.

One she didn't want to see.

'In London?' she asked.

'Yes,' Dominic said calmly.

'We can't afford London—we're barely getting by here.'

'I've already got a place.'

'So I've got to follow you wherever you go?'

'Not if you don't want to,' Dominic had said. Then, 'Jesus, Rachel, that pregnancy just about finished you, and seeing you—' Dominic had halted. 'Seeing him…' His lips had turned white and he'd swallowed hard.

It had incensed her that he still couldn't bring himself to say their son's name. 'His name's *Christopher*!'

'I know his name, Rachel!'

For the first time ever Dominic had shouted, but then he'd reined it in and taken her cold hands in his.

'I know I should have taken better care… I should never have got you pregnant. Look, I've done everything I can to make it right, but…' He'd shaken his head. 'I'm never putting you through that again. I'm never putting *myself* through that again. There isn't going to be another baby.' He'd paused and shaken his head again. *'Ever.'*

Back at their little flat, Rachel had gone to bed. Lying on her side in the darkened room, she'd pretended to be asleep when he'd come to check on her. And there she had lain, hearing the doorbell and then the arrival—for the first time—of his parents at their flat, as well as the conversation that had ensued.

'You can put all this behind you,' Professor Hadley had said.

'Can you please keep your voice down?' Dominic had asked. 'Rachel's asleep.'

'Is she *still* not working?'

'She's just lost a baby!'

There had been more muffled words and then his dad's voice had cut through the gloom.

'You used to have a future. As far as I can see, the only thing she's doing is bringing you down. It's time to put this mess behind you and pick up your life where you left off.'

As harsh as Professor Hadley's words were, it had been nothing Rachel hadn't been thinking herself. Dominic seemed fine, while her whole world had crumbled.

They'd limped on for a couple more months, until finally Dominic had sat down on the edge of the bed she'd barely got out of in those days.

'Listen,' he'd said, and taken her hand. 'What if I ask your dad if we can move in with him for a few months? I can work like crazy and we can get ahead—and you can take some time and focus on retaking your exams.'

She'd looked up at him, up to the dark of his eyes, and then down to the mouth that had never once said the words she'd needed to hear.

'Or *I* could move in with my dad.'

'What are you talking about?'

'Dominic, why did you marry me?'

'Rachel—'

'Why?'

The silence was endless. 'What do you want me to say here, Rachel? I'm trying to do the best I can.'

'But why did you marry me?'

'Because you were pregnant—because it was the right thing to do...'

She'd known all along that Dominic had only married her because of the baby. And now that there wasn't one...

Rachel had removed her hand from his and then she had removed herself from his life.

Mourning both her marriage and her baby had been a mountain it had taken years to climb. Her long-time dream of being a midwife had evaporated, and she'd simply not known who she was any more.

She'd moved back to her dad's, returned to work at the hairdresser's—this time as an apprentice.

There she'd made friends, and later she'd moved out of her dad's. She had finally rediscovered what it meant to have dreams, to want something in the future. But she no longer wanted to be a midwife, so she had applied to study nursing and had fallen in love with Emergency.

It had taken years, but piece by piece she had built a new life.

A good life.

A nice life.

And yet it didn't hold a candle to the bliss she had once known.

The good times with Dominic had been the very best of times, Rachel thought now, as she lay there, recalling the utter joy of lying in his arms, the sheer heady pleasure of their lovemaking. But it hadn't all been sex.

She had never been happier than when they'd scored a lunch break together and would sit in a café or bar, holding hands. Or when they sat at their little kitchen table and he tested her for when she'd retake her exams. When she'd cut his hair. When they'd stood in their little living room, Dominic tall, her massive with her baby bump, and danced and laughed and danced…

She'd never been so happy in all her life.

And later, as she scraped the remains of her lunch from the sandwich box into the little compost bin that they kept under the sink, Rachel herself loathed the analogy, even if it smacked of the truth:

She and Gordon were frittata.

CHAPTER FOUR

BREAKING UP REALLY was hard.

Perhaps more so when you were the one taking an axe to a perfectly good relationship with a nice and kind man.

Had she not bumped into Dominic...

Rachel truly didn't know what would have happened.

But by the end of the week, when she still hadn't told her fiancé that her ex-husband was working at The Primary, Rachel accepted the reason why.

She should have been able to tell Gordon, reassuring him that it wasn't a problem, that Dominic meant nothing. *Nothing.*

She should have been able to say airily, *Oh, that was years ago...* And, *If Dominic was the last man on earth I wouldn't...*

Except, Dominic had been the *first*.

She certainly wasn't breaking up with Gordon in the hope of rekindling things with her ex. It was more that she could not bear the thought of putting Gordon through what she had experienced.

He deserved love.

'Is there someone else?' Gordon hurled the inevitable question at her.

A week ago she would have been able to look him in the eye and say, *No, of course not. Absolutely not.*

Except…

'Rachel?' Gordon demanded.

She truly didn't know how to answer him, for it had hit her then: there had always been someone else taking up too much space in both her mind and her heart.

Dominic Hadley.

Yes, breaking up really was hard to do.

There was a lot of slamming things in suitcases—Gordon.

And a whole lot of silence—Rachel.

She really was still terrible at sharing her feelings.

When the door slammed closed she sat there, in silence rather than in tears, and wondered if she should research if there were any adult education classes she could take in How to Share Your Feelings.

She felt…*defeated*.

It was the best word she could come up with.

Defeated because she had worked so very hard for so many years and tried so very hard to move on.

She had tried to let love into her life. She had moved her world to be with Gordon. But here she was, alone, her world turned upside down…again.

There was never a more honest hour than the one just after a relationship died.

Rachel wanted a family, and she wanted a baby, and while she'd been content with Gordon, she hadn't been as happy as she'd told Dominic she was.

She hadn't loved Gordon. At least not in the white-hot way she had loved Dominic—not that she'd ever dared to reveal it to him. She had always been so good at keeping her feelings under wraps.

But Dominic hadn't loved her.

And she must never forget that fact.

* * *

When she had a couple of days off on the rota, Rachel took the train up to Sheffield to tell her dad that her engagement to Gordon was off.

She wanted to tell him in private, without a running commentary and input from her brothers, but it took some considerable time to find a moment alone with him. The doorbell or the phone were constantly ringing, with one of her brothers or their wives, or one of her ten nieces and nephews, all of whom Rachel adored.

Except today. Especially today. It felt as if she was always the aunt and never the mum, and destined to remain that way for ever.

As if to ram home that fact, Phil and his wife dropped by with the happy news that Rachel would soon be an aunt for the eleventh time. She had never been more grateful for the ability to hide her true feelings.

But finally she stood in the kitchen alone with her dad.

'So, how are you finding the new job?' he asked as he stacked the dishwasher while Rachel made them a cup of tea.

'I like it,' Rachel admitted. 'The hospital's really busy, but the staff are nice. There's a big work do coming up and I've put my name down to go...' Her voice trailed off, and it took her a moment to find it again. 'Dad, I've got something to tell you. I broke up with Gordon.'

She watched as her dad stiffened and then got back to rearranging the mugs on the top rack—the mugs that she herself had put in the dishwasher.

'That was sudden,' her dad said.

'I know.'

'You're okay, though?'

'Dad, it was my choice. I'm honestly fine.'

'Are you going to move back up here?'

'Not yet.' Rachel sighed. 'There's a lease on the flat and…' She shrugged. 'I think I like London.'

'Really?'

'I didn't just move there because of Gordon.'

She'd been ready for change too. But she hadn't foreseen this much change.

She was single again, and in a new city, with a new job and no friends nearby to call on…and her ex-husband working at the same hospital. Not that she would be getting into a deep and meaningful conversation about *that* with her dad.

'I'm sure the right one's out there for you,' her dad said, doing his best to offer relationship advice to his daughter. 'Better to find out now than later.'

Was it?

Rachel wasn't so sure.

How could it possibly be better to find out all these years on, just as you were finally moving on with your life, with an upcoming marriage and the possibility of babies on the horizon, that you weren't as over your ex as you'd hoped?

Of course she didn't say that to her dad, though he had something of his own to add. 'While we're on the subject of romance and such,' her dad said, 'I've got a lady friend coming to dinner tonight.'

'What?' Rachel frowned, because in the twenty-six years since her mother had died there had never been so much as a hint of anyone else. 'Are you saying you're seeing someone? How long has this been going on?' Rachel asked. 'Is it serious? Are you——?'

'Moira,' he said. 'Her name's Moira.'

And that was all Dave Walker had to say on the subject of his love life. Though when Moira arrived he had plenty to say about Rachel's.

Moira, Rachel guessed, was younger than her dad—in her early sixties, perhaps, with straight white hair cut in a rather stunning jagged bob which, given Rachel's brief hairdressing career, she noticed and admired. Beyond the bob, she considered that, since Moira's hair was a beautiful white, rather than grey, she had very possibly been a redhead.

Like Rachel's mum.

And that was more than enough to make Rachel wary.

'It's lovely to meet you, Rachel.' Moira smiled. 'I was sorry we didn't get a chance to meet before you headed down to London.'

'Moira had other plans on the day of your leaving party,' her dad explained.

'No, I didn't, Dave,' Moira said, and Rachel couldn't help but smile. 'You just thought it a bit soon for the kids to be told.'

'Well, you're here now,' Dave huffed. 'Come on through.'

He guided them to the dining room, where they sat down at the table—usually they ate in the kitchen or in the lounge. He handed Moira a glass of wine and soon brought up the reason for Rachel's unexpected visit. 'Rachel's just broken off her engagement.'

'Oh, that can't have been an easy decision,' Moira said. 'Or was it?'

Rachel certainly wasn't about to reveal anything to a stranger, but before she could find a polite response which would make it clear the subject was not up for discussion, her dad chimed in.

'Probably for the best. Never really took to him myself.'

'You've said that about everyone I've ever been out with.'

'Well, you've brought home some right idiots.'

'Dad, I've hardly brought anyone home.'

'There was that Ricky. The one you worked with when you were hairdressing.'

'Ricky's gay.' Rachel sighed. 'We were just friends. I assume you're referring to Dominic?'

'Hmmph,' Dave said, because he loathed speaking about that time. 'That one couldn't stop a pig in a ginnel.'

He looked at Moira, expecting her to laugh, but halted when Rachel got up from the dining room table and walked out.

He found her in the kitchen staring out at the garden and trying not to cry.

'Come on, lass, I'm just playing. I'm sorry to hear about you and Gordon—but, as I always say, there's no point upsetting yourself.'

But it wasn't Gordon she was upset about.

It was Dominic.

She thought back to the eighteen-year-old Dominic, arriving home after a long day working with her father and brothers before heading out for a shift in a bar that night. He'd asked her what the old Yorkshire saying *couldn't stop a pig in a ginnel* had meant.

'Couldn't stop a pig in an alley,' Rachel had translated. 'It means useless, I guess. Why?'

Dominic had shaken his head rather than say why he was asking. 'It doesn't matter.'

He'd looked so hurt that day, so dejected, but she had never, even for a moment, thought the insult had come from her dad.

She'd spent so long looking back on their time together wearing thorn-rimmed glasses, shaded with the resentment and the pain of what had come after, that she hadn't stopped to think what it had been like for him. And Dominic's apology the other day in the hospital about not providing for her had shaken her. While she knew he hadn't been talking about money, the truth was that Dominic had changed all his plans, worked hard day and night, and tried so hard to take care of both her and the baby.

'Is everything okay?'

Rachel glanced up and saw that Moira was standing at the kitchen door, but she said nothing, safe in the knowledge that her dad would soon shut the conversation down.

Except he didn't!

'She's just a bit upset about the break-up with Gordon.'

'It's not Gordon!' Rachel snapped, and then blurted it out. 'Dominic's working at The Primary.'

'What?' The colour drained out of her father's face.

'He's a doctor there,' Rachel said.

'Who's Dominic?' Moira asked.

Dave gave a weary sigh and ran a worried hand over his scruffy grey beard. 'Our Rachel was married to him for a while,' he said, then added, 'Broke her heart, that fella did.'

'It was a long time ago, Dad,' Rachel said, and tried to rally. 'It's fine. Come on, let's have dinner.'

Dinner was an amazing roast lamb, that Dave had cooked incredibly well, but he was very quiet as Moira kept the conversation careering over to Dominic.

'How long were the two of you married, Rachel?'

'About a year,' Rachel said, and took a large slug of wine. 'Have *you* been married, Moira?'

She was making a point—there were some things you just didn't talk about.

'Twice,' Moira said.

Rachel was glad she'd killed that conversation stone-dead…except it turned out that Moira was just drawing breath.

'First time was wonderful—second time a mistake,' Moira said. 'I swore off men and kept to it for fifteen years. But then your dad and I...'

Rachel closed her eyes and wondered if the talkative Moira was going to tell her that she and her dad had been internet dating—but, no.

'Well, I was downsizing and he came to give me a quote.'

'Oh.'

'I don't know what came over me, but I said, perhaps we could work it out over dinner. Still,' Moira said, 'you don't want to hear about your dad and me. How was it, seeing this Dominic again?'

'Moira...' Dave warned, but Moira took no notice.

'I'm just asking. I dread running into *my* ex.'

'It was fine,' Rachel said airily. 'We had lunch together and caught up.'

'Caught up?' Dave checked. 'On what?'

'Just...' She blew out a breath. 'This and that.'

It was clear her dad didn't like the sound of that and was visibly worried.

'Look, maybe you should just come back home,' he said. 'You're not with Gordon any more—there's nowt to keep you down there.'

But Rachel, who had been thinking the same thing, answered as the woman she wanted to be, rather than the one she was. 'I'm not coming home just because my ex happens to work in the same place. It's a huge hospital. With any luck I'll barely see him.'

With any luck!

CHAPTER FIVE

'How were your days off?' May asked.

'Great.'

Rachel's response was a little stilted—and not just because Dominic was sitting at the crowded nurses' station. He was writing up some notes after a frantic morning, during which a serious head injury and a cardiac arrest had arrived simultaneously, all on Rachel's first full shift in Resus.

So much for hardly seeing him!

And she felt particularly awkward because she'd told no one about her break-up with Gordon. There was no need to just yet, she'd decided. After all, it wasn't as if she'd ever worn her ring at work. And it just felt somehow safer to say she was in a relationship when she was around Dominic.

Well, not *safer*.

But there was no point muddying things.

'Did you end up going home?' May persisted with the conversation.

'Yes,' Rachel said, and then checked herself, because she was being aloof. It was only Dominic she had to remember to stay entirely professional and polite with—not her colleagues. 'I had dinner with my dad and his new girlfriend.'

'How was it?' May asked.

'Awkward,' Rachel admitted. 'Though she seems nice and everything.'

'Well, I'm sure you'll soon get used to her.' May smiled and then picked up a large envelope and waved it in Dominic's face. 'I need your deposit for the night out. Cash only—I can't be doing with your apps and things. If you change your mind, you won't get it back.' She read down her list to see who else was on it. 'What about you, Jordan?'

'Heather and I will be there.' Jordan nodded. 'I'll have to get the cash to you another day.'

'What about you, Rachel? Oh, you've already paid. What was your man's name again?'

'Gordon!' Dominic answered for her, with a tart edge that May must have caught because she gave a slow blink. 'So it is!'

'I can't wait,' Tara chimed in, with a smile aimed at Dominic. Rachel felt her nostrils do that pinched thing all over again. 'We're going Greek!'

'Fantastikós,' Dominic said, and took his wallet out and peeled off the necessary notes. 'I'm looking forward to it.'

Indeed Dominic was. Now.

He wanted to be very sure that Rachel Walker didn't think that the fact she'd once been Rachel Hadley gave her any say in how he lived his life.

'Right,' he said, and stood. 'I'm headed up to Maternity before they page me again.'

I've got this, Dominic decided as he made his way.

He and Rachel were all caught up. There was nothing left to say.

There was no way he was going to change his life, or

tiptoe around Rachel. They'd spoken, she'd said she was fine with them working in the same building, and she was engaged to someone else. They had both moved on.

But he couldn't deny he was keen to see this Gordon chap for himself.

The man who made Rachel happy.

His skin crawled at the very thought of it, and his jaw was clamped even as he entered the ward.

'Dominic!' Freya, the midwife who was Richard's wife, greeted him warmly as he stepped into the delivery suite. 'We've been waiting for you.'

'I'm sorry it took me so long.' He introduced himself, and apologised to both the patient and her partner for the delay.

'Just don't run off.' The patient, Sonia, gave a weak smile that soon changed into a grimace of agony.

'The last anaesthetist got paged to go to Theatre just as Freya was getting things ready,' explained Josh, Sonia's partner.

'Well, I can vouch for Dominic,' Freya said. 'He gave me *my* epidural and I've been crazy about him ever since.'

It was one of Freya's funny little stories to relax women in labour.

As Dominic set up, he looked over at Josh, who was comforting Sonia and telling her how great she was doing. They were both so young.

Dominic gave a *lot* of epidurals, and usually he could just shut his mind down on the past and get on with the job. But there were days—and this was one of them— when it was impossible to keep the memories away.

'We'll have you feeling a lot more comfortable very soon,' he said as he washed his hands and then put on surgical gloves.

Sonia was amazing. Her partner held her hand and

shared a worried glance with Sonia's mother, who was stroking back her hair from her sweaty face. There was just so much love and support in the room.

There was no real comparison to when he and Rachel had gone through this, Dominic told himself. This baby, soon to be born, was healthy and full-term, yet for some reason it was just getting to him, when usually Dominic refused to allow it to do so.

With the epidural secured, he stepped back, and Josh, along with Freya, helped Sonia lie back on the delivery bed.

'You'll be feeling much better soon,' Dominic said.

'I think I'm already starting to.'

'Told you he was good!' Freya said.

Dominic ran through his instructions again, and Freya thanked him as he left, but as he stepped out of the delivery suite, it felt as if the sound of all the babies crying in the unit was playing in stereo in his head.

Wah, wah, wah.

He sat there, trying to write up his notes, as the tiny babies cried and wailed. And all he could think was that he couldn't recall the features of his son with the precision he required.

Dominic didn't have so much as a photo of him.

Rachel had them all.

But it wasn't just her reappearance in his life that had him wanting a photo. He'd tried to get one a few years ago, but the hospital where his son had been born had long since closed down.

Wah, wah, wah.

For Dominic, the worst part was that, despite having been told he had died, despite having seen his still, silent heart on the ultrasound while he was still in Rachel's womb—despite all that—when he'd been born, when

Dominic had seen his son for the first time he had still expected him to cry.

Dominic put down his pen and buried his face in his hands, not even noticing that Freya had come to the desk.

'You okay, Dominic?' she checked.

Normally he'd make a joke—especially to a colleague—and laugh it off. But right now he could not make a joke and he could not laugh it off. He was at work on a ward, updating his charts, and about to break down. That would never do.

'Dominic?' Freya checked again.

'I've got a thumping headache.'

He didn't, but for appearances' sake Dominic accepted a glass of water and took a couple of headache pills.

No, he and Rachel were *not* all caught up. They had some unfinished business after all.

He wanted those photos and he was going to ask her for them.

Having made the decision, he headed back down to Emergency. There he found Rachel, restocking the drawers in the Resus nurses' station, and as he tried to decide how best to broach the subject, she shot him a look.

'What?' Dominic said, surprised at the venom in her look when she was normally so inscrutable.

'You know very well what.'

'I don't.'

'You. Earlier,' she said. 'Answering for me.'

'I have no idea what you're talking about.'

'Telling May Gordon's name.'

'So? May forgets names all the time. It was just a little sarcasm aimed at her,' Dominic lied smoothly. 'I was pointing out that even I know your fiancé's name.'

He knew that not for a second did she believe him.

'Don't do it again,' Rachel warned. 'I'm doing my level best to stop this from getting out.'

'Guess what, Rachel?' Dominic answered. 'You don't get to tell me what to do. Don't you remember that conversation we had in the canteen?'

He took a seat and tried to focus on what he'd come here to ask, but Rachel incensed him out of all reasonable proportion with all her no-go zones. Even the scent of her hair as she filled the drawers incensed him— because even all these years on beneath it was the scent of *her*. And it made him speak without thinking.

'I don't see why it has to be such a secret.'

'Don't you?' she checked.

'No. I honestly don't.'

'Perhaps I don't want it to get out that I was married to The Primary Hospital's own resident alley cat.'

'Ha-ha.' He said it sarcastically.

'You've changed,' she accused.

And it wasn't just because he'd become something of a womaniser, thought Rachel. The Dominic she had known had been loyal and faithful. Something twisted inside her as she recalled the slightly shy, somewhat awkward boy she had once known.

But Dominic wasn't apologising for anything these days.

'Of course I've changed,' he retorted. 'From what I recall, the old me wasn't getting very far.' And then he warned her with a pointing of his finger. 'Don't try and police me, Rachel.'

So much for professional and polite!

'I'm just trying to keep the past where it belongs. I've barely been here a week and I do not want to be the topic of gossip.'

She had filled every drawer bar one, and to show him he didn't affect her in the least, she asked him to move—just as she would if it were anyone else—so she could get the last one done.

'Excuse me,' she said.

He shifted his knees to the left without a word, and as her arm brushed his, Rachel wondered if the fire alarms were about to go off, because his very touch scorched.

'Thanks.'

To her displeasure, she knew they were both turned on and trying very hard not to be.

'We clearly need to talk,' Dominic said. 'But away from here.'

'I don't think we do. We've already talked, in the canteen, and said all that needs to be said.'

'There's something I need to ask you and I'm not comfortable doing it at work. Look, I don't want to make any trouble between you and your fiancé...'

She opened her mouth to tell him that she and Gordon had split up, but closed it as he continued.

'There's that pub I told you about, just across the road from the main entrance,' Dominic said. 'I'm on until six...'

Rachel shook her head. 'I finish at four.'

'Then I'll speak to Richard and see if I can get away early. I'll be there around five and I'd really appreciate it if you would join me.'

And she had to concede, while she did not want to go, that if their paths were going to cross at work, it was going to take more than a ten-minute catch-up in the hospital canteen to work out if it was doable.

Perhaps he'd already decided that it wasn't and he was going to ask her to consider leaving.

And if he did say that they couldn't work together

and asked her to go, Rachel pondered as she worked her way through the afternoon, what would her response be?

Righteous indignation and *How dare you try and dictate my life thirteen years on?* Or would she fold over in sweet relief and say *Yes, of course I'll leave, because I'm finding this impossible too*?

But of course she wouldn't say any of that. Far more likely she would fall back on her usual tactic of not giving him the slightest sign that he was getting to her.

Except he was.

There was a very good reason she didn't want their past getting out. She did not want his name attached to hers. She did not want the inevitable questions and she did not want to have to relive or explain her past when she was struggling to picture a future.

Here.

Working alongside him.

When her shift ended she made her way to the changing rooms, but she still didn't know if she was going to meet Dominic or slink off home. From her locker, Rachel pulled out the jeans, jumper and boots she had worn to work that morning, topped them off with a trench coat, and decided she wouldn't bother with make-up—though usually she'd have put on at least a dash of lipstick if she were catching up with a friend.

Dominic wasn't a friend, though.

May came into the changing room as Rachel was running a brush through her hair before pulling on a woolly hat.

'Any plans for tonight?' May asked.

'Not really,' Rachel said.

She was surprised by how much she wanted to confide in May, to tell her she was thinking of going for a drink with her ex-husband, Dominic, and how conflicted and confused she was feeling about it all. But of course she didn't. The habit was too ingrained. Rachel had long learnt to keep her thoughts to herself.

'Just a quiet one,' she added as she wound a scarf around her neck.

'Well, enjoy.' May smiled and took up her bag and headed out.

Rachel doubted she'd be enjoying herself, but decided that she had to be brave. She would meet with Dominic— just to hear what it was he wanted to ask—and then she'd go home.

He might not have been able to get away early, Rachel consoled herself as she stepped into the pub.

Except, despite the pub being busy, she saw Dominic straight away.

Gosh, he looked completely amazing as he sat there sulking in a beautiful grey suit. He was drumming his fingers on the table, but when she walked in he looked up immediately and raised his hand in greeting.

Rachel gave him a wave to say that she'd seen him, and then went to the bar to get a drink.

He'd been waiting for fifteen minutes. Richard had agreed that he could leave early to meet Rachel, and had also enquired after his headache. Clearly Dominic was a hot topic of conversation between his boss and his wife. Still, as much as that irked, right now the person who really irked him was Rachel.

He was actually surprised to see her, as he had braced himself for the fact she might not come. Yet here she was, looking utterly gorgeous and quietly, despite his reluctance, turning him on.

She took off her scarf and then her hat, in a ritual he knew all too well, then shook out her hair—which was lighter than it had been when they were together, and which she wore straight now.

Rachel carried over what he suspected would be grapefruit juice, and placed it on the table before removing her coat.

Dominic had to force himself to remove his gaze, because he did not want to notice her bust in the tight jumper she wore, nor picture the slim pale legs beneath her jeans, or the blaze of gold that lay between them.

'I didn't know if you wanted to eat?' Dominic said. 'I can ask for the menu if you'd like?'

'No, thanks,' Rachel said, and watched as he topped up his sparkling water.

He'd never drunk alcohol—well, only very occasionally—as he always liked to be sharp and had long ago told her he couldn't see the point.

'Was it a problem?' Dominic asked. 'Meeting me tonight?'

She knew he was asking if Gordon knew she was meeting him, and she didn't know quite what to say, but again she chose not to tell him about the break-up.

'No.' She shook her head. 'It's no problem. So, what is it that you want to ask me?'

'I'll get to that. How are you finding working at The Primary?'

He was questioning her as if he were conducting an interview.

'I like it.' Rachel's response was equally wooden, but then she relaxed and gave him an eye-roll. 'Well, apart from the fact I've just found out that my ex-husband works there.'

'How inconvenient,' Dominic retorted, and they finally shared a smile.

'Very,' she agreed, and then asked, 'How long have you been there?'

'For ever,' Dominic said. 'I did my clinical training there and never left.'

'So when did you decide to become a doctor?' she asked, with what she told herself was curiosity but what she feared was a desperation to know more.

'After you and I broke up I took stock, I guess, and I had the grades... To tell the truth, I had thought of medicine before, but wasn't sure I'd be any good.'

'But you're the cleverest person I know.'

'I meant socially,' Dominic said. 'But all that time working with your dad taught me a lot.'

'How?'

He shrugged. Clearly he wasn't prepared to open up entirely. 'So, you say he's seeing someone?' he asked.

'Yes.' Rachel nodded.

Dominic was genuinely curious about his former father-in-law.

They hadn't kept in touch, as such. There had been a couple of phone calls that he didn't want to think about, and it had also taken Dominic two years to pay him back for the funeral.

Every month he'd sent half his wages—more if he could afford it.

And every month he'd got a brief note thanking him for the payment.

Until the final one.

Well done, lad.
We're all square now and I wish you nothing
but the best.
Dave

The note had meant a lot and he'd kept it.

'What's she like?' he asked now.

'Talkative,' Rachel said.

'Really?'

'Opinionated,' she elaborated. 'She's taking Dad shopping next week. Says she's sick of his old jumpers.'

'And he's agreed to go?'

'He's smitten.' Rachel rolled her eyes heavenwards. 'Smitten! I caught them kissing in the kitchen.'

Now, *that* he couldn't imagine, and Dominic felt his mouth gaped for a moment. 'And how do *you* feel about it?'

Rachel tightened her hand on her glass. Dominic had always made her examine things. He'd always asked how she felt. And now, just like thirteen years ago, she didn't know how to share how she felt, so she settled for the classic response.

'Fine.' Rachel shrugged. 'As long as he's happy.'

Only that wasn't quite true, and she could not entirely escape Dominic's piercing eyes. She could almost feel her superpower fading against the scrutiny of his gaze. It dawned on her that apart from her brothers, who didn't discuss such things, Dominic was the only person she knew who might understand the magnitude of her dad dating again.

'It's going to take a bit of getting used to,' she admitted.

'Has there been anyone else since your mum?'

Rachel found she was holding her breath, because in the past he had always been trying to get her to open up about her mum. He'd always slip her into conversation, when in the Walker household the subject of her mum had been strictly forbidden.

'No.' She gave a small shake of her head.

'So she's the first woman he's dated in twenty-six years?' Dominic said. 'Wow.'

Yes, wow, indeed…

It touched her that without asking he could do the maths, that he still knew the dates and anniversaries that mattered so much to her.

'I think it's been going on for a while,' Rachel admitted.

'What makes you think that?'

'Just a couple of things that were said. I actually think she's angling to move in.'

'Good luck to her, then. I remember trying to stack that dishwasher…'

'Oh, it wasn't just you he had a go at about it,' Rachel assured him. 'I don't go near it. He's so set in his ways I just can't believe he's started dating.'

'She must be pretty special,' Dominic commented, 'to have got under that rhino hide of his.'

'Maybe…' she conceded.

He was making her laugh.

He was making her think.

But then, Dominic had always done that to her.

'Give her a chance, Rachel.'

'I am—but what if she does move in?' Rachel sighed. 'And what happens if…?' She stopped then, and blinked, because she hadn't aired her thoughts about this to anyone before. Even when they'd been together she'd kept most of her thoughts to herself.

'If they break up?'

'Yes.'

'You can't stop your dad getting hurt.'

'I know that.'

'At least she won't have to look far for a removal company.' Dominic laughed. 'God, remember when he moved us into the flat?'

Rachel wished he wouldn't reminisce, but she gave a little laugh to disguise her confusion at her fondness for the memories he evoked. 'I do.'

They'd actually had so little to move that it could have been done in a couple of car trips, but her dad had insisted on a lorry.

'That flat's actually up for sale.'

She'd passed the sign when she'd been at home, visiting her dad, but she didn't dare tell Dominic that she'd been tempted to go in and take a look, for old times' sake...

Rachel hadn't known it back then, of course, but both the best and worst times of her life had taken place in that flat.

Dominic bought them both another drink, and they reminisced for a dangerously long while.

About the flat.

About the café across the road.

About the best of times.

But not about the parts that hurt the most—and Dominic knew it was time to get to that.

'Do you want another drink,' he offered, 'or the menu?'

'No, no... I really ought to head off.' She drained the last of her juice. 'What is it that you want to ask me?'

'It's a bit sensitive.'

'It's fine,' she invited. 'Just ask.'

In another version of themselves, Dominic thought, he would take her hand. That was how things had worked for them. Except that wasn't appropriate now, so instead of holding her hand, he steepled his fingers and pushed himself to speak.

'The photos of Christopher that were taken at the hospital… I don't have any.'

'I'll get you some,' Rachel said hurriedly, wishing she had a sip of juice left, because her mouth was suddenly dry and she could hear the roar of her pulse in her ears as Dominic spoke on.

'I did attempt to get some from the hospital, but it's closed down and I hit a wall trying.'

She nodded. 'I'll have some copies made.'

'I don't want to upset you…' He tried to gauge her expression, but it was completely closed off. 'But I'd really appreciate it.'

'If you can give me a few days…?'

'Whenever you have time.'

She nodded again.

'Rachel…'

He knew, despite appearances, that she was hurting. He couldn't *not* take her hand—except she pulled her hand back and took herself completely out of bounds.

'I said I'd get them for you.'

Rachel knew she'd snapped, that she'd overreacted to his touch, but it was either that or break down.

Right now she was mourning not just the loss of her baby, but also all the moments they'd never shared— as a family, as a couple. So badly did she want to take Dominic's hand, take him back to her empty flat and go through those photos together. But they hadn't been able to accomplish that when they were married, so there was no chance now they were not.

She moved to stand. 'I really ought to go.'

'You're sure?' Dominic checked, and she nodded.

But of course it wasn't as simple as just getting up and walking out.

As if she were dressing for a North Pole expedition, on went her coat, the scarf and the hat. But, feeling his impatience, she omitted the gloves and stuffed them into her pocket instead.

'Don't you have a coat?' she asked as they headed out.

'No need. I'm driving,' Dominic said, though she noticed he had not offered her a lift home.

They walked out of the pub together and into the dark car park, both wondering how to end this rather awkward meeting.

Rachel did not recognise his mood. He stood taller than usual, if that was possible, and his expression was serious. Her own feelings were jumbled up after being asked to give him copies of the photos, and it was awkward to know how to say goodbye.

Though it should not be awkward because there was nothing to say—or rather, because there was so much to say that they did not know how to discuss. Their failed marriage and the baby they'd lost, the photos he didn't have and their working together, the attraction that still existed between them.

That persisted.

For, despite all the changes over the years, there *were* parts of Dominic she recognised.

Like the slight glaze that came to his eyes when he wanted her.

The way he stood just a smidge too close and dominated her space.

Or was it that she'd stepped a little closer into his?

And when he looked down at her, and she looked up at him, they both recognised the want in the other person's eyes.

It wasn't fair, Rachel thought. All desire for each other should have been returned with the divorce papers. Every shred of want should have been annulled.

Except it hadn't been.

He was smartly dressed, but end-of-day dishevelled, and he was hungry—she knew it as well as if he had told her himself. She simply knew. And, though he stood still, she also knew he was restless.

In another time they'd be kissing now.

In an older version of themselves they would not have been able to wait for each other's mouths until they were home...

'Are you getting the Tube?' Dominic asked gruffly, and she nodded. 'Then I'll say goodnight here.'

'Sure.'

How to leave him, though?

A little wave? Rachel thought, but that seemed stupid.

A handshake, then? Even worse.

And, anyway, evidently they did not know how to *do* a handshake—because as his fingers met hers she looked down at their hands and saw they were entwined once again, and she could not bring herself to pull her hand away.

A small kiss, perhaps?

Before she knew what was happening, their touching hands led to moving in for a small kiss...

Except it was rather like testing the Christmas tree lights, not really expecting them to be working, but then being stunned by the blazing, breathtaking effect when they suddenly sparked into life.

The instant their lips met they were hurtled back to a time when touch had not been out of bounds. To a time when they had relished each other completely.

Her body lit like a flare, her senses jamming at the return to this bliss.

There was nothing tentative about this kiss.

It was harsh, and thorough, and when gravity wasn't enough to keep her standing, instead of holding her up he kissed her against the cold brick wall of the car park.

He pulled off her hat and it fell silently to the wet ground. He made her want sex in dark places as he filled her senses with his touch, his taste, his smell. His ragged breathing told her that he wanted the same. The frantic tangle of their tongues left them both suddenly desperate.

He went for her belt and parted the fabric of her coat, building to a kiss that was too much for a drink after work on a Monday.

It was a kiss that warned them they could never be just friends.

And then Dominic felt an unwelcome tap on his shoulder. Only it wasn't a person—it wasn't even his conscience. It was the unwelcome thought that they were hurtling towards an affair.

And Dominic, thanks to the less-than-gorgeous lessons of his parents' marriage, would never go there.

'For God's sake, Rachel!' he accused as he pulled back. 'What the hell are you doing?'

'Me?' she shot back, because he knew he hadn't exactly been unwilling. 'It takes two!'

'Yes, but I'm not the one who's engaged.'

Dominic was furious with himself.

While a torrid affair was way down on his list of wants, messing up her life again was way more abhorrent.

'Go home,' he told her.

He looked down at her coat that he had parted, at her tousled hair and freshly kissed mouth. He wished for an eraser that might somehow unsex her—if there were such a thing. For if Rachel had ever come home to *him* looking like that, he'd have known in an instant.

He reached for her belt and started to tie it. 'This never happened,' he said. 'This is never going to happen ag—'

'Gordon and I broke up,' Rachel cut in, and felt his hands still. 'I ended it last week.'

He looked at her then—right at her. And she rather hoped they could get back to kissing…get back to a moment ago, when she had been swept away by the power of their connection.

But now she had cleared the air and finally told him.

Except the bark of his response to the news startled her.

'Why would you go and do that?'

Rachel didn't know what to say.

But that didn't matter because Dominic had plenty to say!

'Don't do this, Rachel.'

'Do what?'

'Don't throw away a relationship over me…'

'I didn't.'

'I mean it, Rachel. We will not be getting back together. I have *nothing* to offer you, as far as the future's concerned.'

His words were so blunt, his statement so absolute, that something inside her shrivelled. And as she stood there being told—yes, *told*—that there was absolutely no chance for them, that marriage and babies were the very last thing he wanted, she knew that hope had just died. The little flicker of hope she hadn't even known existed had just been doused.

Embarrassment and anger kicked her into damage

control mode and she gave a mocking laugh. '*You?* You really think I threw away a three-year relationship over you? What happened to you, Dominic? When did you get so arrogant?'

He let go of her completely then, and there was only one word going through Rachel's head: *deny, deny, deny.*

'Did it not enter your head that I could end a relationship without factoring *you* in?' She breathed in hard and found some strength. 'Gordon and I had only just moved in together, and I realised almost straight away that we'd made a mistake.'

That, at least, was the truth.

'Fair enough,' Dominic said. 'But, Rachel, I have to be sure. Because you and I…' He looked down at her and she recalled the pain and the hell of the end of their marriage. 'We didn't work.'

'Obviously.'

'And, despite what I might have said before, I do want you to be happy. It just won't be with me. And so if my presence *did* have any impact on your decision, I suggest you go back to your fiancé and patch things up…'

'I would never use him like that, Dominic.' She blinked as she tried to fathom him. 'You seem to prefer that I be engaged.'

'I'd *prefer*,' Dominic clipped, 'that you'd never come back into my life.'

It was a horrible thing to say.

And as she turned and walked off Dominic knew he didn't really mean it.

After all, he'd tried to get in touch—not once, but twice over the years.

And now Rachel Walker had arrived back in his life

with a pile of excess baggage—an awful lot of which belonged to him.

And it hurt to examine it.

CHAPTER SIX

THAT KISS SHOULD never have happened, Rachel knew. On so many levels, it should never have taken place.

For it had awoken her to him all over again.

The constant smouldering burn that had never quite died out had been reignited.

She didn't like him now, though, Rachel insisted to herself. This new, arrogant Dominic did not appeal.

And it was starting to show.

'Is your ex the redhead down in Emergency?' Richard asked Dominic after a particularly tense afternoon in Resus. 'Rachel?'

'How did you know it was her?' he asked.

'Because the two of you barely speak.'

'I told you,' Dominic said. 'We've agreed to be professional and polite.'

'With extra ice added?'

'Well, how are we supposed to be?' Dominic snapped. He was doing rather a lot of that of late. 'We're hardly going to be friends.'

But he knew it couldn't go on like this.

He sighed and headed back to the department, for he had to sort things out.

Dominic did *not* want to be in lust with his ex-wife. And certainly he did not want a relationship with her. He was well aware of how badly it had worked out the first time.

Despite Rachel's protests to the contrary, he was still silently panicked that she'd broken off her engagement because of him.

And there she was, with a long-sleeved top on under her scrubs. Because Rachel was *always* cold.

'We need to speak,' Dominic said. 'Alone.'

'This is becoming a habit, Dominic. Won't it look odd?' Rachel said. 'Us hiding in the drug room or the linen cupboard?'

'Can't you go for a break?'

'I'm not due for one. Just say what you have to here,' Rachel insisted.

But when he stood there silently, refusing to back down, with a sigh she led them to an empty cubicle, where she pulled the curtain to give them some privacy.

'I'm sorry about what I said the other night,' he started. 'I was shocked that you and Gordon had broken up and concerned—'

'I don't need your concern.'

'Let me finish,' Dominic said. 'I was concerned that my being here might have factored into your decision to end things with him.'

'Well, it didn't.'

'Good—because it's very clear that we want different things. I like the single life. The only thing I want to be married to is my career, and the last thing I want is a family. In fact...' He took a deep breath and knew the time had come to tell her what he had done. 'I've made sure it can never happen. I had a vasectomy some years ago.'

'Dominic,' Rachel said coolly. 'We were divorced thirteen years ago. You don't have to run your contraceptive methods by me.'

Ha! she thought, laughing in her head at her cool response. *Beat that.*

He did.

'I might have had to the other night,' Dominic said, his eyes never leaving her face as he moved one dangerous step closer, nudging into her personal space.

He took her hand and for a moment she honestly thought he was going to place it on his crotch.

'Because if I hadn't stopped things when I did we might have ended up doing it against the wall.'

'You really think so?'

'I *know* so.'

Rachel thought she deserved a cape, tiara and a wand—because she didn't even blush, despite picturing him doing just that.

The scent of their arousal was in the air she breathed, and his mouth—*that* mouth—was a mere arch of her neck away. But she didn't step back, determined to hold both her position and his eyes.

'Dominic, it was a kiss for old times' sake. Please don't go reading more into it than that.'

The audacity of him!

She shook his hand off hers. 'I'm certainly not rushing around looking for a replacement fiancé.'

'Good.'

'And while we're *sharing*,' Rachel said, 'the reason Gordon and I broke up is because I didn't want what happened to me to happen to him. He's a good person.'

She watched Dominic's eyebrows draw together in confusion at that.

'And I know, better than most, how it feels to be married to someone who doesn't really want to be married to you.'

'What are you talking about?' His eyes widened incredulously at her words. 'I went and told your dad the day I found out about the baby. I asked him for his permission to marry you the same night. I deferred university. I worked two jobs. I even offered to move in with your dad...'

He shook his head, clearly furious at her take on their marriage.

'You didn't love me, Dominic.'

'No.'

He seemed hurt, angry, but the one thing she knew was that they could not go back down the path of *them* again.

'And do you know why?' he asked.

She rather felt that she didn't want to know, but he let her have it.

'Because apart from in bed, Rachel, I found you to be cold.'

Dominic knew that was below the belt. But this woman brought out the worst in him, as well as the best in him, and her return had made him relive every last hurt again.

Trying to reach out to someone who constantly pushed you away. Crying alone in the shower for your baby, then walking into a bedroom where your wife had already turned to face the wall. Knowing the pain you had caused her...knowing what you had both lost.

And even now, when he'd hurt her again, she barely blinked.

'It must be catching, then,' Rachel said, and walked off.

* * *

Rachel knew it now for a fact. Dominic Hadley had never loved her—which meant she had been right to guard her heart.

Luckily there were only ten minutes or so left of her shift, and within the hour she had let herself into her flat. Without even taking off her coat, she went into the bedroom, opened up a drawer and took out a faded cream folder.

The first thing to fall out was her wedding ring, which she'd once so proudly worn. And then she took out an exercise book she'd kept from school—one that Dominic had written his phone number on. There were lots of little messages he'd written to her in class too, but she could read the true intent behind them now.

What time will your dad be back?

So they could have sex.

I got them!

Condoms—so they could have sex.

Has it finished yet?

Her period—so they could have sex.

Teenaged Dominic Hadley really had had sex on his mind—and fool that she was, she'd confused it with love.

Well, no more.

She fed the exercise book into the shredder, page after page, and cried bitter tears as she did it. Then she took out their wedding photo, but could not bring herself to shred that.

There were also certificates—marriage, birth, death and divorce—and those papers were such a neat summing up of their relationship that she could not bear to look at them properly.

And then she got to the photos Dominic wanted. It twisted like a knife in her gut to look at them, but they also made her smile.

There was one photo of the three of them, sitting on the bed, with Rachel holding Christopher and Dominic's arm around her.

And there were several of just Christopher.

She touched his pinched little face and open mouth, his long slender fingers, the fine fuzz of hair on his head.

She would get these reprinted and give them to Dominic, and then all would finally be said and done between them.

No, there had been no need to take off her coat, because in minutes she was out of the door again.

Always be kind.

It was a saying often bandied about, but that evening, when someone tutted as she knocked into them while lining up to print off the photos for Dominic, the snap of a stranger's temper nearly had Rachel giving in and turning to run for home. That single terse 'tut' just about had her heading for King's Cross Station and the first train back to Sheffield, but instead she got the photos copied and was soon back at her flat.

Job done.

When she'd given them to Dominic there would be nothing more to discuss, no more conversations to be had, and the subject of their past would be entirely closed.

Rachel sealed the envelope and labelled it *Photos*, and then put it in her bag. Now she just had to give them to him when the chance arose.

* * *

Except it never arose.

For the first time in her career, Rachel started to put her hand up to work in Minor Injuries rather than the main section of Emergency or Resus.

There was less chance of seeing Dominic there.

'How did you do this?' Rachel asked as she pulled on gloves and peeled back the tea towel wrapped around the hand of a delightful elderly woman who had brought herself to The Primary on a bus.

'Peeling and cutting up pumpkins,' said Miss Tate. 'I make soup for the homeless, and pumpkin soup is supposed to be easy. But, Nurse, they're really hard to cut.'

'I bet they are.'

'But it's a flexible soup.'

'Flexible?' Rachel checked as she examined the deep cut and saw the exposed tendons.

'Vegan, gluten-free, nut-free…' Miss Tate reeled them all off. 'And don't get me started on the health and safety regulations. It's wearing gloves that caused this to happen—I couldn't get a grip of the knife. In my day you just put a bone in a pot, but it's a complicated affair now, making soup.'

As well as hazardous, Rachel thought, picturing these shaky arthritic hands wrestling with a large knife and a pumpkin.

She looked at her patient, and saw that Miss Tate was a little bit grey and was sweating. 'It's rather a long wait,' Rachel said, 'but I can get you on a gurney and lying down…'

'I don't mind waiting.'

'Well, let's make you as comfortable as we can. Is there anyone I can call?'

'No need to trouble anyone.'

Rachel looked up as the curtain swished open and saw May.

'I just need a word, Rachel,' she said.

She paused when she saw what Rachel was dealing with and, instead of insisting on having a conversation, gave Rachel a hand with Miss Tate, chatting away about the pumpkin disaster as they got her up onto a trolley and into a gown.

'Chilli flakes are the secret ingredient to a good soup,' Miss Tate said.

'Ah, but I don't like it too spicy.' May shook her head.

'No, just a little pinch—it brings out all the flavours.'

'Could you not roast the pumpkin first and *then* cut it up?' May suggested.

'Oh!' Miss Tate dwelled on that suggestion for a moment. 'I think that might work. *Roast* pumpkin soup… that sounds very nice.'

With the soup and the patient sorted for now, May pulled Rachel aside. 'We'll miss you tomorrow night,' she said.

Rachel had taken her name off the list for the ED night out. She had come up with loads of excuses to justify it, but mainly it was because she did not want to see Dominic socially.

'I've got your deposit for you,' May said, handing her an envelope.

'I thought it was non-refundable.'

'I always say that,' May admitted, 'but we've got plenty going, so the numbers are fine. It's a shame, though. I was looking forward to meeting your man… What's his name?'

'Gordon.' Rachel smiled, because if she'd told May once, then she'd told her fifty times. Still, there was something she *hadn't* yet told her and there was no time like the present. 'May, Gordon and I have broken up.'

'Oh, my dear! When did that happen?'

'A little while ago. I didn't say anything at the time, because, well…'

'Of course not. You needed time to process it.' May was serious now. 'Does it change anything? I mean, I know you moved to London because of his job. Are we going to lose you, Rachel?'

'I don't honestly know, May.' Rachel told her the truth she was coming to know. 'The flat's too expensive for only me. If I stay then I'm going to have to find somewhere else.'

And, while she liked London, with Dominic so near it was hell. If she was going to have to find somewhere else to live, why not in Sheffield, where her family and friends were?

Well away from Dominic.

She couldn't hide in Minor Injuries for ever. And Rachel knew she *was* hiding.

'You're still on a trial, Rachel, so you only have to give a week's notice, but for what it's worth, I'd be very sorry to lose you.'

'Thank you.'

'Listen,' May said. 'Do you want a shift tomorrow night? I'm having trouble covering the department, what with everyone coming for this night out, and I've had someone ring in sick.'

'I'd love to,' Rachel said. She'd been about to ask May if there were any extra shifts, but the overtime for a Saturday night would certainly help.

For now.

Rachel knew she would have to make a decision soon about staying.

And, despite May's kind words, it was starting to look very unlikely.

CHAPTER SEVEN

DOMINIC KNEW HE had to get Rachel out of his head. And he decided it would be best to do it in a way he knew only too well. He would lose himself in a woman's body.

Since Rachel had been back on the scene there had been none of that.

None.

He knew Rachel had put her name down to be at this social event tonight, but he had decided it was time to set new ground rules. Tonight, he fully intended to re-discover the joys of being single and commitment-free and to indulge in some completely meaningless sex.

Dominic was usually very good at that.

'Dominic! Over here!'

His name was being called from a couple of directions, but Tara waved for him to take the empty seat she had kept for him. They weren't an item, although they'd got it on at times, but instead of joining her, he gave a vague nod as his eyes scanned the room.

Rachel wasn't here, he realised.

He ignored the gritting of his jaw when the flash of red hair, which his eyes reluctantly sought, didn't appear.

Good! he told himself, refusing to acknowledge that the thud in his chest might be born of disappointment rather than relief.

Good, he said again, to himself. It was excellent that his ex-wife wasn't here, policing his moves.

Except instead of heading over to sit beside Tara, he moved towards the empty seat next to Jordan. They went way back, and had been through medical school together. Dominic had even been best man at his wedding.

'No Heather?'

'Nope.'

'Mind if I join you, then?'

'Of course. The babysitter cancelled,' Jordan explained as Dominic took a seat, 'and frankly I don't blame her.'

'Are the twins still wild, then?'

'Completely.' Jordan nodded. 'And Nicholas is following their lead.'

'Sounds like you need a night off,' Dominic said.

He knew very well that Jordan was stressed about some upcoming changes to the paediatric unit, as well as bogged down with work, so adding a young family to that mix must only increase the burden.

'I don't know how you do it all.'

'Oh, I wouldn't have it any other way,' Jordan said as the starter was served.

The *saganaki* was the best Dominic had tasted, yet he pushed it around his plate, for once not particularly hungry.

The whole meal was delectable, but Dominic didn't clear his plate. He wasn't alone—surprisingly Jordan, who loved his food too, didn't finish, but unlike Dominic, he could explain why.

'I promised Heather I'd bring home a curry.'

And just when Dominic was starting to question what on earth he was doing, talking toddlers and happy marriages with Jordan when there was Tara pouting petulantly and no doubt waiting for him to take her home, a memory pierced his mind... Ending his shift at the bar and grabbing a curry—because of course he was starving, but also a very pregnant Rachel had had a bit of a craving for it.

As well as a craving for him.

The memory was so vivid, so real, he could almost *feel* the happiness that had existed between them as he'd walked into their freezing flat. He'd grabbed some plates from the kitchenette, walked into their ice box of a bedroom, holding up the bag of food like a trophy, then stripped off and climbed into their warm bed.

They'd eaten as if they'd been starved for a week, tearing at the naan bread, scooping up the curry and devouring it. And then had come the best bit. Rachel loved *gulab jamun*—sweet syrupy balls that they generally didn't order—but that night he'd surprised her.

They'd already been turned on, but her groan as she'd eaten one had driven him wild, and a gorgeous wrestle had ensued.

Rachel, eight months pregnant and on top of him, sweet, sticky sex, with syrup everywhere, and an orgasm that had had him seeing stars...

It had been followed by a kind of clarity and peace he'd not known since, with his difficult, fickle woman, who revealed so little and only very occasionally blossomed and opened up—but only to him.

And later, with both of Rachel's cravings satisfied, they'd lain there, feeling the kicks of their baby and trying to decide on a name.

It had perhaps been the most pure and simple happiness he had ever known.

'Okay,' Jordan said suddenly, breaking into his thoughts. 'I can't not tell you.'

Dominic turned. 'Tell me what?'

'Heather's expecting.' Jordan beamed. 'We're beside ourselves because we're so pleased.'

Dominic looked at his friend, who was smiling delightedly at news that would have had Dominic running for the hills. *Four!* Four children, by his rapid calculation all under four, including the terrible twins! Yet Jordan had always said he wanted a big family, and he and Heather were, from all Dominic could tell, as in love now as they had been on their wedding day.

More so, even.

'Congratulations,' Dominic said. 'You're a lucky bastard.'

'Oh, I know I am,' Jordan said.

Suddenly Dominic wanted what he himself had once known. He wanted that pure and simple happiness again.

The meal ended and it was then that the party kicked off. This would usually have been the time when Dominic would have really started to enjoy himself. But this evening he just could not get into the swing of it—and it had nothing to do with the sparkling water he was drinking.

'Hey, Dominic!'

Tara was waving him over to the dance floor, but he had absolutely no desire to go over and join her. No desire in that direction at all.

'You're quiet, Dominic,' Jordan commented. 'Do you want a drink?'

'I'll just stick to water, thanks,' Dominic said.

'Is everything okay?'

Dominic glanced up and frowned at Jordan's enquiry. 'Of course.'

'Only with Rachel working in Emergency…'

'What?' Dominic was furious. 'Did Richard tell you?'

'No,' Jordan said. '*You* did—-a couple of years ago.'

Dominic closed his eyes and drummed his fingers on the table. The less said about that night the better.

'You had Heather looking her up on social media, remember—?'

'Don't let on that you know,' Dominic cut in. 'She's adamant that she doesn't want it to get out.' Christ, it was like trying to keep the lid on Pandora's Box. 'I mean it, Jordan.'

'I won't say anything,' Jordan said, 'but I'm here if you want to talk.'

Jordan left it there, and said he was getting up for one quick dance before heading home.

The Emergency Department certainly knew how to party. People were actually dancing on the tables now, and Dominic was being urged to join in.

Only Tara's laugh suddenly grated on him, and he didn't like the possessive way she'd placed a hand on his arm, as if it were up to her to collect him for dancing, so he brushed it off and politely declined.

Tara's nostrils did that pinched thing—not that Dominic noticed as he headed for the bar and ordered another sparkling water, wondering what the hell was wrong with him.

Since Rachel's return to his life all other women seemed to have lost their appeal.

Although sex had never been as good as it had been between him and Rachel.

She had loved it.

He had loved it.

They had loved it.

Except for that awful first time.

He was laughing quietly to himself about that when he heard a crash and, turning around, saw that a table had collapsed—thanks to the weight of the people doing an impromptu Greek dance on top of it.

There should be no better place to be injured than at an Emergency Department party, but it meant an awful lot of people jostling to be in charge.

'I'm the only one sober,' Dominic pointed out as he took over. But one look at Jordan's shoulder told him this would require more than a simple sling. In fact, it was a nasty injury.

'We'd better head back to The Primary,' Dominic said, as he fashioned a sling with his tie and put Jordan's jacket on him back to front, buttoning it up to hold his arm securely in place.

'I'll come with you,' Tara offered.

'No need,' Dominic said, because she was seriously starting to annoy him.

There was no need. He escorted Jordan out to his car and drove him to The Primary.

It was pouring with rain, and so, rather than using his priority parking spot, he pulled into the forecourt. 'Wait there,' he told Jordan, rather needlessly. 'I'll go and find a wheelchair.'

The place was in its usual state of Saturday night chaos, so he knew there was little chance of finding a wheelchair, a gurney or anything useful.

Though there *was* Rachel.

She had on that long-sleeved top under her scrubs, and her gorgeous hair was in a high ponytail. She was the best thing to have happened to him this Saturday night.

But he could never accuse Rachel of being needy, because far from waving and smiling when she saw him, she gave a slight eye-roll as she came over.

'What happened?'

'I couldn't stay away from the place,' Dominic quipped.

But she didn't even reward his pale joke with a smile. 'Jordan fell—he's fractured his right clavicle. I need a wheelchair but I can't find one.'

She left him standing as she went and got one.

'Thanks,' he said when she returned, and went to take it.

But Rachel didn't let the handles go. 'I'll come with you.'

'I can manage. I got him into the car.'

'And how many fractured clavicles have you got *out* of a car?'

None.

'I thought you were going to the do tonight?' Dominic commented as they walked out of the department.

'I didn't know I had to run my social calendar by you.'

'Fair enough,' Dominic conceded, and then admitted to himself that he'd missed her being there tonight. That despite all his earlier chat, Rachel was the only woman he'd wanted to see.

Dominic drove a low-slung sports car, but it clearly did nothing to impress her.

'Even I'd have trouble getting out of that,' Rachel muttered as they approached, but she dropped the attitude as soon as the car door opened.

'Hey,' she said, and smiled to Jordan even as she tried to map out his exit. 'What happened?'

'The Zorba dancing,' Jordan said through gritted teeth as his phone bleeped. 'Heather's been calling but I can't get to my phone. My wife,' he added, for Rachel's benefit.

'Why don't you speak to her when you're a bit more comfortable?' Rachel suggested. 'For now, let's focus on getting you out of the car.'

'I'm sorry about all this,' Jordan said. 'I've had a bit too much to drink…'

'It's fine.'

'Heather's going to freak.'

'Hey,' Rachel said, 'she's only going to freak because she'll be worried about you. Let's get you into the department.' She looked over to Dominic. 'Go into the driver's seat—you can support him from there when he turns.'

Zaima, the night sister on duty, joined them with a porter, and then Ross, the ED registrar on for the night shift, came out armed with a green whistle, which Jordan sucked on as they attempted extraction.

But every move proved agonising for him.

'Why didn't you call an ambulance?' Zaima said to Dominic when they failed the second time they'd tried.

'Because we'd still be waiting for it to arrive!' Dominic replied tartly, though he was beginning to wish he had. 'I'm sure the paramedics have got plenty to do on a Saturday night.'

'So have I!' Zaima retorted, in an equally tart tone.

Then Rachel asked Jordan to lean forward, and with Dominic assisting from the rear, she and Zaima lifted his feet. Soon they had him turned, and his feet on the ground, and then he was in the wheelchair and finally inside the ED.

Dominic went and moved his car.

'I'll get the receptionist to come and take your details,' Rachel said as she wheeled Jordan into a cubicle. 'Let's get you into a gown.'

It was indeed a nasty fracture, and he was given an IV and analgesics before they even tried to get him up onto a trolley.

When Jordan was finally comfortable Ross came in and examined him. 'How soon can we get him up for an X-ray?' he asked.

'We've got two portable chests waiting, and an urgent C-spine,' Zaima responded.

And whatever else had come in in the meantime.

'I can take him,' Dominic offered, as he came in and took a seat on a stool at the nurses' station.

Rachel shook her head. 'He needs a nurse with him, given he's had analgesics.'

'I'm sure I can manage—and, no, before you ask, I haven't been drinking.'

'It's policy,' Zaima said.

And policy would be adhered to—even if sitting on the hard chairs outside X-Ray an hour later with Dominic was the last place she wanted to be.

'How long will we be here?' Dominic asked.

'As long as it takes,' Rachel said.

He looked over to Jordan, who, thanks to the analgesics, was comfortable and fast asleep. She went over and checked the pulse in the arm affected by the fracture.

Jordan stirred and opened his eyes. 'I'm really sorry.'

'Jordan, it's fine,' Rachel said, and gave him the latest update. 'Heather's sorting out a babysitter and is on her way.'

But that only served to distress him.

'No, no...' Jordan said.

'They couldn't get a babysitter for tonight.' Dominic didn't exactly whisper, but he said it in low tones for Rachel's ears and then addressed Jordan. 'I'll call Heather now and tell her that I'll stay with you.'

'Will you tell her that you'll drive me home?'

'Let's see what the X-rays show,' Dominic answered carefully, because he was already certain that Jordan was going to be headed for Theatre, rather than home. 'I'll call her now.'

'Thanks,' Jordan said. 'He's a good friend,' he told

Rachel, and then tried to focus on her. His eyes, thanks to all the morphine, were little pinpoints. 'He made a terrible husband, I'll bet, but he's a good friend.'

'Try and get some sleep,' Rachel said gently, impressing herself with how calm and gentle she kept her voice.

She gave him a nice smile as he closed his eyes and fell asleep.

'Good God!' she said to Dominic as he returned from calling Heather. 'Did you go into the doctors' mess with a megaphone and tell them all your ex-wife was working in the Emergency Department?'

Dominic had the audacity to laugh. 'People talk, Rachel.'

'Well, *I* don't.'

'Normal people, then. Look, Jordan's the most discreet person—honestly, Rachel. He knows me from way back. We went to med school together.'

'Well, when he's sobered up, would you please remind your friend that I don't want this getting out?'

She was cross, but Dominic's laughter was infectious, and she found that she was smiling and feeling just a little bit warm on the inside. Their marriage had mattered enough to Dominic that he'd had to share it with his friend.

'I'll remind him,' Dominic said as the radiographer came out.

Jordan was wheeled in and Rachel went with him.

'Busy?' the radiographer asked her in a dry tone.

'Just a bit.'

Jordan was lovely and co-operative, and didn't need to be told to hold his breath when the chest films were taken, but he did whimper at some of the positions required for other images.

'Stay nice and still,' the radiographer said as she

and Rachel stood behind the lead screen. 'As still as you can…'

Rachel frowned, because Jordan was suddenly restless and pulling the film from under his arm.

'Jordan?' Rachel came out from behind the screen. 'Jordan!'

He was struggling to breathe. She took his pulse and found it was irregular, and saw he was starting to turn blue. The radiographer hit the emergency button that would turn on a strobe light above the room and also in the ED, to indicate that urgent help was required.

'Get Dominic!' Rachel called to the radiographer as she laid Jordan flat.

Dominic glanced up and saw the flashing light. It must have been set off by accident, he told himself as he looked to its source.

Jordan had a fractured clavicle, for God's sake.

But years of experience had Dominic standing, ready to dash in.

He strode into X-Ray and was met with the precariousness of life.

Jordan was blue and Rachel was using an Ambu bag to attempt to breathe life into him. The radiographer was attaching the defibrillator and also an oxygen saturation probe to his finger.

'What happened?' Dominic asked as he took the stethoscope from Rachel's neck.

'He became agitated,' Rachel said. 'Sudden collapse. Should we get him round to Resus?'

Jordan's oxygen saturations were dire, and as Dominic listened to his breath sounds he figured out what had happened. 'Tension pneumothorax,' he said, taking a ten-mil syringe from the emergency trolley. 'I'm going to do a needle thoracostomy here.'

He really must have nerves of steel, he thought, because he shut out the fact that it was probably his closest friend he was stabbing with a syringe. But when there was a popping sound, and the hiss of trapped air being released, he let out a breath of relief of his own.

'What the hell—?' Zaima said as she ran in. 'Oh, Jordan...'

It was horrible—horrible for everyone. But soon they had him back in Resus, though he was flailing and conscious by the time they got there.

'Stay still, Jordan,' Dominic ordered, his eyes like a hawk's, taking it all in as he attempted to stay back and let the team work on his friend.

Soon they had him stabilised, and Dominic took on the less-than-pleasant task of calling Heather to update her.

Dominic didn't look forward to that call one bit.

But Jordan was a lot more comfortable now, with heavy-duty pain relief and a chest tube in, and he would be headed for Theatre as soon as a slot opened up—although they were seriously backed up.

'We might try and get him onto the ward,' Zaima had said. 'At least then he can wait in a comfortable bed.'

Rachel was checking Jordan's blood pressure when Dominic came back from calling Heather. Jordan's face was the colour of putty.

'How is she?' Jordan asked groggily.

'She's okay,' Dominic said. 'Her mother's on her way to look after the children, and then Heather will be here. I said I'd stay with you till she comes.'

'Is she very upset?'

'She's fine. Just annoyed that you didn't bring home her curry…'

He was trying to keep things light, but the truth was it had taken a lot to calm Heather down. He didn't want to stress out Jordan with all that.

The second he'd mentioned the curry, Dominic had glanced over at Rachel and caught her eyes. The porcelain skin that never flushed suddenly had, and Dominic knew that Rachel was remembering that long-ago night before it had all gone so wrong for them.

Of course, neither Jordan nor Zaima had the slightest clue of the history that danced between them…

As Dominic waited for Heather to arrive, he sat by Jordan and watched Rachel work.

Not in an obvious way—more he just sat by Jordan, who was dozing, and she appeared now and then to check his obs, or he caught sight of her wheeling a patient past. She looked ever more tired and pale as the night progressed, and the band holding her ponytail slipped lower.

He wondered why, with all the painted beauty available to him tonight, it was still her.

Had always been her, really.

There had never been another woman who absorbed him as much, and he pondered how her bland expression as she steered a huge singing drunk man in a wheelchair through the department could make him smile.

The queen of deadpan, he'd once called her.

She never fully revealed her thoughts and it had driven him crazy at times.

At other times, though, he had relished the game of guessing what was going on in her mind. The thrill of the chase and the flirtation had never been better with anyone else than it had been between them.

And now it had started again.

She stopped by the trolley where Jordan lay, still sleeping. 'He's first on the list for the morning,' she told Dominic. 'You might as well head home.'

'I said I'd stay till Heather gets here—though it won't be for a while, as her mother lives a good few hours away.'

'Well, I'm going on my break,' she told him. 'Do you want to share my roll?'

'I would love to share your roll, Rachel.'

It was just a cheese-and-salad roll, with a generous layer of Henderson's Relish, and she sliced it into two in the unit's kitchen.

They had shared many such rolls in the past.

On the day he had started at Rachel's school, instead of heading to the dining room, he had sat with her under a vast oak and she had shared her homemade lunch with him.

Now she made two mugs of builder's tea—dark and strong and exactly how he had come to like it. And as he watched her squeeze the teabags and flick them into the bin, he knew not a single person watching would even guess they were flirting. Even if cameras were trained on them and their moves were being analysed, no one would be able to tell.

But they were.

She carried the plates and he carried the mugs, and they went into the large, deserted staff room and sat down opposite each other.

'Still like the relish, I see,' he said in his fake northern accent, after he'd taken a bite and tasted the spicy fruity tang that was a staple in the Walker household—well, everywhere in Sheffield, really.

'Aye!' Rachel said.

'Reminds me of the lunch breaks I'd take when I worked with your dad.'

'I am sorry about that.'

'About what?'

'About my family. They gave you a hard time.'

'Not really,' he dismissed, but then he laughed mirthlessly, because the Walkers weren't exactly sensitive New Age guys and it had been one hell of a time when he'd worked with them. 'Yeah, it was pretty rough—but that said, they were just being protective. I did get you pregnant; they were never going to go easy on me.'

And this time he didn't shrug, but told her a truth instead.

'That year of working with them did me a lot of favours. For all his blundering ways, your dad's actually very good at small talk.' He gave a soft laugh of recall. 'He could chat to anyone,' Dominic said. 'I mean, moving house is one of the most stressful times of people's lives, yet your dad would nail it each and every time, and some of it rubbed off on me.'

'Really?'

Dominic nodded, then watched as she lay back in her seat and closed her eyes—not to sleep, but to sigh. 'What a night…'

'I know,' Dominic agreed.

In the scheme of things, a tension pneumothorax on a Saturday night was something they were well used to, but it felt very different when it was a colleague and friend.

'How was Heather?'

'Terrified,' Dominic admitted. 'I tried to play it down a bit, but she's a doctor herself. She knows it was touch and go for a moment.'

'Not with you there,' she said, opening her eyes and looking right at him. 'Your hand didn't even shake.'

'Well, I wouldn't be much good if it did. I just had to shut it all out and focus on the task, and then panic afterwards...' Then he admitted the truth. 'He'd just told me that Heather's pregnant again.'

'God!'

'I'd literally just told him what a lucky bastard he was...'

'Really?' Rachel said. 'And there I was thinking you'd be giving him the name of your vasectomy surgeon.'

It was a little dig, but it made both of them smile.

He'd never expected her to smile about it...

In fact, Rachel was surprised to discover that what she felt was the oddest sensation of sweet relief. Perhaps, she told herself, it was because it took any future for them—even if it was only in her imaginings—right off the table. Because more than anything Rachel wanted to be a mother some day.

Only that wasn't quite it.

She was looking right at him.

Still.

And the news that he'd had a vasectomy somehow made sex—well, just about sex.

It was actually quite liberating.

It all boiled down to desire.

And that desire was there.

Zaima came in then and broke the spell. She had come for a coffee, rather than her meal break, she said, though Rachel was sure it was actually to find out all the gossip from the Emergency team's night out.

'Who else was up on the tables?' she asked Dominic. 'Was May?'

'No!' Dominic grinned.

'What about Louise from Maternity?'

'I don't think so,' Dominic said.

Usually that would have been something he'd notice, thought Rachel—because Louise, a midwife on Maternity, was stunning.

Zaima pushed for more gossip by bribing him with salt-and-vinegar crisps. 'What about Tara?'

'She was there.' He nodded.

And Rachel was horrified to feel a slight twitch of her nose. Her superpower was fading... But then, it had never been put to the test against the thought of Dominic dancing with another woman before.

Zaima didn't pick up on the tension between Rachel and Dominic because there was nothing to see.

The chemistry belonged entirely to them.

Rachel's internal radar was tuned with precision to him, and she knew, even though he chatted and ate crisps, that his little pauses before answering Zaima's questions were down to her presence.

Indeed, Dominic *was* having trouble focusing on the conversation—because it was killing him not to have Rachel again. And it was killing him to work alongside her.

No, things could not continue as they were. The fault line was shifting. But he was more than happy to suffer any collision that might be ahead if it meant he got to be with Rachel again.

He glanced over to where she sat, watching the television and sipping her tea, as if butter wouldn't melt in her mouth, but he was certain of the fire that was growing between them.

'I'd better get back,' Zaima said.

Rachel glanced up at the clock to see how much of her meal break she had left. 'I'll be back in ten.'

She turned back to the television, but the image on it seemed blurry and she had no idea what else was being said, such was her awareness of Dominic in the room.

'Do you ever think of us?' Dominic asked suddenly.

Rachel swallowed. She wanted to give a dismissive laugh, as if that might shut him down, except it would be a blatant lie. 'Sometimes.'

'Because I've been thinking about us a lot of late,' Dominic pushed, 'and I think you've been thinking about us too.'

'What part of us?' Rachel asked dryly, and continued staring ahead. 'The arguments, the bills, the—?'

'Not those parts.'

She swallowed again. She was tempted to pick up her mug and walk out, but then she turned and looked at Dominic, thirteen years older and somehow all the sexier for it. Which was incredible, because there had not been a single thing she would have changed about him back then. Yet here he was, pale from lack of sleep, with dark shadows under his eyes and unshaven, and he still made her weak with wanting.

'It would be a mistake,' Rachel said, talking about the sex that now seemed inevitable.

'Perhaps,' Dominic conceded. 'However, of all my regrets—and with you there are many—one of the biggest is that I can't remember the last time we did it.'

She was startled.

For once she was actually startled—and not because of what he'd said, more because she had been thinking the same thing.

'Neither can I,' she admitted.

Their sex life had died with their baby. It hadn't felt right to reach out for comfort. For solace. For the moment of peace their lovemaking gave. She hadn't known how.

And on top of all that for Rachel there had been a sense of impending doom that their marriage was about to end.

But she also hated it that she couldn't remember their last time.

She'd tried to think back, but they'd been at it all the time. If she'd known that it was the last time she'd have treated the moment, the memory, with infinite care.

'It might complicate things,' she said now.

'Or it might clear the air,' Dominic said. 'I want to remember our last time.'

There was a warning there—that it would be a one-off—even as he invited her to play this dangerous game.

She could have chosen to take offence, but she didn't, for if she decided to give in to her perpetual desire for him, then it most certainly would be for the last time.

She gave him a smile, but no answer, collecting her mug and returning to work.

Rachel had made her decision.

Richard knew about them, his wife probably knew, and Jordan knew. Very soon everyone would know...

She simply could not work in a goldfish bowl where their failed marriage was gossiped about.

And she could not move on with her life alongside him.

She was leaving The Primary.

Heather arrived at just after seven in the morning, and Rachel walked her up to the ward to which Jordan had been transferred.

'Of all the irresponsible things to do!' Heather said as they took the lift. 'What on earth was he doing, dancing on a table?'

'Letting off steam?' Rachel ventured.

'Killing himself, more like,' Heather said, letting off a little steam of her own.

She was clearly frantic and scared as the ward nurse pointed them in the direction of his bed, in a four-bed pod near the nurses' station.

Dominic was sitting in a chair beside him, but jumped up when he saw Heather and gave her a hug.

'He's going to be fine,' Dominic said.

And Heather stopped being cross as soon as she saw her husband, groggy from medication and with tubes and drips everywhere.

'Oh, Jordan,' she sobbed. '*Look* at you!'

'Heather…' Jordan said. 'I'm so sorry.'

'Stop that now,' Heather said as she hugged him. 'It's just rotten luck.'

It made Rachel feel teary, and she wasn't quite sure why. Their intimacy and obvious affection and love had brought a rare lump to her throat, but she swallowed it down as she heard someone call out to her.

'Staff Nurse Walker?'

She turned at the sound of her name and there, sitting up in bed, smiling at her in the semi-darkness, was a wonderfully familiar face.

'Miss Tate!'

She went over to the bed, delighted to see her elderly patient from the other day. Her arm was in a sling attached to an IV pole, and she wore a white theatre gown.

'How's your hand doing?' Rachel asked, assuming she had had it repaired.

'The same as when you last saw it.' Miss Tate rolled her eyes. 'My surgery has been cancelled three times. There have been a lot of emergencies. Still, hopefully I'll be sorted this morning. I've been put on "Nil by Mouth" again. It's a good way to go on a diet, let me tell you.'

'You poor thing.'

'Oh, I don't know about that. I'm quite enjoying watching the world go by. What did he do?' She nodded in the direction of Jordan's bed.

'I can't tell you that!' Rachel smiled.

'Well, I heard he was dancing on a table.' Miss Tate laughed. 'Good for him, I say. I danced on a few tables in my day.'

'Really?'

'Oh, yes.' Miss Tate nodded. 'And I'd dance on them again, given half a chance.'

So would Rachel.

Well, not so much dance on a table, but she felt a growing need to be with Dominic again.

And later, as she came out of Emergency at the end of a very long night shift, Dominic was standing at the entrance.

'Do you want a lift home?' he asked.

'No,' Rachel said.

She went to walk off, but desire was coursing through her, and she could almost taste the lonely regret she would feel if she climbed into her bed alone and missed out on just one more time with him.

Dominic Hadley was her eternal Achilles' heel.

Maybe sleeping with him once more might just clear her head after all—because she was going crazy.

Perhaps in going to bed with him she could finally put *them* to bed and then move on with her life…?

She knew the arguments were flimsy, but she was too weak to care. She simply wanted to be with him.

And so, instead of walking away, she met his eyes. 'We can go to yours.'

CHAPTER EIGHT

IT WAS RAINING in London.

Just as it had been raining in Sheffield, the sublime second time that they had made love.

'Wait there,' Dominic said. 'I'll bring the car round.'

Rachel stood in the ambulance bay while he dashed through the rain. He had always taken care of those details, Rachel thought. His silver sports car didn't impress her a jot, but the driver certainly did.

He was soaking from his run in the rain. Just as he'd been that time with the stupid golf umbrella when he'd thrown off his parents' warnings about her and made his way to her father's house, Rachel thought as she climbed in.

The wipers swished a little more smoothly than the *thump, thump* of her heart. At a set of traffic lights she turned to look at him, and Dominic turned at the same time, and they smiled their private smile for the first time since they'd met again.

Dominic lived a fifteen-minute drive from the hospital, she found, as the gates opened to a very plush apartment block where they parked in the basement.

They took a lift up to his apartment, but she noticed little about it as she stepped in—just that it was neat and rather large. Because she cared not for the view from the windows…only for the man who took her straight to his bedroom.

He didn't kiss her, and he didn't bother with any pre-amble. Dominic simply went for the hem of her top and she lifted her arms, compliant and willing.

She wore a rather tired white bra that he deftly re-moved, and her skin was so pale that you might almost miss the pale pink of her areolae, already gathered and taut at the prospect of his return…

Dominic did not miss them.

Her nipples were awake, and he stroked them with un-ending fascination, but there was more he wanted to see.

He drew down her trousers and was pleasantly sur-prised by the tiny silver knickers and the jut of gold be-neath.

'God, Rachel,' Dominic said, and paused in the un-dressing just to stroke and admire.

He slipped his fingers in and felt her for a moment, before stripping off himself. And there, in his bedroom, her mask slipped too.

It always had.

So much so that when he retrieved some condoms from his jacket her nose did that pinched thing, and this time her eyes narrowed too.

'Rachel,' he said. 'I bought these with *you* in mind.'

'Liar.'

'Nope,' he said. 'I lied to myself, but I was always hoping to have you last night—if you'd deigned to show up to the staff do.'

She peeled a condom off with a reluctant smile, for here in his bedroom they could admit to their jealous natures where each other were concerned.

Here, standing naked before him, Rachel could forget her own rules and drop her guard. There was so much desire between them, so much want blazing in their eyes, that she felt safe.

She reached out to touch his body. The strong arms, the broad chest, the toned stomach and the swell of his erection had her trembling with want.

'What's this?' She ran a slender finger over an old white scar, low on his stomach, and watched his muscles jerk tight at her touch.

'I had my appendix out a few—' Dominic started, and then stopped explaining as that same slender finger ran up his thick length.

For Rachel it was like the dessert trolley coming round and having to choose. It was either sink to her knees and taste him, or step towards him and have him inside her.

But he made the choice for her and pulled her in.

Their naked bodies met again, and with the feel of his hard, taut skin against hers, his soft mouth was an exciting contrast. Unlike their kiss in the car park, which had been desperate and urgent, now his mouth was gentle on hers, savouring this reunion.

He had a scent, and a taste, and it was like coming home after a long time away.

His hands were warm on her skin, holding her waist and then moving down and cupping her buttocks, pressing her against him.

Her hand was between them, and he moaned into her mouth as Rachel held him again, strong and velvet beneath her fingers. His kiss roughened as tears stung her eyes at the delight of again being naked and close and intimate with Dominic.

She paused only to slide on the condom, the way they had taught each other so many years ago. Except her hands were shaking even more now than then, as a lick of desire stroked low in her stomach. She thought she might come just from touching him…

His kisses became more demanding, guiding her towards the bed, and they toppled onto it together.

His hand reached between her legs, impatiently parting her willing thighs, both of them desperate for him to be inside her. She guided him greedily, crying out as Dominic seared into her tight oiled space.

They were a knot of limbs and hungry, desperate kisses. He held her face and kissed her cheeks, her lashes, then released her and moved up onto his forearms. It was not a gentle coupling for either of them after all this time, and her legs wrapped tightly around him as he thrust into her.

They had been toying with each other all night—the looks, the food, the pauses, the laughs, the warnings, the nudge of memories… All of it had led them here.

He made the air in the room impossible to breathe. He made the thoughts in her head turn off. He consumed her completely.

And then, when she shattered, when she felt the utter relief of crying out his name as she came, he gave that breathless shout she would crave for ever and released himself into her, collapsing on her in the giddy space they'd made.

Here she was, Rachel thought. The woman she'd lost.

CHAPTER NINE

CERTAINLY IT HAD been a mistake, Rachel thought as she awoke in his arms. A glorious, wonderful mistake that she would remember fondly and never regret. But, yes, it had been a mistake—because now she was right back where she didn't want to be: at the start of the long and painful process of getting over him.

Back to being in love with a man who didn't love her back.

'Hey...' Dominic said as she lifted her head.

'Did it help?' Rachel smiled. 'Did we clear the air?'

'We did,' Dominic said. 'Temporarily at least.'

Because she could tell he already wanted her again, and that he'd been lying there thinking about how right they'd felt. And what that meant.

Rachel was thinking the same.

Here, in his lovely warm bed, their limbs lazy and entwined, it would be so easy to give in to the impossible dream of *them*.

But this had been about sex, Rachel reminded herself.

Although it had always been far more than just that for her.

How did men do it? she wondered. Or rather, how did Dominic separate love from sex so easily?

She didn't seek out gossip, but certainly in the weeks

since she'd started at The Primary she'd heard enough to know that Dominic hadn't been lying when he'd said he dated. *A lot.*

It had taken her years to move on and try another relationship—Gordon had seemed ideal, for he had never pushed her out of her comfort zone the way Dominic did. He'd accepted that there were things she simply didn't want to speak about and had left it there—and Rachel had honestly thought she wanted that.

'What are you thinking?'

Rachel laughed to hide her embarrassment—because she could hardly tell him that she'd just been thinking about Gordon!

'It's rude to compare,' Dominic said.

'I wasn't.'

'I should hope not.' He smiled. 'Do you want to know what I was thinking?' he asked.

Rachel wasn't sure that she did.

'I was just thinking about us,' Dominic said as they lay there in the dark. 'If we didn't have a past, and you hadn't been engaged, if we'd met for the first time that morning in Resus, would we be in bed together now?'

'No.' Immediately Rachel shook her head.

'No?' Dominic checked.

'I'd have steered well clear of you,' Rachel said. 'I was warned about you from several sources.'

'I don't believe you.'

But Rachel was insistent. 'If we hadn't already slept together, then I wouldn't be here now. I mean it, Dominic. You're not my type.'

'In what way?'

She lifted one hand from his warm chest and started listing the many ways he did not tick her boxes. 'The reputation, the attitude, the sports car, the vasectomy so you can screw at whim…'

He caught her hand and buried his lips in her palm in a slow, long kiss that she felt all the way down low to her stomach, and when he had made her want him all over again, he refuted what she had said earlier.

'I think we'd be exactly here. In fact, I think we'd have been in bed your first week—possibly even the first night.'

'Oh, no,' she said. 'I take for ever to get into bed.'

'Then *you're* the one who's changed.'

She laughed, a deep low laugh, and it was a forgotten sound that startled her.

Of course there had been laughter in her life since him, but that low belly laugh was one only he had ever elicited—that laugh was private and seductive and it had only ever been heard by Dominic. It was a laugh that provoked, a laugh that begged him to continue this game which always ended in sex.

'I'm telling the truth,' she said.

'Suppose we had just met,' Dominic said.

She wriggled out of his arms and tried to sit up. But he pulled her back down and pinned her to his chest. Clearly he wanted this conversation and would not let her wriggle out of it.

'Suppose you'd come out for the staff do last night and you'd suspended your morals and we had ended up in bed. We'd be getting to know each other now…'

Rachel was rather sure that she wouldn't like whatever he was scheming, but feigned nonchalance. 'By all accounts, I'd have long since been in a taxi on my way home.'

'I'm not that much of a bastard, Rachel.'

His chest hair was tickling the side of her face and

she was focusing on her breathing as she braced herself for his questions.

'So,' he said. 'I would probably be asking are you seeing anyone?'

'Well, I would hope not, given that I'm here...' She cut the rancour and decided to try to play his annoying game. 'No,' she said. 'I've just come out of a long-term relationship.'

'I'm sorry,' Dominic said. 'Do you miss him?' he asked. 'Or her...?'

'Stop it!' Rachel laughed.

'I'm being politically correct, given we don't know each other at all. So,' he asked again, 'do you miss your ex?'

Not as much as I should, Rachel thought as she lay in Dominic's arms. *Not as much as I missed you.*

She settled for, 'It's early days,' and then asked him, 'What about you? Are you seeing anyone?'

'Not really.'

'What sort of answer is that?'

'Okay, no, I'm not seeing anyone seriously.'

'Have you, though?' she asked. 'Have you ever been in a long-term relationship?'

She wanted to fill in the missing years. She loathed that appendix scar—couldn't bear it that he must have lain on an operating table as she went about her day. Her hand moved involuntarily down to cover it.

'No. Well, apart from—'

But Dominic stopped himself from saying *you*, because they weren't supposed to be admitting to the fact that they'd once been married.

He also stopped because her hand was creeping down his body, so he removed it from the danger zone and caught it again. He was doing his best to tread carefully as he coaxed her out of her shell.

'I think I might need to mend my ways,' he admitted, and was relieved when she gave that low laugh. The one that signalled him to go on.

He didn't quite know what to ask next, because every question led back to them, and so, while he had her warm in his bed, he tried to imagine not knowing the little she'd told him.

He picked up a coil of her thick red hair. 'I love your hair,' he told her. 'Where does it come from?'

He felt her tense even at that simple question.

'My mum,' Rachel said.

'So she's got red hair?'

'Yes,' Rachel said. 'And green eyes like me. She's Irish.' She looked up at him, as if to explain why she was keeping it in the present tense. 'I don't tell all on first dates, Dominic.'

You don't tell all ever, he wanted to bite back, but he did not want to send her hurtling from his bed.

Finally, as they lay silently together, he was rewarded for good behaviour.

'My mum died when I was six.'

'I'm very sorry,' Dominic said carefully, and gave her shoulder a little squeeze. He honestly was. And then he asked what he had asked all those years ago, and awaited her same evasive answer even while hoping for more. 'Do you miss her?'

'Yes,' Rachel said.

'Do you remember her?' he asked, remembering that she'd always said she didn't, really.

'Bits,' Rachel admitted.

And then she allowed him a glimpse of her memories. 'I remember feeling confused when she was teaching me to read. I'd try to follow her finger but I didn't understand how what she was saying could mean "cat". She spun stories,' Rachel explained, and he liked her soft laugh beneath his cheek. 'A short book took for ever for her to read because she would always elaborate and make up new threads.'

They lay in silence and it was she who broke it.

'What about your family?' she asked.

'They're…' *The same*, he was about to say, and then he remembered they were pretending not to know about each other. 'My parents are the poster couple for staying together for the sake of money. They are miserable and it shows,' Dominic said. 'I've barely seen them since…'

It was getting hard for Dominic to play by the rules. Their lives were inextricably linked—a tapestry of a thousand threads, with each stitch linking the next— and it was almost impossible to separate them.

'Do you miss them?' she asked.

'No,' he said. 'In fact, I breathe a huge sigh of relief when the Christmas visit is done with and I don't have to see them again for months.'

'So you only see them at Christmas?'

'And at the odd awards night for my father. I send flowers to my mum on her birthday, and I call her, but again, there's the same breath of relief when I hang up.'

'They must miss having a relationship with you?'

'I don't really know—and to be honest, I don't really care.' He sighed. 'I put myself through medical school, Rachel. They said they wanted to help, but I told them it was way too late for that. It was about then that I stopped trying to look out for everyone else and decided to look out for myself instead. I chose to focus on my career rather than relationships, and while some might call me a bastard, that's only out of hours. I am brilliant at my job.'

'You don't think you can have both?'

'I don't *want* both!' Dominic snapped.

He didn't want to be in lust with his ex-wife, yet clearly he was—given they were wrapped around each other and her hand was back on his appendix scar and all he wanted to do was move it down.

He'd been so certain that he didn't want a relationship with her.

Yet here he lay, not wanting her to leave.

And he'd been so *completely* certain that he didn't want children that he'd gone and had the snip.

And yet he'd recently checked the success rates of having it reversed.

The rules were falling away, and they could no longer play this game that they were strangers who had only met last night.

Dominic decided that the trouble with bed was... Well, you were naked, and together, and it was all too easy to take one kiss, one deep kiss, and lose yourself in it. Take two, perhaps...

But Dominic would deny them that.

'Rachel...?' He peeled her warm body from him— which was a feat indeed, because he was warm and willing too. 'Why don't I go and get us something to eat?'

It had been a long time since they'd shared her roll in the staff room after all, and perhaps if they could remove all temptation they would be able to speak some more.

As Rachel watched Dominic pull on his trousers and shirt, and retrieve his wallet, his words were still hanging in the air.

'I don't want both.'

He gave her a haphazard kiss on the side of her mouth and tucked his shirt in. 'I won't be long,' he said.

After he'd gone she sat up and hugged her knees.

What the hell was she doing here? Rachel asked herself. What was she doing, playing Dominic's little getting-to-know-you game?

She didn't want her ex-husband to know she was crazy in love with him.

Still.

Still!

What was the point in handing over more of her heart when she knew it was something he didn't want?

She had been lying in her responses right from the start. When he'd asked her if they'd have ended up in bed had they not shared a past, of course the answer had been yes.

Yes, yes, *yes*!

Even if it was thirty years from now that Dominic appeared, even if he hobbled in on a walking stick with grey hair and arthritis, he'd have the ability to throw a hand grenade into her life.

Here was the proof!

Right when her life had finally been put in order, here she was back in Dominic's bed.

But only by chance.

Had she not moved to London and inadvertently taken a job at the hospital where he worked, then she might never have seen him again.

Dominic hadn't sought her out—he hadn't looked her up or tried to get in touch during their thirteen years apart.

It was just sex.

And, while sex with Dominic was bliss, Rachel wanted a relationship that was about more than that. And, as Dominic himself had just clearly stated, he didn't want that.

She wanted more than to warm his bed while he nipped out for a takeaway.

No doubt by Monday they'd be back to attempting to be professional and polite.

And failing.

Rachel knew that if she stayed they'd end up sleeping together again. It was the one thing—the only thing— they could get right.

But this really had to be their last time, because she could not be on call for Dominic and his libido.

Before she left she took out the envelope she'd been carrying in her bag since she'd had the copies of the photographs made and placed it on his dresser, propped up against a bottle of expensive cologne.

And then she wrote a little note and left it on the pillow.

At least now we can remember our last time.
  Rachel

They were all caught up now.

Dominic stepped into the bedroom and saw the empty bed and the note on the pillow.

He would never understand her.

Just when they had started talking—*properly* talking— she had withdrawn again.

Just when they had finally been getting somewhere, Rachel had crawled back into her shell.

And then he saw the envelope on the dressing table.

These were the photos he had asked for, and he'd been absolutely right: it hurt to examine the past.

They both looked so young.

So very young that he finally forgave himself for not knowing what the hell to do at the time.

Even now he wasn't sure he would know what to do.

Because there was no such thing as the perfect still-birth, and no right way to grieve for the loss of a child.

But tonight he was finally starting to.

And as the food went cold, he sat on the edge of his bed and cried for his son.

For the first time he was angry with Rachel.

She should be here, doing this with him.

He had tried so hard with her—he really had. But where was the effort from Rachel?

Had she just handed him this envelope on Friday, he'd have been grateful to look at the photos alone, but she had just left his bed.

Just left his bed and abandoned him to do this alone.

He'd been right all those years ago.

Rachel Walker *was* cold.

CHAPTER TEN

Miss Dorothy Tate
Eighty-two
Tendon repair

DOMINIC'S INTENTION WAS to skim through the notes and then assess the patient for himself—except Rachel's handwriting jumped out at him as if it had been written in neon.

He knew that writing almost as well as he knew his own, and he found that he smiled as he read it. Even her sparse notes said so much about the patient.

Cut hand making soup for the homeless!

He walked into the anaesthetic area and introduced himself. 'How are you, Miss Tate?'

'To be honest, I'm feeling like rather a nuisance.'

'Absolutely you're not,' Dominic refuted. 'Accidents happen. I know your surgery has been cancelled and rescheduled a few times over the weekend, and I'm sorry about that.'

'Well, there have been a lot of emergencies…'

'There have been, but hopefully you've been well looked after?'

'Very much so.' Miss Tate nodded.

Dominic made more small talk as he put in a second IV, in case it was needed. 'What were you doing playing with knives with these hands?' he asked when he saw her gnarled fingers.

'I was making soup.'

'So I read,' Dominic said. 'For the homeless.'

'Well, someone has to take care of them.'

'Yes,' Dominic agreed. 'But how about you let us take care of *you* now?'

He went through the procedure with her and explained that she would be having a regional block rather than a general anaesthetic.

'You won't feel a thing, but I can give you a light sedative if you like.'

'I don't want a sedative. I like to know what's going on. Will you be with me, Doctor?'

'The whole time. So if you change your mind just let me know.'

'I won't change my mind.' Miss Tate smiled.

She watched him as he worked and Dominic could feel her eyes on him.

'You look tired, Doctor,' she said.

'Not at all,' Dominic lied.

'Were you on call last night?'

'No.' He shook his head, and of course he didn't add that he'd been up most of the night looking through photographs.

'You were there on Saturday night,' she commented.

'Where?'

'With Jordan—the one who fell off the table dancing. Such a lovely young man. You stayed by his bed until his wife arrived.'

'Yes.' Dominic nodded.

He went through her medical history. Apart from some arthritis in her hands, there wasn't much of note.

'What's your secret?' he asked.

'I never married,' Miss Tate said, and smiled.

Dominic gave a wry laugh and decided he liked this old girl.

'What about you?' she asked.

He looked down into shrewd bright blue eyes and realised she knew. No doubt she had heard Jordan bringing Heather up to speed—and after he'd asked him not to say anything as well.

Seeing those blue eyes that had seen a whole lot more than he had, Dominic told the truth. 'Once,' he admitted, and saw the eyes of the anaesthetic nurse look up in surprise.

'Married?' the nurse said. 'You?'

'Yep.'

It was a relief to admit it. Dominic was sick of playing by Rachel's rules. Whether she liked it or not, they had once been a couple—a couple who had had a son. He couldn't keep hiding the past, when it was here in front of him, in plain sight.

His past wouldn't be there for much longer, though. Rachel was at this very moment taking herself out of his life.

'Could I have a word, please, May?'

She should have done this the very first day she saw Dominic.

For some people, working alongside an ex might be no big deal. For Rachel, it had proved to be something far worse than hell—it had been a glimpse of impossible bliss.

'I'd really appreciate it if you didn't let on to anyone

else that I'm leaving,' she told May. 'I've only been here a few weeks and I'd really rather just slip off.'

And she'd be slipping off very soon, given that she had been here less than a month, which meant there wasn't even any notice to serve. But she agreed to see out the week.

'What about the flat?' May asked. 'Are you going to lose a lot of money for breaking your lease?'

'A bit,' Rachel admitted.

'What price your peace of mind, though?' May smiled. 'We'll be sorry to lose you, Rachel. You're a wonderful emergency nurse. Though I have to say I'm surprised you lasted as long as you did. When you told me you and Gordon had broken up, I expected your notice the next day.'

Gordon.

What a time for May to finally remember his name.

But it was like hearing the name of a song she'd once known—familiar, but the lyrics were a little hard to recall.

Then she took a patient up to the orthopaedic ward, and there, standing at the end of Jordan's bed and having a chat with him, was her song.

Or rather, there was Dominic.

Dominic was the song that made her heart lurch in recall, the song that dragged her up to the dance floor each and every time, the song she sang in the shower, the song she turned up the second she heard the introduction, the song she sang at full volume...

Dominic Hadley was her song.

And she simply had to stop listening to it.

Dominic glanced up and saw her and, still smarting from her walking out on him, turned his back and returned to his conversation with Jordan.

It didn't go unnoticed by Miss Tate, and as he left the ward, she gave him a look.

A look he knew only too well.

A look that told him, *You can behave better than that.*

CHAPTER ELEVEN

HER LAST SHIFT at The Primary.

A late shift.

It was a gorgeous spring day—her first warm one in London—and to celebrate, Rachel had put on a flimsy dress that tied at the side and topped it with a white cardigan and some flat sandals.

She wasn't the only one. Cheered by the first glimpse of sun, everyone seemed to have taken the chance to lose their dark coats and boots. There were people outside the cafés and flowers in pots outside the pub.

It was as if London were pulling out all the stops and trying to persuade her to stay, because she had never seen it so vibrant and pretty.

It was rather a different case at The Primary.

May and a porter were running through the car park with a gurney. Rachel considered going to help, then saw them helping a heavily pregnant woman to stand up and realised it was all under control and she might be needed more inside.

There were ambulances and police cars lined up, and police officers in the corridor when Rachel stepped inside. In fact, the place was so busy that there wasn't even time for a handover.

She went quickly to change into scrubs, then put

her hand up for Minor Injuries, where she practically lived now.

Or rather, where she practically hid.

When she went for her coffee break, before the early staff headed off, thankfully there was no Dominic in the staff room.

'Rachel!'

Just as she had on her first day there, she heard May calling her down to the main section.

The timing could not have been worse—because as she walked through the department, she saw Richard and Dominic there.

'I need a word with you before I head off,' May said as she wrote on the whiteboard and then took off her glasses. 'What a day!' She closed her eyes and massaged her temples. 'I have not drawn breath since I got here this morning. That poor woman fainting in the car park... hostage negotiations with a psych patient...'

'Sounds like I missed a bad one.' Rachel pushed out a smile, relieved when she saw that both Dominic and Richard had stood up and were clearly about to leave.

'We're heading back to the ITU, May,' Richard told her.

'But Labour and Delivery are looking for you,' May said.

Richard rolled his eyes. 'We're not covering them.'

'Please, Richard,' May said. 'It's for a patient who was here earlier.'

Richard took the phone with a sigh, and told L&D the same, but then he fell quiet. 'Okay, I'll be right up.'

'I can go.'

'No, no...' Richard said, but then his pager buzzed in his pocket.

Rachel glanced up when he sighed.

'Actually, I have to go to the ITU, so if you could go to L&D? Epidural…'

'Sure,' Dominic said.

'I'll fill you in on the way up.'

This would be the last time she saw Dominic, Rachel thought. Standing there sullen and ignoring her. And she would miss him for ever.

'Poor lass…' May tutted. 'She was going to leave it all to nature, but they must have decided to induce her…'

'Who?' Rachel asked.

May was too busy to answer her, but her words were enough to have Rachel looking at the admission log.

Vanda Callum, aged twenty-seven, was the 'poor lass' who had fainted in the car park.

She'd been in the Emergency Department for all of fifteen minutes, and had soon been transferred to the maternity unit, but there was enough written in the notes for Rachel to know that she had suffered a death in utero.

This type of patient was the very reason that Rachel hadn't been able to face midwifery.

Well, that and the healthy pink babies who cried, too.

How did Dominic do it? Rachel wondered as he and Richard headed off. Because she felt sick inside.

How did he do this? Dominic asked himself as he arrived at Labour and Delivery and Stella, the associate unit manager, handed him the notes.

'Thanks for coming. I know you're not covering us today, but I couldn't get anyone else. Freya's set up for you. Full term,' she said, and went through the history. 'Vanda came up from Antenatal this morning, when they couldn't find a heartbeat. She and her husband decided to go home and have some time there, wait for a natural delivery, but on her way out she fainted in the car park and came back up to us via the ED. She had an ECG and bloods, but it was a simple faint. Just overwhelmed and grieving.'

'Okay,' Dominic said, looking carefully at the heart tracing and blood results as Stella continued to bring him up to speed.

'Dr Mina induced her, and initially Vanda said she didn't want an epidural, but it's all getting too much for her.'

Dominic nodded.

The Primary was a very busy hospital, with a huge maternity unit, so naturally he had dealt with this sad situation many times, and it was never easy on anyone. But for Dominic, who normally did his level best to keep his memories at bay, today was proving a struggle.

Since seeing those photos, since being with Rachel, it felt new and raw again—as if it had happened only recently.

He slipped quietly into the dark room.

'Here's the anaesthetist now,' Freya said to the patient, with her signature light touch, and she gave Dominic a smile.

Vanda's partner looked up with a grim, helpless and desperate expression that Dominic recognised—for he'd once worn that same expression himself.

'I'm Dominic Hadley, the registrar anaesthetist. What would you prefer me to call you?'

The patient didn't respond.

'Vanda,' her husband said for her. 'And I'm Greg.'

Dominic shook his hand and then explained to Vanda what would be happening. 'I know I can't take the pain of your loss away,' he added. 'But I *can* make you more comfortable.'

He checked all her vitals himself, and then the epidural

was quietly done, with Freya holding Vanda as Greg sat with his head in his hands—trying, Dominic guessed, to summon the strength for the next bit.

Rachel hadn't wanted an epidural either.

He remembered standing in a small interview room, with her father and four hulking brothers, trying his eighteen-year-old best to explain to her father what was going on against the background sound of Rachel's pained moans.

'Can't they give her something?' Dave had come close to shouting. 'Can't she have an operation?'

'The doctor says there are risks with surgery.'

'But can't they numb her or something?' Dave had started pacing. 'Can't they give her something to take away her pain? She shouldn't have to go through this. She won't be able to handle it,' Dave had said. 'I'm going to speak to the doctor myself...'

He'd stormed off and Dominic had gone after him, desperate to avoid her father bursting into the delivery suite and causing a scene.

'Dave, I really think we should listen to Rachel...'

'What would *you* know? This is all your bloody fault!' Dave had flung at him.

And then he'd given Dominic a look—*such* a look—for all the ways he had made his daughter suffer.

Dominic had forced himself to speak. 'Dave... Can we put things aside for tonight, please? Just keep it down for Rachel's sake? She needs us to be calm.'

'You don't get it. It's going to be like when her mum died all over again. She was inconsolable, Dominic...'

Dave had pressed his fingers into his eyes and Dominic had stood there, not knowing what to say because he simply hadn't known this side of Rachel.

'We were all upset—of course we were,' Dave had

continued. 'I was devastated. But Rachel was terrible. Every night she cried herself to sleep, and then woke up crying the next day. I had to fetch her out of school more times than I can count.'

'I didn't know that,' Dominic had admitted. 'But, Dave, I can only go on what she's telling me now. And she's telling me and the midwife and the doctor that she doesn't want anything for the pain...'

Dave had started to cry then—only the second time he'd seen Rachel's father's tears. The first time had been when Dominic had told him his daughter was pregnant and Dave had said he wished her mother was here. He'd said the same thing again.

'I wish her mother was here. She'd know what to do.' And then he'd wiped his eyes and blown his nose and taken a big breath. 'Tears aren't going to get us anywhere. You're right, lad. We have to listen to Rachel. We both want what's best for her.'

'We do,' Dominic had said, relieved that her father wasn't going to make a scene. 'I'd better go back in.'

He did not want to relive that night.

But he was doing it—he was—and he ached for this young couple and their journey ahead.

'There you go,' Dominic said as he secured the epidural. 'It's all done. It will start to take effect very soon.'

He helped Freya get Vanda lying back in the bed, and then slipped away to write up his notes.

A short while later Freya joined him. 'Thanks for that.'

'No problem.'

'I'm just giving them some space,' Freya said, and then sighed as she sat down. 'I've got the best job in the world most of the time, but nights like this kind of redress the balance.'

Dominic made no comment. He was in absolutely no mood for a chat.

Freya looked over to him. 'You were ever so nice to her.'

'I would hope so,' Dominic clipped.

He did *not* want to talk about this, so he quickly concluded his notes. But as he headed off, he ran into Richard coming out of the lift.

'Everything okay?' he asked.

'Yep.' Dominic nodded. 'Freya's at the desk.'

'I'm not looking for Freya—I came to check on you.'

'Why?'

'Because I saw your ex-wife's face when she looked at the admissions log. Because there's an obvious reason why teenagers might feel they have to get married. And because, assuming you don't have a teenager of your own that you haven't told me about, this patient will have been difficult for you. Freya and I—'

'Oh, for God's sake!' Dominic retorted. So that attempt at a chat from Freya had been for *his* benefit. 'Leave it, Richard,' Dominic warned him—except the muscles in his jaw knitted and he was appalled to feel that he might break down in the hospital corridor.

He strode off, cross with Richard for discussing it with Freya, but all the while knowing he would have done the same had the situation been the other way around.

He didn't need them meddling in his love life.

Love life?

What a joke.

He leant against the wall and closed his eyes.

He'd hurt Rachel so badly, and taken away the chance of the one thing she wanted most. They'd been over before they'd even started. They couldn't even speak about their son...

Or rather, Rachel wouldn't.

Nor would she speak about the end of their marriage.

And neither would she speak about her mum.

Yet she'd been inconsolable when she'd died—Dave had told him as much. Or rather, Dave had said she'd been *terrible*.

He thought of his own stunned reaction to the matter-of-fact way she'd spoken about her mother all those years ago, then pressed his knuckles into his mouth when he thought of Dave Walker and his brusque, insensitive ways dealing with a grieving six-year-old child.

Rachel wasn't cold. Dominic knew that then. The poor thing was frozen.

And he couldn't blame Dave, because he didn't know how to talk about it either—especially with Rachel. There was so much other stuff that got in the way...

And then he looked back to the L&D unit and thought about the couple in there, and he hoped that they'd do better than he and Rachel had.

They had to speak about Christopher. But it always got mired in other stuff—their marriage, their break-up, their families...

Dominic took a breath, and summoned those nerves of steel he'd fought to acquire.

At work he could shut out the world and focus only on the task.

And that was exactly what he needed to do now.

'See you, Rachel!' Tara said.

Probably not, Rachel thought, but smiled and gave a little wave as Tara headed off.

And that was that.

She'd said goodbye to May when she'd finished at four—that had been the reason May had called her down—but apart from May, no one knew her time at The Primary was done.

What on earth had she been thinking to wear a flimsy dress when it was only March? she wondered. Because that lovely warm spring day had turned into a blowy cold night when she stepped out into the draughty corridor.

And there waiting for her was Dominic.

'Rachel,' said Dominic, and pushed off from the wall he'd been leaning on.

'Oh, did we agree to have sex again?'

Rachel was at her sarcastic best.

'Only, I must have forgotten to pencil you in.'

'No.' Dominic couldn't help but smile as she sniped at him. 'I came here so we could talk.'

'Well, I don't want to talk to you,' Rachel said.

'I know you don't,' Dominic said. 'You've made that abundantly clear.' He called out to her departing back. 'You're walking off now just as you walked out on us the other night—just as you walked out on our marriage.'

She turned furiously to him. 'I did not walk out on our marriage.'

'You withdrew,' Dominic said, but then he caught himself—because he had not come down here to row about their marriage, nor about the other night.

Focus on the reason you're here, Dominic reminded himself.

'I came down to ask if we can speak about Christopher.'

'You're at work, Dominic.'

'I've asked a colleague to cover me for as long as it takes, and Richard's loaned me his office so we won't be disturbed.'

He didn't want to do this at work, but neither did he

want this conversation to take place in a bar or restaurant. And as for his home—well, there was the distraction of a bed.

And he and Rachel did *not* need the distraction of a bed.

Here at work he could focus better, and right now he was entirely focused on *her*. On the jut of her chin, the glare in her eyes that warned him to stay back.

Well, no more.

'I don't want to talk about it,' she said.

'Why?' Dominic persisted, refusing to back off.

He saw her blinking rapidly.

'Why can't we talk about it?'

Rachel could feel the flutter of her pulse in her throat and her eyes darted to the entrance as she planned a swift exit.

'He was our son and I think it's time we spoke about him together, but you have to want to,' said Dominic.

She'd *always* wanted to, but she was terrified of breaking down, scared of showing the depth of her pain.

'I might get upset,' she said.

'Yes,' Dominic agreed, looking at her.

To the rest of the world they might look as if they were discussing the weather, but she knew there was so much more if only she could let him in.

'You probably will get upset, and no doubt so will I.'

She looked at him, standing so steady and together and strong.

'I can take your pain, Rachel,' he said. 'If you'll let me.'

'What if you can't?' Her voice was hoarse with strain.

'Rachel, I *can*.'

He sounded so certain that it steadied the panic that clawed at her throat.

She knew this was her last chance to speak of Christopher with him, given she was leaving, but more than that, after Dominic's admission that he too might get upset, she finally felt ready.

'Come on,' he said.

They walked together up the long corridor, not touching, but then she shivered, and he must have seen her, and not caring that someone might see, nor what they might think, he put an arm around her and held her hand.

She was grateful for his warmth.

He put on the *Do Not Disturb* light outside Richard's door and, barring all hell breaking loose in ED, for now it was just the two of them.

There was a picture on Richard's desk, of him with Freya and their baby, and her eyes were drawn to that because she wanted that happy family photo so badly.

Instead of the one she had tucked inside that folder.

'Thanks for the photos,' Dominic said. 'Though not...'

He'd been about to say, *Not for the way you left them*, she thought, but stopped himself.

'It's good to finally have them.'

'I should have sent them to you years ago,' Rachel admitted. 'Although I didn't know where. Still, I should have tried...'

'Rachel, I wasn't ready to look at them...' Dominic paused. 'Until the other night.'

He took out his wallet and opened it up, and then positioned it so that a picture of the three of them now sat on the desk. She gazed on the photo for a long moment and then looked at Dominic, at his pale face and lips and the shadows under his eyes, and then she blinked in surprise when he gave her a slow smile.

'He was beautiful.'

She nodded.

'He had your hands,' Dominic said, and he took her hand and examined it, as if confirming that his memory was correct as he held her long fingers. 'I remember holding him and thinking I'd never seen such perfect hands apart from yours.'

He had been too delicate to be held for very long, but there had been those treasured cuddles, and she shared one of her memories now.

'He had your mouth.'

Beautiful lips that she had wanted so desperately to see stretch and cry and one day smile if only he'd had the chance...

'Why couldn't he have lived?' she asked.

'I don't know.'

'Why?' She asked the impossible question again. 'I feel like everything died that day.' She started to cry—not loudly, but tears were beginning to spill out. 'Not just Christopher, but us, and everything I ever wanted to be, all just died with him.'

'I know.'

Rachel really cried then, and for the first time since her mum had died, she wasn't reprimanded for it. Or told to 'Hush', or 'Enough now', or be taken to the park.

Dominic moved his chair close to hers and held her and let her cry.

'His legs...' Rachel said, and Dominic crumpled, when he thought of those sturdy little legs that had never kicked, never walked, never run.

He wanted the quiet glory of running with his son.

That feeling when you knew you had just conquered the world.

He should have seen his son shoot out of the starting

blocks and on to victory. His legs, even in the bewilderment of death, had been present and strong.

When Rachel looked up and saw that Dominic was crying too, she didn't know how to react. There were tears on his cheeks and in his velvet brown eyes. She'd never seen him like this in her life, and somehow it helped to see him cry for their little son.

'There was nothing I could do for him,' Dominic rasped. 'Nothing. I couldn't even warm him.'

She remembered Dominic tucking a blanket around him and holding him close, and that made her cry all over again, but it felt better to cry with him, to witness his love and to share their grief together.

'I wanted him back inside me, alive and growing,' she said. 'It was like when Mum died.'

She had never told him that, but had always wanted to, and they weren't going off track now—they were finally on it.

'What was it like?' he asked.

'I just wanted it all to go back to how it was, but everything had changed.' She felt as if she were choking. 'Then everything did go back to how it had been—everything just carried on except *without* her. I don't even know if they miss her...'

'Of course they do. Rachel, it's just the way your dad is, but I know for a fact he misses her. The night we lost Christopher he cried, and said he wished your mum was there.'

'Dad cried?'

'Yes—and he cried and said exactly the same thing to me on the night I told him you were pregnant.'

She'd never known what had been said that night—

just that Dominic had come to the pub and said they would marry.

'Your dad loved your mum, just as he would have loved Christopher. And you know that. You *do* know that. It's just his way, Rachel.'

'But everyone said he was a mistake.'

'Yes,' Dominic said, 'and even I thought the same at first. But once I got used to the idea—well, he stopped being a mistake, didn't he? We *both* wanted him.'

They had—they really had.

'I'm not going to hide him any more,' Dominic said, and she looked up at his words. 'I don't have a child but I *did* have a son—and he changed me and the direction of my life. I'm a doctor because of him.'

And that made her cry all over again, because it was something so tangible in a sea of what-ifs, and something good to come out of so much grief.

'There's always going to be a part of me missing, but, Rachel—'

Dominic cut himself off and dragged in a breath, reminding himself not to cloud this conversation. This was about Christopher and what he had brought to their lives. The rest they could deal with in the fullness of time.

And, while he wanted to ask her when they could speak again, when they could talk about *them*, he did not want to push too hard too soon.

And so, rather than talk about trying again, and vasectomies and things, and the terror of doing it all over again, he moved back to their little lost son.

'He was wanted and loved.'

And now that Rachel had taken off those thorn-rimmed glasses, shaded with resentment and pain, she could recall softer, kinder times—Dominic coming home after a long shift at the bar and crawling into bed exhausted, holding both her and the bump of their baby as she slept in his arms.

She spoke to him about the little pair of socks that she'd kept. Remembering how he'd come home with them one evening because they were cute.

And together they recalled the two of them cuddled up under blankets on the sofa, because they were saving to feed the electricity meter when their baby was born, and the flat would need to be kept warm.

It was nice to remember all this, but also terribly hard to do so. And so, when they were all wrung out, she closed up his wallet and handed it to him and watched him slip it back into his jacket. It was nice to know the photo now lived by his heart.

'You know,' she said as she peeled some tissues from the box, 'despite the tears, I do feel better.'

'Good,' Dominic said, and took a couple of tissues for himself.

'Will you be all right to work?' she asked.

He nodded. 'I'll get you a taxi home.'

'Don't be daft,' Rachel said, and she looked at him, this man who might not love her but who had always taken care of her. 'I'll be fine. Thanks for this,' she said, and she meant it.

Because talking about her son, being able to share her memories of Christopher Hadley with his father...

It had meant the world.

CHAPTER TWELVE

'WHO ARE YOU here to see, Dominic?' May was updating the whiteboard. 'The surgeons are—'

'I'm actually here to see Rachel,' Dominic cut in.

He had given her a few days' space, so as not to cloud their conversation about Christopher with the other issues surrounding their relationship, but he could no longer hold back.

Now Dominic *wanted* to cloud the issue. It was time. They belonged together. There could be no doubt.

'Rachel Walker,' he elaborated when May frowned.

'But Rachel's not here.'

'When's she back on?'

'She's not,' May said, and carried on writing on the whiteboard. 'Rachel left last week.'

'What do you mean, she left?'

'Just that.'

May wasn't exactly forthcoming.

'It was supposed to be a three-month trial, but it wasn't working out, so she left before the end of it and headed back to Sheffield.'

'May, I really need to speak to her. Can you give me her mobile phone number?'

'I'm not about to give you one of my nurses' contact details.' May gave him a rather scornful look. 'I'm not the keeper of your little black book, Dominic. It would be a full-time job, that's for sure.'

'May…' Dominic was appalled that Rachel had gone and was way past caring about keeping secrets. 'Rachel is my ex-wife.'

'Jesus, Mary and Joseph!' May put down the white-board marker. 'Are you sure?'

'I think I'd know.'

'But you never let on.'

'Rachel didn't want me to,' Dominic said. 'Anyway, it was years ago.'

'Yet you're standing here asking for her number.'

'Because I *have* to speak to her.'

May was kinder then, but still adamant. 'Dominic, I won't be giving you her phone number. If she'd wanted you to have it you would have it.'

Rachel exited the train station at Sheffield and returned to her life without Dominic.

There was blossom on the trees, and everything looked gorgeous and green as the taxi carried her back to her dad's. She wore the same summery dress she'd had on when she'd last seen Dominic, but despite the attire, and the familiar sights of home, tears kept stinging her eyes and she wondered what on earth she'd done.

Since that night, talking with Dominic, she'd been like a leaking tap—only her tears weren't all about Christopher.

He'd told her in bed that morning that he wanted to work rather than to have a relationship. He'd outright said that he didn't want both. And even at their most intimate, holding each other and crying about their son, Dominic hadn't wanted to talk about *them*.

She had to accept it. Because she could not go through it again and again.

Rachel felt like a failure as she paid the taxi driver and hauled out her case. She was thirty-two years old and moving back in with her dad. Well, just for a couple of weeks, until she found somewhere of her own.

As she walked up the garden path she saw the front door open.

'Dad!' She barely recognised him. His beard was gone, his scruffy grey hair was freshly cut, and he was wearing, of all things—

'What are you doing in a *lilac* jumper?'

'It's blue,' her dad insisted.

'It isn't,' Rachel said as she hugged him, and then pulled back when she saw his lady friend coming out of the kitchen. 'Oh, hi, Moira,' she said, when what she really wanted to ask was, *What have you done to my dad?*

Rachel did not want to be back living at her dad's. And now she couldn't even hide herself away in the kitchen, as Moira seemed to have that under control.

'Dinner won't be long,' Moira said as Rachel took a seat in the very tidy lounge on a sofa that had new cushions.

Clearly it wasn't just her dad that Moira was sprucing up!

Moira lived here, Rachel realised. Or if she didn't quite live here fully yet, she soon would.

For dinner they were no longer formally seated at the dining table, but squashed on the sofa in the lounge, eating spaghetti bolognaise from trays on their laps.

And when they'd finished eating it was Moira who went to take the plates.

'I'll do it,' her dad said, and stood up, no doubt to micromanage the stacking of the dishwasher.

'Sit down, Dave,' Moira said. '*I'll* do it.'

And when her dad sat down, and allowed someone else to stack his precious dishwasher, Rachel knew just how serious the two of them were. On top of that, he patted Moira's bottom as she walked past.

Oh, God—Rachel could not bear the thought of them in bed together!

'I'll probably stay at Nicola's,' Rachel said, mentioning a friend oh, so casually. 'I'll just borrow my old room for a couple of nights.'

'No rush,' Dave said as Moira came back in.

And as they watched a replay of a dancing show on TV, Rachel found out that he and Moira were thinking of taking up ballroom dancing!

The whole world was moving on and having relationships and falling in love and having babies. All except for her.

Rachel could feel the sting of tears at the back of her eyes.

'Our Phil's dropping in,' Dave said during the adverts. 'He's bringing over the gender-reveal cake, but he's taping it up so we can't peek. We're going to have a little party here.'

How did her dad even know what a gender-reveal cake *was*? Things really were changing here...

But she knew her dad loved nothing more than a little party, with all the family present, so Rachel pushed out a smile. 'When?'

'Tomorrow. If it's a boy, it's going to be called Robin, but if it's a girl—'

'Don't start, Dave...' Moira sighed.

'Pixie!' her dad said, in the most scathing of tones. 'I've lived too long—I really have. Eleven grandchildren and one of them called *Pixie*!'

'You have twelve grandchildren,' Rachel said, her voice shaking.

It was only the fact that she now knew her dad had cried about Christopher that made her brave enough to raise it.

'You have twelve—but, oh, that's right... We don't speak about Christopher.'

'Because I don't want to upset you.'

'Has seeing Dominic stirred things up?' Moira asked.

Rachel pursed her lips at the intrusive question. Clearly Moira had been told all about it. But even as she did that, tears were trickling down her face, and there was nowhere to go, nowhere to hide except her old bedroom, and somehow the thought of that just made things worse.

'Come on, love,' Dad said. 'Don't go upsetting yourself.'

'I think you need to tell her, Dave,' Moira said.

'Moira!' he warned.

Rachel looked up. 'Tell me what?'

'It's nothing,' he said. 'It was years ago.'

But Moira was insistent. 'She still needs to know.'

'Very well,' Dave said. 'Dominic called me.'

'When?' Rachel asked, and her heart soared with hope. But of course it was a false alarm.

'A couple of years after you broke up.'

'Oh.' She sagged back in the seat.

'You know how he insisted that he'd pay me back for...' He swallowed. 'For Christopher's funeral. I always said there was no need. I was more than glad to take the strain off the two of you...'

Somewhere in the recesses of her mind, lost in that appalling time, there was a memory of that. Her dad saying he would take care of things and Dominic swallowing his pride, insisting it was to be just a loan.

'When?' Rachel croaked. 'When did he pay you back?'

'He'd send some money every month until he'd paid me back. It was just something he felt he had to do. I didn't want to go worrying you with talk about it.'

It made her feel very small to realise that her assumption that Dominic had walked off without a backward glance could not be further from the truth. He had told her that he'd put himself through med school, and now she was finding out that on top of that he'd been paying her dad back—doing what little he had been able for their son.

'He called to thank me for the loan and he wanted to know how you were…said that he was studying to be a doctor…'

'What else did he say?'

'Nothing much.' Her dad shrugged. 'He just wanted to know how you were.'

'Dave!' Moira said again. 'Tell her about the other time. Two years ago.'

Rachel turned and looked at her father, and despite the new jumper and the fresh haircut, she could see the strain on his features, and she noticed that he was clinging on to Moira's hand.

'Your dad told me a few things after you were here the last time. Well, I dragged it out of him,' said Moira.

'What?'

'I think he'd been drinking,' said her dad.

'Dominic?' Rachel frowned, because Dominic didn't drink—well, not much—but it would seem that one night two years ago he had.

'It was his thirtieth birthday and he was all mawkish. Said he wanted to get in touch and find out for himself how you were. He wanted your phone number.'

'And?' Rachel said.

'He said he'd tried to find you on social media and the like.'

'What did you say?'

'That perhaps there was a reason you didn't want to be found,' her dad said. 'I told him you had started seeing someone... Gordon. That you were back on track and for the first time in years you actually seemed happy. I said that if he cared about you—if he really cared about you—then it would be better for all concerned for him to leave well alone.'

Rachel hadn't known it was possible to feel so cross, and yet so relieved, so bewildered, and yet so clear-headed, all at the same time. Dominic—arrogant, confident, alley cat Dominic—had struggled too.

'Why the hell didn't you tell me?'

'Because I didn't want to bring up old hurts,' her dad snapped. 'That man caused you no end of problems...'

'I loved *that man*, though,' Rachel choked.

The doorbell went. No doubt it was Phil with the cake.

Her dad, glad of the reprieve, jumped up to get it while Rachel sat silent, with tears coursing down her cheeks.

'He meant well,' Moira said. 'It's been eating him up.'

'I know he meant well.' Rachel felt her anger towards her father fading. He'd been the one who'd had to deal with the fallout of their divorce after all, and she could understand his desire to protect her.

'I'm sorry for your loss, Rachel,' Moira said.

'Thank you,' Rachel responded politely, and then tried to pull back from discussing it further with Moira. 'It was years ago, though...'

'And tidied up and put away still festering.'

'Yes,' Rachel said, and she looked over at Moira with less wary eyes.

Dominic had been right. She must be pretty special to have got all that information out of her dad.

Rachel was starting to see how much she had lost by keeping her distance from people, and as her father helped Phil in with the cake, she relaxed and opened up to Moira.

'Does it change things?' Moira asked. 'Knowing that he called?'

'A bit,' Rachel admitted. 'Although I know he was trying to get hold of photos and things. Still, it helps to know that he paid for the funeral.'

They watched the dancers on TV for a moment, but then Rachel had a question for Moira.

'How did you get Dad to tell you?'

'I asked him,' Moira said. 'After that dinner we had I knew there was something bothering him, but when I asked what it was he said it was none of my business.'

'What did *you* say?'

'I didn't say anything. I went and got my coat,' Moira said. 'And when he asked why I was huffing off, I told him that if he wanted me in his life, then it most certainly *was* my business. That I'm not going to be fobbed off.'

And apparently there was someone else who refused to be fobbed off.

'Er… Rachel…' Her dad stood at the living room door, his face bright red and clashing with his lilac jumper. 'You've got a visitor.'

And there behind him stood Dominic.

He did not stand quietly, for there was such a presence to him, dressed in black jeans and a black jumper, unshaven and pale.

She couldn't take her eyes off him.

'Dominic.' Moira stood and introduced herself. 'I'm Moira—a friend of Dave's.'

'It's nice to meet you, Moira.'

Rachel watched as Dominic walked in and shook Moira's hand. It was all so terribly polite and so very odd to have Dominic Hadley back in the Walker living room.

It was more than odd for Dominic. There was the strangest feeling of déjà vu as he stood at the fireplace where he all those years ago had told Dave Walker that he'd got his daughter pregnant.

He'd been terrified then, but he wasn't terrified now—because he was here to finally put things right.

'I'm sorry to mess up your evening,' Dominic said to the one friendly face in the room.

'No, no,' said Moira, 'it's no bother. We were just watching the television.' She glanced over to Rachel, whose skin was bright red, her eyes all puffy and glassy from crying. 'And having something to eat...' she added rather lamely.

'Rachel.' Dominic turned to her then. 'I was hoping that we might speak.'

She nodded—what else could she do?

'Perhaps we could go for a walk?'

'Sure.' She pulled herself up from the chair and gave a thin smile to her worried-looking dad.

'Take care,' Dave said, and his voice was gruff.

Dominic could feel his reluctance to let her leave, but he stepped back and allowed the two of them to pass.

Rachel couldn't quite believe he was here. Her head was still whirring from the fact that he had called her dad. Twice. That the man she'd thought had walked away without a backward glance had spent two years sending money to her father.

That was the Dominic she had known—the man she had loved from the start.

'He's watching us from the window,' Dominic said as they walked. 'I can *feel* it.'

'I know…' Rachel sighed. 'He means well.'

'He does,' Dominic said. 'He's a good guy.'

She gave a mocking laugh, because she knew the two men she loved did not get on.

'He really is,' Dominic said. 'I can't imagine losing the woman I love and then having to run my own business as well as raise five kids.'

'Nor can I,' Rachel admitted.

'And then, just when he'd got them almost done—just when the youngest was close to finishing school—along came some guy and got her pregnant.'

Her cheeks were sore from the tears that were still trickling down as they walked familiar streets, passing their old school and the tree where they had shared her roll on the first day of the school year—where she'd smiled her metallic NHS braces smile at Dominic Hadley as she'd handed over her heart.

Because she had fallen in love at first sight.

And love could be so hard.

Impossible, even, when you were told it was just a crush, that you were too young, and your feelings would fade.

They paused a moment at the school gates, where she'd stood waiting for him to finish his exams so she could tell him about the baby, and she remembered watching his smile fade.

'Come on,' he said, and they walked on past the school and towards the park.

'Why did you leave without saying goodbye?' Dominic asked quietly.

'Because we'd said all we had to say.'

'Had we?' Dominic checked. 'Because there are an awful lot of things I want to say to you that I haven't, and I've always felt you've been holding back.'

'That's right. I'm cold.'

'You're not, though,' Dominic said. 'Are you?'

'No.'

They arrived at the park—the same park where her brothers had swung her and bounced her, so she'd return home with a smile rather than admit to her pain. The same park where she'd lain on the grass next to Dominic and told herself she could never have him.

There were so many hurts, but there was one in particular that still festered beneath all the others that were beginning to heal.

'I loved you,' she told him, without looking at him.

'Yet you never once told me that.'

'Because I was scared to,' Rachel admitted. 'Because I loved you and you didn't love me.'

'You don't know that.'

'But I *did* know that,' Rachel said, and turned to face him. 'I loved you the day I met you and I had to hold back from telling you over and over. I would have married you baby or no baby—would you really have wanted to hear that?'

He was silent.

'The day we got married I wanted to come to this park and spin and dance like I was Maria in *The Sound of Music*. I wanted to cry because I was so happy. Yet there was a part of me that knew you'd only married me because of the baby.'

'Perhaps, but—'

'No buts,' Rachel said. 'Please don't lie to me here, Dominic. You married me because I was pregnant. I knew it, you knew it, and everyone else knew it too. And so, yes, I held back. I was so happy, but I felt guilty for being happy, so I tried to hold back, because I didn't want to smother you. I didn't want to be hanging-off-the-lampposts happy when the truth was we were only together because of the baby.'

'No,' he said. 'We were together first.'

'You didn't love me, Dominic. At least not the way I loved you.'

Rachel felt oddly relieved. The truth was out and there was nothing to hide any more.

Dominic opened his mouth to speak and then closed it. Because her revelation had been unexpected. Because he'd thought he might have to coax an admission of love from Rachel.

Now he faced the force of it, as they sat on the bench in silence and looked out at the park.

Dominic needed to think about this—not just dismiss her deepest thoughts, or sugar-coat things just to white-wash their history—and he took a moment to consider.

She was right, and she was wrong, and she was all shades of everything in between.

'You say you loved me, Rachel, but you never trusted me. I know you were grieving and depressed after we lost Christopher, and I'm sorry for my handling of that, but you pushed me away right from the very start.'

'No—'

'Yes,' he said firmly. He stated it calmly and as fact. 'You never let me in. Even when I asked about your mother...'

'You didn't want to hear all that.'

'Of course I did,' Dominic refuted. 'I didn't expect you to open up the day you first told me, but even over the weeks, over the months, over the years, you never gave me the parts of you that mattered the most.'

He said it not as a criticism—in fact, he held her hand.

'I get it, Rachel. I didn't then, but I do now. You were shut down by your family. But as for me not loving you...'

He was trying to be logical, but he was also bewildered.

'I didn't know what love was back then, Rachel,' he admitted. 'And I'm not making excuses—it's the truth. My parents told me they loved me in the same breath as they told me all the things they did for me. But that didn't feel much like love. And then everyone told me I'd ruined both our lives and that we'd never make anything of ourselves, and that didn't sound a lot like love.'

Rachel turned and looked at him.

'I know that I wanted to look after you, and that I failed to do so.'

'It wasn't your fault.'

'It felt as if it was at the time,' Dominic said. 'You say I didn't fight for us—but I tried. I even offered to move in with your dad! And when you said it was time to put it all behind us, to move on with our lives, that all we'd done was make each other unhappy, I believed you meant what you said. You know how I felt about my mother staying with my father. I would never have wanted to keep you in an unhappy marriage.'

'I overheard your dad talking to you,' she admitted.

'He never spoke *for* me. Those were *his* words—never mine. I've barely spoken to him since that day. Why didn't you just ask me what I wanted? How I felt?'

'Because I was scared to,' Rachel admitted. 'Because I knew how much I loved you and I didn't want to hear that you didn't love me.'

'And do you still?'

'Still what?'

'Rachel!'

'Do I still love you?'

Rachel looked at his velvet brown eyes and she was simply too tired to deny, deny, deny. It was finally time to be honest, no matter what the consequences.

'Yes, Dominic, I do.'

'Then what were you doing walking out on me the other day? You left me with those photos, Rachel, and that hurt.'

'You'd just told me you didn't want both a relationship *and* work,' she reminded him, 'and then you headed out to get takeaway.'

'We were *talking*, Rachel. For the first time in years we were properly talking… Okay, maybe it wasn't the best time to pause the conversation, but I was trying to get us out of bed and actually speak. Because if you love me…'

'I *do* love you.'

'Even if I can't give you babies?'

'Of course I still love you.'

Oh, she wanted a baby, wanted a family, but the love she felt was independent of that.

'You *get* me.'

'When you let me.' Dominic smiled.

'I'm sorry I'm not good at sharing my feelings.'

She decided to try hard and let him know some of the things that made her love him so.

'I love how you hold my hand, even when we row.'

It was one of the nicest of things he did. Even during difficult conversations he was still holding her and looking out for her.

'And I love how you make me smile, even when I'm

trying not to, and I love your terrible attempts at a northern accent. I love how you're so patient with my dad, and how you paid him back...'

She saw the press of Dominic's lips, as if it was he who was having to work hard to hold his feelings in now.

'That means everything to me. And I also love that you called him twice...'

'He told you?' Dominic closed his eyes, looking both embarrassed and relieved that her father had told her.

'Was it about the photos?' she asked.

'In part,' Dominic said, and then stood. 'Come on.'

'Where?'

'It's just easier to do this while we're walking.'

He was nervous, Rachel realised, and that was so unlike the Dominic she now knew.

He cleared his throat. 'After I'd paid him back, I had a letter from your dad. I've still got it,' he admitted as they left the park. 'He said that we were square, and he wished me all the best. But I didn't want it to be over, Rachel, and I just had to know if you were okay. When I called, your dad said you were getting there, and that me getting in touch would only make things worse. I couldn't argue with that.'

They turned in to the street where they had once lived, and she smiled when she saw the little flat they had shared.

'And the second time?'

'It was my thirtieth. I don't usually drink, but I went out with Jordan and he told me Heather was expecting. I don't know... It just got too much. I told him about Christopher and you, and I realised I'd never come close to finding what I'd once found with you. I missed what we'd once had. You say that I didn't love you, but looking back, I know I did—I just didn't know it at the time. That night we had the curry…'

She blushed at the memory.

'I was in love with you then, Rachel, and I love you now. I've never stopped loving you.'

She looked up into his eyes, and felt his hands on her cheeks, his fingers wiping away her tears. 'Please don't just say it.'

'Why would I just say it? If I didn't want us to be together, why would I have got in my car this morning and driven all the way up here to put us through this? Why have I been finding out about vasectomy reversals…?'

'Stop it.'

'But I have been,' Dominic said.

'Since you looked at the photos?'

'No, since we had that awful lunch in the canteen.' He smiled at her frown. 'I was absolutely certain when I had it—right up to when you came to The Primary. But I'm not so certain now. I don't want to take away our chances.'

Finally, after all this time, she dared to say what she had wanted to for so very long. 'Can we try again?'

'We'll do more than try,' Dominic told her. 'I love you, Rachel Walker, and I'm going to spend the rest of my life proving that to you. Come on,' he said again.

'Where?' Rachel frowned as she was trotted off again. 'Here.'

She frowned again as he reached into his jeans and took out a key, opened the door. 'What are you doing?'

'I didn't come straight to your father's when I arrived in Sheffield,' Dominic said. 'And I didn't fancy a hotel, nor having to show up at your father's door whenever I wanted to see you. I decided we'd done enough of that and I went to speak to our old landlord. The flat is ours for the next two weeks. I figured that might give us time to work things out. I didn't know you'd be so easy to convince...'

She was stunned, but smiling, and a little overwhelmed to be walking through this door again.

And then Dominic picked her up and carried her—as he *hadn't* done on their wedding night.

Yes, she liked this rather more arrogant version of him. And there was another new side to him too...

He put her down in the little lounge, where there were fresh-cut flowers in a vase on the table.

'You've been shopping,' she said.

'There's food in the cupboards,' Dominic said as she peered into the kitchen, 'and I've made us roast pumpkin soup.'

'Seriously?'

'I got the recipe from a patient. Chilli flakes are the secret ingredient to a good soup, you know.'

'I *do* know.' Rachel smiled. 'But how do you?'

'It was a *very* lengthy tendon repair.' Dominic smiled. 'Miss Tate could teach us all a thing or three...'

Miss Tate had chatted not only about soup, but also about the importance of flowers, and being kind—all the things he hadn't learnt from his parents. And then she'd told him how, if she had her time again, she would take more chances and maybe not hold back on love.

They hadn't been talking about Dominic, yet he'd felt a little as if they had. And it had been a pleasure to sit on his stool beside such a wonderful lady.

'Dominic, it all looks gorgeous,' Rachel said.

There were flowers on the little table too, where once there had been doctor's letters and bills.

'What time did you get here?'

'I went to see May this morning, around eight, and left pretty soon after that. Richard has said he doesn't want me back until this is sorted. Although I was prepared for quite a lengthy negotiation.'

He led her to the bedroom, which had the same brown walls and grotty curtains, the same heavy wooden bed, but...

'New sheets?' She smiled.

'New everything,' Dominic said, and then he pulled her to him. 'A brand-new start. Rachel, will you please marry me?' he asked, and then added, 'Again?'

'You mean it?'

'I have never been more certain of anything in my life,' he said. 'In fact, I've still got my wedding ring.'

'So have I!' Rachel laughed.

'And this time you're getting an engagement ring.'

'I don't need one.'

'Well, you're getting one,' Dominic said. 'This time we're doing it right, and that starts tonight. I've already told your dad I'm asking you to marry me.'

'When?' Rachel frowned.

'When he came to the door. He was about to send me away until I pointed out that that hadn't worked in the past. I said that if you didn't want me in your life, then I had to hear it from you. I said I loved you, and that I was going to do whatever I could to make things better.'

'You told him that?'

'Yes—and I reminded him of what he said on the night Christopher died. That we both want what's best for you. And that I believe I am best for you. And that I wasn't asking his permission to marry you—I wanted his blessing.'

'Oh!' Rachel breathed.

'Then he took me into the dining room and said, "Put wood in 't 'ole, lad". What does that even mean?'

'Shut the door.' Rachel smiled at his terrible northern accent.

'Well, I did shut the door, and your dad asked if I had a ring. I said we'd choose one together, but he said that you might want this…'

He took out a ring—a gorgeous pink ruby surrounded by little diamonds. It was a ring that Rachel had loved all her life.

'It's Mum's ring.'

'Yes.'

'I remember it,' she said.

It had glinted in the bedside light as her mum had turned the pages of her bedtime stories. She could remember her smiles, and the scent of her perfume, and she wasn't scared to share those memories with him any more.

'Will it hurt too much to wear it?' Dominic asked. 'Because if that's the case…?'

'No, no,' Rachel said. 'I absolutely love it.'

'You really do have beautiful hands,' Dominic said as he slid the ring onto her finger.

And they were even more so now, with the perfect ring on them.

He kissed her then—a slow lingering kiss that tasted of patience rewarded and a very deep love.

He took the little bow that tied her dress and undid it, sliding his warm hands inside. His kiss was still tender as he undressed her and then pushed her back onto *their* bed.

As she lay watching him undress, she felt choked up, especially when he climbed into bed and held her. Because she knew how lucky they were to have been given this second chance.

'I'm sorry for all the hurt,' Rachel said, and she knew the part she had played in their demise.

'No more saying sorry about that,' Dominic said. 'Maybe we were too young for a love this big?'

He kissed her again, and now it was more consuming, with the roughness of his jaw and the weight of his naked body warming hers.

He kissed her slowly all over, his mouth tasting her, pinking her skin and making her burn all over, burying himself in her, discovering her all over again.

And when she came to his lips, nothing could stop him. No sheath, no barriers. They were together again.

He drove into her with such passion, and she met him with the same force, until they were moving together, loving each other. And then she looked up and saw those velvet brown eyes closing as he lost himself in her.

They were locked in rhythm, with no secrets between them, no feelings unshared and no needs unmet...just her building moans that made him move faster and faster.

Then Dominic opened his eyes and watched the delicious frenzy of her climax as she unravelled beneath him and he spilled into her.

And then there they lay, facing each other again, her hair back to curly, his eyes back to kind.

Lovers and loving each other all over again.

CHAPTER THIRTEEN

'IT'S *YOUR* WEDDING DAY?'

The hairdresser gaped in surprise at the calmest bride in the world, sitting in her chair.

Rachel deliberately hadn't gone to the place she'd once worked, because their wedding was a secret and just about them.

'Yes.' Rachel smiled.

'But you booked a "hair up for a wedding…" Usually brides like to have a trial…'

No trial had been necessary.

There was to be no family this time.

No pregnancy either—although Dominic was working on that!

No pressure.

The sun was bright and shining high as they met at a quarter to eleven outside the Town Hall.

It was a gorgeous listed building and there were people milling around outside, a newly married couple stepping out to the sound of cheers.

'I can't wait to marry you again,' Dominic said. 'You look beautiful.'

Rachel wore a flowery dress from a high street store and some wedge sandals for the occasion. Her red hair was curly and piled high and she carried a bunch of sun-flowers—because they made her feel happy.

Dominic looked completely immaculate, of course. He wore a dark grey suit, a white shirt, a silver tie and a smile. He'd had his hair cut and gone for a hot towel shave. She could not wait to get her hands on that smooth jaw. In fact, she ran her hands over it and moved in for a kiss.

'Not until we're married, cheeky,' he said, and then offered his arm.

Together they walked in.

Their register office wedding was a very tiny one, because with two witnesses pulled at random from the street, they held hands and looked only at each other as the registrar spoke.

'The purpose of marriage is that you may always love, care for and support each other, through all the joys and sorrows of life. It is a partnership in which two people can pledge their love and commitment to each other; a solemn union providing love, friendship, help and com-fort to you both through your life together...'

Hearing those beautiful words, Rachel started to cry. They had been here before, had heard those words before, but this time there was such certainty in the air that it was for ever, and it made the words sound extra-poignant.

'We know we can do this now,' Dominic said gently. 'Whatever life brings.'

She nodded and they made their vows, and she smiled as his ring slipped back on her finger, where it belonged.

And then her ring was back on his. And finally they were husband and wife again. And Dominic kissed the woman who was clearly destined to be his bride.

There were people everywhere as they stepped out of the small ceremony room. Love was in the air, and there were kissing couples and gorgeous bridesmaids trotting past as they were offered congratulations by people they didn't know. It was, for both of them, the most perfect wedding.

Rachel felt as if her heart might burst with happiness as they stood on the gorgeous staircase inside the Town Hall, with its crimson carpet and ornate banister, and had photos taken on their phones by a passing stranger. Especially when she felt Dominic's arm holding her tightly and she turned and saw his proud and confident smile as the moment was captured for ever.

They sent a photo to both sets of parents and some close friends to announce their union to the world.

'Your dad will be annoyed at missing out on a chance to party,' Dominic warned her.

'I'm sure he'll have a little party in our absence tonight, and we can head over tomorrow with a cake. Anyway, it's his turn next.'

They would be back at the Town Hall in precisely two weeks, for the wedding of her father and Moira.

Dominic had been right to tell Rachel to give Moira a chance, for her father too had found love again, and Rachel could not be more thrilled for him. She was starting to adore her new stepmother—this woman who was willing to reach for her coat rather than sit quietly by and be shut out of their family.

At last Dr and Mrs Hadley walked out of the Town Hall and into a taxi, to go for a very special wedding breakfast.

'This is my favourite place in the world,' Rachel told him as they walked in the gorgeous grounds of Chatsworth House and looked at the cascade of water in the fountains. Then, when they had selected their picnic spot, Dominic took out a bottle of champagne.

'Here's to us,' he said as they clinked glasses.

It felt so right to wear his ring, and so pleasurably strange to see Dominic wearing hers again.

But Dominic really was a lightweight, because one glass of champagne in, he was making her laugh as he stood up and ran across Capability Brown's perfectly manicured grounds. He started to spin like Maria in *The Sound of Music*, and she joined in, and they spun till they were dizzy, and then, the best part of all, they lay together on the grass and looked up to the bright blue sky.

'I'm sorry I never gave Sheffield a chance,' said Dominic. But he was more than happy to do so now, as he put on his terrible accent. 'I might even have gravy on me chips tonight.'

They were delirious with love, messing about on the lawn like the two teenagers they'd once been, and then lying back and relishing the fact that they were husband and wife.

Rachel sighed. 'I love it here.'

'I know you do,' Dominic said. 'Are you sure about us staying in London?'

'I'm very sure.' Rachel nodded. 'I like working at The Primary.'

May had been thrilled to have her back—and, of course, despite refusing to give Dominic her phone number, she'd had no problem in sharing the juicy gossip that Dominic and Rachel had once been husband and wife.

Rachel didn't mind. It had given people the heads-up about their relationship, so she didn't have to tell everyone, and even Tara had managed a smile and offered congratulations when they'd gone back.

'We'll be back up here often,' Dominic said now. 'We've got the flat, remember?'

It was their wedding present to each other. The little flat where they had started married life the first time around would be their heavenly escape when they came back to visit her family.

But for now it was on to Bakewell in the Peak District, where they had rented a gorgeous little honeymoon cottage, nestled in clouds of soft heather on the wild moors. There were low wooden beams and a log burner, and a welcome basket of food that they would explore later.

It felt as if it were just the two of them alone in the world, save for the sheep, and Rachel enjoyed a feeling of peace she had long forgotten—a sensation of utter contentment that wrapped around her like a hug. Dominic made her smile, but he also allowed her to cry and express all the emotions in between.

There was grass on his suit from where they had lain on the ground, and she felt the eternal thrill of Dominic as he took her in his arms and kissed his bride again.

'So... Are you happy?' Dominic asked the same question he had on the day she'd returned to his life.

And she knew he asked because it would always matter to him.

For Rachel there was no need to pause or examine her answer this time. 'So very happy.'

For she was back with the man she had always loved.

EPILOGUE

NIGHT FEEDS WERE the best.

Rachel loved nothing more than to sit in semi-darkness and just relish the quiet time with their little girl.

Araminta Aoife Hadley.

Minty.

'Minty?' her dad had barked when he'd come to visit them at the hospital. 'Oh, I've lived too long—I really have. First there's Pixie and now Minty. I'll be laughed out of the pub!'

'Oh, give it a rest, Dave,' Moira had said, and she and Rachel had shared a smile.

And then Rachel had teared up as she'd watched her dad holding little Minty, telling her just how very precious and loved she was.

Dominic's parents had visited too, and agreed she was beautiful indeed, and Dominic had had to borrow Rachel's superpower to push down his resentment as he'd accepted their congratulations and smiles.

Minty was now six weeks old, and while Rachel's pregnancy had been terrifying, she and Dominic had faced it together this time, sharing their hopes and fears and taking it in turns to be strong.

She had silky dark hair, a sweet rosebud mouth, fat cheeks and long fingers, and Rachel took her time to trace them all as she fed her. Her feet poked out from the little sleep suit and Rachel could not resist counting her tiny toes.

She was rather certain that Minty smiled.

When she'd finished feeding, instead of heading straight up the stairs, Rachel stood and cuddled her for a moment, rocking her as she held her, enjoying the sweet, milky baby scent and the softness of her hair as she gently paced the room before coming to stand at the fireplace.

They had, as both she and Dominic as well as all their visitors agreed, the best mantelpiece in the whole world.

At one end there was a photo of them on the steps at Sheffield Town Hall, both smiling—Dominic probably in terror and Rachel trying to contain her love.

At the other end there they stood again, thirteen years older and a whole lot surer of their mutual love.

And between them there were photos of Minty, and of Jordan and Heather's newest son, Andrew, who was Rachel and Dominic's godchild.

Richard's wife, Freya, was expecting again, so there might be another photo to add soon.

And there was Pixie, and her other nieces and nephews too. And there, nestled within the other photos, next to the beautiful portrait of her mother, the much-mourned Aoife Walker, with her gorgeous red hair and smiling eyes, was Christopher, in the arms of his parents.

They were both a part of their journey and a part of their family, and would be for evermore.

'If you throw me out I'll come back,' Dominic said, and his delightfully tricky wife smiled as she realised he had come downstairs to join her. 'And then we can get another wedding photo to put in the middle—because I'm just going to keep on marrying you.'

'And I'll just keep on saying *I do*.'

Rachel smiled, and when he held out his arms she handed him little Minty.

They were, they both knew, simply meant to be.

* * * * *

BABY BOMBSHELL
FOR THE
DOCTOR PRINCE

AMY RUTTAN

MILLS & BOON

For my readers.
I wouldn't be here, at this milestone,
without all of your support.
Much love.

CHAPTER ONE

Toronto, Ontario

DANG IT!

She was late.

Imogen hated being late. Especially on the first day of the medical conference, in her first lab of the conference. This was a lab she'd specifically signed up for. This was her number one reason for coming to the conference and she was late.

Jet lag. It was jet lag and that was the story she was sticking to.

She'd been in Yellowknife a long time and hadn't traveled in a while. Jet lag usually didn't bother her.

Except today, of course. It had to be today.

She slipped into the room, hoping no one clocked her or noticed she was late for the simulation lab that was the talk of this conference. It was the whole reason why she had come. If it hadn't been for the lab and workshops, she would've stayed in Yellowknife, in her safe little bubble where she knew her routines, knew her patients, knew her work.

She tried to move quietly at the back of the lab, looking for any open seat.

"Dr. Hayes?"

She cringed as her name was called out.

"Yes. Sorry," she responded.

The instructor looked less than impressed. "Join group five over there. They've already started without you."

Imogen's cheeks heated with embarrassment as she slunk over to group five.

She sat down. The other two doctors briefly filled her in, but she knew they were annoyed she was late.

She was too. The last thing she wanted was to be the center of attention. She hated it, and arriving late had done exactly that.

Her ex, Allen, had craved the limelight and she didn't.

She loved helping her patients. She loved Yellowknife, but Allen had wanted more.

She was mortified to be the last one here.

"Another latecomer," the instructor piped up. "Honestly, people, let's not make this a precedent. Join group five, please."

Imogen looked up to see the other straggler, hoping to find a kindred spirit with whom she could commiserate. Her mouth dropped open when she saw who was walking toward her group.

He was six-three, at least, broad-shouldered, blue-eyed, and he had a neat beard. He reminded her of all those Viking heroes that she would see on the covers of her best friend's mother's romance novels. The ones she and her friend would sneak out and read at slumber parties.

It was like he had walked straight out of the pages of a book.

She was pretty tall herself, at five-eleven, so it was rare for her to find someone who towered over her and made her feel like she could actually wear a nice pair of heels with him and be swept off her feet.

Allen had never liked her to wear heels, as he was already an inch shorter than her.

What are you thinking about? Why are you thinking like this?

It had to be the jet lag. She wasn't thinking rationally. She shook those thoughts from her head.

He sat down next to her, smiling politely at her; she met his gaze, which was intense. It was as if he could read exactly what she was thinking and he in turn looked her up and down with a brief flick of his eyes.

She really hoped she wasn't blushing, because suddenly it was very hot in this room, especially after the chilly reception she had received from the others and the hotel air-conditioning, which was cranked up full blast.

"I'm Dr. Hayes," she whispered. "And I was late too."

He smiled. "Dr. Vanin."

He had an accent she couldn't quite place, but there was no time to talk, as they both had to catch up on what they'd missed.

And she got the feeling, by the way he sat so stiffly beside her, that he wasn't the chatty type. After the instructor gave them all directions, their group went to work in the simulation lab that had been set up. She was paired off with Dr. Vanin as they practiced using robotic technology to perform a surgery she would usually do with a laparoscope.

Their operation on the silicone abdomen was removing a gallbladder with a gallstone that was lodged in the common bile duct. One that could not be retrieved after an ERCP and that needed to be surgically removed.

Thankfully, this was her forte.

She was one of the top general surgeons in the Northwest Territories.

"Have you ever used this technology before?" Dr. Vanin asked.

"Robotic, no, but I'm pretty familiar with laparoscopic surgery, but when there's a situation like this with a stone lodged in a duct, I usually do a full laparotomy at that point. It's why I'm here, to learn how to do this kind of surgery in the most minimally invasive way possible."

He nodded, seemingly impressed. "I do not do much general surgery, especially delicate work with laparoscopes. My specialty is trauma. I'm here to hone my skills."

"Well, I can help guide you." She stepped to the side. "Why don't you go first?"

He smiled warmly. "Thank you, Dr. Hayes."

"No problem." Imogen stood beside him. Her heart raced like she was a young girl standing beside her first crush. It was silly, but there was just something about him that made her feel out of control.

And she didn't like to lose control.

Control protected her. It had got her where she was today.

And she was kicking herself for offering to guide him with the instruments. The last thing she wanted to do was crow about her achievements. Allen used to get so defensive when she was lauded over him.

Allen's not here. He's gone.

"If I'm overstepping…" she started to say, and he looked up at her, confused.

"How? I appreciate the help from a more experienced general surgeon. Please, you are not overstepping."

She blushed. "Okay."

He nodded and turned his attention back to the instruments.

She watched him use the robotic controls easily. He was picking it up quickly.

"What stitch do you use on the common bile duct?" he asked.

"A running stitch using a monofilament absorbable suture. That allows me proper repair of the anastomosis of the bile duct. And it will hold well; the last thing a patient needs is a leak, which would lead to sepsis."

"Show me how you do it." He stood up and she took his spot. She showed him her running stitch, which she could do blindfolded.

"You do that so efficiently," he remarked.

"Thank you."

"No need to thank me. It is the truth," he stated.

She blushed. "Still, thanks."

Imogen couldn't remember anyone, other than her late father, complimenting her. But her father had *had* to compliment her—he was her father. He had been supportive and loving, but he'd also been biased.

Allen had never complimented her, but she'd never really worked much with him because the way they'd started out had been through professional rivalry, a torrid romance, then her broken heart when he'd left because he couldn't handle her popularity or life in the north.

She'd sworn she'd never again date another doctor.

Of course, with her workload in Yellowknife, she never had time to date, and the only people she interacted with besides patients were doctors, paramedics, nurses...medical people.

So she never bothered dating. Never thought about it.

And if she didn't think about it, she had control over her feelings. She didn't feel so alone or hurt.

Why are you thinking about it now, then?

She had to get a grip. She was not at this conference to date. She was here to work. Even if her friend and boss, Jeanette, had told her to loosen up and enjoy herself, Imogen had no time for that.

Once she finished her part of the lab, and the class was over, she was going to ask Dr. Vanin out for a cup of coffee. But when she looked up, he'd already left the room. She was disappointed, but it was probably for the best that she keep her distance.

All week she saw him. And as much as she tried to avoid him, they always seemed to sit next to each other and during labs they always partnered up. But when the class was done he'd disappear. Even though she made other acquaintances at the conference, when she'd spot Dr. Vanin, he was always on his own and he always seemed to disappear before she had the chance to really talk to him.

He wasn't really talkative, but he was smart and knowledgeable and, oh, so sexy.

So when she walked into the hotel bar for the mixer at the end of the conference, and saw him brooding at the bar rather than conversing with the rest of the physicians, she steeled her resolve to go and talk to him.

Even if this was so not her usual modus operandi, she didn't know anyone else. If she took control of the situation, then she could make a new friend. She could even call it networking, since he was a fellow professional and she absolutely, definitely was not going to date anyone medical ever again.

The way her own parents had ended up had made her

a little gun-shy. Her father had been perpetually waiting for her mother to come back, but she never had.

She shook away the thought of the mother she'd never known.

This wasn't dating. This was a mixer and she didn't work with Dr. Vanin. All she was doing was going to talk to someone interesting.

And sexy.

Her stomach flip-flopped as she approached him.

"Dr. Vanin… Lev, isn't it?"

Dr. Vanin turned around on his bar stool and smiled. "Yes. And you're Dr. Hayes, if I remember, yes?"

"Yes, but you can call me Imogen." She extended her hand. "May I sit?"

He nodded and motioned to the empty bar stool next to him, and suddenly she felt very awkward and out of place.

Say something.

"We seemed to have been at every workshop together. Quite a coincidence, eh?" She cringed inwardly at using such an obvious Canadian colloquialism.

"That we do," he said. His eyes twinkled and she hoped he found her awkwardness cute rather than goofy.

"Where are you from?" she asked.

"I'm from Chenar."

"Where exactly is that again?" She knew it was in Europe but felt silly for not having a better grasp of geography.

He smiled and nodded. "Northeastern Europe. Our country was founded by Viking traders looking for access to the Silk Road by land instead of by sea. It's why we appear more Nordic than Russian. I get asked that all the time. Not many people know where it is. They just assume I'm Romanian or Russian."

"Now I remember. It's a small, unique country. I've been there, but a long time ago."

His smile brightened. "You've been there? How unusual."

"My father loved to travel. It was just the two of us and we went to a lot of places when I was young."

"Does your father still travel?"

"No. He passed a couple of years ago." Imogen tried to swallow the lump in her throat as she thought of her father, a scientist, who had been working up in Alert. He'd passed away from a major hemorrhagic stroke. Gone before he'd even hit the floor.

Imogen had been traveling to smaller communities up in Nunavut when it had happened. It was a sore spot for her that she hadn't been there when he'd passed. He'd been her only family. It had been just the two of them for so long.

Her throat tightened.

"I'm sorry to hear that," Lev said gently.

"Thank you." She cleared her throat, trying not to cry.

"And now that I have thoroughly depressed you," he teased, "what should we talk about next?"

Imogen smiled at him. "No. I'm fine. Really."

He cocked an eyebrow. "Are you sure? I mean, this social thing is kind of sad, and then I went and depressed you further…"

"You're not depressing me."

"Good." He took another sip of his drink. "I would hate to drag you down with me."

Imogen glanced over her shoulder. He wasn't wrong. It was summer and this was Toronto. She'd lived in the city when she was at university and then medical school.

They were in a stodgy hotel with cheap drinks and bland food. Outside, Toronto was just coming to life.

"Do you want to get out of here?" she whispered conspiratorially.

He perked up. "Really?"

"I used to live in Toronto. I could take you on a quick tour if you'd like?"

Lev grinned and there was a twinkle in those deep blue eyes. "I would like that very much."

"Good." She set down her drink. "Let's go, before someone else decides to talk to us."

Lev finished the rest of his Scotch and followed her out of the bar.

It was kind of exciting to sneak out of the hotel, dumping their name badges on a table just outside the reception room.

In only a few minutes they were out of the hotel and on Front Street. The sun was only just beginning to set, though it wasn't late. Where she lived now, in Yellowknife, the summer sun wouldn't set for hours. It was one of her favorite things about living so far north, but there was still something magical about sunset in a bustling city like Toronto, with the city lights coming on and reflecting in the water of Lake Ontario. Toronto never seemed to sleep. It was exciting and thrilling. She'd forgotten that.

"There is one thing I want to do," Lev said as they walked along Front Street. "Something I've wanted to do since I came to Toronto."

"What's that?" she asked, curious.

"Go up that!" Lev pointed to the CN Tower.

"Sure. We can see if it's still open." Without thinking,

Imogen took his hand. She froze for a moment when she realized what she'd done, but he didn't pull away or seem to mind as they headed in the direction of Union Station. They ran across the road, dodging and weaving through the parked cars and the small evening traffic jam in front of the train station.

There were people on their way to some concert at the Scotiabank Arena and there were others trying to make their way home, taxis dropping off and picking up in front of Union Station. She led him through the train station and to the walkway that connected the station to the major attractions that hugged the Toronto waterfront.

They were lucky and able to get two tickets, which Lev insisted that he pay for because she was his tour guide.

It was a quick elevator ride up, and Imogen had to plug her ears as they popped. Soon they were on the observation deck of what used to be the tallest freestanding structure in the world.

They stood side by side, looking out over the city, which was lighting up as the sun sank on the west side of the city. Lev didn't say much and Imogen stood beside him, her pulse racing with the anticipation of something new and exciting.

Something she hadn't felt in a long time.

"So big," Lev whispered. "This city is about the size of my country."

"It's a pretty big city. All the years I lived here, this is my first time on the observation deck."

He cocked an eyebrow. "Really? Why?"

She shrugged. "I was at medical school. I was focused. I didn't make time."

She hadn't made time for a lot of things and that saddened her.

They wandered along the perimeter of the observation deck until they were looking south at the lake. When she looked out over Lake Ontario, she closed her eyes and imagined she was back home in Yellowknife, on her houseboat and listening to the sounds of Great Slave Lake. She hated being so far from home. No matter where she and her father had traveled, they'd always come back to Yellowknife. She opened her eyes and looked out over the city and Lake Ontario.

Lake Ontario was smaller than Great Slave Lake, but you couldn't tell when on the shoreline, as both were vast and she didn't really care to think about it. Not now. Not when she was standing next to a man who made her body thrum with excitement, in a way Allen never had.

It's just lust.

Allen had been her boyfriend for three years, and lust didn't last forever.

She'd just met Lev. He was new.

She needed to get a grip on these crazy emotions. She had to get back in control. Only she liked this feeling of living a little. It was fun and new. It wasn't going to be anything serious.

This was what she should've done when she was younger, but she'd been too afraid. She was still afraid, but she was going to savor tonight. It was the first step she needed to take, to put the burning mess of what had happened between her and Allen behind her.

Her first step in moving on.

Even if Allen had moved on a couple of years ago.

"I have never seen a lake so large."

"This is the seventh largest in Canada." She winced. Her father had always called her an encyclopedia and Allen had hated her little trivia facts.

Lev's eyebrows rose. "Only seventh? Which is the largest?"

Imogen frowned. "Uh, I think Lake Superior. It's farther north, but still in Ontario."

Lev leaned forward. "I like Canada. I have only been here a short time and I wish I could stay. A man could get lost here."

He said the last bit almost wistfully, like he wanted to get lost, and she didn't really blame him for thinking that way. It was why she liked working in the north. Even though Yellowknife was a city, it was far from anything else.

Only a thirty-minute drive out of the city and it was wilderness, trees and rock that had been exposed by glaciers.

It was easy to get lost up there, but it was a place where she'd found herself after Allen had broken her heart and her father had died.

"What is on the islands?" Lev asked as they watched a ferry slowly make its way from Queens Quay to the islands.

"Some homes, parks, a nudist beach," she teased.

Lev chuckled. "Wouldn't it be cold?"

"Not in the summer. We don't all drive a snowmobile to work." She did, in the winter.

"I never thought that. Do people think that?" he asked.

"Some," she said dryly.

He shook his head. "Well, I just meant it's night and the water looks cold."

"Yes. It can be cold, but I doubt people are at the beach now."

A lazy grin spread on his face. "Why not? Darkness hides a lot."

Her heart skipped a beat and she felt the blush rise in her cheeks as she tried not to think of the two of them alone on the nudist beach with only the moon lighting up the sky.

"Where can we get a drink?" he asked, breaking the tension.

"I know a nice place down by the waterfront."

"Good. Lead the way." Lev took her hand and it sent a jolt of electricity through her. It just felt right to hold his hand. It made her forget all the rules she'd set up to protect her heart. It made her feel carefree. It made her feel hot and gooey, all the things she'd never really felt before. Or if she had, she'd forgotten and Lev had woken something up inside her.

And as they walked slowly along the waterfront toward the patio, it felt like they had been doing this walk for some time. They didn't talk much, but then, during the whole week at the conference they hadn't really spoken a lot. There had just been this instant camaraderie the moment they'd both walked into the robotic lab late. Like they knew each other, even though they'd never met before.

Kindred spirits. Although she didn't believe in that. Not really.

Still, she felt at ease with him.

Like this was right.

You're crazy. He lives halfway across the world from you.

She knew all her friends in Yellowknife had told her to let loose and live a little when she was down in Toronto, but this was ridiculous. She couldn't be interested in Dr. Vanin. Long-distance relationships never worked and she wasn't leaving Yellowknife. She couldn't.

She'd tried it when she'd been a traveling doctor and it had crashed and burned, hard. She wouldn't date someone from far away again.

Who said anything about dating?

All this was… Well, she didn't know what it was, but she was enjoying herself. She couldn't quite believe that she was here with Lev, walking along the waterfront, hand in hand, talking about the city, enjoying the summer evening.

She didn't want to go to the patio and be around other people, because she liked this so much. It was as if they were in a little bubble together and she didn't want anyone to burst it.

Of course, it would burst eventually when they both went home tomorrow, but for now, it was nice, just the two of them.

They stopped and Lev leaned over the railing, watching the water and the city lights reflecting in the lake.

"It's a beautiful night. It's nice out here. So calm. So quiet."

"It is a nice night, though I would hardly call Toronto calm or quiet."

"Well, it seems quiet here."

"I prefer the country," she said.

"Do you?" he asked, surprised.

"Why are you shocked by that?"

"I thought you were a city girl."

"What made you think that?" she asked.

"You could navigate that traffic outside the hotel. You seem not to be bothered by crowds of people."

"I went to school in Toronto for many years. I'm used to it, but I'm not a city girl. I much prefer a quieter setting. A smaller setting."

"Tell me about it."

"What would you like to know?" she asked.

"You're a surgeon where you're located?"

"Yes. I did some work with a flying doctor service, but now I'm based in a hospital."

"Flying doctor?" he asked. "I have heard of this, but I'm intrigued about how it works."

"There are so many small communities that have no other way to connect them. You're at the mercy of the weather, though, as a flying doctor. Food and medical supplies are all brought in that way for some communities."

"And if the plane can't fly?" he asked.

"People can die." She thought of her father again. Maybe if he'd been in a city...

She shook that thought away. His stroke had been so catastrophic that even if he'd been in a hospital, he would've died.

"You have to be tough to live there."

She nodded. "Being a flying doctor is not for everyone."

"It's for you, though," he said softly, and he touched her cheek as he said that, which caused a flush to bloom in her cheeks. "When you blush, you look so...beautiful."

Imogen's heart raced. Her body seemed to come alive at his touch. His compliments made her swoon. It had been a long time since someone had touched her so intimately, and the fact it was Lev made her heart beat just a bit faster.

It was like she'd been asleep for years, walking around in a haze.

Numb.

"Well, your job as a flying doctor is admirable," he stated, breaking the heady tension that had fallen between them.

Another compliment. It caught her off guard.

* * *

*"You could be so much more if you'd leave Yellowknife,"
Allen huffed, annoyed with her.*

*"Why would I leave Yellowknife? My services are
needed here."*

*Allen shook his head. "Being a flying doctor? You
could earn so much more if you came south."*

*"Are you asking me to marry you and come south?"
She was shocked and a little thrilled at the prospect of
marrying Allen.*

*"No," Allen said bluntly. "I'm going south. You can
come if you want, but you know I don't believe in marriage."*

"I'm not going south."

*Her heart broke, but she couldn't choose a man who
couldn't commit.*

*"Then I guess this is it." Allen turned his back on
her and left.*

"How is it admirable?"

"I take it not many physicians want to do what you
do," Lev said, interrupting her thoughts.

"No. You're right. They don't." It was an ongoing problem that the north had a hard time keeping people. "I
don't anymore. I do like the hospital I work at."

"Still, you amaze me."

"I don't know why. I love my life. Perhaps I'm selfish," she said sheepishly.

"No. Not selfish. Not to live like that. I'm envious of
you. In Chenar, I work in the capital city and deal with…
the elite of my country. It's not what I like. Not at all." His
tone was one of dissatisfaction. "I much preferred my military work, but that came to an end and I was discharged."

"You don't sound happy."

"No. I'm not. I enjoyed it, but...my time was up."

"You could always leave," she offered. "Go somewhere else."

"If I could, I would." He took her hand again. "I wish I could be free like you, Imogen. I envy you."

Was she free? She didn't feel free.

"Last time I checked, Chenar was a free country. Sure, there's a king...but I don't think he's cruel."

A strange smile passed over his face. "No. Not at all. But let's not talk about it anymore. You promised me a drink."

"I did. It's just over here."

It was a short walk to the patio that she had been thinking of, but when they got there, it was closed. Instead, a small boutique hotel had opened up in its place. And though it didn't have a public bar, it had a rooftop patio for guests.

"Well, that's a shame. We can find somewhere else," she suggested.

"Didn't you say this was a good place?" he asked.

"I did, but the bar is only for hotel guests."

He grinned, a devious look in his eyes. "Let's get a room together."

Her pulse quickened. "What?"

"Get a room so we can have a drink."

"You're crazy." It was a mad idea, but still kind of thrilling.

"What do you think? We get a room, have a drink and then leave."

Live a little.

"Okay," she said excitedly. "Let's do it."

This was perhaps the craziest thing she'd ever done, but this whole night was so out of the norm for her, it was exciting. Her heart was not in danger and then she'd return to Yellowknife and her normal routine.

Lev was going to take a room just so they could have a drink on the rooftop. All that was left was a penthouse suite, but he paid for it anyway.

Soon they were on the rooftop patio of a penthouse suite that overlooked the lake, drinking glasses of champagne, like it was the most natural thing in the world.

"I still can't believe we did this," she said.

"Have you never done this?"

"No." She laughed.

He grinned and clinked her champagne flute against his. "Well, there's a first time for everything."

"Oh?" she asked, intrigued. "You do this a lot, do you?"

He took a sip and shook his head. "No. This is my first time too."

Her blood heated when he said that and she tried to swallow the bubbly liquid, but it was hard to do that with her heart racing, her body trembling, while the rational part of her brain was still trying to process why she was here.

The limbic part of her brain told her she was in the right place and it keenly reminded her that Allen had left a long time ago and she was single and had been alone for quite some time.

One glass of champagne led to another and another. It was a beautiful summer evening and somewhere they could hear the muted strains of jazz music from some piano bar, somewhere down there.

"I would like to dance," Lev announced, setting down his flute and standing up. "Dance with me."

"Does everyone follow your orders?" she teased, although she wanted to dance with him too. She'd been swaying to the music because she couldn't help herself. The champagne was getting to her.

"Yes. Because where I work I am the Chief of Staff." He grinned. "Dance with me, Imogen, and then we'll get a cab back to the conference hotel."

She set down her flute and took his hand, letting Lev pull her into his strong arms. It felt so good to be held by him, one hand holding hers and the other on the small of her back as they slowly moved together to the echoing music that was intermixed with the sounds of the waves lapping against the shore. Her body thrummed with desire.

It was magical and she didn't want the night to end. She didn't want the moment to end and she didn't want to go back to the conference hotel.

Warmth bloomed in her cheeks as she thought about kissing him.

She wanted to kiss him.

He smiled down at her. "You look so beautiful I almost don't want to leave."

"I don't want to leave either." She bit her lip and then leaned in, standing on her toes, because she'd worn flats and he was so much taller than her. She pressed her lips against his for a quick kiss.

She was doing what she had always been afraid of doing—getting involved with a doctor.

You don't work with him. He won't hurt you.

This was out of her comfort zone, but she was really enjoying what it felt like to live a little. There had been so many times that she'd been afraid to take a chance on something she'd wanted and had let the moment get away. This time, with Lev, she wasn't so afraid. She was only afraid she would regret *not* having this stolen moment with him.

The kiss was light at first and then deepened. His arms went around her back, pulling her close, and suddenly it was no longer a light, butterfly kiss but something deep with longing.

It had been so long since a man had made her feel this way. Since she had felt this need to relinquish her careful control and just feel.

The kiss ended.

"I'm sorry, Imogen. I didn't mean for that…" he whispered against her ear, his voice deep and husky.

"Don't apologize," she whispered, and kissed him again, running her hands through his overlong blond hair, wanting to have more of him.

Even if it was just for one night.

She didn't care. She wanted something to remember him by. She pressed her body against him, not wanting an inch of space separating them as she melted in his arms, his hands hot through the thin fabric of her summer dress. She couldn't help but wonder what they would feel like on her skin.

All she knew was that she wanted more.

"Imogen, are you sure?" he asked.

"I am." She had never been so sure of anything. Even if nothing came of this, even if she never saw him again, she wanted this moment.

She'd been wandering in a fog for too long and Lev had awakened something deep inside her. He scooped her up in his arms and carried her off the patio into the room. She was glad it was just the two of them, far from the rest of the conference, far from what they both knew.

Just the two of them in this moment.

CHAPTER TWO

LEV WATCHED HER SLEEP. He couldn't help himself—she was so beautiful.

He'd thought so the moment he'd first laid eyes on her at the conference when he'd arrived late. She'd been the only friendly face in the crowd.

And a beautiful one at that.

Usually he avoided women.

He'd been so in love with Tatiana.

His father hadn't approved of her, but he hadn't cared. He'd believed they were meant for each other. He'd been about to propose to her when he'd caught her cheating.

She'd acted like it was no big deal. His father had cheated on his mother. It was all about position and wealth in Tatiana's eyes. There was no such thing as love.

To the world they had seemed perfect, but Lev remembered how sad his late mother had been in her marriage and he felt that same sadness and hurt too. He'd broken it off with Tatiana and joined the Chenarian armed forces as a trauma surgeon.

He'd been burned before. They never saw *him*, only his position.

His plan had been to keep far away from Imogen, but the fates seemed to have another plan, because every time he turned around, there she was.

And he was glad to see her, even though he knew he should keep away, but there was something genuine about her.

He knew he shouldn't have gone to that mixer, he knew he shouldn't have engaged with her, but he couldn't help it. She was beautiful, with long, soft, silky light brown hair, big expressive blue eyes, and her pink full lips were ones he could kiss for a long time. He liked it that she was tall and could almost look him in the eye. She held her head high with confidence, and she was funny, intelligent and dedicated to learning and furthering her career as a surgeon.

When they had been working in the simulation lab, he'd seen her ace the new surgical technique with skill, and the way she'd handled a laparoscope with such grace had been admirable. And she'd been willing to help him.

As a trauma surgeon, he had to get in fast and do repair work, but he wanted to learn all he could.

Imogen's had been the only friendly face in the crowd.

Everything about her was admirable.

His father and brother would not find that particular quality, intelligence, something to admire in a woman, but that was what he always looked for. He wanted an equal partner, and in his circle of Chenar society, that was almost impossible to find. Especially after Tatiana.

Imogen was a rarity in his world and he wished he could stay here forever with her. He hadn't planned on making love to her tonight, but he was glad it had happened. It had been a momentary lapse when he had forgotten who he was and who his family was. He had been caught up in the moment with her.

One stolen moment with her…

He reached out and touched her arm. She murmured in her sleep but didn't wake up. He smiled and couldn't help but think of how it felt to taste her lips against his, have those arms wrapped around him and be buried deep inside her.

Everything else in his life was a complete blur.

It was just her and him at that moment. It was an escape. One he desperately wanted.

Lev's phone buzzed and Imogen stirred in her sleep. He cursed inwardly, angry that it was intruding on their time together, and picked up his phone, to see a stream of texts that he'd ignored all night.

The last one made him angry as he realized that they had tracked his phone's GPS and were in the lobby. His bodyguards. Lexi and Gustav had been plastered to his side all weekend, not giving him a chance to breathe, and he felt bad for them. He knew they were bored out of their skulls, attending a medical conference, but his father had insisted when he'd given Lev permission to attend.

Lev wasn't to leave Chenar without Lexi and Gustav. His father had become so overprotective lately, not that his father really showed any affection. It was all about preserving his male heirs.

It was why his father had forced him to leave the military. His father had ordered it so. In his father's words, it was high time he used his foolish medical degree for the benefit of the cream of Chenar society.

He was actually surprised he'd been able to slip away from them at the mixer with Imogen. It had been an act of defiance, and a thrill of freedom to do that.

He didn't want Imogen to know who he really was. He didn't want the truth of his family to cloud her judgment of him, like it almost always did when women found out that Dr. Lev Vanin was just an alias. He was a doctor, but he tried to keep it quiet that he was the spare to the heir and really Prince Viktor Lanin of Chenar.

Women, once they found out who he was, changed. They wanted the fantasy. The prestige and power of being with a prince. Women like Imogen put their careers first, instead of duty to a country, and he couldn't begrudge them that. He envied Imogen's freedom and he would give almost anything to stay here in Canada and move to the north to get lost.

He loved the wilderness and loathed the pomp and ceremony surrounding his birth. Especially his ever-present bodyguards.

Lev quickly got dressed and texted Lexi that he was on his way down, that there was no need to come up. He'd get rid of them and then he would go back to Imogen and tell her he had to leave and why—because of who he was.

It would change everything. He was sure it would—it always did, even if part of him wanted to think that Imogen was different.

He slipped out of the room and headed downstairs. He knew that Lexi and Gustav, who had been with him since medical school, would be more than annoyed that he'd managed to give them the slip and go to an unsanctioned hotel with a woman.

And he was sure his father, once he found out, would be none too happy, but Lev didn't care. He didn't regret a single moment of his stolen freedom. It had been worth it.

The moment he got off the elevators he could sense there was something in the air. Lexi was acting strangely and his stomach knotted. Something was wrong. Gustav was on the phone, Lexi's gun was visible on his holster, and he was pacing. Outside, through the glass doors connecting the small lobby to the outside world, he could see black SUVs waiting and more guards.

Canadian bodyguards.

Something was wrong.

"Lexi," Lev said, coming forward, speaking Chenarian, which had developed over centuries from a blend of Norse and Romanian, so that no one else would understand. "What's wrong?"

"There's been a coup," Lexi responded, his face somber. "Your father... I'm sorry, Viktor."

Lev couldn't breathe for a moment as Lexi's words sank in. That his father had been overthrown and was dead. It was something his father had talked about. It was one of the dangers of ruling a country with an unstable government, and though Lev had logically known something like this could happen, he'd never really thought it would.

He lived in an idyllic bubble where his father and his family were impervious to the machinations of those who sought power.

"What about Kristof?" Lev asked.

"Missing in action and presumed dead, but in reality he's safe. He just wants the world to think he's dead... and he wants you to go into hiding. Here," Gustav responded, ending his phone call. "It's a mess in Chenar. We've been speaking with the Canadian government and we need to protect you in case..."

"In case something happens to Kristof," Lev finished.

"The insurgents don't know where he is or where you are, because they don't know your alias. They don't know you're a surgeon," Lexi said. "The Canadian government has agreed to hide you. Embassy cars are outside and a plane is waiting. We have to go."

"I can't go into hiding. My father, my brother...our people."

"There is no choice, Your Highness," Gustav responded. "Our allies are sending in troops. This will be resolved, but until then we need to keep you hidden and safe."

"I cannot hide away. Not when there's trouble in Chenar. I need to go and—"

"Your Highness, there is no other option. This plan was put in place by your father if something like this were ever to happen."

Lev was furious. It was just like his father to do something without telling him or Kristof what was going on. And even though he had no desire to be King or even a prince, for that matter, he hated knowing that his people were in danger.

That there was suffering, violence, and he was powerless to do anything.

He was safe and that was not right. He clenched his fists in frustration, but he knew he couldn't make a scene. It was late at night and he didn't want to draw attention to himself or his bodyguards, who were just as worried, upset and powerless to do anything to help their country.

They are helping their country by keeping you safe.

And then it really hit him that his father was gone and he didn't know where his brother was. At least Kristof was safe, or that was what he'd been told. He really didn't know.

He was being selfish by standing here and arguing with Gustav and Lexi about what needed to be done. Even though it drove him mad that he couldn't be on the front line, giving help to his people during this time of crisis, he had to do his duty and he had to go into hiding.

Imogen.

He looked back to the elevator with regret. He wanted to tell her everything now more than ever. He wanted to tell her why he was disappearing, but that wouldn't be safe.

It certainly wouldn't be safe for her.

Lev knew he had no choice but to leave. He was glad

the room was paid for and that Imogen could just check out. He grabbed a piece of hotel stationery and quickly scrawled a note, apologizing to Imogen for his abrupt departure but not telling her why.

"Would you please give this to my guest when she leaves tomorrow morning?" he asked the concierge.

"Of course," the concierge responded, taking the envelope.

"Thank you," Lev said.

He wished he could go up to the room and tell Imogen in person why he was leaving. He wanted to tell her everything, but couldn't. She was the sacrifice he had to make for his country.

He couldn't let his people down. He couldn't let his brother down.

He couldn't let his father down.

"Your Highness," Gustav said gently. "We have to go."

"I know." Lev sighed. "Let's go."

Lexi and Gustav walked beside him. Their guns were visible at their sides, and Lev felt ill as he exited the hotel and saw the heavily armored dark SUVs waiting. The Canadian government had come to take him away to who knew where.

He just hoped that, wherever he went, he could still practice medicine while he waited for news from Kristof about when he could safely return to his country and mourn his father.

Properly.

CHAPTER THREE

Three months later, August
Yellowknife, Northwest Territories

"YOU CAN'T LIVE on a houseboat with a baby!" Dr. Jeanette Ducharme proclaimed, bursting into the doctors' lounge. Imogen knew instantly that the comment was directed at her for two reasons. She was the only one currently pregnant who worked at the hospital and the only one of the physicians who lived on a houseboat.

Imogen cocked an eyebrow in question at the Chief of Staff and her best friend in Yellowknife, who rarely got involved with people's lives, but seemed overly protective of her as of late.

Probably because she had been the one who had told Imogen to "live a little" at that conference in Toronto, which was how she had ended up pregnant in the first place.

Imogen liked to think that Jeanette felt bad, but only just a bit, and usually only when Imogen was having a really bad case of morning sickness.

Really, it was Imogen's fault she'd had a one-night stand in the first place, for throwing caution to the wind and momentarily forgetting she'd had her IUD taken out a month before because of the horrific migraines it had been causing. She'd forgotten in the moment that she'd had no other form of birth control, and she hadn't wanted Lev to stop.

Kids had never been in the plan, but now she was going to have a baby.

It was still kind of shocking, but she was excited and scared too.

Really scared.

She'd been raised by a single parent. She could do this. *Can you?*

There was a fair bit of self-doubt buried deep down inside that told her she was crazy for even thinking of doing this alone. Her father had given her so much love and support, but there was always that piece missing, the weight of not knowing her mother.

Always wondering, always envious of those who had mothers.

She worried her baby would feel that way about not knowing its father.

It broke her heart and scared her.

Focus.

There was nothing to regret about her one night with Lev.

It had been unplanned, but she could do this.

She cleared her throat. "What're you talking about? Why did that thought just randomly pop into your head? Lots of people with kids live on the lake like me. It's called environmentally friendly living. I'm leaving less of a carbon footprint."

Jeanette rolled her eyes. "It has nothing to do with that. You're by yourself. What if you go into labor and there's a storm? Or your motorboat won't start or your anchor gives way and your barge just drifts away out into Great Slave Lake…"

"Jeanette, calm down. I'm only three months pregnant. The baby will come in the winter."

"Exactly. What if there's a blizzard or the ice hasn't formed…?"

"Right. Blizzards do happen in the winter," Imogen teased, trying to make light of a situation that she'd been thinking about too. "I don't live that far offshore and I have contingency plans. The ice should be formed by then and I have my snowmobile."

"Ice thickness has been tricky these last few winters. Winters are getting warmer… Ice road season is shrinking. Take it from me—I've lived here my whole life. It's not freezing as thick! Look how warm our summer was."

Imogen sighed and rubbed her temples. "Jeanette, what has gotten into you?"

"You know I like to think ahead." Jeanette sat down on the couch next to her. "I worry about you. Out there all alone and stuff."

Imogen chuckled. "I'm fine. Really."

What Imogen didn't tell her was that those thoughts had crossed her mind from time to time too. Ever since she'd found out she was pregnant and that she was alone. Truly alone. Her father was gone, she'd never known her mother, and she didn't have any extended family. She didn't have anyone to rely on.

It was just her. The way it had been for some time, and she was comfortable with that.

And Lev was gone.

The moment she'd found out she was pregnant she had called the Chenarian Embassy—or what passed for an embassy in the wake of the coup. She'd wanted to relay a message to him, but the consulate and Canada had repeatedly said they didn't know where he was, other than that he had returned to Chenar and was lost.

Lev was missing in action. No, not Lev. Prince Viktor Lanin. That had been a surprise she hadn't expected. A bigger shock to her than news of her pregnancy would be to him, she had thought.

It made her feel ill, thinking he was dead, but there was simply no information on him. Just reports. Prince Kristof and Prince Viktor were missing, and King Ivan was dead.

There was no sign of him and she'd tried all she could to find him.

Lev had vanished the morning all hell had broken loose in Chenar. There was no reliable communication with the war-torn country.

Her heart broke, thinking he might be dead, and she had no way of finding him or telling him about the baby. She also had a hard time believing he was gone—perhaps he had only got mixed up in the chaos and was unreachable? She knew she was foolish to cling to the hope that he was still alive, but somehow she couldn't let it go.

It upset her she couldn't tell him about the baby and that Lev might never know their child.

Would he even care? He was a prince and you were just a fling.

She didn't know. She liked to think Lev would care. After finding out Lev was really Prince Viktor, she'd looked him up online to try to force her brain to accept the truth. There were a few photos of him when he was young, but there weren't many of him as an adult—or even pictures of Dr. Lev Vanin, his alias.

Prince Viktor Lanin was different from the man with whom she'd had the one-night stand. His long blond hair was short and clean-cut. There was no beard, and he was clean-shaven and regal. It was the eyes that gave him away.

But now it was just her and her baby.

And she couldn't tell anyone who the father was.

And, anyway, there was no proof and she wanted to protect her child. She didn't want attention drawn to her or the baby, especially with such a politically unstable situation in Chenar.

She was terrified of being on her own, of carrying an heir to the throne of a country in chaos, and she was scared that she was living alone on the lake in the home her father had bought for himself to live in when he'd retired from his work in Alert.

All Jeanette's fears were her own. It was just that Imogen didn't want to say them out loud. If she said them out loud, it made them real. Not that they weren't real, but it was a way for Imogen to compartmentalize it all. Of course, Jeanette had done that for her instead, by stating the obvious.

"I didn't mean to freak you out," Jeanette said.

"I'm not freaked out." Although she was.

"You looked freaked."

Imogen sighed. "I'm okay. Truly. You don't need to worry."

"I just feel responsible."

"You didn't get me pregnant," Imogen said dryly. "I did that on my own...sort of."

She grew sad as she thought of Lev and the night she had thrown caution to the wind; when she thought of how he'd made her feel.

Lev was gone and her baby could never know his or her father. Imogen knew how that felt, how it felt not to know a parent.

Her mother had left shortly after she was born and her dad had never remarried.

She'd always had a feeling of being incomplete and she never wanted that for a child of her own, but here she was.

Alone. She touched her belly—not that she could feel anything, but it gave her comfort to ground herself. To think about all the possibilities. That was what she wanted to do right now—she wanted to think of the positives, because focusing on the negatives was just too scary.

Whatever happened, she was going to do right by her child. Her father had given her all he could, and although she had mourned and wondered about her mother, she had never been lacking in love.

And neither would her baby. Even if it completely freaked her out.

Jeanette chuckled, interrupting her chain of thought. "No, I don't suppose you conceived this baby on your own. I'm just worried about you. You're not only my colleague. You're my friend."

"Thanks, Jeanette. I appreciate it. I feel the same way about you, you know." She smiled.

Jeanette grinned. "I'm glad and I'm sorry for freaking you out slightly. That was not my intention."

"Well, to put your mind at ease, I've actually leased out the houseboat for the winter to a couple of scientists from Alert. They were colleagues of my father. They're coming down for an extended research trip and needed a place to stay, so they're taking over the houseboat for the winter season. I've found an awesome rental for the winter, which is not far from the hospital, so I'll be on the mainland for some time. I promise you the ice, or lack thereof, won't be a problem when the time comes."

"Oh, my God, that's so good to hear!" Jeanette gave her a side hug.

"So that's all you wanted to talk to me about on my

break?" Imogen asked quizzically. "You just wanted to discuss my temporary living arrangements?"

"Yes. Well…no. I have a new assignment for you!"

Imogen groaned. Jeanette's code word for assignment meant a new doctor to the territory. When Jeanette used the word *case* it meant a new patient but *assignment* meant a difficult new doctor who even Jeanette was struggling with.

"Really?"

Jeanette stood. "I'll go and get him. He should be finished with Human Resources and you can show him the ropes."

"Why me?" Imogen sighed, getting up from the couch where she'd actually been enjoying a quiet morning until now.

"Because you're so lovable."

Imogen frowned. "I don't think that's it."

"Fine. Because you can handle these stubborn newbies."

"You're the Chief of Staff!" Imogen complained.

"Exactly! Which is why I'm so busy and need your help and your gentle but firm touch here."

Imogen rolled her eyes as Jeanette left the doctors' lounge, essentially giving Imogen no choice in the matter. As much as she didn't want to take over and show this new doctor the ropes, she knew that in a few months she'd be leaving Jeanette short one surgeon, in a place where there was already a shortage of doctors.

The least she could do was help this new doctor settle in.

She took a deep breath as Jeanette opened the door.

"Dr. Imogen Hayes, I'd like to introduce our newest member of the Yellowknife medical community, Dr. Lev Vanin!"

* * *

Lev took a step back, his eyes wide as he looked at her, and Imogen did the same, but she tried not to show her shock for too long. She didn't want Jeanette to suspect something, but Lev appeared just as shocked as she was. At least Jeanette couldn't see his expression.

And Jeanette wouldn't know he was a prince. He looked very different from the official photos online and he was using his alias.

Still, she couldn't believe he was here and he was alive! Her brain was trying to rationalize why a missing prince of a war-torn country was standing in front of her, in Yellowknife, of all places, while her heart was leaping and skipping. Of course she was glad he was still alive, but she was scared about what the future held for her unborn child.

She wasn't going to keep her child from its father, but really what did it all mean? All she could think was that her baby was in danger and there was no way to control the unknown. Her anxiety ticked up a notch.

Focus.

She had to keep calm so Jeanette wouldn't suspect anything.

"It's a pleasure to meet you, Dr. Vanin." Imogen stuck out her hand, hoping her voice didn't crack or sound too awkward.

"The pleasure is all mine," Lev said, taking her hand briefly.

"Dr. Hayes will show you around. She is Chief of General Surgery here in Yellowknife—at least until the winter, before she goes on maternity leave."

Imogen winced and could hear herself internally screaming. This was not how she wanted him to find out.

Lev's eyes widened again, his gaze falling to her belly,

which really wasn't showing under her dark blue scrubs, as she was only three months along.

"I'm sure Dr. Hayes will fill me in on everything here," Lev said slowly. "Thank you, Dr. Ducharme, for such a warm welcome, and my apologies for the hiccup earlier."

Jeanette nodded. "Well, I'll leave you two to it."

"Thank you, Jeanette." Imogen was trying not to shake as Jeanette left the room. When they were finally alone, Lev crossed his arms.

"Pregnant?" he said, sounding astounded.

"Well, it's nice to see you too, Dr. Vanin. Or should I say Your Highness?"

Lev winced.

He suddenly remembered that he'd told her the truth in the note he'd left for her at the hotel. He'd wanted her to know why he'd left. Why he'd had to leave. He'd thought he would never see her again.

He hadn't known where she worked and Canada was so large.

He was stunned to see her. Overjoyed to see her.

Since everything had fallen apart in Chenar, he'd been moved from one place to another. He had wanted to return to her that night, he hadn't wanted to leave her in the lurch like that, but he'd had no choice.

His brother, Kristof, who was also in hiding, had demanded Lev stay in Canada.

And, since their father was dead, Kristof was technically King and Lev had no choice but to obey. And he'd been shuttled from location to location ever since.

Lexi was in Yellowknife with him, but Gustav had had to return to serve in the military. Lexi wasn't alone in his duties. The Canadian government had provided protection.

Lev might be able to walk around freely, but he knew Lexi and the others were not far away.

Even though he was in Canada and hidden, he still wasn't free and he really didn't care about that. With his father gone and his brother also in hiding, Lev felt an even stronger sense of duty to his people. Once the situation in Chenar had de-escalated he would go back.

He'd go back to Chenar and properly mourn his father. They may have had their differences but Lev had made peace with their cold relationship.

He'd made peace with a lot of things since his homeland had been plunged into turmoil and he was stuck in Canada, powerless.

He couldn't let his grief take hold of him right now. The only way he'd make it through this whole ordeal was focusing on what he could do, and that was being a trauma surgeon...if he could just stay in one spot for more than a week at a time. He hoped the Canadian government and Lexi would agree that Yellowknife was a safe place for him and leave him here.

But then he saw Imogen and heard she was pregnant.

That took him a moment to wrap his mind around. Imogen was pregnant and not far along.

It might not be yours.

And that thought brought him back to reality.

Imogen was his secret joy, and he liked to remember their time together when the weight of everything that was happening to him dragged him down. She was the one good thing he could think of, even though he'd thought he would probably never see her again.

And now here she was, standing in front of him, and she was pregnant. Pregnant! And he could be the father.

Most likely he was. Children had always been something he'd wanted, but it was hard to imagine that with his life the way it was right now. He was also terrified because he'd never had his father's love or affection. How could he be a good father?

So he never thought about kids. He'd entertained the notion when he'd been with Tatiana, but then she'd shown her true colors and all those hopes of having a real family had been dashed.

And now with Chenar in turmoil, he didn't want to put a child of his in danger.

"Am I the father?" he asked. In one way he was hoping that he was the father, because that meant there was no other man who had captured her heart, but he also worried about the burden of his family and the situation falling on his child. The thought of something happening to his child, to Imogen, because of who he was was too much to bear thinking about.

"Yes," she said quickly, apparently annoyed. "You are."

Not that he could blame her for being annoyed. First he'd left her, leaving behind a hastily scribbled note with a bombshell of his own, and now he was questioning her integrity.

"I would ask why you didn't tell me, but I have been a bit out of touch with the world." Lev scrubbed a hand over his face.

"I know," she said gently. "The world says you're missing in action. I thought you were dead. You just vanished."

"It's better that way," Lev said quickly. At least Kristof seemed to think so. Lev wasn't so sure.

"Where have you been?" she asked.

"Everywhere, but no location was safe. Yellowknife

is a small enough city that your government feels like I can be protected and work as a doctor, thus keeping up my secret identity."

"Okay," she said, but there was an odd edge to her voice. He didn't blame her. He was pretty sure he knew what she was thinking. She was as confused as he was. And he was terrified about her safety as well as his child's.

And he knew she was probably worried about their child.

Their child.

He was still having a hard time wrapping his mind around that fact.

His stomach twisted in a knot. All he could think was that the danger that plagued his country now posed a threat to his child.

To Imogen.

It terrified him.

How was he going to protect his child? How was he going to protect Imogen?

Is it really your child, though?

And that niggling thought ate away at him. He remembered what had happened with his brother. His brother had fallen in love with a woman who was not of their father's choosing and that woman had become pregnant, supposedly with the next heir. Kristof had been over-the-moon happy. He'd been thrilled, and there had been a wedding planned.

And then it had come out that his brother's intended had been duping him. Just like Tatiana.

That the child was not really his.

His brother had been so broken and Lev never wanted to feel that kind of pain. He was wary about entering into relationships. He didn't want to feel that betrayal his brother felt.

He couldn't let himself get too excited. He had to protect himself, just as he wanted to make sure that Imogen wasn't in danger because of her association with him.

Why is she in Yellowknife?

She'd been safer when he hadn't known where she was. How had he not known she lived here?

Because she never said where she lived.

All she'd said was that she lived in the country and had been a flying doctor at one point.

Yellowknife was small, but it was a city. This was not country.

"You look like I feel," she said.

"How is that?"

"Stunned."

Yes. He was stunned, but he didn't want to talk about it.

"Why don't you show me to where I'm supposed to work?" Lev said, breaking the odd tension that had fallen between them. "I'm eager to get started. That's what I'm here for."

Imogen nodded. "Of course. I'll take you down to the emergency room. Follow me."

Lev followed her out of the doctors' lounge and through the halls. It wasn't a long walk from the emergency department. He would only be seeing those who required emergency surgeries. There were people in the emergency room who didn't have a regular family doctor, or those seeking help for mental health. Those patients fell under other doctors' jurisdiction. As much as he wanted to help more, he couldn't draw attention to himself. If someone figured out who he was, the truth could get back to Chenar and he'd be moved again…and now he knew where Imogen was, he didn't want to be moved.

"This is the emergency department. I'll take you over to the nursing station so you can be filled in on the protocols for triage. I know you're a trauma surgeon, but you'll be assessing more than traumatic injuries here. We're short-staffed and it's all hands on deck."

"That is not what I was told," he said.

"Well, that's how it is in the north. I made it clear that was how it was when we met," Imogen snapped.

"No. Not really," he said. "I had no idea you lived here."

If he'd known she was here, he would have told someone in the consulate so he wouldn't have been assigned here. He dismissed the wrench in his gut that said he would have done everything to ensure he was brought straight here.

"I told you."

"No. You said you lived in the country. This is not the country."

She rolled her eyes. "So I did, but I mentioned flying doctors to you."

"You did, but Canada is so large."

She sighed. "Well, you're here now."

"I am."

"And that means all hands on deck. As I said, we're short-staffed." Then she leaned over. "Sometimes we have to fly into remote communities. You will have to do that as well. Especially if there's an accident."

"I was not informed of this."

"Well, consider yourself informed." Imogen turned on her heel and headed toward the nurses' station. He followed after her, annoyed for a moment about the whole situation. Yes, he was practicing medicine, but all he really wanted to do was go back to Chenar and assess the damage. Those were the people he should be helping. It was obvious his presence here in Yellowknife was not welcome. Lev could understand her coldness and knew it was for the best she keep her distance.

It would be the best for both of them.

It was safer for her and the baby. The baby…

And yet she was someone he could not get out of his mind. All those lonely nights, the nights he couldn't sleep and didn't know where he'd end up, he'd seen her face.

She'd been a comfort during all the chaos.

He didn't want to stay away from her, even though it was for the best.

She'd unknowingly been his rock since the collapse of his country. But now they were here in Yellowknife, things had to change. He didn't want to stay away from her—he was drawn to her. But he had to protect them.

Protect Imogen. Protect their child. And protect his heart.

CHAPTER FOUR

HE WAS OKAY.

Of course she was relieved he was alive and not lost.

But she was also angry that the embassies had lied to her about not knowing where he was. She knew, logically, it had been to protect him. But that didn't change the emotions coursing through her body.

Imogen sat behind the nurses' station in the emergency room, watching Lev assess a patient. He was looking at the patient's imaging at one of the many computers in the central part of the trauma bubble, where all patients went when they had been triaged and there was a bed available.

When she'd received his note that first morning, she'd been floored. It had shocked her, and she'd thought of nothing else the whole way back to Yellowknife. Then the stick had turned blue and her world had come crashing down.

After she couldn't get hold of him, when she didn't know where he was—or whether he was even alive— she'd had to accept that she'd be raising this baby on her own. And she'd grieved the loss of him for her child. She'd grieved that her child would never know its father.

She knew what it was like, always wondering what they thought of you. Why they'd left. Worrying that you were the reason they'd left. That you hadn't been good enough for them. She'd never wanted it for a child of her own.

And suddenly there he was, standing right in front of her, in Yellowknife and under her supervision.

And she had to pinch herself to see if she was dreaming.

It felt like she was dreaming.

Lev glanced in her direction, as if sensing she was watching him, and she looked away quickly, but not gracefully. It was obvious she was watching him and she was mortified, but she couldn't help herself. Even though she was conflicted, she still found herself drawn to him.

Attracted to him.

Knowing exactly what it was like to be with him and craving that pleasure again.

Pull yourself together.

She sighed and tried to return to her work.

You don't get involved with or sleep with people you work with.

Only it was too late for that! She didn't regret their night together, but she was still reeling from the shock. Lev was here, alive and hiding in Yellowknife, working with her.

The missing Prince of Chenar was actually a trauma surgeon, and he was here, working in Yellowknife…and she was carrying his baby.

This seemed like something out of an offbeat comedy.

That ended with the hero and heroine falling in love and living happily ever after.

She snorted at that thought and went back to her charting.

There was no way that could happen. She couldn't make the mistake of believing it could, of trusting someone in that way.

Allen had hurt her. She'd thought he was her home, her family, but he hadn't been. He'd left. Just like her mother had.

She didn't want their child to get hurt if it ended—or rather, *when* it ended. Lev still deserved to be involved in their child's life and her baby deserved to have both of its parents. But she didn't want her child to feel the same rejection she did. The pain of being left behind.

Love was fleeting and never seemed to last. Not really. It was rare and Imogen had a hard time believing in happily-ever-after. There had been no happily-ever-after for her father. He'd been crushed when her mother had left him and he'd pined for her his entire life.

And then there was her one real, long-term relationship. That had ended badly and broken her heart.

Love was a fantasy not in the cards for her.

She wasn't going to get hurt. Lev could be involved with their baby, but not with her.

She had to protect her heart.

She couldn't—and wouldn't—deny her child access to its father.

She never wanted that for her child. But she couldn't pretend it wouldn't have been easier to tell her child that its father was dead, as cruel as that sounded, but it was the truth. Telling your child that it had been abandoned because its parent hadn't wanted it was a lot more painful.

"You can explain to her why you're not coming to see her. She's been looking forward to seeing you."

Her father looked at Imogen sadly as she stood by the door of their home in Toronto, waiting for her mother, who had promised to come and take her for the night.

Waiting for a woman who never came.

"Denise, this... Fine. Fine." Her dad hung up the phone and sighed.

"She's not coming, is she?" Imogen asked sadly, not unfamiliar with this disappointment.

"No, honey. She's not. How about we do something together?"

"No. It's okay, Dad. I'll just go read in my room for a bit."

Tears stung her eyes and Imogen swallowed the painful lump in her throat. She was angry at herself for letting that memory intrude. She didn't like to think of her mother. Didn't like to think about the pain and the disappointment she always felt when she was promised something and constantly disappointed.

Allen had promised her that they'd stay in the north. That he'd remain faithful to her.

That he loved her.

But all that had changed when he'd got a better job offer.

He'd just left.

The only constant in life had been her father, but he was gone, and she was terrified that Lev would leave and not be there for their child.

Either way, she'd be the constant in their child's life.

She wasn't going to leave, but she wasn't going to force Lev into something he wasn't comfortable with. The moment the stick had turned blue, she had made her peace with the fact that she was probably going to do this on her own.

She glanced up again and Lev had moved on.

At least he was doing his work. Jeanette might've found him difficult, but really Lev wasn't being all that difficult, other than seeming not to understand the concept about the doctor shortage.

Not many physicians, nurses or even teachers came to the north. Yellowknife had it better than most communities, because it was a large city in the territory, but attracting qualified professionals to remote places was difficult.

The phone rang at the main station and Imogen answered it, because it was a call from the dispatch phone and the nurse was working on triage.

"Emergency," she said over the line.

"We have an ambulance en route. Three injured. Boat capsized just off Jolliffe Island. One patient had to be intubated and vitals are weak," the ambulance dispatch answered.

"How far out?" Imogen asked, standing and motioning for the trauma team with hand signals they were used to.

"Five minutes."

"Okay. Thanks." Imogen hung up the phone.

Lev stepped out of the pod where he'd finished with a patient. "What's going on?"

"Incoming trauma," Imogen said. "You're the trauma surgeon on duty. I'll show you where to meet the ambulances."

Lev nodded and followed her as they quickly grabbed disposable gowns and gloves to cover their scrubs. He followed her outside, where they could hear the distant wail of the ambulance.

"What happened?" Lev asked.

"A boat capsized in the lake. One of the patients had to be intubated. You can take that patient and I'll assess the other two for injuries and then help you if you need it."

Lev nodded and she was glad he was here. His specialty was trauma, and though she'd worked on emergency situations, she much preferred the operating room over the accident scene. But this was the north, specialists were in short supply, and, as she'd tried to tell him, everyone mucked in when they were needed.

The ambulance pulled up and the doors opened.

Lev took over, as the first ambulance had the intubated patient. The ambulance driver rattled off instructions, while Lev did his own assessment, helping the ambulance crew push the intubated victim into the resuscitation room.

The second ambulance pulled up and the third followed. Imogen pointed one of her residents in the direction of the second ambulance when she realized the patient there had a superficial head wound that required stitching.

In the third ambulance, the patient had what looked to be a dislocated shoulder.

"What happened out there?" Imogen asked as she helped the ambulance crew to wheel her patient into another room.

"Wind whipped up pretty fast on the lee side of Jolliffe Island. It was something strange for sure and their boat wasn't that sound. Looked like it had seen better days."

Imogen nodded. "Gotcha. So it was probably taking on water."

The ambulance driver, Dave, nodded. "Yeah."

"I told my dad to get the boat fixed, but he said it would be fine," the young man said, grimacing as the ambulance crew helped him off the stretcher onto the hospital gurney.

"You're not from Yellowknife, are you?" Imogen asked, not that it mattered, but she wanted to distract her patient from the pain while they set him up with an IV, which would give him the pain meds he'd need to go through the X-ray and while they popped the joint back into the socket.

"How did you know?" the young man asked.

"I've never seen you come through here and I live out by Jolliffe Island. I notice new boats when they putter by."

The young man chuckled. "We're from Edmonton. Thought we'd come up a bit farther to do some fishing."

"What's your name?" Imogen asked, as the nurses working with her prepped his arm and she examined his dislocated shoulder.

"Tom."

"Are you allergic to anything, Tom?" she asked.

"No."

"Good. We're going to get an IV started and give you some pain meds, and then we're going to get some imaging on your shoulder here, which I think is dislocated. Is your father the patient in the first ambulance, the one who had to be intubated?"

Tom nodded, his face pale. "Yeah. My brother and I were able to get to shore and call for help. We thought Dad was behind us."

"I'll check on him. Is there anything I need to tell my team about your dad?"

"No. He's pretty healthy for sixty."

Imogen smiled. "Good. You just relax the best you can and we'll take care of you. Jessica, start an IV and give him some morphine for the pain. Let me know when his imaging comes back."

"Yes, Dr. Hayes," Jessica said.

Imogen left Tom to the capable team of nurses and checked on Tom's brother, who was getting sutures, and then she made her way to where Lev was working.

"How is he?" Imogen asked, joining in as the team worked on Tom's father.

"He has a head injury. Looks like he hit his head on a rock and he has water in his lungs. He had a brief moment of tachycardia, but we have his heart rate under control. There was no asystole," Lev said. "He's stable and his pupils are reactive. I just want to get some imaging done on his head. We have a central line started and I would like to keep him intubated until after the imaging."

"Okay. Well, let's get him down to CT." Imogen helped Lev wheel Tom's father out of the resuscitation room.

They got their patient down to CT and waited together while the imaging came up.

"How are the other patients?" Lev asked, as they waited.

"Well, one of the sons has a superficial laceration to his head that's being stitched up and my patient has a dislocated shoulder. I just want to make sure that I can safely pop the joint back into place and that he doesn't need surgery."

Lev opened his mouth to say something when they heard an alarm.

"He's going into cardiac arrest," the CT technician said over the speaker as they hit the code button.

"Page Cardio!" Lev shouted as he dashed out of the room to the patient.

Imogen paged Dr. Snell and then joined Lev as they got the patient out of the CT machine and began chest compressions, and the nurse handed Imogen a dose of epinephrine.

Dr. Snell was there within a few moments and took the lead as the three of them rushed the patient out of CT and up to the OR floor.

"I have it from here, Doctor," Dr. Snell said, as his team took over the patient outside the OR. Imogen could tell that Lev wanted to continue to help, but Dr. Snell was one of the best cardiac doctors north of sixty.

Lev stood back. "I should be helping."

"Dr. Snell has it. And wasn't it you that seemed confused you would be doing more in the emergency room than you have in the past?"

A half smile crept on his face. "Yes. This is true."

"Be thankful we have Dr. Snell. He's the best in these parts." Imogen got a page that her patient's imaging was back. "Looks like my patient's X-rays are in. Want to help put a shoulder back in place?"

"Don't you have an orthopedic surgeon?"

"We do, but he's not on duty today, and it's most likely a simple fix. I'm sure you can handle it."

Lev nodded. "I've done a few."

"Come on, then. I much prefer the scalpel to popping a joint back into place."

By the time they got back to the pod where Tom was waiting, he was pretty high on pain medication, which would make their job easier.

"The images you ordered, Dr. Hayes." Jessica brought up the imaging on the computer and Imogen was relieved to see that it was a simple dislocation.

"Thank you, Jessica. If you could assist Dr. Vanin here, we'd be grateful."

Jessica nodded and smiled shyly at Lev, who didn't pay much attention to her. A small pang of jealousy hit her. It surprised her. She shouldn't care. Lev wasn't hers, but it bothered her that another woman was interested in him too.

Don't let it bother you.

She understood exactly what Jessica was feeling. Lev was sexy and charming. He was handsome and a doctor. Three months ago, Imogen had been feeling it too when Lev had swept her off her feet. Or maybe she had swept him off his feet. Either way, sweeping had happened, and now she was pregnant. She thought about that night. It flashed in her mind. It made her blood fire.

Focus.

"Are you ready, Tom?" Imogen asked. "Dr. Vanin here is going to put your shoulder back into place."

Tom grinned up at her. "You're tall! She's tall!"

Imogen rolled her eyes while Lev chuckled. "Yes, Tom, she is."

Tom's eyes widened. "You're like a Viking! You know there are Viking graves up here, eh?"

"Is that so?" Lev said, trying to hide his amusement. "Now, brace yourself, Tom. This will hurt for a moment. One, two…"

Lev didn't finish his countdown as he popped the joint back into place. Tom let out a shriek and then passed out.

"Is he okay?" Lev asked.

"He's fine," Jessica said. "Vitals are good."

"Good. Thank you," Lev said, and then he looked at Imogen. "How much pain medication did you order for this man?"

"The standard amount for his size." Imogen left the trauma pod and Lev followed behind her.

"I have never been referred to as a Viking before, although our ancestors are Scandinavian and not Russian. My mother was from Sweden."

Imogen chuckled. "Well, the first time I saw you I have to admit I thought the same thing. I thought you were more Nordic. That was before I knew where you came from."

Lev's brow furrowed in puzzlement. "What about me says Viking to you?"

"You're taller than me."

"Other men are taller than you," he stated.

"Not many. I'm five foot eleven."

Lev shrugged. "What else?"

Imogen felt her cheeks warm. "I don't know."

"Come on. There must be something?"

Imogen felt embarrassed. She didn't want to be talking about this with him in the middle of the emergency room.

She didn't want to talk about how blue his eyes were, how broad his shoulders were.

How strong he was.

How he'd made her feel when he'd taken her in his arms.

She shook her head.

"We're at work."

"And a patient said I resemble a Viking, so I want to know if this is some kind of Canadian thing," he teased.

She rolled her eyes. "Fine. Your beard is trimmed, but it's very Viking-slash-lumberjack. And your long blond hair with the shaved sides. You're muscular, fit." What she didn't mention was the tattoo she knew he had on his upper thigh. That strong, muscular upper thigh with its Nordic design. Maybe it was more Baltic—what did she know?—but either way, it was dead sexy. It crept up his thigh and onto his abdomen.

Warmth spread through her body and her pulse thundered between her ears.

Don't think about that.

"It's more hipster, surely?" Lev grinned.

"What is?" Imogen asked, clearing her throat and forgetting the thread of what they had been talking about.

"My look. Less military and more hipster."

"I suppose. But if you start wearing flannel you could fit in with the best of the lumberjacks," she teased.

Lev laughed. "I do like that wilderness look. So different from my military uniform and…well, I do prefer this look. I can blend in like this."

"I like how you look too." She groaned inwardly as she realized what she'd just said out loud.

Lev grinned. "Do you indeed?"

"I think you know I do. I don't usually rent a hotel room with a man I hardly know."

He smiled, the corners of his eyes crinkling. "That was a magical night."

"It was." Her pulse began to race and she was very aware of how close he was standing to her.

"Do you think about that night often?" he whispered.

Her heart skipped a beat. Yes. She did think of that night, but she wasn't going to admit it. She had to remove herself from this situation.

"I'm not answering that," she said dryly.

"Why not?" he asked.

Because I refuse to get involved with someone I work with.

Because my heart can't take it.

Because you will leave.

Because Yellowknife is not your home.

Only she didn't say those things. They were hers to know. No one else.

"We're at work. At work, we talk about work things. That's it. I don't like to discuss my personal life here and definitely not in the emergency room when there are patients waiting for us." She blurted it out, hoping he wouldn't press her further.

"Then perhaps we should have a meal or something together tonight so we can talk? I think we have a lot to talk about."

CHAPTER FIVE

THEY DID HAVE a lot to talk about. Lev wanted to ask her so many things, especially about her pregnancy. He was still having a hard time wrapping his mind around that.

He was struggling to believe her. He'd been hurt by Tatiana, had watched his brother be betrayed and watched his mother's heart break every time his father had cheated.

Imogen is different.

Was she?

He couldn't be sure. He wanted to believe she was, but he barely knew her...other than intimately. He tried not to think about her saying she liked the way he looked, and he tried not to think about the way her cheeks had flushed pink, and he definitely tried not to think about how her creamy skin would flush pink in the throes of passion.

How her full lips would swell with their passionate kisses.

Focus.

Imogen was obviously struggling with this whole situation too. He couldn't blame her. She'd all but admitted she'd thought he was dead. And she was smart enough to know that his true identity put the child in danger. He struggled too with all the implications.

It was overwhelming.

Yes, they had a lot to talk about. He'd have to talk to

Lexi about a safe place they could go for dinner. Lexi would need time to make sure the place was cleared of all security threats. He didn't want Imogen in any danger.

"I would like to talk more about it and would like to have dinner with you tonight, so why don't you come to my place?" she asked.

"Where is your place?" he asked. "I have to have my security team do a sweep."

"I live on the lake."

Now he was confused. "You live by the lake, you mean?"

"No, I live on one of those houseboats out in the bay. Near Jolliffe Island. I have a motorboat instead of a car. We can walk to the docks and I can ferry you out to my houseboat and take you back to shore afterward. That's if your security team would be okay with that. I mean, my place is pretty private."

"If it's private, I'm sure it will be fine." Imogen lived surprisingly unconventionally.

Lev couldn't be one hundred percent sure how Lexi would feel about Imogen's home, but he was intrigued by the prospect of Imogen living on a houseboat. In Chenar there were people who lived on barges. They weren't very big, but they were long and able to maneuver the slender canals and lakes in his country and the neighboring countries.

As a boy he'd been fascinated by the lifestyle that came with barge living. Until he'd grown to be over six feet tall and realized very quickly that the small, cramped confines were not for him. Imogen was tall too, so he couldn't see her living in a cramped space.

He was excited to see what the houseboats out on the bay looked like on the inside. When he'd first seen them a couple of days ago, he hadn't been able to believe what he was seeing—dozens of brightly colored homes floating out on a huge lake.

And the fact that Imogen lived on one of those boats just solidified what he had suspected about her when he'd first met her: she was interesting as well as sexy.

Don't think like that.

She could never be his woman.

Not with the state of things back home. He didn't want to put her life in danger, but her life was already in danger because of the baby. He had to talk to Lexi and the Canadian officials about extending protection to Imogen.

At least until this whole situation with his government was settled.

Until Kristof said it was okay to come out of hiding.

And even though he and his brother had never had the best relationship, the thought that his brother was in danger ate away at him every single day.

Lev hadn't been in Chenar when everything had happened.

He hadn't been there when his father had been killed.

He hadn't been there.

"I can come back to Chenar," Lev said, annoyed that he was being denied by Kristof again. *"You can't keep me here in Edmonton with nothing to do."*

"No. You're to stay in Canada. It's for the best."

"How? I can't help here, Kristof."

"You need to stay," Kristof said coolly.

"No. I don't. I must get back to Chenar and do my duty!"

"Your duty is to your King and country."

"Father is dead!" Lev snapped.

"I am your King!" Kristof shouted. *"You will do as I*

say and not be so selfish as to put your life and Lexi's at risk. You will stay there until I order otherwise!"

And maybe that was what Kristof had meant by saying that Lev was selfish.

Maybe he was. He just felt so helpless.

"So how about I meet you down by the docks off Franklin around seven?" Imogen said, interrupting his morose chain of thoughts.

"Okay. I don't know where that is," Lev said. "I haven't been here long enough."

"Any cabdriver knows the way and it's not a long walk from here. It's down near the Bush Pilot Monument."

"And I will be able to find your berth easily?"

Imogen chuckled. "Yes. You'll be able to spot me."

"Okay. I will see you at seven, then."

"Good. I'll see you then."

Lev watched her walk away and he scrubbed a hand over his face. He wasn't sure how he was going to explain this to Lexi, but he and Imogen needed to talk about what was going on.

He finished up his first shift and then made his way outside.

There was a heaviness in the air, a smoky quality that caused a haze to settle over the city, even though it was still light outside.

Lexi was waiting in front of the white pickup truck he'd acquired in Edmonton, Alberta. It had dark tinted windows and Lexi said it would help them blend in. At the time Lev hadn't been so sure, but as they'd made their way north, he'd seen that Lexi was right. Everyone seemed to drive a big white truck.

Lexi had taken his job seriously and had blended in. Gone was the clean-shaven military look he usually adopted.

He too had grown a beard and let his hair grow longer, but only on the top.

He no longer wore designer suits, but had settled into denim and plaid, just like Lev.

"How was your first day?" Lexi asked, opening the door for him.

"I thought we talked about this," Lev said gruffly.

"What?" Lexi asked.

"You can't act like my bodyguard any longer," Lev said, as he slipped into the passenger side and closed the door. Lexi came around and got into the driver side.

"Force of habit," Lexi responded gruffly. "I suppose you want your own vehicle."

"Yes. In fact, I do, and you're going to have to figure out something else to do while I'm working. I know it can't be easy on you, being here with me and just doing nothing."

Lexi grunted. "It does not matter. Your father tasked me to protect you and that's what I'm doing."

Lev rolled his eyes. "I appreciate that, but I'm well looked after."

"I can't go back to Chenar. I don't have family like Gustav, and I was discharged from the military because of my shoulder. What am I to do? This is all I know. All I know is protecting you."

Lev could feel his frustration. He felt it too.

"Lexi, I just feel bad you're stuck here with me."

Lexi grunted again, but he was smiling. "Your Highness, I've been watching over you since you graduated from medical school, and before that we were in school together. I know you're my Prince, my leader, but you're also one of my best friends."

"Thank you."

He sighed. "I suppose I could work down at the wharf. I spent the last couple of days watching them load float-planes. I could do that work."

"You still have your pilot's license?" Lev asked.

"Yes," Lexi said cautiously. "Why are you asking?"

"You can be a bush pilot."

"I'm not leaving you in Yellowknife alone!" Lexi snapped. "The Canadians are doing a good job, but I promised your brother. I'm not becoming a bush pilot."

"So you just want to load planes at the docks?"

Lexi shrugged. "It's something to do. I can walk there and you can take the truck."

"Well, if it gives you something to do." Lev glanced out of the window. "What's with the smoke?"

"Wildfires, but they're not nearby. Apparently the jet stream causes the smoke to settle down here in Yellow-knife. I don't mind it."

"It's a bit heavy out there, the air." Lev was trying to approach the subject about Imogen and the baby, but he didn't know where to start. "I'm going out tonight."

"Pardon?" Lexi said, stunned.

"Do you remember the woman I met in Toronto? The surgeon I—?"

"Yes."

"She's here."

Lexi's knuckles went white as he gripped the steering wheel tight. "So we have to leave?"

"No."

"Does she know who you are?"

Lev sighed. "Yes."

"Then we leave. I will call the consulate when we get back to the apartment."

"Lexi, she's pregnant."

"She's…what?" Lexi asked.

"Pregnant. With my child." If he said it clearly and simply, it would help him believe it too. Help him believe he'd been the only one since their night together.

Lexi didn't say anything for a few moments, but Lev could tell he was fuming.

"You've done a lot of irresponsible things…"

And he had.

He'd become a surgeon against his father's wishes, had been a military trauma surgeon and on the front lines, also against his father's wishes. He'd often left without the protection of his bodyguards; he'd rejected life at court.

"Did I know this was going to happen?" Lev snapped. "No! And I didn't know that my father was going to be assassinated and that our country would implode, trapping me here. I didn't know these things."

His guilt was heavy on his heart. It weighed on him like a rock.

"My apologies, Your Highness. I will speak to the Canadians about this delicate matter, but only after we confirm that the child is indeed yours."

"Well, that won't be for a few months," Lev grumbled. "Unless she's open to diagnostic testing beforehand, but I won't force that on her."

"I don't know if our Canadian friends will agree to protect her. If word gets out…"

"I don't even want to think about it. And how could they not protect her?" Lev snapped.

"What if she's lying? You said she knew who you were. May I ask, sir, with the utmost respect, what if it's not your child? Look what happened to Kristof. He was duped. And Tatiana…"

Just the mention of Tatiana brought the shame of being

fooled right back up to the surface. He'd been foolish and, yes, selfish for not listening to his father about her, but that was in the past.

"You don't need to remind me of that," Lev snarled. "I'm fully aware of what happened."

"So, this going out tonight is with this other doctor?"

Lev nodded. "Yes. She has a houseboat out in the bay. She wants to take me to her place for dinner."

"You're not going out on a houseboat," Lexi stated.

"Lexi, you can hire a houseboat and do perimeter sweeps if that makes you feel better. She's not a threat and her houseboat is more than secure."

Lexi groaned. "I suppose so. I would like to meet her, though."

"Not yet. Let's not overload her. She was shocked to see me too. The world thinks that I'm missing, presumed dead, and she thought that I was dead too."

"All right, but I'm not happy about this, sir." Lexi pulled into the driveway of their small rental apartment, which was located at the top of a row house that sat down by the docks.

"I know you're not. I'm not either, but if the child is mine, I need to protect them both."

And he hated it that he had said *if.*

The child was his.

Imogen wasn't like Kristof's former fiancée. She wasn't like Tatiana. She was a different woman.

Is she? How do you know?

Lexi nodded. "I agree."

"Good." Lev climbed out of the passenger side and glanced out over Yellowknife Bay. He could see all the houseboats dotting the water from their vantage point on the top of a small hill, and he couldn't help but wonder which of those brightly colored homes was Imogen's. She was so close to him, yet still so far away.

After her shift, Imogen raced to the North Store Co-Op and grabbed something to make for dinner, since all she had in her fridge were a couple of yogurts and a really brown head of lettuce. She hadn't felt like cooking much recently and had yet to make it to the grocery store.

Usually when she got back to her houseboat after a long shift she made herself a bowl of soup and went to bed.

Tonight was different.

Tonight she wasn't so tired. Lev was here. So instead of feeding Lev a dinner of brown lettuce and yogurt, she opted to heat up a frozen lasagna and bought some garlic bread.

She'd been exhausted lately from the pregnancy and trying to figure out how she was going to make everything work on her own, but she wanted to talk to Lev and to hear what he had to say and how they were going to deal with this.

The water of the bay was calm and it was an easy short ride from the docks to her teal blue houseboat that was moored off the edge of Jolliffe Island. Her plan was to get the lasagna started, do a quick clean and then watch for Lev to get to the docks.

She wasn't far from there, so she'd be able to see him when he got there and then she'd head over to pick him up.

Pick him up?

It made her stomach swirl at the thought he was coming here. There were so many emotions she was feeling.

What if he doesn't show?

That thought subdued her. How many times had her

father waited for her mother to show, only to be disappointed?

Lev's not like that.

But she didn't know. She wanted to believe he wasn't, but she didn't know.

Feeling anxious, she started to tidy. It kept her mind off her swirling thoughts and nauseous belly.

She cleaned up and straightened a few things and had the lasagna on in her propane oven. She checked her water tank, which was still full, and then wandered out onto her deck to watch for Lev.

It was getting close to seven and she hoped he'd be punctual, because from what she recalled during that surgical conference in Toronto, he tended to be a bit late to sessions. Now she understood why.

He probably had a security team trailing after him and they likely wouldn't let him go anywhere without them.

Oh, no. What if his team is coming with him?

Imogen bit her lip, worrying that she didn't have enough food for his bodyguards and worrying about what her neighbors would think seeing guys in dark sunglasses and suits standing on her houseboat. If Lev wanted to keep his identity hidden, then that was not the best way to go about it.

This is a bad idea.

The only problem was she had no way to call him off.

There was no way to change plans until she met him at the docks. She was worrying about all of this when she saw him arrive and look around, and she was relieved to see he was alone.

Her stomach did a flip-flop. She'd never thought she'd see him again.

Now he was waiting for her. He'd come to the dock, like he'd promised, and it was a relief.

Be careful.

She had to control herself.

All they were going to do was talk about the baby and managing their co-parenting.

That was it.

Is it?

She got into her motorboat and pulled away from her houseboat, making the short five-minute ride to the docks and pulling up close to Lev.

"Hey!" she shouted over the engine as she moored her motorboat.

Lev grinned and waved at her as he made his way down the long dock to her berth. "I thought I was late and you had given up."

"No. Not late. I live just over there and I could see you approach." She pointed behind her. "The teal houseboat is mine."

"Ah! I was wondering which one was yours." Lev climbed down into the boat with relative ease and Imogen looked around.

"Is it just you?" she asked.

"Yes." Lev motioned up the hill where some row houses sat. "My place is just up there. Lexi, my…"

"Roommate?" Imogen offered, suddenly aware that he might not want to admit that Lexi was really his security guard.

"Yes. He's watching. He wanted to meet you, but I said that might be a bit overwhelming, given that you only found out I was alive this morning, and, you know, the baby…"

"Does Lexi know?" Imogen asked as she released the moorings on her boat and handed Lev the lines as she untied them.

"He does. I told him."

"I'm sure he's thrilled," Imogen said.

"He has…concerns."

She chuckled. "How very diplomatic of you."

There was a twinkle in Lev's eyes. "Well, I am a bit up on international relations."

"It's a short ride, so have a seat and I'll show you my place."

Lev settled into the seat next to her and she started the engine and navigated her boat away from the dock and headed out over the calm waters of Yellowknife Bay, before pulling up beside her houseboat. Lev helped moor the boat and then climbed out with ease onto her dock and then helped her up, lifting her slightly like she weighed hardly anything.

She stumbled slightly and fell into his arms.

"Whoops. I've got you," he said as he steadied her, his arms around her, holding her. She remembered the last time Lev had held her like that. She could feel herself blush, her blood heating as she looked up into his eyes.

She was so close to him again and she had forgotten how he made her feel. How good it felt with his arms around her. When it came to him, she was so weak.

She hated that.

Focus.

"Thank you!" she said breathlessly, pushing herself out of his arms. "Let me show you around."

"Sure."

Imogen opened the door and motioned for Lev to go in ahead of her.

"It's so spacious!" he said in shock.

"I'd hardly call it spacious."

"I do. Compared to the houseboats in Europe." Lev walked around her living space. Her place was open concept with the living room and dining room one big open space. There was a bathroom off to the side and another door connected to a small shed where she kept her snowmobile in the summer months and her motorboat in the winter months. Also housed there was her father's canoe, which she barely used anymore, but which she didn't have the heart to part with.

Her bedroom was up a set of stairs. It was a loft over the kitchen. And she had a lot of windows and a couple of good skylights to let in the sun when she could. In the winter it was a bit harder to get the sun in, but it was nice to lie on her bed at night and watch the aurora.

"Is this your childhood home?" Lev asked, staring up at the ceiling.

"No. My father had a house on the mainland, but this was always a dream of his and my mother..."

She trailed off, not wanting to think of her father's broken dreams. "When he died I couldn't bear to sell it. He built it, so I had to take it over."

"He built this?" Lev asked, impressed. "Amazing!"

"The houseboat doesn't leave a large carbon footprint. My water comes from the lake. There's a large freshwater tank and filter through here, as well as the septic system and the panels for my solar power and propane." She opened the door to the shed. Lev stepped through and examined everything, taking it all in.

"Your home is fueled by solar power too?"

"Only in the summer when I can take advantage of the midnight sun. In the winter, I rely on propane or hot water."

"It's incredible," Lev said with awe.

"Yeah. It was always my dad's passion to live off grid. I finished off the rest of this barge when he died."

"I'm sorry that your father never got to live here."

"Thanks, but I don't want to dwell on that." She didn't

need extra emotional turmoil on her plate tonight. They were here to talk about the baby. "Do you want something to drink? I don't have any alcohol."

"Water is fine."

"Good." Imogen went to get a cup of water from the tap and watched as Lev wandered around, staring up at the ceiling. She handed him his glass of water. Lev took a seat on her couch and she sat down in the easy chair nearby. "So, I suppose you have questions."

Her stomach did another flip-flop as she braced herself for questions she wasn't sure she could answer because her brain decided to skip out on her.

Lev nodded. "When is the baby due?"

"February. Around Valentine's Day, funnily enough."

"I'm really concerned about how to protect you both, and my bodyguard Lexi is afraid that the baby is not mine. I'm sorry—he's not a very trusting individual. He's been trained to question everything."

But there was something in his tone that made her think that maybe he didn't quite believe the baby was his either. And although it hurt her, she couldn't blame him.

They were strangers.

Strangers who had shared one incredible night.

Don't think about it.

"I get it. I'm sure if you do the math, you can figure out the conception date, but I am willing to do paternity testing if that's what would make you and Lexi happy."

Lev set down his glass of water and scrubbed his hand over his face. "I don't want to put the baby at risk by doing invasive testing."

"I'm going to be having an amniocentesis. There are some genetic tests I want to have done, some genetic concerns on my side, and honestly, when I thought you were dead, I wanted to see if there was anything else I should be concerned about. I had no information about your side of the family."

Lev smiled gently. "There is nothing overly debilitating in my family, as far as I know. When is your amniocentesis scheduled?"

"In a couple of weeks. You're more than welcome to come—that way you can get the paternity confirmed and put your mind at ease."

Lev's brow furrowed. "I have no doubt that it's my child you carry."

"No doubt?" she asked, skeptical. She had a hard time believing that he would blindly trust her. She didn't think he was as foolish as she'd been.

"You wanted to be sure of the paternity."

"There are extenuating circumstances. I was skeptical, but... I believe you."

"I'll say," she said. "I just have a hard time trusting you."

"I believe you, Imogen." Lev stood and then knelt down in front of her. "I believe that it's my child you carry. I know I don't know you well, but my gut tells me it is the truth. Lexi may have his reservations, but I don't care. I want to protect you and our child. The only way I can bring about the same level of protection that I have is to make you my wife."

"What?" Imogen asked, stunned. "Say that again?"

"It's simple, Imogen. To protect you and our unborn child, you need to become my wife. I want you to marry me."

CHAPTER SIX

"What?"

Her world had stopped turning there for a moment, and she felt like she was going to be sick.

She was pretty sure that it wasn't morning sickness. She was a thousand percent sure that it was shock.

"What?" she said again, her heart racing. "I didn't hear you correctly."

"I'm asking you to marry me," Lev said, annoyed. "I thought I was clear."

Imogen got up and sidestepped around Lev, who was still on one knee in front of her chair. She needed to put some space between them.

This was just supposed to be a dinner to talk about the baby, to talk about what had happened since and what would happen next. To talk about what was going on in Chenar and how it would affect her and the baby.

She was not expecting a marriage proposal. Neither could she accept one. This was just too crazy. And all she could think about was when Allen had left her, when she'd thought he was proposing but wasn't, and how foolish it had made her feel to think that anyone could want to be with her.

Her mother certainly hadn't.

And then there was her parents' marriage. That had been a disaster.

"I think… I think you may have lost your mind," she stated, her voice shaking in partnership with her body.

Lev frowned. "How have I lost my mind?"

"You're proposing marriage to me. We barely know each other."

"We've had sex." He smiled knowingly.

She was very aware they'd had sex. She thought about it often, and if that wasn't enough, there was a baby growing inside her. But sex didn't mean they had to get married.

They were strangers.

"Sex doesn't mean you know someone. Like whether or not you like them as a person with a real personality or whether you can live with them or tolerate them. Sex is just…" She didn't even know how to finish that sentence. She ran her hand through her hair. Didn't know what to say.

"Something is burning."

"What?" Imogen asked, confused.

Lev stood and pointed, and she spun around and remembered she had a lasagna in the oven.

"Crap!" She ran over to the kitchen, grabbed her oven mitts and pulled open the door. Thankfully, some had just bubbled up over the side and had burned on the bottom of the oven, but the rest of the lasagna was perfectly salvageable for dinner.

It was at instances like this when she remembered she didn't like cooking. Not really. She didn't mind grilling, but anything else to do with the oven beyond boiling a pot of water on the range top she didn't seem to have the aptitude for.

"Is it okay?" Lev asked.

"Yeah. Some bubbled over. It's just a ready-made one I got. I've never actually bought a frozen lasagna before." She peeked under the tinfoil. "It looks okay."

Lev came over. "Test the middle."

She cocked an eyebrow. "The Prince of a kingdom is familiar with frozen lasagna?"

"What do you think I've been living on since I went into hiding? Lexi and I have learned to cook a variety of things. Frozen meals being the most common. Do you have a knife?" he asked.

Imogen reached into the drawer and pulled out a knife. He took it from her and cut into the middle, pulling it out and touching the side of the blade.

"It's hot. It's done. I'm sure it's excellent. Not as good as home made, but it will do at a pinch."

Imogen cocked an eyebrow. "And you've made one from scratch?"

"I have. I told you, Lexi and I have learned to manage things. I don't mind actually." He proceeded to cut the lasagna and then pulled out the garlic bread, which hadn't fared as well and looked a little blackened.

"You're full of surprises."

Including proposals and coming back from the dead.

"Well, seeing how you said we're strangers, I suppose that shouldn't be surprising…" His eyes twinkled and Imogen groaned.

"It's true, Lev. We're strangers and Lev isn't even your real name."

"No. That's true. But it is my middle name. Vanin is just a combination of my given name and my last name."

"See, this is why I can't marry you. I don't know you."

Lev sighed. "I know it's not ideal and it's not like I'm expecting anything from you."

Imogen's eyes widened and her pulse raced. "What

would you be expecting?" Although all she could think of was sex.

Would that be so bad?

She shook that thought away. Last time she'd thought like that she ended up pregnant.

"To share my bed."

Her cheeks heated. "What?"

"Wifely duties."

She cleared her throat. She wouldn't mind a few "wifely duties" with Lev. When it came to Lev, it wouldn't be a duty and she would never think of it that way.

Nothing about that one stolen night they'd shared had resembled anything unpleasant. In fact, it had been the exact opposite.

Focus.

Imogen cleared her throat. "What are you talking about?"

"Imogen, it would be a marriage on paper only. That way you and our child would be protected."

"Because we're in danger," she stated.

Lev sighed. "I don't know. I really don't. Lexi seems to think so, as do the Canadians. There have been some unsettling experiences when I was placed in other locations and then was moved quickly, but mostly I was moved because they were worried I'd been recognized. I'm afraid that once they get wind of you, I will be moved again, and I don't want to leave you or the baby."

Imogen chewed her bottom lip. "I don't know, Lev. I mean, it's one thing to say it's a marriage of…I guess convenience, if that's even a thing, but wouldn't it raise suspicions if you were to marry me and not live with me?"

"I won't invade your life, Imogen."

"You already have, Lev," she said in bemusement, and touched her belly.

"Yes. I suppose I have." He smiled and her heart skipped a beat.

Imogen sighed. "I can't marry you."

"Think on it. Please."

Lev had never thought he would ever be asking anyone to marry him after what had happened with Tatiana, but he couldn't leave Imogen so exposed. He didn't want her or the baby at risk, and the only way he could offer her protection was to have her marry him. It was his duty to protect them.

At least on paper she would be protected.

Once this was all over and he knew that she and his child were safe, he would grant her a divorce. He didn't want to trap her into a life of protocol. He didn't want to take her away from this place she seemed to love so much.

And he understood why she felt that way about the north.

Despite being forced to come to this place for his protection, despite his every step and every move being watched, he still saw the appeal of life up here.

The drive up from Edmonton had been eye-opening. Endless farm fields, bright yellow with canola, to forests of birch, pine and cedar, crossing mighty rivers surrounded by rolling hills that reminded him of the badlands in America's Midwest.

The land had changed the farther north they'd traveled, and then the traffic had dropped away. Once in a while they'd drive through a small town or meet a transport truck going south, but then those signs of civilization would melt away into forest and rough rock that jutted through the loam, like the soil had been scraped away, the only sign of life the occasional bear or bison crossing the road.

Trees were slender, some burned away from a previous fire, but all reached up toward the large blue sky, reaching their leaves and needles to catch the last rays of summer sun as the days grew shorter.

And the quiet.

That was hard for Lev to get used to, but he liked it.

And then coming here to Imogen's simple houseboat. He could get used to living this way.

You can't.

It was all just a dream, because he couldn't have this life. He was a prince. He had responsibilities. He'd known that his whole life.

Lev set the knife down.

"Are you okay?" Imogen asked as she set the table.

He didn't even realize that she'd gone about setting the table. The last thing he could remember was asking her to think about his proposal and then his thoughts had run away with him.

"What?" he asked, shaking his head and picking up the lasagna tray with the oven mitts again.

"You drifted off there. You totally zoned out."

"I'm fine. I was just…thinking." Which wasn't a lie.

"I will consider your proposal, Lev, but I can't see how it would be a good idea." Imogen went to get a couple of glasses of water while Lev served the lasagna onto the plates. He got it. It really wasn't a good idea.

"You could always move in with me and Lexi." Then he frowned, because his place with Lexi was even smaller than her houseboat and Lexi wasn't thrilled that Lev had got someone pregnant.

"I don't think so." Imogen chuckled. "Those places on the hill are okay, but they're tiny."

"I could move in here. I mean, we work together and your couch looks comfortable enough."

Imogen's eyes widened and Lev pulled out her chair for her at the table. She sat down and was still sitting there looking stunned.

"You want to live with me?"

"If we were going to pretend to be married to keep you and the baby safe, you're right. We would have to live together to keep up pretenses, and it makes no sense for you to cram into my apartment with Lexi. So I'll move in here with you."

"Do you think my houseboat is safe?"

Lev shrugged. "It is exposed, but to move you would seem suspicious."

"And what about Lexi?" she asked.

"He'd stay where he is. He would be close enough to keep watch. He's already keeping watch."

"What do you mean?" she asked.

"The boat that keeps going by, which you probably haven't noticed, that's Lexi."

Imogen went to stand but Lev motioned for her to sit.

"Don't draw attention to him. He won't like that. This is the only way I could get him to agree to allow me to come out here."

Imogen sighed. "We're talking like we're going to go through with this charade and get married."

"It makes sense, Imogen, and it protects you and the baby. Please, let me do this for you. I feel so helpless right now and so worried about you both."

"I will think on it. That's all I can offer right now, Lev. I'm sorry."

He got up from his seat and knelt down beside her. "Don't be sorry. I'm sorry I got you into this predicament."

"I think I had a little bit to do with it too," she teased.

Lev smiled up at her.

Yes. She was definitely involved in their little mistake. He couldn't forget that and he didn't want to forget it.

The memory of that night together haunted him, and if he weren't now heir to the throne of Chenar and in hiding, he would go about this differently.

You don't really know her. She's right about that.

And that niggling thought brought him back to reality. Imogen was right. They really didn't know each other beyond that one night, and lust wasn't something you based a marriage on. His parents' marriage had been based on that and they had both been miserable.

They'd remained married, but neither of them had been faithful to the other, and his mother had died unhappy.

He didn't want that kind of marriage. He didn't want a marriage of duty. He wasn't sure he wanted a marriage at all. None of this had been in his plans.

"How about we eat before the food gets cold?" Imogen suggested. "Besides, my stomach is growling."

Lev nodded. "Sounds good."

He returned to his seat and they ate their lasagna and slightly charred garlic bread. The sunlight was slipping away and it was growing darker.

"What time is it?" he asked.

"About nine."

"I thought this was the land of the midnight sun?" he said, as he picked up his dish and took it to her sink.

"Only near the summer solstice. We're headed into autumn and it'll get dark earlier and earlier. The aurora should be coming back soon too."

"I hope to see it." He turned on the tap and let the sink fill.

"You don't have to do the dishes. I can do that. You're my guest."

"And the only reason I'm your guest is because you're carrying my baby and I'm apparently resurrected from the dead," he teased. "I have this. It's okay."

"Thanks." She packed up the leftovers in a plastic container. "Maybe Lexi would like some dinner."

Lev nodded. "He probably would. Knowing him, he hasn't eaten."

"Will he stay out there on that boat until you head back to the mainland?"

Lev nodded. "Probably. He's not only my bodyguard—he's my friend. We grew up together. Went to the same military school. My father wanted me to be a soldier like my brother, Kristof, but I preferred healing to anything else. Lexi was in the military for a while, until an injury forced him out and my father appointed him as my personal bodyguard. I was a bit reckless in my youth."

"Oh?" Imogen asked, intrigued.

"I liked to party a bit too much, even though I was training to be a military doctor, and Lexi helped me see the error of my ways. He takes his job a little too seriously sometimes."

Imogen smiled. "It's nice to have someone looking out for you."

Lev shrugged. "I suppose, but why should he have to? He has no real life of his own. He used to be a pilot in the military and I know he would like to fly again. I suggested he take a job as a bush pilot if we're up here for the foreseeable future, but he won't do it. I'm his job, but I know he's bored."

"Well, he could get a job at the hospital."

Lev frowned. "What?"

"There are security jobs to fill in the hospital. He would still be close to you and doing something."

"Why are you insisting on torturing me?"

"I thought you said Lexi was bored. I was offering a solution." Imogen put away the dishes he had just washed.

She was right. It was a perfect solution, even if he hated the idea that Lexi would be so close. But maybe that way he could protect Imogen, the baby and himself all at the same time. Lexi would definitely like it.

Imogen was staring out of the window and she was worrying her bottom lip, thinking. She did that often. He'd noticed it when they'd been in Toronto and again at work today.

Those lips he remembered kissing. How he wished he could take her in his arms and kiss her again. She was so beautiful, and the memories that sustained him did not do her justice.

He couldn't think about her like that, though.

He had to keep his distance. This marriage was to protect her and his child from the situation at home. He refused to trap her into a life of protocol.

She belonged here in the north.

She deserved to be free. Even if it meant free of him.

"Lexi must really think there's a threat," she whispered.

"Yes. There is a threat. I've been moved all over. I've had places compromised. There are insurgents out there, trying to finish the job and eradicate all the heirs to the throne of Chenar." He reached down and, with a quick check to make sure it was okay, touched her belly. He knew he wouldn't be able to feel anything yet but he couldn't stop himself. "All heirs."

"Okay." She turned to face him. "Okay."

"Okay?" he asked, mystified.

"I'll marry you." She worried her lip again.

"You will?" he said, stunned but also relieved that she was agreeing to the marriage.

"But there will be some ground rules," she said.

"Ground rules?" he asked.

He couldn't help but wonder what kind of trouble he'd got himself into.

CHAPTER SEVEN

"What kind of ground rules?"

She could tell by his expression, his furrowed brow and pursed lips, that he was worried.

"Well, the marriage is on paper only. That much we've established."

Lev sighed. "Right. I understand."

"You're moving in here."

"Yes, but I don't think Lexi will approve," he groused.

"I understand that, but my place is bigger."

"Okay, what else?" Lev asked. He sounded exhausted and she felt bad.

"The baby... I have custody after this marriage ends." She was worried he wouldn't agree, because her child had royal blood, but she couldn't leave Canada for an unstable country. This was her home. This was where she wanted her child to grow up. Yellowknife was all she knew.

"I would never take the child from you, Imogen."

She was surprised. "You wouldn't?"

"Of course not. A child needs its mother more than its father." There was a hint of sadness in his voice.

"A child needs its father too," she said sadly, as she thought of her own father. And she couldn't really comprehend a child *needing* a mother because she had never had that experience, though she had surely wished for it.

"My late father was not…loving. He wasn't very warm and I rarely saw him. My mother, she loved me. She loved to be with me, but I lost her when I was seven and then spent many years being raised by governesses."

She felt bad for the little boy he had been.

"I didn't know my mother," she said. "But I wouldn't trade my time with my father for anything. Lev, I want you to be in our child's life."

She did. She just couldn't leave Yellowknife. This was her home. It would be their child's home.

She was scared. She couldn't see into the future, she couldn't control the future, and it felt overwhelming.

Lev took her hand. "I appreciate that, but when our marriage ends, our child will stay with you. It's better for our child that he or she grows up away from the life I knew. I'm not doing this to take the child from you. I'm doing this to protect you."

"I know," she whispered. And she believed him, but she was terrified of being hurt or her child being hurt.

"Come on," he said gently. "I think I've overwhelmed you enough for one night. Let's get me back before Lexi loses his mind."

Imogen chuckled. "Good idea."

They walked out and he helped her untie her motorboat. She made her way slowly to the mainland, the lights on shore and years of experience guiding her through the darkness.

"Lexi will be around here somewhere. I would like you to meet him and I'll explain to him what's going on." Lev got out of her boat and helped her tie up.

"Do you think that's wise?" she asked as she handed him the lines.

"Why wouldn't it be?" Lev asked.

"I don't think he'll exactly be thrilled."

"Thrilled about what?"

Imogen startled as Lexi, or the man she assumed to be Lexi, seemed to materialize out of the shadows.

"Lexi, I want you to meet Dr. Imogen Hayes." That was all Lev said but she knew he would tell Lexi about their agreement later. She knew they couldn't talk about it out in public, and anyway, Lexi looked like he was still processing this whole thing too.

Imogen got where he was coming from.

"It's nice to meet you." Imogen held out her hand, but Lexi just crossed his arms and nodded.

Lev said something under his breath in what sounded like Chenarian and Lexi took her hand grudgingly.

"I was thinking that Dr. Hayes could come up to the apartment and we can go over plans."

Lexi cocked an eyebrow. "If that is what you wish."

His bodyguard seemed a bit grumpy, but she couldn't blame him.

Lev reached out, took her hand and led Imogen away from the dock and up the hill toward where their apartment sat.

"Where is Lexi?" Imogen whispered to Lev.

"He's behind us somewhere. He'll show up."

"This is kind of freaking me out." She wasn't used to this kind of thing at all. What had she got herself into? She knew she should have kept away when she'd seen Lev at the conference. Why had she listened to Jeanette about living a little?

You don't regret it. You know you don't.

Even though this whole thing was more than she was expecting, more than she really wanted to deal with, in reality she was glad that she was pregnant and she was glad to have had that night with Lev.

Lev, as if sensing her apprehension, squeezed her hand

in reassurance. They walked up the steps that led to the top of the row house and he unlocked the door.

The apartment was smaller than her houseboat and had what appeared to be two bedrooms, one bathroom and a kitchenette that connected to a small living-dining area. There was a set of windows that overlooked the bay, and from this high up on the hill she could see beyond her little houseboat to where the bay became Great Slave Lake.

There was just a hint of pink from the sun setting in the west, and with the remnants of the smoke in the air, there was a haze to the sky, and a few stars were starting to peek out.

The apartment was sparsely furnished, but that was to be expected given that Lev had nothing. Only what he'd brought with him to the medical conference and whatever he'd accumulated since.

She felt bad for him.

She couldn't imagine being cut off from the only home you knew and being forced to stay in a foreign country, not knowing what had happened to your loved ones. Although she did know what it was like to be alone.

"Have a seat." Lev motioned for her to take a seat on the couch. She sat down just as the door opened and Lexi came in.

"Everything is secure," he murmured.

"Good." Lev poured Lexi a cup of coffee, which Lexi took, but he didn't sit down. He remained standing. "Dr. Hayes has agreed to marry me."

A strange look passed over Lexi's face. It was as if he had expected it, but she got the distinct impression he was still mightily suspicious. As if he thought she was agreeing to all of this because Lev was a prince. Like this had happened before.

"I fought him," Imogen blurted out, annoyed with the

face Lexi made. "I didn't want to marry him, but if my baby is in danger I don't see what choice I have."

Lexi didn't respond to her. "What is the plan now, Your Highness?"

"You need to obtain a license for me to marry Imogen and we will get married as soon as possible. Then I will live with her on her houseboat," Lev stated.

Lexi said something in Chenarian and Lev snapped back, causing Lexi to stand down.

"You don't want him to move out to the houseboat, do you?" Imogen asked. She didn't understand Chenarian, but she knew by his body language that Lexi was against all of this.

"No. He does not," Lev said. "But to protect you and the baby, it is the smartest decision. It is the only decision. You can see the houseboat from here, Lexi."

"I can't protect you out there, Your Highness. Neither can I properly protect your wife and heir."

"I'm not moving in here," Imogen stated. "No offense, but this apartment is very small, and so is my place. I'd offer you my couch, but that's where Lev will be sleeping. And, I might add, I wouldn't even be considering this if not for the dangerous political crisis that's happening right now in your country."

Lexi bowed at the waist. "My apologies, Dr. Hayes. I do understand your frustration. We shall try and make it work. May I be excused, Your Highness?"

Lev nodded. "You may."

Lexi gave another curt nod and retreated to his room.

"Not to be bothersome, but how am I going to get home?" Imogen asked.

"There's a Canadian agent waiting downstairs to escort you." Lev held up his phone. "I've explained the situation to those in charge of my protection, and the prime minister has been informed as well."

Imogen did a double take. "The prime minister knows?"

Lev nodded. "It's a matter of national security. This is how I can protect you and the baby."

"Okay." Imogen nodded. "Well, I guess this is going to come as a shock to those in the hospital. I mean, our marriage... I know they can't know the real reason we're getting married. I just don't like everyone knowing my business and now everyone will know you're the father."

"I understand. I value my privacy too, but this is the only way, Imogen."

Imogen nodded. "Let me know when we need to go to the courthouse. Or let me know if there's anything else I can do."

Lev closed the distance between them and placed his arms around her, and then took her hands, bringing them up to his lips for a kiss. His blue eyes were focused intently on her, making her heart skip a beat. The feel of his lips on her skin sent a tingle through her body.

She hated this effect he had on her. Both hated and loved it.

"Thank you for doing this, Imogen."

"Good night, Lev." She opened the door and headed down the steps where a plainclothes Canadian security agent was waiting to escort her down the road to her boat.

Usually, she wasn't all that bothered walking down Franklin at night, even though it was down by the docks, but tonight she felt like there were a million eyes on her. She felt unsafe for the first time in her ten years in Yellowknife, felt like she wasn't safe in her own city, and she didn't like that.

She didn't like having to rely on Lev for her safety.
For her baby's safety.

Her father had taught her to be resilient. To take care of herself.

Relying on someone usually just brought disappointment and heartache.

Like all the times her mother had promised to come and see her. Like Allen promising he'd never leave her, and that he'd stay in the north with her.

She felt powerless.

She felt helpless and it scared her that all these feelings involved Lev.

She was scared of it all.

"Wait, hold up… What?"

Imogen groaned inwardly. She looked up from her chart and saw that Jeanette was headed her way.

Here we go.

"Hi, Jeanette. What's up?" But Imogen knew exactly what was up. She knew exactly what Jeanette was going to say to her, because Imogen and Lev had gone to Human Resources to fill out the documentation that dealt with spouses working together at the hospital.

"You know what's up!" Jeanette said. "We need to talk."

Imogen sighed, set down the chart she was reviewing and followed Jeanette into an empty exam room. Jeanette flicked on the lights and closed the door.

"Imogen, I know I told you to show the new guy around, but…marrying him?"

"Jeanette, he's the father of my baby. Remember how you were bugging me since I got back from Toronto about the mystery guy I hooked up with, the guy who got me pregnant? It was Lev."

Jeanette's mouth opened in shock, and she sat down on the wheelie stool, sliding back to the wall. "I had no idea."

"Well, we didn't exchange emails or anything. I mean…" She had to straighten out her story. She couldn't tell Jeanette the truth. She couldn't tell Jeanette that Lev was from Chenar and she hadn't known where he was for a couple of months, and she couldn't let Jeanette think that her marriage to Lev was a marriage of convenience either. "It was supposed to be a one-night stand and I wasn't expecting anything to happen but something did. We connected and… I was embarrassed to tell you that your newest surgeon was actually the father of my baby."

Jeanette's eyes narrowed. "There's something else you're not telling me, but I'm too tired to figure it out."

"We're going to have a quick civil ceremony tomorrow afternoon and Lev is moving out to my houseboat. We're going to raise this baby together."

Liar.

She didn't know how long she had with Lev, but she wasn't completely lying.

She hadn't wanted Jeanette to know when she was getting married, because she didn't want her to make a big thing about it, but it was no use trying to hide it from Jeanette. She seemed to be able to figure stuff out and find out information so quickly. She was good at reading people and that was why she was Chief of Staff.

"What're we doing for the wedding?" Jeanette asked, going straight into planning mode.

"Nothing."

"Nothing? You can't have nothing. You need to do something."

"I just want something simple, Jeanette." Imogen shook her friend's shoulders playfully. "I don't need anything complicated or crazy."

"What're you going to wear?"

"I don't know. What I usually wear?"

Jeanette frowned. "You're not going to wear buffalo plaid and denim. I'll get you a dress."

"No. I don't need a dress."

Jeanette made a dismissive hand motion. "You're getting a simple, nice dress, and I'll pick it out for you and I'll be your witness."

"Okay." Imogen knew when she was defeated.

"What if we have dinner at the Grayling after?" Jeanette was smiling. "I can make a reservation."

"Sure. Lev's best friend is in Yellowknife too, and he'll be there, so if you and Dave come, make the reservation for five."

Jeanette nodded and then hugged her. "This is awesome. I feel like I'm responsible."

Imogen cocked an eyebrow. "How are you responsible?"

"I hired him and I sent you to that conference in Toronto where you hooked up!"

"Wasn't it a federal transfer?" Imogen asked.

"Yeah, but I had the spot." Jeanette winked. "Okay, I'll take care of the dress and the Grayling for dinner after. This is so exciting."

Imogen just shook her head as she left Jeanette to plan. She wasn't sure how she was going to break this to Lev and she was pretty positive that Lexi wasn't going to like the idea too much. Lexi hadn't said much to her at all, but Imogen knew that the government agents had made sure that their house, the dock and the hospital were now secured.

She was being watched now too, but none of it made her feel any more at ease. It didn't make her feel safe at all. She'd lost control and she hated that.

"Imogen!"

She turned to see Lev coming toward her.

"What's up?" she asked.

"I have an emergency appendectomy in the ER. It's about to rupture and I'm hoping you can help me in the operating room. I know from a certain simulation lab you're pretty handy with a laparoscope."

She was surprised Lev had asked for her assistance. Allen never had, but then, Allen hadn't liked to be upstaged. Especially not by her, which should've been a huge red flag, but she hadn't seen it at the time.

Now she knew better and she was happy Lev thought nothing of asking for her help.

"I'll meet you on the operating room floor in ten minutes."

Lev nodded and ran off back toward the emergency department. Imogen took a deep breath to calm her nerves. She couldn't think about government agents watching her or the fact that she was going to have to marry Lev just to protect her baby.

She had an emergency appendectomy to do.

She had her job to focus on and a life to save.

Lev was glad to see that Imogen was already in the scrub room by the time the emergency patient was being wheeled into the operating theater.

"So, tell me about the patient," Imogen said, scrubbing at the sink.

"The patient is thirty-two-year-old Fudo Fushita, a tourist from Japan. No territorial health card—this is a travel insurance job. He was complaining of worsening stomach pains the last day or so when his wife brought him in. Pain over the McBurney point and worsening pain on release rather than when I press down."

"Did you get an ultrasound?" she asked.

"I did and blood work. The appendix is about to rupture. I started the patient on a course of antibiotics, in case it did before we could get to it."

"Well, let's get in there before it does." Imogen headed into the operating room. The patient was already under general anesthesia in preparation for the procedure, so Imogen took her place on her side of the operating table, waiting while the scrub nurses finished draping and sterilizing the field. Lev stood on the opposite side of the table, ready to provide assistance to her in her role as general surgeon and the lead surgeon on his case.

Usually he had a hard time letting go and relinquishing control over one of his patients, but he didn't feel that unease with Imogen. He was just glad that he was able to assist, and as they started the surgery, he was pleased to realize how easy it was to work with her in the operating room.

They were in sync, like they had always seemed to be when running simulations at that conference. It was like she knew exactly what he was thinking. She made the same moves that he would and her skill was unsurpassed.

It made Lev admire her all the more.

She was such a strong woman. He couldn't believe she was here in Yellowknife and that she was so close to him now. When he'd kissed her hands last night it had made him want to kiss more than just her hands.

He wanted all of her, but he couldn't have her. He didn't deserve to have her since it was his background and circumstances that had put her life in danger.

He rolled his shoulders, trying to ease the tension in his back as he assisted Imogen on the surgery.

And as they removed the appendix and stabilized the patient, he was glad that she was here in Yellowknife, even more than he had been before.

They closed up and the patient was taken in a stable condition to the post-anesthesia recovery unit. They got out of their surgical gear and were at the sink, scrubbing out.

"I need to let the patient's wife know that he'll be okay, but she only speaks Japanese," Lev said. "Do you know where I can find an interpreter?"

"I know some Japanese. I can speak with the patient's wife."

Lev was surprised. "You know Japanese?"

"My father traveled a lot when I was young, remember. Also, I felt it was important to learn some basics, as Yellowknife gets a lot of tourists from Japan in the late summer, fall and into the winter. They come to see the northern lights. This isn't the first tourist I've worked on."

"I didn't know Yellowknife was such a tourist hot spot."

"It is when it involves the northern lights." Imogen smiled. "I also know French and Dene."

"Dene?" he asked.

"It's an indigenous language. My Dene is rusty, but Jeanette is Dene and her husband is Métis, and they've taught me a few things to get by."

"You'll have to teach me," Lev said. "I would like to know, because I don't know much about the indigenous people in Canada or even what Métis is."

And he did want to know. He was intrigued, and if he was going to be staying here for some time, he wanted to get to know the people. He wanted to be able to blend in. It would be safer for all of them if he could.

Imogen smiled. "There's time for that. Come on. Let's

let Mrs. Fushita know that her husband is going to be okay."

"Right." She and Lev left the scrub room and made their way to the waiting room. Lev introduced Imogen to the patient's wife, and Imogen explained the procedure, how Mr. Fushita was faring and that someone would come soon to take her up to him, as well as making a translator available.

After Imogen had reassured the patient's wife, they left the waiting area.

"So, we're going to have a reception," Imogen blurted out as they walked down the hall.

"A what?" Lev asked.

"Jeanette found out that we're getting married. I had to tell her you're the father of my baby."

Lev stiffened. "What else did you tell her?"

"That we had a one-night stand in Toronto and that we're going to raise the baby together."

"And she didn't suspect?" Lev asked.

"No. She's just excited she was matchmaker. Or she thinks she was."

He frowned. He wanted to believe she was telling the truth, but something was bothering him about it. The way she was acting was a bit odd.

"You okay?" he asked.

"Yes. Why?"

"You seem out of sorts."

Imogen sighed. "Just nerves. Jeanette is making a big deal out of this wedding."

"Oh." Lev's stomach knotted. He was worried too. It was getting out of hand. "It'll be okay."

But he wasn't so sure. If something slipped, Lexi and the Canadians would make him leave.

And if he left, he wasn't sure that Imogen would follow.

And he couldn't blame her for that.

CHAPTER EIGHT

IMOGEN PACED NERVOUSLY on the deck of her houseboat. She'd lent her boat to Lexi when he'd dropped her off and now he was headed back to pick up Lev and his meager belongings so that Lev could move in with her, so they could start this pretense of being a happy couple, in love and getting married and about to have a baby.

Is it a pretense?

When he'd disappeared, she'd thought about him. She'd wished she'd got to know him more and been able to tell him about the baby.

Now they were getting married.

All so that Lev could protect their child, because of who he really was.

The whole thing seemed absurd. And she had to remind herself it wasn't real.

After Allen, she'd never wanted to get married. Marriage didn't last. So logically she knew this was fake, but it still seemed crazy and over the top.

You agreed to it.

She was doing the right thing for her child. She knew that. This was the right thing.

Is it?

"Why am I so nervous?" she said out loud, almost as if to ground herself.

It wasn't like she'd never lived with a man before, but she remembered how that had turned out before. She'd thought she and Allen had been in it for the long haul, because they'd been together a long time, but it hadn't worked.

It had hurt her.

She had felt rejected when Allen had left. Just like her mother had left.

She didn't want to have another broken heart. She couldn't.

This isn't real. You're not in love with Lev.

It made her question whether she had ever really been in love with Allen at all. She thought she had, but not the way her father had been in love with her mother and had ached over her mother's abandonment of them.

She'd got over Allen and learned from her mistakes. But her father had never moved on from his heartbreak.

"Why did you never move on, Dad?" Imogen asked.

"Why are you asking me this?" he asked, puzzled.

"I was always curious."

"I loved her."

"But she clearly didn't love you as much as you loved her."

"I know, Imogen, but try as I might, she still has my heart, broken as it is. I can't move on."

She wondered if she was incapable of such a love, and that made her even more wary about any kind of relationship. She had walls and her walls protected her. But they also protected Lev.

He just didn't know it yet.

And she didn't know why she was thinking like this. Right now.

Anxiety.

Which made sense. Her mind would not stop running.

The boat pulled away from the dock on the mainland and headed toward her. She took a deep breath. She had to keep reminding herself that this wasn't real.

Her marriage tomorrow would only be on paper. This was all for their child. This was to protect their baby. That was the important thing.

Their baby.

The only reality about this situation was that she was still attracted to Lev. She cared about him and she recalled how she'd felt when she hadn't known where he was, the shock she'd felt when he'd walked into the doctors' lounge. That was why she was doing this, and she had to keep reminding herself of it in order to make it through this whole charade.

But there was another part of her that desperately wanted this to work so her child could have two loving parents, but she banished that thought.

She didn't want to get her hopes up.

Yellowknife was her home, not Lev's, and one day he'd return to Chenar.

The boat pulled up to her dock. Lev was by himself.

"How did you enjoy your first solo ride?" she asked as she took a rope from him, tying it off.

"It was fine. Do people swim in this lake?" he asked, changing the subject abruptly. Which took her mind off her anxiety and jumbled thoughts.

"Some. It's quite cold. Why? Do you want to swim?"

"I might. I liked to swim back home, for exercise."

"It's cold, but I suppose if you wanted to you could. Will Lexi approve, though?"

Lev frowned. "You're right. Probably not."

They stood there awkwardly, a weird tension between them. It was like they were frozen in their respective awkwardness.

She worried her lip and he stood there, his back ramrod straight.

"Why is this so hard?" Imogen finally asked, breaking the silence.

"I don't know," Lev mused. "That's why I talked about swimming, to be honest. I didn't know what else to say."

Imogen smiled. "I thought as much."

"Perhaps because we're living a lie. A noble lie, but a lie nonetheless," he offered.

"Yes. Maybe," she said, but she wasn't completely convinced that was the only reason. "Well, we might as well get this thing started."

She opened the door to her home and Lev followed her inside.

"I'll have to show you how everything works," she stated. "How to pump water and turn on the propane."

"Yes. That would be helpful. I don't want to be a burden to you." He set his duffel bag down on the floor by the end of the couch.

"You're not a burden. I agreed to this as well. For the baby." She folded her hands in front of her and still remained frozen to the spot by the door. "Are you ready for tomorrow?"

"As much as I can be." He gave her a half smile. "I'm sorry to have dragged you into this situation, Imogen. I didn't want to entrap you in my complicated life."

"I wasn't exactly dragged, if you recall." And she blushed, thinking about it. No, she hadn't been dragged. She'd gone quite willingly with him.

And you'd do it again too. Admit it.

She shifted awkwardly because she was trying not to think about Lev and their night together.

Say something.

"Would you like a cup of tea or coffee?"

"I would love some, but please show me where and how to do it and let me make you a cup of tea."

"Okay."

It was a simple task to put on the kettle, but it kept her mind off worrying as she showed him how the kitchen was laid out and how to work the stove. When the tea was steeping she showed him how the solar panels worked and how to pump water from the lake. Then they took their cups of tea and headed out to the back of her houseboat, where she had a couple of Muskoka chairs sitting on the deck.

She liked sitting out there in the evening, watching the water and listening to the waves lap against Jolliffe Island. It always calmed her down.

They sat there in silence.

"This lake is larger than the one in Toronto?" he asked. "You told me there were larger ones."

Her heart fluttered. He remembered their discussion. He remembered their night in detail like she did.

"Yes. It is. It's a world record breaker, in fact, but there's one farther north of here that you can access by plane and it's even larger."

"What's it called?" he asked.

"Great Bear Lake."

He chuckled softly to himself. "It seems almost impossible to me that there is more to this country. I've been all over it and it still amazes me how large it is. How vast. I can't believe there is more."

"Well, it's a bit different up there. The tree line ends

and it's mainly tundra. You can see musk ox and caribou migrating."

"That's what I love about Canada. The scenery is so different. It can change in a moment."

"Why don't you tell me about Chenar? I have been there, but it was so long ago," she said, though she knew she'd broached a touchy subject when she saw his lips purse.

"It is difficult for me to talk about it. It's small, and for the most part it resembles Romania with green forests and mountains. There are castles and old buildings, older than in your country, but you can see the Scandinavian influence in the style."

She smiled. "And that's what I love about Europe, about small countries like Chenar."

He nodded. "I just hope that I can return there one day."

"I hope so too." And she meant it.

Then that thought made her sad because she couldn't go with him if he left.

Yellowknife was where she belonged.

She was safer here.

She knew this place. This was where her father had been planning to retire. This was where her roots were firmly planted.

"I just never planned on returning there without my father as King." He set down his mug. "Kristof will be King. I am not prepared for that reality."

"Kristof is hiding too, right?"

"He is but my father is…" He trailed off and Imogen understood what he didn't say.

It was the grief talking now. If he didn't say it, then it wasn't true. When she'd first heard her father had died, she'd hoped they were wrong, that when she got up to

Alert her father would still be alive. Deep down, though, she'd known that he was gone.

But not saying it out loud had given her control of the situation.

It was compartmentalization.

It was survival.

"I hope your country returns to its former glory too."

Lev smiled. "Thank you, but I would like to change the subject if it's all the same to you."

"Of course. What would you like to talk about?"

"Tomorrow. What is happening? Lexi is in a state and knows nothing. Jeanette has phoned me twice to ask me about a suit, which I do have, but what is going on?"

Imogen groaned and then laughed. "Jeanette has insisted on me wearing a dress and that we have dinner afterward—her, her husband, us and Lexi—at the Grayling Bistro."

Lev grinned. "Ah, so that is what Lexi was grousing about. I thought it was just about me moving in here with you."

"Oh, dear." Imogen sighed. "I do feel bad for Lexi. I'm sorry this whole thing is stressing him out."

"He's not the only one," Lev said dryly.

"This is all so complicated." She sighed again.

"A child does that. Especially an unplanned one."

Imogen was taken by surprise by that statement, but Lev had a point. This child had changed their lives already. Everything was so complicated now.

"Perhaps we should set some ground rules so we can live together comfortably." She didn't want to talk about rules, but they had to find a way to make this arrangement amicable.

It was a marriage of convenience, not a love match.

Give it a chance. It could be...

She dismissed that thought. It couldn't be.

"Like what?" he asked.

"Like what will be done when this marriage comes to an end?"

"What do you mean?" he asked.

"Well, if your country is settled you'll have to return back to Chenar. You said I could keep the baby."

"Yes, I've been thinking about it, and for the sake of the child you would come with me. I wouldn't divorce you."

Imogen blinked a couple of times. "What?"

"You both would come with me. I have no desire for this marriage to come to an end. Imogen, it will be a long time before things settle down at home, and even then there will always be danger for an heir to the royal family."

He knew she was shocked, but it was the truth. He'd been thinking about it a lot. He wanted to be in his child's life. Imogen would have to come to Chenar to make that happen.

He wished he could stay in Canada with them both, but that was not an option. His duty, as a prince, meant he had to reside in Chenar. Even if he'd rather stay here.

Sure, he groused about being trapped, but the more time he stayed in Canada with Imogen, the happier he was.

The freer he felt.

But he had been born into duty, and one day he'd have to go back to Chenar and the life he'd never wanted.

It wasn't ideal, but the baby would be his heir and this way he could protect them both. Forever.

"I'm not going to go with you," Imogen stated. "I'm doing this to protect the baby, but I'm staying here."

"And if the worst happens and something happened to my brother, I would become King and you will need even more protection."

"Lev, I'm not leaving Canada. I'm not leaving the north," she said firmly. "This is my life. I belong here, and if you can't handle that, if you try to force me to leave, then I won't marry you."

Lev said nothing as she got up and went back inside.

He sat there for a few minutes.

Imogen was stubborn, but so was he.

He knew he had scared her, because he was terrified too.

This might be a marriage of convenience, but he didn't intend for this marriage to end, not where his child was concerned.

He had not planned to marry Imogen, but now that it was to be done, he wasn't going to end it. He was going to change Imogen's mind about the whole thing. One step at a time.

He followed her inside, where he saw her cleaning up in the kitchen, wiping the counter quite vigorously, like she was trying to wipe her way through it.

"Are you all right?" A foolish question. Clearly she wasn't.

"No. I'm a bit bowled over by what you said. I thought I made it clear when I agreed to this arrangement. It wasn't going to be forever. It wasn't going to be permanent." Her voice was shrill and anxious. He couldn't blame her, but he was only stating the truth.

He'd been thinking about this since last night.

As much as he wanted to let her go, he couldn't.

"Fine," he agreed, but only so she wouldn't change her mind. "You're right. We agreed to do this for as long as I am in the country."

She cocked a thinly arched brow and he knew she didn't believe his capitulation. She was perceptive, he was learning that, but to be a good surgeon you had to be.

"Are you sure?" she asked.

"Yes. You're right—it's what we agreed to. I can't force you or my child to come with me. So I will do everything in my power to protect you after our marriage ends, but for now, let me do this."

"Okay. Everything will go as planned tomorrow. Or as Jeanette planned tomorrow."

He laughed softly. "Yes. As Jeanette planned."

Lev nodded and headed back out on the dock, this time to the front of the houseboat. He could see that Lexi was out on their small balcony. Lev didn't wave to him because Lexi wouldn't like the attention, but Lev was annoyed that Lexi was stuck here too.

Lexi had the freedom to go back to Chenar, except for his vow to his father to protect Lev, and Lexi took vows seriously.

So do you.

Lev sighed.

He hoped Kristof got the situation in Chenar straightened out soon.

He wasn't completely sure that he wanted to go back, if it came down to it, but Lev had already let his father down so much and he wouldn't do the same to his brother.

Being unable to move, to be hidden and trapped here, was one thing, but to be free to make his own choice was another, and he envied Imogen and even Lexi their freedom.

Lexi straightened his tie. Lev could tell Lexi was anxious. As was he. He told himself that this was for the baby.

For Imogen.

"You're sure?" Lexi asked.

"Yes. It's the right thing to do. It's my duty to protect them."

It might be his duty, but he *wanted* to protect Imogen and the baby. The thought of something happening to them was too much to bear and it unnerved him how much Imogen affected him.

Lexi nodded, but he couldn't relax, which was making even Lev more nervous.

The doors opened and Imogen walked into the courtroom. She looked both a bit green and a bit pale at the same time. He hoped it was morning sickness and not that she was ill at the prospect of marrying him.

He wasn't exactly thrilled with it either, but he hoped he was hiding it better.

As she approached him, his anxiety melted away. She looked so beautiful.

He smiled at her. He was glad it was her. If he had to fake marry someone, he was glad it was Imogen.

She smiled back and he took her hand as they were married by the justice of the peace.

The only one in that room who was anywhere near happy was Jeanette, and by extension her husband, Dave.

The newlyweds had to put on a show.

They had to appear happy while they were out in the public eye. Everyone, including Jeanette, had to believe that this was real.

That they were in love.

You could be.

Only he didn't let himself think like that. There had been a brief time, before everything had happened at home, when he'd thought he could be, that he might want to fall in love with a girl like Imogen, but that wasn't a possibility.

He would stay married to her to protect her, but he wasn't sure he could open his heart to her without feeling a sense of guilt for burdening her with a life she didn't want. Every day he struggled with this sense of guilt.

And he hated himself for it.

After a very awkward dinner at the Grayling, it was time, as Jeanette put it, for the two newlyweds to go home.

Home.

This wasn't his home, but there had been times in the past when he hadn't felt that Chenar was his home either. Not since his mother had died. The longer he stayed in Canada, the more comfortable he was here.

"Are you okay?" Imogen asked, as he helped her tie up her motorboat at their houseboat's dock. *Their* houseboat.

"Yes. Why?"

"You seem a bit shell-shocked."

Lev chuckled as he finished securing the boat. "Maybe a bit. Marriage wasn't…"

"Me neither," Imogen said. "But it's for the baby."

"Yes." And that was what he had to keep reminding himself. It was for the baby.

She opened the door to their houseboat, and they went in. Lev sat down on the couch and watched Imogen putter around her place. He smiled. She was wearing the flowery dress Jeanette had picked out for her.

It was flowy, but still clung to all the right places, showing off her curves and a slight swell in her abdomen where his baby grew.

His baby.

She turned, a pink flush in her cheeks that made his blood heat as he thought of the flush in her cheeks when she'd been in his arms back in Toronto.

"What?" she asked.

"What do you mean, 'What?'"

"Why are you staring at me?"

"Just admiring you." Which was the truth. She was beautiful. He always thought that.

She blushed again.

"So, in the morning, is Lexi going to meet us to drive us? He doesn't have to. We can walk."

"Lexi will be there. I know you two were arguing about that, but unless you want to move into our place, we have to let Lexi do his job."

"I can deal with that." She stood up. "I'm exhausted. I think I'm going to bed."

Lev stood and took her hand. It was so small and delicate.

Don't get attached. This isn't permanent.

Nothing about his life was permanent.

"Good night, Imogen." He kissed her hand, hearing her gasp ever so slightly. She took her hand back. He'd stepped too far, but he couldn't help it when he was around her.

"Good night, Lev."

Lev made them tea. Decaf for Imogen and the real stuff for himself. The morning was a bit awkward. He knew he shouldn't have kissed her the night before, but he hadn't been able to help himself. All he could do was pretend it had never happened, even if he couldn't stop thinking about it.

"Morning," she said, but her voice sounded a bit tense.

"I made you tea." He held out a travel mug. "It's decaf."

"Thank you. I wish it wasn't decaf, though," she murmured.

"I know, but full caffeine is not good for the baby."

"I know." She sighed. "You ready for today?"

"Work?" he asked. "I always am."

"I mean work as a married couple. I'm sure there will be a lot of gossip."

"Why do you think that?" he asked.

She worried her lip. "I have made a point not to date anyone I work with."

"We're not dating. We're married," he teased.

"Be serious…"

"It'll be okay, Imogen."

"Sure." Though he could tell she wasn't. They left the houseboat and Lexi was waiting for them at the dock to drive them to the hospital.

She was tense and worried, and he didn't know how to ease her anxiety.

On arriving, they went their separate ways. He went to the emergency department and she went up to the post-operative care floor to check on her patient.

He was hoping that some distance between them would help him not worry so much about her and what her association with him had put her through.

He knew that was a pipe dream. She was his wife. He wouldn't stop thinking about her.

"Dr. Vanin, there's a patient in bed three who is in some distress," Jessica, the nurse, said, handing him the triage report.

"Thank you." He glanced at the chart and the labs that had been done. He went straight to the patient, who was not so much in distress as in pain. Lev suspected it was acute cholecystitis.

"Can you page Dr. Hayes?" he asked Jessica.

"Of course." Jessica left the pod.

"Mrs. Doxtater? I'm Dr. Vanin. Your blood levels are showing elevated pancreatic enzymes. You're having a

gallbladder attack and I'm going to have a general surgeon talk to you."

"Thank you, Dr. Vanin," the patient said weakly.

"I'm going to give you something for the pain." He
injected some pain medication into her IV line.

Imogen showed up a few minutes later.

"What's going on?" she whispered.

Lev handed her the chart. "I think this patient needs
a cholecystectomy."

Imogen read through the chart. "I think you're right.
Based on the levels of enzymes in her blood, her pan-
creas is taking over. I'll check her."

Imogen slipped behind the curtain and he listened to
her talk to the patient. She was so gentle and sympathetic,
instantly easing the patient's anxiety.

And she was good at cholecystectomies, or so she had
said at the conference when they'd done their first simulation together. It was one of the first things he'd found
attractive about her.

He was watching her now as she stepped out from behind the curtain, making notes in the chart, and the more
he watched her, the more he started to feel for her, and
that was a dangerous thing indeed.

You can't feel this way.

More to the point: he didn't deserve to feel this way
about her.

Why not?

How could he love someone when he had never had
a shred of love from anyone? How could he give love
when he didn't know what it was? He didn't deserve
it. Especially not when he was safe and the people of
Chenar weren't.

Lev sighed and scrubbed a hand over his face.

He was exhausted from all this guilt, from all these feelings.

"You were right," Imogen said, coming up to him, leaning over the nurses' station where he had been sitting.

"She needs her gallbladder removed?"

Imogen nodded. "The ultrasound showed a gallstone the size of a golf ball, possibly bigger, and the gallbladder is elongated. I'm worried it could rupture. Do you want to assist me?"

"Of course. When do you want to do the surgery?" he asked.

"Tomorrow morning if I can. I've admitted her, and I think she's stable for now. I gave strict instructions for her diet and to start her on some antibiotics."

Lev nodded and stifled a yawn. "Good."

She frowned. "Are you okay? You seem a bit distracted today and tired."

"To be honest, it's your couch. It's not that comfortable."

"I'm sorry about that. Maybe you should take the bed tonight?"

"Absolutely not. I'm not pregnant."

"Maybe we can check the furniture store and see if they have a futon or a pullout? Of course, Lexi will hate that, running errands," she teased.

Lev chuckled. "Yes. He will."

"Why don't you let him work here at the hospital?" she asked. "He's coming here every day as it is. He would do well as a security guard and it would give him access to both of us while we're here."

"Security guards work irregular shifts. He won't like it much if he has to work and we're not here. He would be fired for leaving his post."

"True. I never thought of that," she said. "I feel bad that he's alone."

So did Lev.

Lexi really had no life and he knew how much his friend wished he could be in Chenar.

"It was a good thought, though."

"We should have him over to dinner tonight," Imogen said.

"I'm sure he would like to come for dinner." Although Lev wasn't completely positive that was true. They may have lived together, but Lexi tried to keep his distance when he could, because he didn't want people to think that they were connected. He didn't want people to recognize him or Lev.

Not that Lev was in the spotlight. The world knew who Kristof was. They didn't care much for the spare.

And he preferred it that way.

Still, Lexi tried to keep a low profile where possible, but Imogen hated to see him on his own. She might act like a tough surgeon and not be bullied by patients or co-workers, but there was a soft side to Imogen Hayes that he really admired.

"Oh, there's Lexi now," Imogen said.

Lev glanced over at the door to the emergency room and saw Lexi had walked in and was scanning the room.

"I'd better go and see what he wants." Lev got up and walked to the waiting room, catching Lexi's eye and motioning him forward. Lexi looked concerned and they found a private spot to speak.

"I have news," Lexi whispered.

"I'm listening."

"Your brother has sent word about the situation in Chenar. It won't be long until it is over and we can go home!"

CHAPTER NINE

IMOGEN WAS WATCHING Lev and Lexi. Something was up and she hoped it wasn't bad news.

Lexi left and Lev returned.

"Is everything okay?" she asked.

"I think so." But he hesitated like he wanted to tell her more and couldn't.

Then she thought it might be the location of where they were standing. They were in the hall of the hospital and anyone could walk by.

"Do you need some air?"

"That would be great," he said, sounding relieved.

They headed for the ambulance bay and stepped outside, where they were hit with cool crisp air, a sure sign that autumn was on its way. The cooler air was nice as they stood outside in the empty ambulance bay, taking in deep breaths.

"Seems early for this change in weather," he remarked, but she had a feeling that wasn't what he wanted to talk about.

"Autumn comes early here." She'd noticed the other day some of the trees were starting to change color. "So, what did Lexi want?"

He smiled. "You don't beat around the bush, do you?"

"I can't help it."

"Just word from my brother. He's fine… Well, he's more than fine. The situation in my country may be over soon."

"Well, that's wonderful!"

"Is it?" he asked, his voice tense.

"Isn't it?" she asked, confused.

"I would have to leave."

"Oh." Then it hit her. He would leave her. Just like she'd known he would all along.

You knew this could happen.

The only reason they'd got married was for the baby, and though she knew he wanted her to go with him to Chenar, she wouldn't leave Yellowknife.

This was her home.

"Imogen, right now I'm here," he said as if reading her thoughts and trying to reassure her.

"Right." His words did little to reassure her.

Nothing in life is permanent.

Except her home here. Yellowknife had never failed her.

"This is your home, Imogen," her father had said. *"Never forget that. Yellowknife has never failed us or let us down or left us. It's home."*

"So is Lexi leaving, then?" she asked, clearing her throat, trying to forget all the self-doubt she was feeling.

"Yes. For now. Some restrictions have been lifted. I can't leave the territory, but there's no immediate threat and Lexi needs to go to my brother."

"So you have some freedom?"

"A bit. Not much."

"Maybe we can go together on my rounds in Fort Smith?" she suggested, trying to change the subject from him leaving her and their unborn child.

Lev smiled. "I'd like that. Work will help keep my

mind off everything. I'd like to keep busy until..." He trailed off, but Imogen knew what he'd been about to say.

Until he left.

Even though she had built up these walls to protect her heart, it was hard to breathe at that moment. When had she let him in? She'd known this would happen, she'd reminded herself of it at every turn, so why was it so hard to contemplate him leaving?

You could go with him...

She shook that thought away. Her pulse thundered in her ears. It was deafening and she felt like she was going to be sick.

You knew this wasn't forever.

Her emotions were in turmoil and she had to put some distance between herself and Lev.

"Imogen, you look pale. Are you feeling well?" he asked, putting his arm around her, like it was habit. But it wasn't.

She stepped away from him.

"I'm fine." Which was a lie. She was trying to process everything, all the emotions she seemed to have lost control over. "I've finished my shift early and I was going to walk back to the dock. I can get a water taxi to take me to the houseboat. I'll leave my boat for you."

Lev nodded. "Okay, but be careful and I'll be home as soon as I can."

Home. But this wasn't his home. He'd made that clear.

"Sure." Imogen walked away from him. She had to get her purse and change out of her scrubs. She needed space to calm down and process the fact that Lev would be leaving sooner than she'd thought.

She shouldn't have got her hopes up because she'd known this was coming.

And she'd been disappointed too many times.

* * *

Imogen tried to stay up and wait for Lev, but she had a headache when she got back to the houseboat.

She was so tired and she was worrying about what Lexi had said to Lev. She didn't have the strength or stamina to deal with her emotions tonight.

She had to clear her head properly and make plans to move on. But when she got home, she went straight to bed. All this turmoil was making her feel nauseous and exhausted.

The moment she got home she fell asleep, and when she woke up the houseboat was quiet and still, and it was dark out. She wasn't sure how long she'd been out.

She got out of bed, but didn't turn on the lights, because she didn't want to blind herself and she was hoping to take herself back to bed until the last remnants of her headache were gone. She crept down the stairs and headed straight for the bathroom, only to walk straight into a wall of warm, wet flesh.

"What the heck!" she screamed as she jumped back, knocking over a vase that was on a small end table.

"Imogen, it's me!" Lev said in the darkness.

She rubbed her eyes. She could barely see him because all the lights were off downstairs and there was no moon tonight, a rainstorm having moved in from the northwest. She took a deep breath to calm her racing pulse after being scared senseless.

"Lev, what are you doing, lurking around in the dark?"

"I had a shower."

"Okay." Imogen moved past him to turn on a light. There was no sense hanging around in the dark now.

"No, don't…"

But it was too late and she'd already flicked on the light, gasping when she saw that Lev was standing in her kitchen stark naked. All she could do was stare and admire Lev in her kitchen, the intricate tattoo she thought about often, his well-defined muscles and a few other attributes that she admired on full display.

Don't think about it.

She tried to look away, but she couldn't. Her heart, which had been racing before because she'd been scared, was now beating faster for a completely different reason. Staring at him, standing there naked, she recalled every little detail about him and how he'd made her feel that night.

His strong hands on her skin, caressing her. The taste of his lips on hers and the hot, heady, endless pleasure they'd shared that night. Her blood began to heat, her pulse thundering, and she bit her bottom lip in a desperate attempt to keep the blush she felt from rising in her cheeks.

She turned away quickly. She had to regain control. She hated the way he had this effect on her body; that she was so attracted to him, that she still thought of him and the way he made her feel. Where Lev was concerned, she couldn't resist. He seemed to be the exception to all the rules she'd put in place, and it drove her crazy.

"Why are you standing in my kitchen completely naked?"

"I told you, I took a shower. I'm not dripping over your floor. I did dry off in the bathroom and hung up my towel. I thought you were asleep and that's why I didn't turn on the light, but your bathroom is small and I preferred to put on my boxer briefs out here."

She spun around and saw that he was standing there still, with his hands on his hips, not in the least embarrassed that he was naked. She wasn't exactly embarrassed either. It was just rather too tempting to see him this way and right now she was in no mood to tempt fate.

He had an amused smile on his face, which was a huge change from the frustrated and tense man she'd left behind at the hospital. This seemed more like the fun guy she'd met at the conference.

"You need to put some clothes on," Imogen said, her voice shaking.

"Fine." He walked over to the couch, pulled his boxers out of his suitcase and slipped them on. "Is this better?"

No.

Only she didn't say that aloud. She much preferred him naked, although the boxers made it easier for her to have a rational conversation with him, despite not really hiding anything.

She could still see his tattoo, peeking out from the top of his briefs and a bit from the bottom of the leg. It was hard not to stare at it. It was intricate, sexy and in an intimate spot she was all too familiar with.

"You like my tattoo?" he teased.

"What?"

"You're staring at it." He sat down on the couch, which he'd made up into his bed.

"It's quite large." Her face flushed again and then she groaned, laughing, while Lev chuckled.

"Thank you."

She rolled her eyes. "I was talking about the tattoo."

"I know, but this whole situation is actually quite funny. You brought me out of my funk."

"Good." She wandered over and curled up in her chair. Truth be told, she was feeling better too.

"How was the rest of your shift?" she asked.

"Quiet. Lexi left for the airport. He's off to see Kristof."

He sighed. "The Canadians arranged it. I don't know where he's going."

"You sound a bit upset."

"I'm worried about Lexi leaving. He's the only connection I have to Chenar."

"Funnily enough, I'm going to miss him too. I miss seeing him standing out on his deck with binoculars or going by in a boat," she teased, trying to lighten the mood.

Lev chuckled. "Yes, well, as I said, he takes his job seriously. Although we never did get him to buy that futon."

"Well, we can go to the furniture store tomorrow, after I do that surgery and after my prenatal checkup."

"You're having a prenatal checkup tomorrow?" he asked. "Why didn't you tell me?"

"I booked it before I knew you were still alive and before we got married. It slipped my mind until now. It's routine. You're more than welcome to come. I hope you know that."

Lev nodded. "I would like to."

"I'll book my amniocentesis, so eventually you should get positive proof of your paternity."

"Thank you."

"You never told me why you need this. I mean, you married me. Do you really not believe that the baby is yours?" She wasn't sure she wanted to know the answer.

Maybe if she knew his real reason she could rationalize it and make sense out of this whole situation.

"It was because of two things." Lev sighed. "First was my brother. He fell in love with this woman and she became pregnant. He was thrilled, although our father was less than thrilled that she was pregnant and they were not married. Kristof was going to rectify that, though.

He was head over heels for this woman. Actually, we all cared for her, and so in a way it hurt us all."

"What happened?"

"Kristof discovered she'd been having an affair. The baby he'd thought was his was not. He was so excited to be a father and to get married, but she was just after the title and the money. She didn't love Kristof. He never trusted anyone again and the pain he was put through was unbearable to watch."

"And the second one?" she asked.

"It was me."

"You?" she asked, confused.

"There was no baby, but I fell in love with a woman who also betrayed me. I was going to marry her. I was planning a life, a life she didn't want." Lev scrubbed a hand over his face. "Women don't see the man. They see only the title, the prestige."

"I'm sorry," she said gently.

"No woman, besides you, has ever got pregnant and claimed it was mine, but I have been burned before. I tend to keep out of the spotlight. I'm not as actively pursued as Kristof. And after Tatiana, a wife and child were never in my plans."

"I understand. That would test the faith of anyone."

"I'm sorry that I couldn't trust you right away."

"No apology necessary. This pregnancy wasn't in my plans either. I never thought I would have a family—I wasn't really sure that I wanted one."

"Why?" he asked.

"My mother abandoned me. She broke my father's heart and… I never really knew any extended family. It was just me and my dad for so long. I guess I was afraid."

"So you've never had a long-term relationship before?"

"I have." She didn't want to talk about Allen, but he

had been so forthright about his brother and why he'd wanted to prove the paternity, she wanted to be truthful with him too. "I was in a long-term relationship with another doctor. I thought I knew what love was, and we were building a future together. He knew how important it was to me to be up here in the north. He knew that was my plan and told me he wanted the same, but he didn't and he left, but…"

"But what?" he asked.

Her cheeks heated in embarrassment. "I thought he wanted to marry me, but he didn't. He said that was never in his plan, but when he left here… Well, he's married now with a child. Of course, his wife could never upstage him like I apparently did."

"Upstage him?" he asked, confused.

"He liked the limelight and hated it when I got accolades. Between him and my mother, it's hard."

"So it's hard for you to trust too, then?" Lev asked.

"Yes. It is."

It was hard to trust anyone, because everyone eventually left.

No one stayed.

Not even her mother.

"Well, we certainly know how to have a good conversation, don't we?" Lev teased.

"Yes. We do." Imogen chuckled. "Well, I'm going to go back to bed. We have an early morning tomorrow and a surgery. I hope you're still able to come and assist?"

Lev nodded. "Of course. When is your prenatal?"

"One o'clock on the third floor. I hope you're able to come to that too."

"I will be there. For both. What time would you like the alarm set?"

"Five in the morning should do the trick."

"Very well. Good night, Imogen."

"Good night, Lev." She got up from her chair and quickly used the bathroom. After she was done she flicked off the light and made her way back up to her loft. She looked back once to see Lev spread out on the couch, looking uncomfortable and cramped as he moved around, trying to find a comfortable position.

He couldn't sleep like that. Not when they had to get up early in the morning to do a surgery.

"That's not working," she said, from her loft.

"I know, but I'll eventually find a comfortable spot," he answered back.

"I doubt that." And even though she knew it probably wasn't wise, she knew she had to offer. "Why don't you come and sleep beside me? I have a queen-size bed. You need a good night's sleep for surgery tomorrow."

"Do you think that's wise?"

No.

"It'll be fine. We're married. We're supposed to be sharing a bed anyway. At least for sleeping."

"Thank you. I wouldn't mind a good night's sleep." Lev got up, taking his pillow, and followed her up the stairs to the loft.

She climbed in on her side and Lev took the other side. Imogen tried to get comfortable, without disturbing Lev too much, and she hoped that she would be able to sleep tonight, but it was hard, knowing that he was so close.

Within arm's reach.

And it was dark and private here.

"Good night, Imogen," he whispered in the dark.

"Good night, Lev."

It wasn't long before she heard him breathing deeply,

asleep, but she knew that it would be some time before she would find her own rest. She just hoped that she'd be able to get some more sleep before her long day tomorrow.

Imogen stifled a yawn from behind her surgical mask and blinked a few times. The one thing she hated about being pregnant was the fact she couldn't have her usual caffeine intake. She missed her black, fully caffeinated coffees in the morning.

Especially when she had spent all night tossing and turning, very aware that Lev was sharing her bed.

At least she had managed to go home early the night before and have that nap, but just thinking about the nap had brought back another keen memory of her walking into Lev when he had been naked and fresh out of the shower.

Just thinking about him standing there made her blush, and it didn't help matters that he was standing on the opposite side of the table, assisting her with the cholecystectomy.

Don't think about it.

She rolled her shoulders and turned her focus back to the monitor as she maneuvered the laparoscope to remove the inflamed gallbladder.

"Dr. Vanin, can you move the camera five degrees to the left?"

"Yes, Dr. Hayes."

Lev was operating the camera and light portion of the surgery while she was in there, working to seal off the bile duct and making sure she didn't nick the liver or the common bile duct while she removed the gallbladder. She wanted to make sure she took the whole thing out with the stone intact.

Usually, these were simple operations that she could do with her eyes closed, but truth be told, she was a bit worried about the size of the gallstone and whether she could remove the whole thing out of the belly-button incision. She didn't want to have to open the poor patient up.

With an adjusted movement, Imogen breathed a sigh of relief when she carefully separated the gallbladder and was able to bag it with the gallstone still in place. She was worried that the extremely inflamed gallbladder, which had some necrotic patches, might erupt.

She also didn't want a piece of the large gallstone to chip off and get lodged in the common bile duct, which could then cause pancreatitis.

And damage to the common bile duct could cause a whole mess of other issues for the patient. She'd have to open up the patient and the surgery would be longer. It reminded her of the simulation lab at the conference she'd done with Lev.

The robotic equipment made a bile duct injury very simple, but they didn't have that new equipment here. The only good thing was that Lev was familiar with the procedure and he was here, working with her.

She hoped it didn't come to that.

Thankfully, she was relieved when she was able to bag the nasty gallbladder and remove it with relative ease through the small incision she had made, with no damage to the bile duct.

"There!" she said with triumph as she removed the laparoscope with the bagged gallbladder hanging on the other end. "Got it!"

"Excellent work."

"Now, to make sure everything else is okay." She did a last check of the cavity, making sure she hadn't nicked a biliary artery or left something behind. Her sutures were all in the right place and the ducts had been clear. There was no sign of gallstones or pieces of gallstones anywhere.

Everything looked good. The patient's vitals were strong and she was happy to pull the laparoscope out and suture up the small incisions. Once she had done that, the patient was wheeled out of the operating room and she went to work recording the procedure on the patient's chart so she wouldn't forget later.

"I'm glad that was easy," Lev said, as he headed to the scrub room. "When you told me what was going on with her morning blood draw, I was worried that the gallbladder might have ruptured, which would have been worse."

"I was worried too," she said. "If it had ruptured I wouldn't be making it to my prenatal. I would be doing a much larger surgery and trying to clean up a mess."

"So what is being done at the prenatal today? You told me you had an appointment, but other than booking your amnio, you haven't told me what else is involved."

"It's just a routine checkup. I can't remember when they do the dating ultrasound, but I'm pretty positive that's not right now."

"That's too bad. I wouldn't have minded seeing it. I could use some cheering up."

"Yeah, I wouldn't have minded either, but what can you do about doctors, eh?" She was teasing, hoping to get him to laugh again. Even though they had reached an understanding about the nakedness incident, there was still a sadness about him. Even if he didn't want to admit it, she knew that Lev was worried and that he was anxious to get home to Chenar.

And she wouldn't go with him.

She couldn't.

She wouldn't.
Yellowknife was her home.
Yellowknife had never let her down.

CHAPTER TEN

OF ALL THE places he'd imagined he'd be in his life, this was not one of them. He never thought that he'd be sitting in a prenatal exam room in Yellowknife with his wife, hoping that his baby was okay.

He'd already accepted that this baby was his.

Are you sure?

He hated that voice of doubt. He knew what had happened to Kristof and how Tatiana had shattered his trust, but Imogen was nothing like them.

Imogen was different and he had to keep telling himself that.

Stop. Focus on the baby.

He closed his eyes and took a deep breath to center himself. As much as he tried to clear his mind, all he could think about was last night. The way Imogen had looked at him, the flush in her cheeks, and then sharing a bed with her.

He'd been worried about that, but he'd been so tired he'd fallen asleep easily.

When he'd woken up she'd been snuggled up against him and he'd hated having to disturb her so they could go to work.

He hadn't wanted to leave. It had been so nice to have her in his arms.

It had felt right. It had felt like a home, although he wasn't sure what a real home felt like, but he liked to think it felt like this.

Warm. Safe.

He knew she wanted to stay, but if he wanted any relationship with his child—or with her—he had to convince her to leave with him when it was time to go. Even if he wanted to stay too, he couldn't. It was his duty to go back to Chenar.

Just because the unrest in his country was ending, Imogen was still carrying a royal baby. It was his duty to protect her. He was torn. He wished he could stay here in Yellowknife, but he couldn't be in two places at once. He had to make a choice.

He had to help Kristof rebuild Chenar. It was his duty. But he also had a duty to Imogen, to his child, as well as a duty to his country. His late father had always put the country before his children and had tried to teach his sons that too.

Lev was torn between guilt over duty and his longing to stay here and live a normal life.

Then he thought of her again, as she had been last night. It had not been his intention to have Imogen catch him unawares like that.

When he'd arrived home from his shift, he'd found the place dark, and for one split second he'd feared the worst, until he'd crept up into the loft and found out she'd been sleeping soundly.

If he hadn't been so uncomfortable and so tired that night, he wouldn't have slept in her bed, but it had been so nice to finally be able to stretch out completely and not be confined to such a narrow berth.

Why did it feel so right with her?

He'd never wanted this.

Yes, you did.

After Tatiana his life had been too complicated. Now it was even more so. And he couldn't do charting or see a patient to ease his anxiety.

He was in an exam room, waiting to hear what the doctor had to say about his wife and his baby.

"You're fidgeting," she said.

"Am I?"

Imogen reached out and took his hand. "What are you worrying about?"

"Nothing much. It's nothing really."

He wanted to tell her how he'd enjoyed waking up beside her and watching her sleep, but he couldn't say any of those things because he knew she didn't feel that way.

She'd made it clear that this marriage was on paper only and that she was staying in Yellowknife no matter what. How could he put his heart at risk?

Lev shook that thought away.

There was a knock on the door and the obstetrician, Dr. Merton, came into the room.

"Good afternoon, Dr. Hayes. How are we today?" Dr. Merton looked up from her chart. "Oh! Is this the baby's father?"

"Yes," Imogen said. "Dr. Merton, I would like to introduce you to my husband, Dr. Lev Vanin."

Lev stood up and shook the doctor's hand. "It's a pleasure to meet you."

The doctor stared at him for some time. "Do I know you, Dr. Vanin?"

He could feel the blood draining from his face and he worried that he would be recognized.

"Well, he's been working here for a couple of weeks now, Dr. Merton. I'm sure you've probably seen him in the halls. He's our new trauma surgeon," Imogen explained, seamlessly covering up the truth.

Dr. Merton nodded. "That must be it."

Lev breathed a sigh of relief and squeezed Imogen's hand in thanks. He'd never seen Dr. Merton before, even in passing, but it was enough to change the subject and throw Dr. Merton off the scent.

"Well, your blood work came back normal," Dr. Merton said, not missing a beat. "I would like to check the baby's heartbeat today through my stethoscope. You're far enough along now that we can probably pick it up."

"Probably?" Lev asked, worried. "You mean you weren't able to pick it up before?"

"No," Imogen said sadly. "No, but Dr. Merton doesn't think it's unusual early on. We've used Doppler before to hear it."

"Have you had the first ultrasound?" he asked.

"Yes," Dr. Merton said. "At twelve weeks and everything was fine."

Lev was disappointed. He'd missed it. A couple of weeks ago he'd been in limbo in another town. He'd missed out on so much already.

"I'm sorry," Imogen whispered.

"It's okay. I'm glad the baby is healthy. That's the main thing."

"Now, lie back on the table and lift your shirt. We'll find that heartbeat and take measurements," Dr. Merton said.

Lev stood, helped Imogen up onto the exam table and stood by her head.

"Sounds strong." Dr. Merton measured her. "And your measurements are right on track."

"I don't suppose you could use the Doppler again?" Imogen asked. "Lev was traveling before and missed out."

Dr. Merton smiled. "Of course."

Dr. Merton pulled out the Doppler and placed it on Imogen's abdomen. At first all Lev heard was static. Imogen squeezed his hand and he could tell she was a bit anxious as well. They were both a bundle of nerves.

Then they heard it, whooshing from the placenta and then a fast heartbeat. Dr. Merton smiled and Imogen let out a sigh of relief. He couldn't stop smiling. He looked over at Imogen and she was smiling too, her eyes twinkling. They both were sharing in this moment, the first time he was hearing the heartbeat.

It was amazing.

And surreal.

As a resident, he'd done a round on the obstetrics floor, like every good surgeon in their training, and he'd heard other babies' heartbeats. He was familiar with Doppler and ultrasound, but it was something quite different when it was your own child's heart.

The only thing he wished was that his life wasn't in such a topsy-turvy state.

He wished he could provide stability, wished his child wouldn't need bodyguards and security. Where there were always people watching you.

For that he was sad.

"That's a good strong heartbeat," Dr. Merton said as she finished up.

"Thank you, Doctor." Lev glanced down at Imogen. She was still smiling. "When will you perform the amniocentesis?"

Dr. Merton was recording measurements. "Between fifteen and twenty weeks. I like to wait until a happy medium between the two. Dr. Hayes, were you still thinking of having the procedure done?"

"Yes," she said, and she worried her bottom lip. He

knew she was embarrassed. "I'm hoping you can also confirm paternity."

Dr. Merton looked confused. "We can in the amnio, but you two are married... Surely...?"

"There's a complicated situation, Dr. Merton," Lev interrupted. "Quite delicate and we'd both appreciate it if you could."

Imogen's cheeks bloomed pink and he knew she was embarrassed and worried that rumors could spread. He hoped that Dr. Merton wasn't the kind of physician to spread rumors. It was bad enough that people in the hospital were gossiping over their hasty marriage.

"The test can confirm paternity and it will be kept between us, I assure you," she said quickly. "I will remind you there are risks with the procedure."

"I'm aware," Imogen said.

"Risks?" Lev's heart sank. He'd forgotten that and now he wasn't so sure it should be done.

He didn't want anything to harm his child because this was *his* child. No matter what a test said.

"Perhaps we shouldn't," Lev said.

"I'm having it," Imogen said.

"It's a standard procedure," Dr. Merton tried to reassure them. "But, as with any procedure, there are risks."

"Thank you, Dr. Merton. I know that." Imogen sat up. "I would like to schedule one for week eighteen."

"I will have my secretary call you." Dr. Merton closed her chart. "And I will see you for your regular checkup in a month. My secretary will also call you with the date for your second ultrasound and with information about some more blood work and the glucose tolerance test."

"Fun!" Imogen replied sarcastically to the glucose test.

Dr. Merton smiled. "I know. Get used to it. Have a

great day, Dr. Hayes, and it's a pleasure to meet you, Dr. Vanin."

Dr. Merton left the room and Imogen let out a sigh of relief. "That was a lot more awkward than I thought it was going to be."

"I'm sorry. I didn't mean to blurt it out..."

"No. It's okay. We had to ask or they wouldn't have tested for it and I understand your reasoning."

"Do you think Dr. Merton will keep our request secret? There has already been some gossiping and I don't want to embarrass you further."

"She'll keep it secret. She's a good physician." Imogen stood. "You seem distracted today. Any word from Lexi?"

"No." He let her think that he was worried about Lexi, but he wasn't. Not really. He was worried about her, the baby, about having to leave before he could convince her to come with him. So he let her think it was about Lexi and Kristof.

"I'm sure Lexi is fine." She touched his arm.

"I'm sure." They left the exam room and walked back together.

"Why don't we go out for dinner tonight?" she asked. "Just the two of us."

"I would like that, but you know that it won't be just the two of us," he teased.

He realized it was the first time he'd thought about the baby beyond being something he had to protect. Hearing that heartbeat had made it a reality for him.

"Well, I know that there will be agents watching and that they're never really far away, but they don't have to eat at the table with us, like Lexi does."

Lev chuckled. "True, but that's not what I meant."

Imogen looked confused. "What did you mean, then?"

He stopped and touched her belly. Although he couldn't feel anything, his heart warmed, thinking about the life growing inside her.

"There will be three of us."

She smiled, tears welling up in her eyes. "Right. The three of us."

"I would like a dinner with you two tonight."

She cleared her throat and blinked a few times. He moved his hand and they continued walking.

"Great. So we'll go back to the houseboat, change, and I'll take you to one of my favorite places. Of course, I will have to rent a car."

"Lexi left me the truck. We can take the truck." He cocked an eyebrow as they stopped at the junction. One way led to the emergency department and one way back to the general surgery floor, where she was working today. "Where is this place? We usually just walk everywhere."

She smiled. "You'll see."

"Should I be nervous?"

"Nope. I'll see you at five downstairs by the main entrance?"

"Yes."

She nodded and he watched her walk away. He couldn't help but wonder what she had planned, and then he smiled when he realized that she'd succeeded in getting his mind off everything he was worrying about.

The night they had met, he'd been stewing over something as well. Something that wasn't important and he couldn't even remember what it was, but it would have been trivial compared to what was on his mind now, and she had walked up to him and just started talking.

And he'd forgotten everything.

He'd forgotten who he was when he was around her.

And that was a dangerous thing indeed.

* * *

"Where are we going?" Lev asked. She could tell he was curious and possibly slightly worried, but he was intrigued all the same.

She knew he was feeling a bit lost without Lexi, even if he had complained about Lexi's constant presence in his life, and he was in a bit of a rut. He'd been moved from place to place for the last four months. Everything about his life was dictated by government agents or by Lexi or by his job.

So Imogen had taken it upon herself to arrange a little outing. She'd cleared it with the security detail and they wouldn't be far away, but she wanted to take him out of town. There was a small restaurant about twenty kilometers down the highway, just outside the city off Highway 3.

It looked like a little hole-in-the-wall place, but appearances were deceiving. Inside was a great little restaurant that she rarely got to visit unless she rented a car. And Imogen knew it would soon close for the winter.

This was their last chance and she thought it might be a nice change of pace for Lev. It would get his mind off whatever was worrying him and it would distract her too.

"To a restaurant I like."

"So you said, but where is it that we have to drive out of Yellowknife to get to it?"

"You'll see." She reached over the console and punched the coordinates into the GPS. "Just follow the directions and you'll be fine."

Lev cocked an eyebrow. "I don't know if I should trust you."

He was teasing and she laughed gently. "I think you can trust me."

"Can I?" he teased.

"Would you just drive?"

He was laughing as he pulled out of the parking lot onto the main road headed for downtown Yellowknife. "Fine, but I should also point out I don't like listening to the GPS too much."

"Well, you don't want to end up going in the opposite direction or we'll be driving until the road peters out and there's not much east of Yellowknife."

"So we're headed west onto the highway?" he asked.

"Yes. And make sure you watch for bison."

"I remember," he said dryly.

"Oh? You've had a run-in with one before?"

"Yes. We were delayed by a large group of them that decided to walk down the middle of the highway. Lexi had already been warned that there wasn't much he could do and, really, those beasts are massive. I didn't want the truck wrecked."

"You should meet a moose."

"I have yet to see one. I would like to."

"Not if it's walking in front of your car you don't! Working as a trauma surgeon, you'll probably soon get a case or two of people involved in an accident with a moose. It can prove to be fatal."

Lev frowned. "That's good to know and I really hope I don't encounter one of those traumas."

"I hope not either, but I think it's inevitable."

They drove in silence past the large Yellowknife sign and out past the airport until they were on the Mackenzie Highway, also known as the Frontier Trail Route. Back when she had still been with Allen, they would take his car out as far as Fort Providence, having picnics in the different territorial parks that lined the highway.

One time, they had taken a few days and driven over the Deh Cho Bridge and headed down toward Fort Smith and Wood Buffalo. They hadn't stayed long, as Allen didn't particularly like hiking or the town, but Imogen loved it there. She wished she could go back.

She didn't mind long car trips.

Not in the summer, anyway.

"This really is out in the middle of nowhere," Lev remarked as they drove past the Yellowknife Golf Club and Fred Henne Territorial Park. "Now I'm worried what you have in store for me out here."

"Well, since we're both off tomorrow, I thought it would be the perfect time to take this short trip. Also, the place we're going to is seasonal and will be closing for the winter shortly."

"It's not even fall."

"We get snow in October," she reminded him. She had told him this before.

"That sounds awful, if I'm honest."

She chuckled. "It's not so bad, but, yeah, you don't want to be stuck on this highway in a snowstorm. It's not impassable, but it's slow. A simple eight-hour drive to Fort Smith can take somewhere around sixteen hours in a snowstorm."

"Sixteen hours?" Lev winced, and then frowned at a diamond warning sign on the side of the road.

"You need to slow down when you see those diamond signs," she warned, because he wasn't slowing down.

"Why?"

"It's where the permafrost has buckled the road. If you hit it the wrong way your car could get some air!"

Lev slowed. "What is get some air?"

"It can cause your car to roll, quite violently. It's the worst kind of bump you could imagine. It's fun for no one, and your wallet will hate you for the repairs needed on your vehicle's suspension."

"Okay." They took the dip slowly, but even then it was rough enough to cause her stomach to slosh and do a flip.

"So, this place is a seasonal restaurant?" Lev asked.

"Yes."

He made a face again. "Is it Ratchet Ronnie's?"

"It is! Have you been there before?" she asked, excited.

"That place looked like a dive when Lexi and I drove past. We opted to eat what we bought in Hay River at the North Store rather than test the water at that place."

"Appearances can be deceiving. It's a great place."

He shot her a look that said he wasn't too convinced.

"Trust me," she said.

"You've been asking me to trust you a lot tonight, which makes me even more worried."

"Look, I won't steer you wrong about the food. Trust me."

They drove for about an hour until there was a little gravel road turnoff from the highway. Ratchet Ronnie's sat not far off that gravel road and there was a sign with neon blinking lights to show that it was open. There were several vehicles in the parking lot and Lev pulled the truck alongside them and stopped.

"See," she said triumphantly. "People love this place."

"It just looks like a clapboard shack. Like something out of an old horror movie."

"Just wait!" she teased. "I haven't steered you wrong yet."

"Well, you did once."

"What do you mean?" she asked.

"That little bar on the waterfront that you swore was wonderful, but it turned out to be a hotel. That was a pricey drink," he teased.

She'd forgotten about that momentarily. She had wanted to take him to that little bar after they'd gone up the CN

Tower, only to find her favorite little haunt had turned into a boutique hotel. They had impulsively rented a penthouse suite because it had been the only room available and had drunk champagne on their own rooftop terrace before they'd made love.

It had been a wonderful night.

Of course, taking that suite had had bigger consequences than just a hotel bill. They were married. They were going to be parents.

Don't get used to this.

She had to keep reminding herself of that. Even though they were married, that didn't mean it was permanent. She could still end up raising this child alone.

Don't think about it now.

Right now, all she wanted to focus on was having a nice dinner at Ratchet Ronnie's. She didn't want to think about their marriage of convenience. She didn't want to think about security guards, lines of succession or danger.

"It was expensive," she admitted.

"But worth it." He took her hand and kissed it, making her melt and forget her worry.

"Come on. Let's eat!" She took Lev's hand and led him inside the restaurant.

The look of surprise on his face when they walked into a retro fifties-style diner, complete with red leather booths, jukeboxes and chrome, made her smile, and she gave him a small punch on the arm.

"See? What did I tell you? Appearances can be deceiving."

"This is amazing and it's in the middle of nowhere," he said, astounded.

"Yeah, it's a local secret only to be discovered by adventurous travelers."

They were led to a corner booth and they took a seat to look over the menu. It was classic diner food, featuring things like milkshakes and hamburgers, but also had a touch of territorial traditional foods like bannock, buffalo and arctic char.

"I have to say," Lev said after they'd ordered. "This is a nice distraction."

"I thought it might be."

"You're very pleased with yourself."

"I am rather," she teased. "We have a couple of days off and I thought it might be nice for you to see something outside the city."

He smiled and nodded.

"And we're going down to Fort Smith in a couple of days to help the doctors there."

"Where is Fort Smith?"

"South of here. It's my turn on rotation to do some surgeries at the hospital there. Just routine stuff. I get flown down, as it's an eight-hour drive. So I spend a day there and fly back in the evening. I asked Jeanette and cleared it all—you can come too if you'd like. I could use the help."

"I would like that. It would be a good change of pace."

"My thoughts exactly."

"So what is there to do in Fort Smith, besides work?"

"To do?"

"I would like to see something besides a clinic. I want to enjoy my time here."

Before he left.

He didn't have to say it, but Imogen knew that was what he was thinking.

"Well, you need more time there to see everything. It sits inside Wood Buffalo National Park, which is bigger than Switzerland."

Lev's eyes widened. "Impressive. It amazes me how vast your country is."

"We could go on a small hike in town to see the pelicans in Slave River before they migrate back down south."

"That sounds like a plan."

"Other than that, there's not much to do there." She remembered the way Allen would complain. He hated Fort Smith.

Looking back, she should have realized he hated the north.

"You okay?" he asked.

"Yes. Why?"

"You zoned out and you seemed sad."

"I was thinking of my ex. He hated Fort Smith. He preferred the city."

"Don't think about him," Lev said. "The city has merits, but I prefer this rugged place. Of course, I was used to mobile military hospitals."

"You're a prince," she whispered. "Surely you're used to much more glamorous cityscapes?"

"Used to and like are two very different things."

Her heart swelled. She was glad he liked it here. It gave her hope.

Of what?

Just because he liked it here it didn't mean he wanted to stay, or could stay.

Don't think about it.

She shook those thoughts from her mind. She just wanted to enjoy tonight.

The rest of their evening at the restaurant was exactly what they both needed: a distraction from everyday life. They didn't think about Chenar or work or anything. They enjoyed each other's company, just like they'd done when they'd first met. Imogen was sad to see the evening come to an end, but they had to drive back to Yellowknife and the restaurant would be closing soon.

They paid their bill and walked outside. There was a nip in the air and it was dark but clear.

"It's cooler than the other night," Lev remarked.

"I told you fall is coming, even though it's still August. September isn't far away. Just a couple more days."

Her phone buzzed and she glanced at it. She'd set up an alarm for an app that tracked a certain phenomenon, one she knew Lev wanted to see.

The alert was telling her the chances were high and it would happen soon.

"Is everything good?" he asked. "Is it the hospital?"

"No, but let's go down the road a bit. There's a park and I want to show you something away from this artificial light."

"What?"

"Just trust me."

They got into the truck and drove down the highway to one of the many territorial parks that lined the road.

Not a soul was there.

It was just the two of them.

They got out of the truck and walked toward a lake, which was calm. The only sound was the gentle lapping of waves against the shoreline. Above them was a clear, dark sky.

"So what have we come here for?" he asked.

"Just wait," she whispered.

Then what she'd been waiting for, watching for, happened.

Across the sky a wave of undulating colors broke out against the inky blackness. The green light glowed, danced and arced above their heads in true aurora borealis fashion.

Her heart soared with excitement. She was used to seeing it, but she never got tired of seeing a full aurora moving and rippling across an inky dark sky.

It was magical.

Lev stood there and stared, his mouth open in awe.

"I've waited a long time to see this," he whispered.

"It's beautiful, isn't it?"

"It is." Lev continued to stare up at it, but then he turned and looked at her, touching her face. "It is beautiful, but not as beautiful as you."

Before she knew what was happening, he leaned down and kissed her, gently.

And even though she shouldn't, she melted in his arms as the kiss deepened. It was a brief kiss, but it made her pulse race in anticipation. She didn't know what to say. There was nothing to say as they stood there in the darkness next to the truck, watching the lights dance across the sky.

His arm slipped around her, pulling her close, and she leaned her head against his shoulder, enjoying this stolen moment with him.

Savoring it, while she had the chance.

CHAPTER ELEVEN

IMOGEN COULDN'T STOP to think about that kiss they had shared while watching the northern lights by the shore of Great Slave Lake. The kiss had been gentle, controlled, but nevertheless it had been like a kiss from a lover. It was nothing like their first kiss in Toronto, which had been fueled by passion and champagne.

This was deeper, emotionally.

It had been so simple, so innocent, but it had made her feel connected to him.

It had made her feel safe.

It had made her feel wanted.

Something she hadn't felt for a long time, and it scared her because she didn't want to rely on that feeling. The only person she could rely on was herself. It was what her father had taught her.

Her self-reliance and survival had got her through her father's death and Allen's departure.

She was a safe bet.

Lev was not.

They hadn't said much to each other on their drive back to Yellowknife. Imogen had gone to bed, but Lev had wandered out onto the back dock with a cup of tea to watch the northern lights dance over the water.

She wished she could have joined him, but she was

exhausted and she had an inkling he wanted to be alone. And she too needed to be alone to process what had happened.

So she'd gone to bed and when she woke in the morning he wasn't next to her in bed or on the couch. She panicked. She checked out the back porch to see if he'd spent the night on one of the Muskoka chairs, but he wasn't there. She headed out onto the front deck and her boat was still there.

Where had he gone?

He couldn't have walked anywhere.

He left you.

Panic started to rise up in her. Last night had felt so right. She'd let her guard down and now he was gone. Or someone had taken him.

She took a deep breath. There was a rational explanation.

The sun was shining and that cool nip in the air from the night before was gone. It was warm, unusually warm for late August.

It was almost September and fall had been in the air last night.

And then she saw the towel on the deck and his head in the water.

Swimming.

She did a double take as he swam toward her.

"You're insane," she said, when he stopped and saw her.

He looked up from where he was treading water. "Why?"

"It's cold!"

"It's not too bad. I had energy to burn and I used to spend a lot of time swimming in Chenar, so I thought why not."

Imogen shook her head. "I still think you're crazy. Where did you swim to?"

"To the shore and back," he said nonchalantly, as if it were nothing.

She raised her eyebrows. "You're joking."

"No. It's not a bad swim." He swam over to the edge of the dock and hoisted himself out of the water. Imogen squeaked when she realized that not only was he swimming but he'd been swimming au naturel.

"What is with you and being naked?" She handed him the towel.

He chuckled, a devilish glint to his eye. "It was refreshing."

"I should say so." She chuckled.

He grinned. "It was fine. No one saw me!"

"Oh, no?" Imogen waved to her neighbor, Mrs. Smythe, an elderly woman who was staring from her deck, where she had been enjoying a cup of coffee. She was now staring at Lev, mouth agape. "Good morning, Mrs. Smythe!"

Her neighbor waved, barely, still staring at Lev.

Lev's eyes were twinkling and he was trying not to laugh. "I didn't know she was there. I swear."

"Well, she might not have been there when you started out, but she certainly got an eyeful when you came out of the water."

"I'm glad you think it's an eyeful," he teased.

She shook her head at his bad joke, trying not to laugh. "Aren't you cold?"

"I am getting a bit chilly now."

"Let's go inside and I'll make you a cup of tea while you dry off and get dressed."

"That sounds good."

They headed inside, where Lev proceeded to dry off

in the living room, buck naked, and Imogen tried to focus on making him tea and not stare at him.

Get a grip.

"I'm glad you're so comfortable here that you don't mind changing in front of open windows," she remarked dryly.

Or changing in front of me.

She kept that thought to herself.

Lev laughed. "No one is out there."

"You almost gave poor old Mrs. Smythe a heart attack!"

"I told you I didn't know she was there. I had a hard time sleeping and I decided to burn off some nervous energy. Besides, I'm a doctor. I could have resuscitated her."

"What are you anxious about?"

He sighed. "Lexi and Kristof. I'm glad things are settling down, but not knowing is driving me crazy."

"You mean if you stay or go?"

"Yes," he said quietly.

She swallowed a lump that formed in her throat. She didn't want to think about all of that. Not when last night had been so wonderful. And she felt foolish for panicking that he'd left her. She hated it that he was creeping in through her walls. Hated it that she cared whether he stayed or left.

You cared when he was missing.

"How late did you stay up, watching the northern lights?" she asked, changing the subject.

"Late. I think I tried to go to sleep about two in the morning."

"Did you get any sleep?" she asked, shutting off the kettle and pouring the water into the teapot.

"Not really, but I don't feel tired. I just feel like doing

something." He pulled on his jeans and then picked up a plaid shirt and buttoned it up, his long hair tied back.

"We could go to the museum today."

"Museum?" he asked. "There's a museum here?"

"Yeah. You can learn all about the Mad Trapper."

He gave her a strange look. "There was a mad trapper?"

"Well, you'd have to go to the museum to find out."

He snorted. "You don't know about this mad trapper either. You just heard the name."

She narrowed her eyes. "Fine. I don't. I've never been to the museum, but I thought it might be nice. It would be something to do and maybe we can hike up to the bush pilot monument."

"I've been there," he said. "It's a beautiful lookout."

"I haven't been there either."

He looked at her, confused. "How long have you lived up here?"

"Shut up!" She laughed and handed him his tea as he came over to the island counter. "I was working. Before I started at the hospital I did a lot of flying to remote communities. When I was home, Allen and I would travel outside Yellowknife, but only when the weather was good."

His expression tensed when she mentioned Allen.

"He was a fool."

"I wanted to stay in the north and he didn't. So he left." It was more complicated than that, but she didn't want to talk about Allen. She didn't want to think about him. "I should've seen the signs before I got involved."

"It's not your fault," he said softly.

Only it was. She'd let Allen in and it had caused nothing but pain, just like Lev would cause her pain too.

"Let's not talk about him," she said.

"Well, I guess I can go to the museum and then we

can go to the bush pilot monument. It's still early. When does the museum open?"

Imogen glanced at her clock. "Not for a while."

Lev finished his tea. "Then I'm going to go for a walk."

"What? Where?" she asked, confused.

"On the island behind you." He motioned out of the window.

"What?" she asked, setting down her mug.

"The island behind you. It's not a far jump. It seems to be mostly rock and I'm going to climb to the top of it and see what's on the other side."

"You're crazy."

"Come with me if you want. Have you ever done it?"

"No." She worried her bottom lip. "Fine."

She followed Lev out onto her back dock. There was a small gap between the houseboat and the island.

Lev easily leaped across and she hesitated.

"Come on." He held out his hand. "I've got you."

She reached out, took his hand and made the quick jump onto the rocky shore. His arms came around her, steadying her. It felt good to have his arms around her.

"Was that so hard?" he asked gently.

"No, but I still think you're a bit crazy."

He chuckled softly. "We can all use a bit of crazy once in a while. Come on. Let's see what's at the top."

He held her hand as they scaled the rocky island, using trees to balance, picking their way through the brush to the top.

"I can tell you what's at the top," she said, as her calves screamed in pain from trying to balance while walking up the slanting slope. "More rock and tree and lake."

"Still, it's something different." He got onto level ground and helped her up the last little bit. His hand was strong and steady. It was reassuring. Suddenly, it didn't seem like a silly thing to do.

It felt fun.

"Come on. Haven't you ever explored this place?"

"No. I work and that's about it."

"Where's the fun in that?"

"Your attitude has certainly changed."

"Yeah, well, I have to live while I can before I can't take any more risks like this."

She felt bad for him, but she was enjoying this moment with him as they made their way to the top of Jolliffe Island. When they got there they could see the other side of Yellowknife Bay and the road to Detah.

To the south of them Yellowknife Bay opened up like a great mouth to the rest of Great Slave Lake.

"This is also a pretty nice view," he said.

"It is. I don't know what took me so long to come up here." But she did. She'd got completely wrapped up in her work so she didn't have to think about anything else. So she didn't have to deal with the pain of her father's passing or the fact that Allen had left her. Or that her mother had left her.

Yellowknife was the first place her father had put down roots. He'd still flown to remote villages, but Yellowknife was the first place she had called home.

It was her home. Her work was her life, and that was the way she liked it.

Until recently.

Lev had changed everything.

He had made her see that there was more than work. When she was around him, she wanted to do more and see more.

"I can see why you love it here."

"Of course," she said. "It's my home. My father always came back. I was born here. It's where my mother was from…" She trailed off.

She knew why her father had stayed in Yellowknife. It was where he had met her mother.

Some part of him had always hoped she'd come back.

"Anyway, Yellowknife is my home," she said gently.

"It's a beautiful home," Lev said with a hint of sadness in his voice.

She was going to say something else when her belly fluttered. It was a quick flutter that shocked her and she gasped, touching her belly, startling Lev.

"What is it?" he asked. "Are you okay? Is the baby okay?"

She laughed and smiled, tears stinging her eyes. "Yeah, I'm fine. It was the quickening. The baby, I felt the baby for the first time."

The baby zoomed across her belly again and she laughed.

For all the people who had left her, this baby would be with her always.

This baby was her family.

"I wish I could feel it," he whispered.

"I wish you could too."

She smiled up at him and touched his face, and then this time she initiated it. This was what she wanted. She was in his arms again, kissing him, and she didn't want it to end. But it had to end. This wasn't permanent and she couldn't let him any farther into her heart.

She broke off the kiss, annoyed with herself for starting something she couldn't finish.

"Why don't we get back and head to the museum?"

A strange expression crossed his face. "Of course."

Imogen turned her back and made her way slowly down, back to her boat, her home.

She was angry at herself for kissing him.

And she was mad that she hadn't wanted the kiss to end.

She would've liked it to go on a lot longer.

Maybe even forever.

But that was not in the cards and she had to remind herself of that fact.

When they got back to the houseboat her phone was ringing. She rushed to grab it off the counter and saw that it was Jeanette.

"Jeanette, what's up?"

"We need Lev. There's been a major accident on the highway and we need a trauma doctor to go out to the scene. Seemed a truck collided with a herd of buffalo and flipped over, trapping a car."

"I'll go too," Imogen said.

"Great. Thank you. Get here fast," Jeanette said.

"On our way." Imogen hung up the phone and turned to Lev. "It looks like our trip to the museum is canceled. There's been an accident on Highway 3 and they need us to go out to the scene of the accident with the paramedics."

"Moose?" Lev asked.

"No. A transport truck driver thought he could plow through a herd of buffalo and flipped himself over, but there were other cars involved too. Lots of injuries."

Lev nodded. "Let's go."

Imogen grabbed her purse and locked up. They got into her motorboat and made their way to shore. They went to the truck in the parking lot and Lev drove them to the hospital, where they changed into their scrubs. Lev packed emergency gear with Imogen before they got into an ambulance and headed off down the highway to the airport, where they'd be transported to the scene by helicopter, with the ambulances following as quickly as they could by road.

As they sat in the back, the rocking movement of the ambulance made Imogen start to feel a bit sick, and she popped an anti-nausea pill. She wasn't the best on helicopters either and there was something of a breeze picking up.

Lev helped her out of the ambulance and into the helicopter, buckling her in. The helicopter took off and Imogen tried to focus on the sky rather than the ground as they headed south, cutting over the choppy water of Great Slave Lake toward Behchokǫ̀ Rae-Edzo.

It didn't take long before she could see smoke rising in the sky and the flashing lights from the RCMP and other emergency personnel from the surrounding villages who had come out to assist in the accident.

The surviving buffalo had been corralled and moved off so the emergency crew could go in and help those who were injured.

The helicopter landed with a small bump, and once it was safe to get out, she followed Lev through all the chaos, the noise and the smoke of the accident scene.

"Are you two the surgeons from Yellowknife?" an RCMP constable asked.

"Yes," Imogen said.

"Great. We have the driver pinned and then there's another man we managed to extract who's in bad shape. We managed to get his wife out, but he's trapped."

"I'll help with the pinned man. I've done complicated extractions before," Lev said. "You check on the man they've already pulled out of the wreckage."

Imogen nodded.

She followed another paramedic to where the man

was. A fire team from Behchokǫ̀ was putting out a smoldering car, and nearby, on a tarp, covered in a blanket, was a man. Her heart sank to the soles of her feet when she saw how badly injured he was, barely conscious, under the blanket.

She knelt down beside him and took his hand, assessing his vitals. He was in bad shape; his vitals were not good. She needed Lev's help, but he was working on someone else who was pinned under the transport truck.

She motioned for a paramedic and an RCMP officer to help her move the injured man away from the rubble. She could tell from the bruising on his abdomen as she assessed him that he had a ruptured spleen and would need surgery.

"Is he okay?" a woman asked, coming forward. She was heavily pregnant and had her arm bandaged. "I'm his wife. Marge."

"What's his name, Marge?" Imogen asked.

"Henry," Marge said nervously. "His name is Henry."

"We need to get Henry to Yellowknife." Imogen needed to order a CT scan and get Henry into the operating room, but she didn't want to put any more stress onto Marge. "Get him to the hospital," she said to the paramedic, "and I will be there as soon as the other patients have been helped."

The paramedic nodded and loaded Henry into another helicopter that had landed to transport the seriously injured to the hospital.

Lev came from behind the other side of the wreck, looking grim.

Her heart sank.

"The driver?" she asked.

"There was nothing to be done. He was gone."

"I need to get back to the hospital to work on my patient—"

There was a sharp cry and she spun round to see Marge, Henry's wife, clutch her belly.

Imogen and Lev raced to her side.

"Marge, are you okay?" Imogen asked.

"I was in labor when we left our home in Behchokǫ̀"

Imogen's eyes widened. "You're in labor?"

"With the accident…" The woman cried out again. "…it stopped."

"It's started again." Lev turned to the RCMP officer who was with him. "I need some blankets. I think we're about to deliver a baby here!"

"Have you done an emergency delivery?" Imogen asked.

"Yes. It wasn't always soldiers I attended to."

While paramedics were dealing with the other minor injuries from the multicar crash, Imogen and Lev were able to get Marge into the back of an ambulance.

Lev checked her while Imogen assisted.

"The ambulance won't make it to the hospital in time. The baby's head is crowning," he said. Imogen looked and saw there was no way they'd make it to Yellowknife.

"Marge, you need to push when I say," Imogen coached.

"What about Henry?" Marge cried.

"He's on his way to Yellowknife to get help. Dr. Vanin and I will take care of you now."

Marge nodded.

"Come on, Marge. Push!" Imogen urged, as she braced Marge's shoulders while Lev helped guide the little life into the world.

The birth happened so fast it startled Imogen.

Lev cut the cord and took the baby to the other side of the ambulance, where there was another gurney and oxygen.

Her heart sank.

"My baby?" Marge asked.

"Your baby has been born. Dr. Vanin is assessing—"

"It's a boy," Lev said.

"Your son is being assessed." Imogen helped Marge deliver the placenta and cleaned her up, but she was bleeding heavily and they needed to get her help too. Imogen watched Lev cradle the little, silent new life.

The baby was so small and fragile in Lev's big strong hands. He was so gentle, the way he cradled the infant, studiously keeping the baby warm and holding the large oxygen mask over the baby's face.

"Come on," he whispered. Then he said something in Chenarian.

It sounded like a prayer and Imogen's heart sank, but then a thin little wail sounded in the back of the ambulance and Imogen smiled, relieved, a tear slipping from her eye.

Lev beamed. "He'll be fine. Your son is fine, Marge."

Marge cried and Imogen helped Lev bring the baby and oxygen over to Marge.

"He needs some oxygen support," Lev said, carefully placing the wrapped bundle back in her arms. "We need to get you two to the hospital."

"There's a helicopter ready now, Dr. Vanin," the paramedic said.

Lev nodded and turned to her. "You go with Marge. Keep the oxygen over the baby's face. Keep him warm."

"Why don't you go?" Imogen asked. "You delivered him."

"You need to get back to operate on her husband. Go."

Imogen nodded. The paramedics wrapped and stabilized Marge, who was bleeding more heavily than Imogen would've liked, while she held on to the precious bundle. They were loaded into the helicopter.

"I'll be back soon," Lev said, and then he kissed her forehead before the door to the helicopter shut.

Imogen sat back as the helicopter rose and Lev grew smaller and smaller.

She didn't want to leave him behind.

She didn't want him to go, and it had nothing to do with leaving him behind at the crash site and everything to do with the fact that she wanted him to stay in Yellowknife, for her, as well as for their child. But she knew he wouldn't.

He couldn't.

CHAPTER TWELVE

LEV FINALLY ARRIVED back at the hospital. The baby was in the pediatric critical care unit, but he was assured the boy was doing well. Then he went to check on Marge, who was stable and resting. It was then he learned that Imogen was still in the operating room with Henry, Marge's husband.

He went to the viewing gallery, where some residents were observing the surgery.

He kept to the back to watch Imogen work. He'd done emergency splenectomies in the field, but he was glad for the patient that a hospital had been a short trip by helicopter away and that Imogen was the surgeon working on him.

A smile crept over his face as he watched her. She'd remained so calm under pressure in the field and she'd been a true help when delivering that baby, especially when he hadn't been sure the baby would live.

He'd attended a birth like that in a war zone. Only they hadn't had oxygen and a hospital had been hours away. Both mother and baby had died. It had torn him apart back then. This time the story had ended better, but it made him worried about what would happen to Imogen if he wasn't there when her time came.

She had to return with him to Chenar. He couldn't leave her behind. He had to be there for their child's birth.

He wasn't going to miss that.

And what if she won't come?

He didn't know what he would do if she didn't come with him. He wanted to do everything in his power to make sure she came, but he also knew how strongly she felt about staying in Yellowknife, working in this community. No matter what he did, someone would get hurt.

Maybe this trip to Fort Smith would decide it. It would be just the two of them together and he could woo her and convince her to go back with him.

You could always stay.

It would be a dream to be free to make that choice, but he had a duty.

Imogen had to go with him.

The surgery finished and he left the gallery to meet her on the OR level, outside the scrub room.

She looked exhausted, but she smiled when she saw him.

"You're back!"

"I am. I checked on the baby and Marge. Both are well. How is Henry?"

Imogen sighed. "He lost a lot of blood. The spleen was a mess. I couldn't resect it, it had to come out, but I'm hopeful he'll pull through. He's on his way to the intensive care unit now. He's stable, but, still, you never know."

"You look tired."

"I am," she said wearily. "I am really tired, as a matter of fact. This is not much of a day off."

"No. Not really."

"I still have to pack for Fort Smith."

"I'm looking forward to that. I hope I can be of some help."

"Of course you can. I really appreciate you coming."

They walked side by side down to the cafeteria. He wanted a coffee and she wanted a tea.

Imogen had been in the operating room for hours and Lev had stayed behind to make sure all those who were injured were taken care of.

They got their drinks and sat down at a table.

"So, did you find out how the accident happened? I mean, I know there were buffalo involved."

Lev took a sip of some old, bitter black coffee. "The transport truck collided with a herd. One of the bison was thrown up and over the truck as it hit one of those dips you warned me about. As the truck was thrown, the bison bounced onto Henry and Marge's truck. Then it was a chain reaction of a couple of vehicles behind them."

Imogen winced. "It's unfortunate that the driver of the transport truck was killed."

"Yes, but lucky that no one else died. You seemed surprised when Marge mentioned they'd left Behchokǫ̀. Is that far?"

"Yes, about two hours, but there are currently no nurse practitioners, no doctors or midwives in their village. They had no choice but to come to Yellowknife. No one wants to stay in the north."

"Except you?" He felt bad all over again about trying to snatch her away. If he could stay, he would, in a heartbeat, but his life was not his own. It belonged to Chenar. And now he'd forced that same duty onto Imogen and their unborn child.

"Why don't we go back to our place and get ready for our flight tomorrow?" she suggested.

"Good idea."

They finished their drinks and made their way to the

doctors' lounge to change out of their scrubs and collect their belongings before they headed back to their home.

Or rather, her home.

Not their home.

It could never be that. Even if he wanted it to be.

The first stop the next morning before their trip south was to the hospital, where Imogen picked up the supplies she was taking down to Fort Smith.

Lev helped her pack up.

"This is a lot of mini first-aid kits," he remarked. "What are these for?"

"I like to take them down to Fort Smith and hand them out at the community center. They're for emergency situations, or for people's cars. There's a lot of national park and no decent cell service in a vast area. I want them to be prepared. Plus, there are always the natural disasters, rock slides, forest fires…tornadoes."

"Tornadoes in Fort Smith?" he asked, confused.

"They had one recently. It's rare, but it happens." Imogen zipped up her duffel bag. "It's part of the outreach program I do. I'll hit some other communities too. Fort Smith has a great hospital… They just have a shortage of surgeons. I promised to cover today and I thought it was a good time to distribute the kits."

"It's a good cause." Lev did up his duffel bag. "You ready to go?"

"Yes. I think so. I don't think I'm forgetting anything."

"Did you check on Henry?" Lev asked.

"Yes. I did. He's still in the intensive care unit and the surgeon on call will keep me informed. I've left instructions."

"Good." Lev smiled and slung the duffel bag over his shoulder. "Should we make our way to the airport?"

"Yes. There's a cab waiting and a chartered plane. It should be a short trip. We'll be back late tomorrow night. We'll stay overnight in Fort Smith and I'll do the couple of surgeries I have booked tomorrow morning. Today we'll see patients."

"Okay" was all Lev said.

He was acting odd. He seemed to be on edge.

He's probably worried about not hearing anything from Lexi or his brother.

Still, something was eating away at him. She wasn't convinced it was that.

You don't have time to think about it now.

There was a lot of work to do and she had to get her head in the game. The cab took them to the airport and the private jet was waiting for them. Once the plane was taking off, Lev seemed to visibly relax.

"Are you okay?" she asked.

"Why wouldn't I be okay?"

"You just seemed tense."

"I am a bit nervous about this trip. Nervous about my newfound freedom, I suppose."

"You are?" She had a hard time believing that. It didn't seem like him, or the man she thought she knew.

The man she was falling for.

Don't think about him like that.

But it was hard not to. Before the accident, she'd enjoyed that moment on Jolliffe Island, when he'd put his arms around her and they'd kissed. And the prenatal appointment, and the kiss under the northern lights. It had all seemed so perfect. Then the baby had moved for the first time and everything had just seemed so right.

If anyone had been looking at them, they would have sworn they were a real couple, totally in love.

And that sobered her. It reminded her that their marriage wasn't real. They weren't really in love, no matter how she felt when she was around him.

She couldn't fall in love with him. Except she already was.

When that helicopter had taken off and she'd left him behind, she'd cried. It was silly, but she had. She didn't want him to leave because she couldn't go.

Why can't you?

She shook that thought away. She hated it that he was getting past her walls. She was terrified of the hurt it would bring. And she was scared of delivering her child alone. Seeing Lev hold Marge's baby so tenderly had made her wish for a future she simply couldn't have.

It made her sad.

And her sadness scared her. She was losing control. Unless she could convince him to stay. Although he was the heir to the throne now, he wouldn't be King. His brother would have children, and they would have children, and Lev could be free. Why couldn't he stay in Canada?

The flight was a quick up-and-down flight.

In Fort Smith they were picked up by another taxi and taken to a small hospital that was in the center of town.

Lev frowned when he saw it. "I thought you said this was a hospital."

"It is…sort of. They have the facility. It's just they don't have the surgeons. They have a nurse practitioner and a doctor, so my postoperative patients will be in good hands."

Lev didn't seem convinced, but didn't say too much else. She was worried he'd realize he hated the north, just like Allen, and leave.

Like her mother.

They were taken to a modular home that was owned

by the hospital to put up surgeons and specialists who flew in, and they dropped their bags.

It was a cramped space and the couch was in no way big enough for either her or Lev to sleep on. There was one bedroom and one double bed.

"It looks like we're sharing tonight," he stated, and cleared his throat uncomfortably. "Are you okay with that?"

"Of course. I guess they didn't think too much about it when I told them my husband was coming."

"I remember the first time we shared a bed," he teased, taking a step closer to her, smiling deviously.

"I haven't forgotten," she said, her voice cracking, her body coming to life just at the thought of him. Of that kiss they'd shared on Jolliffe, of the night they'd shared together in Toronto.

The night they'd conceived their baby and the evening out under the aurora.

And now, here in Fort Smith, they were alone. They were away from everyone who knew them. It was just the two of them in a very confined space.

"Well," Imogen said, clearing her throat. "We'd better get these supplies over to the hospital. It's a short walk and my first appointment is in about an hour. I'm hoping you can check on the preoperative patients for me?"

Lev cleared his throat and took a step back. "Of course. Let's do that."

"Good."

Imogen took a couple of calming breaths as she collected up the medical equipment she'd brought. She needed to calm down and not think about Lev in that way, although it was getting increasingly harder to do that.

Lev was distracted.

Before, he had been worrying that he'd be caught, that

Imogen would find out he was disobeying orders by accompanying her to Fort Smith to protect her, but now he was distracted by her.

When he saw that they would have no choice but to share a bed in that small little cottage, he couldn't help but think back on the kisses they'd shared, and then his mind had gone to that night in the penthouse suite in Toronto.

To the way she'd felt in his arms.

The way she'd felt when he'd been buried deep inside her. How sweet her kisses were. How he wanted no one else and had never wanted anyone like he wanted her.

And all he wanted to do was whisk her away and show her how much he desired her. How he'd never stopped thinking about her. But he didn't want to scare her off and he knew that she didn't want to leave Yellowknife.

He couldn't do that to her. He couldn't drag her away from her home.

Who said you had to?

He wouldn't force her, but he'd put up a fight to make her want to come. It was all he could think about. This was tearing him in two.

And he was terrified she didn't feel the same things he was feeling. That she'd hurt him and he would have to leave her behind. He wasn't Canadian and Kristof would force him to return to Chenar. Force him to give up medicine and push him into a life of politics and court.

It would be better for his child to be raised here because Chenar would take years to rebuild. Canada was stable.

Lev knew he should keep his distance, that their marriage was just so he could protect them, but, try as he might, he just couldn't stay away from her. He loved being with her and he was glad he was here now, helping her in this small community to provide much-needed surgical care.

He was helping to save lives and that was what he'd always wanted. Politics had never been his thing. It had been his brother's thing, but then, Kristof had been trained for that life.

Medicine was his passion.

All he knew was medicine.

All he wanted to know was medicine.

And Imogen.

He cleared his throat and went back to his filing, but he couldn't help but watch and admire her from afar as she moved from exam room to exam room.

As if she knew he was looking at her, she glanced over and smiled. Her smile was infectious and he smiled back.

What is this spell she's put on me?

He didn't know, but he was losing the battle. He was falling in love with her.

"You ready to go back and get some dinner?" she asked.

"Are you done?"

"I am." She folded her hands on the counter of the nurses' station. "I think everything should go smoothly tomorrow."

"With you at the helm, I'm sure it will." And he meant it.

"Thanks. Are you hungry?"

"I am."

"Good. We can get changed and then head out for something to eat."

"How about I go and get some groceries and cook you something?"

She cocked an eyebrow. "I'm intrigued. You did tell

me you and Lexi cooked, but I haven't tasted one of your creations yet."

"*Yet* being the operative word," he said. "Tonight you will."

"Okay. Well, there is a fully equipped kitchen and the grocery store isn't far from our lodging. But remember I am pregnant, so no raw fish or things like shark or swordfish."

He gave her a weird look. "Where am I going to get shark in Fort Smith?"

"Good point."

"I will be mindful, Imogen. I promise." He placed a hand on his chest and bowed at the waist ever so slightly.

She laughed. "Okay, well, let's get going."

Once they had changed, he left her sitting out on the small deck under the awning with a warm cup of tea as he strolled down the street to the co-op store.

The leaves had turned here already. There were bright yellows, reds and oranges mixed in with the green from the cedar and pine.

It was a sleepy community, but there were a few people who stopped and stared at him for a few moments because he was new to town—at least he hoped that was why they were studying him.

Not that it much mattered now. The news was reporting that Kristof had returned to Chenar. The coup had been put down, but Lev had heard no details. Which didn't surprise him. He was an afterthought to his brother.

Still, it would've been nice to have been told.

Of course, peace meant his time here was almost over, and the thought of leaving Imogen made him feel ill.

Don't think about it.

The problem was he couldn't stop thinking about it. It was at the forefront of his mind. Always.

He gathered up ingredients to make a beef Stroganoff with egg noodles. Something his governess used to make. It was comfort food for him and he could use some of that starchy comfort just about now.

He bought a few other things for the night, some snacks, just in case Imogen got hungry, and then carried the bags back to where they were staying.

Imogen was sitting outside still, sipping her tea and reading over files in preparation for tomorrow's surgery. She looked up when he came up the gravel drive.

"How did it go?" she asked.

"The cost of food up here is ridiculous," he groused. "But I had fairly good luck. I'll see what I can make of it."

"I really can't wait to find out what you're making."

"Well, you'll just have to wait." He tried to open the door, but couldn't. "Could you help?"

"Sorry!" She got up and held open the door for him. He slipped inside and set the groceries down, and she followed him in after she'd retrieved her tea and files.

"You'll ruin the surprise if you watch me," he stated.

She shrugged. "Oh, well, I want to know."

"You're so impatient," he teased.

"I know." She rummaged through the bags. "Oh, sour cream. Interesting."

"That was expensive," he muttered.

"Yeah, it can be pricey. Seriously, what are you making?"

"You're kind of a pain."

She frowned. "You're mean."

He chuckled. "Fine. I'm making beef Stroganoff. It's cool out there, the leaves are changing, and it's a comfort food. My nanny used to make this a lot for us, especially when we had a bad day at school or something."

"I guess your mother really didn't have to cook. You guys had servants."

He nodded. "Well, my mother was raised to be Queen and she died when I was young. My nanny was very caring and doting. When I make her recipe it reminds me of her."

"I'm sorry. I forgot. You did tell me you lost your mother young."

"It's okay."

She sighed. "Well, at least you had a nanny who loved you. I had no one, save my father. I never knew my mother."

"You don't talk much about her," he said, as he started to prepare the food. "What happened to her? I'm sorry if it's insensitive, but did she pass on when you were young?"

"No. She left us."

"She left?"

Imogen nodded. "She didn't want to be a mother or a wife. She didn't want to move around so much with my father and his research. She wanted a completely different life, so she left and my father raised me."

"I'm sorry. I thought she was from Yellowknife?"

"She was."

"Did she have parents who lived in Yellowknife?"

"They died before I was born. Truth be told, Dad said she hated Yellowknife. Dad and I traveled, but we always came back to Yellowknife. I think he lived in hope she'd come back."

And then he finally understood why she didn't want to leave, but he kept that thought to himself.

"Well, I'm sorry all the same."

"Thanks, but I can't mourn a person I never knew."

"True, but you can mourn that you never knew her."

She smiled at him, her expression soft. "I suppose so. Either way, I want you to know that I'm here for this baby and I don't plan on leaving him or her. I may not know what it's like to have a mother who stayed, but I had a loving father who taught me so much about being a good parent."

"Then you're one up on me. My father wasn't very loving," he said, as he dumped the chopped meat into the skillet and then washed his hands. "I didn't know my father at all."

Yet he still mourned him. It hurt that his father was gone and he wouldn't get the opportunity to know him. Their chance was gone. There was no turning back, and though he grieved the loss of what could have been, he didn't have time to process it. Over the years Lev had tried to reach out to his father and had been met every time with a cold reception.

Maybe Imogen was right. You couldn't mourn someone you never knew.

"We should think of something happier, like this delicious meal that I'm preparing for you." He grinned and she laughed at him.

"Deal. I look forward to trying it."

"That's a lot of pressure to put on me," he teased.

"I'm sorry, but it does smell good and you seem to know the recipe by heart, so that's encouraging!"

He grinned. "Well, I hope I please you."

"You do." And then he saw a blush creep up her cheeks, as if she was embarrassed he'd caught her admitting something that she might not want him to know, and it thrilled him.

Lev tried to stifle a yawn as he scrubbed out after a simple cholecystectomy, one of the two general surgeries

Imogen had performed today. He hadn't got much sleep last night and it was all his fault. He'd opted to sleep on a very hard floor rather than risk temptation and sleep next to Imogen.

Dinner had gone well and thankfully Imogen didn't think his cooking skills were a waste. She had cleaned up—since he had cooked, she'd said—and then they'd both gone outside to enjoy an autumn evening before their early morning start.

The problem was that in that small double, Imogen had kept rolling over to curl up against him. He would try to move and invariably brush something or touch something he shouldn't.

It had been hard to sleep with her curled up beside him. So instead of trying to make the most of a tight situation, he'd slept on the floor, and now he had a crick in his neck and was exhausted. If he was going to be exhausted, he should have just opted to stay in the bed with her. At least then he wouldn't have had a crick in his neck all day.

"You okay?" Imogen asked, as she came into the scrub room.

"Tired."

"I woke up in the middle of the night and saw you on the floor."

"You were taking up most of the bed," he groused.

"I'm sorry."

He shrugged. "It's okay."

"Well, at least we'll be back in Yellowknife tonight and you can get a good night's sleep."

They finished cleaning up and headed out, but when they got their gear to head to the landing strip, they were told by the director of the hospital that all flights were grounded. There was a massive thunderstorm in Yellowknife and there wouldn't be any flights tonight. That meant they were stuck and both of them were too tired for a hike to the rapids.

So they went back to the modular home. Lev hoped he wouldn't have to spend another restless night on the floor.

The weather in Yellowknife might have been grim, but in Fort Smith it was beautiful. They sat outside, watching the sun go down and waiting for the stars to come out.

"It gets so dark here," he said. "And it's so quiet. Quieter than the city."

"That's because Fort Smith is in Wood Buffalo National Park and it's a dark night preserve."

"It's nice just sitting out here with you." He looked over at her. "I hope we see the northern lights again."

"Me too. It's a bit early for that."

"Well, it's worth the wait."

"It's a spectacular show."

"My favorite part about that night was being with you."

He saw her blush.

"Lev, that... I liked being with you too."

"Do you?" he asked.

"I do. I often think of that night in Toronto." She tucked a loose strand of hair behind her ear. "You made me feel alive that night, Lev. I've never forgotten it."

Her words stirred his blood. Ignited him. It thrilled him to know that she thought of him the same way he thought of her. That she desired him the same way he desired her. The way he wanted her and no one else.

He got up from where he was sitting and knelt in front of her. "I've been thinking about something."

"What's that?" she asked, her voice quiet.

"I've been thinking about that kiss the other day. I've been thinking about how this fake marriage of ours is actually very real to me. You make me feel alive, Imogen, and I haven't felt alive in quite some time."

His words stirred something deep inside her. "I feel the same way about you too, Lev." She ran her hand down his face. "I've never wanted someone more than I wanted you. More than I want you." And then she kissed him and she forgot all the reasons why she shouldn't, because she too had been thinking constantly about their kisses, about Toronto, about him.

She couldn't get it out of her mind.

Lev touched her cheek, brushing his knuckles down her skin, making her tremble with desire. She remembered the way he made her feel before and she wanted to feel that again, even if only for a moment.

If he were to go, she wanted one more night with him. One more chance to savor a moment with him and never forget.

"When you touch me, Lev… I forget everything. All I want is you," she whispered.

"I care about you, Imogen. I've never stopped thinking about you."

"I never stopped thinking about you either." A tear slid down her cheek. She was falling in love with him, only she wouldn't say it out loud. She couldn't. She was scared of what it all meant. Of how much it would hurt.

"I know we can't make any kind of commitment, but I want you, Lev. I know it's a bad idea, but I want you."

Imogen wanted just one more night with him. Just one night so she could get on with her life and know there would be nothing to hold her back. And she wanted more memories of this fantasy, memories of her Prince to sustain her. "Please."

Lev didn't say anything. He just pulled her into his arms and kissed her with such intensity she melted. His touch felt so good. Being in Lev's arms was so wonderful it was just what she needed. Lev made her feel safe and secure. He made her body tremble with desire and her blood sing.

When she was with Lev she forgot everything else. All she thought of was hot, sweet passion that made her blood fire and her toes curl.

She pressed her body against him.

"Imogen, how I've missed you. I've thought of you constantly since that night I had to leave you."

"I've missed you too."

Lev scooped her up in his arms and carried her to the bed they had shared the night before, when it had been awkward and he'd ended up on the floor. They'd both been so restrained since their wedding, but now there was no holding back.

Her body was humming with anticipation. They sank onto the mattress together, kissing. Lev's hands were in her hair, down her back, skimming up her thighs and between her legs, making her mew with pleasure.

There was no more talk. The only sounds were their hearts thundering in their ears, their breath catching, as they slowly undressed each other.

She ran her fingers over the tattoo on his thigh. It was a tree branch, the ink black and the design intricate. She traced the design with her fingertips, causing him to moan.

"You drive me wild," he murmured against her neck.

She smiled, but didn't say anything. Her body was shaking with need and she brought him close. He kissed her all over. Down her neck, over her breasts, making her body arch.

She wrapped her legs around him, urging him to take her, to possess her, to be with her.

Lev slowly entered her. She bit her lip as pleasure coursed through her. Never had anyone made her feel this way. She only wanted Lev.

Even though it scared her, she didn't want anyone else. Ever.

Just him.

She didn't want this night to end. She just wanted this moment to go on and on, the two of them moving together in bliss. It wasn't long before both of them came together in shared pleasure.

When it was over, he held her close, tight against his chest, as if he was afraid to let her go, and in return she clung to him.

He couldn't stay and she couldn't go, so they just lay there and held each other in the darkness.

CHAPTER THIRTEEN

IMOGEN WOKE UP to an empty bed. Lev was nowhere to be found.

She frowned. Her stomach churned. They had spent a blissful night together, and when she'd first woken up everything had seemed so rosy, so perfect.

So wonderful.

She got dressed and headed out into the kitchen, sighing in relief when she saw Lev was outside. She walked outside to join him.

"Good morning," she said, trying to stifle a yawn and hoping she didn't sound stressed, like she had been a moment before.

He smiled at her. "Good morning. Our taxi will be here soon."

"What time is it?" she asked, confused.

"Nine. Our flight leaves in an hour."

"Why didn't you wake me sooner?"

"I wanted to let you sleep." He wrapped his arms around her and kissed her. She laid her head against his chest, listening to his heart beating. It was comforting.

"I'd better get ready," she mumbled.

"Yes."

Imogen kissed him again and headed back inside. Her

heart was still hammering. She'd thought he'd left. Her paranoia was killing her.

He was still here.

But for how long?

It frightened her.

And she hated that.

It didn't take her long to pack, so she was ready when the cab came, and they boarded their flight back to Yellowknife. She planned to go straight to the hospital and check on Henry. She hadn't expected to be away this long and she hoped he was okay and out of the intensive care unit.

"What are you thinking about?" Lev asked.

"Lots of things." She didn't want to tell him she'd been afraid he'd left, afraid he didn't like Fort Smith, afraid he hated the north. He'd seemed so unimpressed, like Allen.

History seemed to be trying to repeat itself.

"What did you think of Fort Smith?"

He looked confused. "It was fine. Small, expensive groceries, but fine."

"No, seriously. You seemed underwhelmed when we landed."

"Not underwhelmed," he said. "More like sad that such a large town is so cut off and so lacking in care."

"Oh." She was surprised.

"It made me think of Marge and Henry having to drive more than two hours for medical care."

"Yeah. It's a serious issue. No one wants to stay."

A strange look passed over his face and instantly she regretted saying it.

It was a short flight, and as they were landing, Imogen saw government vehicles waiting on the tarmac.

"What's going on?" she asked. Then her heart sank. They were here for Lev.

The plane landed, and as soon as the door opened, Lexi walked into the cabin.

"Lexi," Lev shouted happily.

"Your Highness, it's over. We can go home!"

Lev grinned and started speaking Chenarian. Then he clapped Lexi on the back as Lexi left the plane.

"Isn't that wonderful?" Lev asked.

"It is. It really is." Her heart was breaking.

"It means we can go back to Chenar."

"Who's *we*?"

"You and me and Lexi, I suppose. Kristof has ordered me to return."

Imogen sighed. "I'm not going!"

"What?" Lev asked.

"I'm not going. I told you. Yellowknife is my home."

They didn't say much else. The car ride back to the hospital was tense. They were escorted into a private meeting room to discuss plans and details for Lev's return to Chenar. The staff now knew who Lev really was. There was no more need for secrets. He was safe.

Finally it was just the two of them again in a room and the tension between them was palpable.

"What happens now?" she asked, her voice trembling.

"You know what happens. We leave," he replied sternly.

"No, *we* don't."

His gaze locked on hers, his eyes sparkling. "I have no choice. It's my duty and I have to obey my King."

"But I do. I have a choice. You know that. You said this was to protect the baby and me, and now the threat is over."

"You married me!"

"For protection. This is my home."

"If our marriage was so fake, why did you spend the night with me? To manipulate me like other women have tried to?" It was like a slap to the face.

"I beg your pardon?"

"You heard me," he said. "You're selfish and you're afraid."

"How am I selfish? How am I afraid?" she demanded.

"Your past relationships failed because you refused to bend. You refused to leave Yellowknife! You refused because you're afraid to lose anything, to take a risk because of what happened to your father. You stay here thinking your mother will come back, but she won't, yet you refuse to go because here you have control. You're afraid, Imogen, and you're selfish."

His words stung and she didn't want to admit that there was an ounce of truth to them. She was too hurt for that.

"You're the selfish one. You lied to me. You promised me you wouldn't force me to go. Did you sleep with me in the hope I would blindly follow you? I'm not one of your subjects! You used me. Trying to seduce me to convince me to go when you knew it was the last thing I wanted. And for what? You don't love me. How can you? If you loved me, you'd know I can't go. You're not King. Why do you have to go?"

"I didn't ask to be born into this life. I didn't want this, but it's my duty. You know that."

"But it's not *my* duty."

"I'm not free. I have to obey Kristof." Lev's eyes narrowed. "You are my wife and you are part of the royal family now, and I order you to come with me."

"You *order* me? Don't be ridiculous. I'm only your wife on paper. That's it," she snapped.

"You carry my child!"

"You don't believe that."

"What are you talking about?" he asked coldly.

"You don't trust me. Not really. You think we're all like Tatiana, but we aren't. I didn't sleep with anyone else, but still you demanded a paternity test, so why do you care about me or the baby?"

"I care."

Imogen's eyes filled with tears. "If you cared for us, you wouldn't be giving me this ultimatum."

"It's no ultimatum, Imogen. It's the truth."

A tear slipped out of the corner of her eye and she hated herself for falling in love with him. She hated it that she was afraid to leave with him. So many people had left her, had hurt her.

Even her father had left her.

She was angry at herself, but how could she be with someone who didn't trust her, someone who didn't listen to her, who ordered her to follow him? Someone who called her selfish. Someone who didn't love her.

"Goodbye, Lev."

She turned to leave, and though she could hear him calling her name, she wouldn't look back. She couldn't. She was too hurt.

She felt betrayed. He'd lied to her and she didn't know how to come back from that, or if she even could.

Why not?

She shook that thought away and closed the door, knowing that she would never see her baby's father again.

And she hated herself for being too scared to follow him.

Lev stood outside Henry's hospital room door. Henry was awake and Marge was showing him their baby. Lev smiled at them. Then felt a pang of longing. He didn't want to leave, but he had no choice.

He'd let his father down enough. He had to be what Kristof needed.

He had hurt Imogen and he was hurt himself that she didn't love him enough to go with him.

You knew she wouldn't.

He sighed and walked away. He'd been too hard on her. If he wasn't duty-bound, he'd stay here with her. He could be so happy here. Being with her here felt like home. It felt right, but there was nothing he could do. Lexi found him wandering the hall.

"We're trying to get Kristof on the phone again," Lexi said. "He's heard about your wife."

"She's not coming to Chenar."

Lexi sighed. "So I heard."

"I have no choice but to leave."

"You do have a choice," Lexi stated.

"No, I don't. You know Kristof. I'm honor-bound to him. I was a disappointment to my father and selfish practicing medicine. Now Kristof is alone and has to re-build by himself. I have to go."

"No, you don't. Talk to Kristof."

"He won't understand. He's just like my father."

"In some ways, but not all ways." Lexi rolled his eyes. "You're a fool, Your Highness, if you let her go. Don't be so afraid. Don't use your duty as an excuse not to make difficult choices. There's nothing standing between you and the life you want."

"I thought you didn't like Imogen."

"I never said that. I was worried about you both. She was just one more person to worry about, including the baby."

"What if she actually doesn't want me?" Lev asked. "Most women just want my title. If I stay here, I give that up."

"She doesn't want that and you know it." Lexi sighed. "You can be so distrusting, but it's time to let go of the past."

Lev scrubbed a hand over his face. "I've ruined everything. I don't want to leave Yellowknife. I like it here, but I am a prince…"

"You have a choice. You can stay, but are you willing to make a life here? Is Imogen willing to make a life with you?"

"I doubt it. I hurt her."

"You can make it up to her."

"How?" Lev asked.

"You can grovel." Lexi smiled. "Talk to Kristof. He will understand. The situation in Chenar has stabilized and everyone is focused on rebuilding. I will go back to help."

"And if I have to return, she won't follow. She had relationships that ended because she wouldn't leave Yellowknife. She lives on that houseboat that belonged to her late father and she won't leave."

"Perhaps she's still grieving. Perhaps she's afraid. Just like you."

The words sank in. He was afraid. Afraid he wasn't good enough. Afraid he wouldn't be a good father. He used Tatiana as an excuse to keep women away, to keep Imogen away. He was not his father and neither was Kristof. He had a chance for happiness here, if he'd only take it. Lev knew what he had to do. He had to find Imogen and tell her. He had to make it right. He loved her and he'd hurt her deeply. Of course she was grieving. Everyone she'd loved had left. And he'd broken her trust trying to convince her—and then order her—to come with him, two things he'd promised he wouldn't do when she'd agreed to marry him.

"I have to find Imogen."

Lexi nodded. "Good. Go and make it right."

He was going to make sure she didn't feel afraid. He wanted her to know that he was just as afraid as she was. He was uncertain of the future and what it held. He didn't know what was going to happen with his country.

The only thing he knew for certain was that he loved her and he couldn't let her go. He couldn't leave her behind and he wasn't going to force her to come with him either. As much as he loved being a surgeon, as much as he loved saving lives, he would give it all up to be with her.

Lev ran down the hall, searching for her, but she was nowhere to be found, and then he caught a glimpse of her with her coat on and she was leaving.

"Imogen!" he called out.

She turned around and frowned when she saw him, then turned back to continue walking away.

He ran after her and grabbed her by the arm.

"Let me go," she whispered under her breath.

"No. I won't let you go."

She stepped back, stunned. "What are you talking about?"

"I won't let you go. I'm not leaving."

Her expression fell. "You have to leave. You said so yourself. You're duty-bound."

"No. I'm not. And I'm not leaving you or Yellowknife. If this is where you need to stay, if this is where you need to raise our child, then I'm staying."

"Lev, a prince can't stay in Canada."

"This one can. Kristof will understand. I'm staying here with you. This is my home now."

"Everyone at the hospital knows who you are."

"Then I won't work here." He shrugged. "All that matters is that we're together."

"You love being a surgeon... You can't give that up!"

"I can, to be with you. To stay with you. I love you, Imogen. I lost you once before and I won't lose you again. I can't live without you."

Imogen couldn't quite hear the words that were coming out of his mouth. She couldn't quite believe it.

It was what she had been wanting to hear for so long, she just didn't believe that it could be happening.

"I love you too, but..."

"I know you're still struggling with your father's death and your mother's abandonment. I know that's why you don't want to leave, but you've lived in other places before."

Her lip trembled. "This is where I was born and this is where my father was going to stay in case she came back. That's why I was staying here."

Lev pulled her in close and he held her. She wrapped her arms around him.

"Then this is where I'll stay. I need to stay with you. I can't lose you or the baby."

Imogen wiped away a tear. "What about the paternity test?"

"I know it's mine, Imogen. You've never lied to me. Never. The best I can do is ask for your forgiveness and hope that you will forgive me. I love you. I'm sorry I tried to force you to make a decision I promised you would never have to make."

"Oh, Lev." She kissed him and then leaned her forehead against his. "I love you too and I'm sorry. I will go anywhere with you. You're right. I was holding on to something that is never going to happen. I thought that by planting myself here, my mother would come and find me, but she won't. I don't even know if she's dead or alive, and I have been mourning what I don't know and what I'm never going to know my whole life. I do know one thing. If I let you leave without me, I'm throwing away something I've always wanted—a family. I'm throwing away a chance for our child."

"I love you, Imogen."

They kissed again and then they walked hand in hand back to where they knew the government officials were waiting to take him away.

He was going to tell them that he was staying. He'd talk to his brother and explain. This was his family. He would always be there for Chenar and, if it came to it, he now knew that Imogen would be there with him.

They were each other's family.

That was all that mattered.

When they walked into the boardroom she could sense a change in the air. There was a buzz and Lev felt it too.

"Your Highness," Lexi said as he bowed.

"I've come to tell you that I'm not leaving my wife. And I'm not leaving Yellowknife. I'm staying here."

Lexi smiled. "That is fine. King Kristof wants you to stay and be an ambassador for Chenar in Canada."

"An ambassador?" Imogen asked.

Lexi nodded. "You'll have to spend some time in Ottawa, though, at least half the year."

"Can you live with that, Imogen? Can you do that for me?" Lev asked.

"Of course," Imogen said.

Lev's eyes filled with tears and he held her close.

"It seems, Your Highness, that you don't require so much protection anymore. The civil unrest is over and your brother is King. You will be safe here in Canada."

Imogen hugged Lev and he pulled her in close.

"What does this mean now?" she asked. "Do we need to go to Ottawa now?"

"No. Prince Viktor still has to remain here and we're trying to patch through another call so he can talk to his brother. From there, we'll work with the consulate and the government to figure out the next steps. For now, you're both staying in Yellowknife."

Lev smiled. "Thank you, Lexi. I appreciate all your help. I will miss you."

"You might as well both go home and we can patch a call through onto your cell phone," Lexi said.

Lexi turned back to the others in the room as they went to work, making arrangements and figuring out the next steps.

"What would you like to do now?" Imogen asked.

"I would like to go home."

"Home to Chenar or the houseboat?" she teased.

"The houseboat. Wherever you are is my home, Imogen. One day, when my brother needs me, I will go back, but for now, there's a lot to figure out and I have to take care of you and our child." He reached down and touched her belly. Although he couldn't feel it yet, there was a nudge, and she placed her hand over his.

"Let's go home."

EPILOGUE

A year later

THE PLANE TOUCHED down and Lev's heart was soaring as he glanced out of the window and saw the familiar sights of Chenar.

A place that, at one time, he'd never thought he would see again.

His home.

Or at least the country of his birth. His home was now in Canada with Imogen and their daughter, Aurora, but he was still glad to be back for his brother's coronation, his wife and daughter by his side.

As the plane taxied toward the private hangar, he could see the royal motorcade waiting. He spotted Lexi right away, standing at the end of the red carpet.

Imogen was holding Aurora, who, at seven months old, wouldn't remember any of this, but at least she had the freedom now to come to Chenar with him. To understand her roots.

"Lexi is out there," Lev said happily.

Imogen smiled. "I'm glad he's here. I know your brother is working hard to rebuild, but I'm still worried."

"No more worries. Lexi will take good care of us, just

like he took care of us in Yellowknife. At least this time we won't be out on the water. We'll be in the palace."

"Aw, I kind of miss him driving by in his motorboat or hanging out in his apartment with his binoculars, watching."

Lev chuckled. "Don't tell him that or he'll come back to Yellowknife."

"Maybe he should. Maybe he wants to."

"I'll leave that up to Lexi. This time he can live on the houseboat instead of us renting it out to tourists."

"What? You don't want him living in our house near Jackfish Lake? There's lots of room to build him his own place."

"No! Don't get any ideas, Imogen. I lived with that man for too long and had him control my life. He's not moving into the guesthouse."

She laughed, but he could tell she was nervous about meeting Kristof and being formally introduced to the country as Prince Viktor's wife. She had a hard time thinking of him as anything other than Lev.

Lev didn't want her to think of him as anyone else. With her, he could be himself, whatever name she called him by.

In Yellowknife, he was still a trauma surgeon and she was still a general surgeon, or she would be when she returned from maternity leave.

He liked his life in his new home, but he was also glad to return to Chenar and hold his head up high. And most of all he was glad that his brother was restoring their country. The only downside to the formality of the coronation was that he had to shave his beard off, which he'd grown fond of, as well as cut his long hair, which his wife liked.

When they got back to Canada he could grow it all back.

The doors opened and Lev stood.

"Are you ready for this?" he asked.

"Yes. I think so."

"You'll do fine." He took her hand and kissed it. "You're with me and I'm so proud of you. Both of you."

He kissed his sleeping daughter on the forehead.

"I'm glad you're both here. I couldn't do this without you."

"You could have," she said.

"Perhaps, but the point is I don't want to. I was a fool when I almost walked away from you. I don't know what I was thinking."

"You were afraid, much like I was. I never thought I would ever get married, not after what happened to my parents. I didn't think that love and marriage could last. I didn't think it was possible, not for me."

"Me either, but I'm so glad we were wrong."

"Me too."

"And I'm glad that I'm able to bring you both to Chenar so you can see where I grew up and see my home. I wouldn't want to do this without you both."

Imogen kissed him on the lips. "And you don't have to."

Lev nodded. The door to the private plane opened and Lexi appeared. He had cut his hair and shaved his beard too. There were times neither of them had thought this day would come, when Chenar would be a safe place for everyone again.

Lev hugged Lexi in the privacy of the plane. He'd missed his friend, even though he tried to deny it. He'd missed having Lexi in Yellowknife.

"It's so good to see you, my friend," Lev said. "I've missed you nagging at me in Yellowknife."

"I've missed you—and Yellowknife too, if I'm honest." Lexi gazed at Imogen. "Your Highness, it's so good to see you and the little Princess are healthy."

Imogen stepped forward and kissed Lexi on the cheek. "It's so good to see you too, Lexi. I've missed you."

Lexi laughed. "Now, that is a bare-faced lie."

"How is Kristof doing?" Lev asked.

"He's ready to become crowned and he's thrilled the three of you are here. How long do you plan on staying in Chenar?" Lexi asked.

"A month at least, but then we have to get back before the fall…before the winter storms."

Lexi looked wistful. "I don't suppose you want a bodyguard? I mean, someone has to protect the little Princess."

"We would love to have you back in Yellowknife, Lexi," said Imogen. "In fact, we have a bunkhouse on our property…"

Lev glared at her, but only in jest.

Lexi bowed. "Thank you. You are too gracious. Now, if you'll head out, the car is waiting and I will follow."

Lev took a deep breath and took a step outside. His country's anthem was playing once again and there was a small group of people cheering. He waved, waiting for Imogen to come down the stairs. She was wearing heels and a dress, which he knew made her uncomfortable, just like his military uniform made him uncomfortable, but it was only for a short while.

Soon they could go home, to the north, where it was just the three of them.

A prince, his wife and their daughter.
A life where he was free and could be himself.
His home.

* * * * *

COMING SOON!

We really hope you enjoyed reading this book.
If you're looking for more romance, be sure to
head to the shops when new books are
available on

Thursday 28th May

MILLS & BOON

Coming next month

FROM HAWAII TO FOREVER
Julia Danvers

It had been like this for the past few days. He was able to focus just fine during the emergency jobs. Just like always, when Jack was in the middle of an emergency, he was at his peak performance. There was something about getting caught up completely in the moment to focus on a medical emergency that allowed him to re-center himself, no matter what kind of emotional turmoil he might be going through.

But during the quieter times, when his mind had time to wander…it wandered straight back to Kat.

And specifically to that kiss with Kat. He was completely mortified by his lack of professionalism. He'd been struggling to maintain a detached, clinical demeanor, and he'd utterly failed. Kat had been vulnerable and afraid, and he'd taken advantage of her vulnerability. He couldn't have felt worse.

But couldn't keep his mind from returning to the way his hand had fit perfectly around her hip. The softness of her skin. The way her hair tickled his face when he buried his nose in it, and inhaled the faint tropical scent that wafted from her.

To make matters even worse, not only had he failed to hold himself to a professional standard…he'd liked kissing Kat. He'd felt… desire.

The plain fact was, he wanted more of Kat. Try as he might to deny it, he knew, deep down, that he wasn't going to stop thinking about her. His body burned to finish what they'd started.

But would Kat even want to talk to him, after he'd let himself get so carried away? They'd known each other for a little over a month, and yet this was already the second time he'd been unprofessional with her in a medical setting.

And yet, during their kiss, he'd felt her hands clutching at him, sensed her body pressing against his. In the heat of that moment, she had wanted him, too.

He had tried to give Kat plenty of space since the quarantine had ended. He didn't want her to feel that he expected any more of her than she wanted to give. If she were interested in him, then she could make the next move.

He wouldn't blame Kat if she never wanted to see him again.

Which was why he was completely surprised when he turned around with his supply box and saw her standing in front of him.

"Sorry," she said. "Didn't mean to startle you."

She walked up to Jack and took the supply box from him, setting it onto the floor. "Well, this takes me back," she said. "It's been a couple weeks since we were in such close quarters together."

Was she angry at him?

Her face bore the same resolute look, with the same determined set of her lips that he'd noticed while in quarantine. Whatever she wanted to talk to him about, he realized that there was no avoiding it. Not when she looked like that.

"I've been thinking," she said. "We're both adults. We've gotten to know each other quickly, in a pretty short amount of time, due to circumstances beyond our control. But no matter how unusual those circumstances may have been, they don't change the fact that we're in this situation now."

"And...what exactly is our situation?"

She took a deep breath. "I've been thinking a lot about that moment in quarantine."

He waited, without breathing. He thought his heart might have stopped.

She went on. "You know the moment I mean. When we...kissed." Her eyes flickered straight to his, and he knew his heart hadn't stopped after all. It was pounding jackhammer-hard.

"I don't know about you," she said, "But I've had a hard time not thinking about it. The kiss, I mean. And I know that you said you don't believe in relationships. Well, neither do I. But in a way, that makes us kind of ideal for one another, right now."

He wondered where this was going. "How so?" he said.

"Well," she continued, looking nervous but determined to carry her point through, "anything involving emotions would probably be a terrible idea, for both of us. But then I started thinking that not every relationship has to involve emotions. Some relationships have a more...physical... basis."

He was suddenly very aware that without the supply box in his arms, there was nothing between the two of them. He would barely have to reach to slip an arm around her waist. Her nose was inches from his. It was very hard to think clearly, with her standing so close.

"Emotions are complicated," he agreed, his voice growing husky. "Are you suggesting that we try letting things get more...physical...between us?"

Continue reading
FROM HAWAII TO FOREVER
Julia Danvers

Available next month
www.millsandboon.co.uk

MILLS & BOON

THE HEART OF ROMANCE

A ROMANCE FOR EVERY KIND OF READER

MODERN

Prepare to be swept off your feet by sophisticated, sexy and seductive heroes, in some of the world's most glamourous and romantic locations, where power and passion collide.
8 stories per month.

HISTORICAL

Escape with historical heroes from time gone by. Whether your passion is for wicked Regency Rakes, muscled Vikings or rugged Highlanders, awaken the romance of the past.
6 stories per month.

MEDICAL

Set your pulse racing with dedicated, delectable doctors in the high-pressure world of medicine, where emotions run high and passion, comfort and love are the best medicine.
6 stories per month.

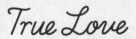

Celebrate true love with tender stories of heartfelt romance, from the rush of falling in love to the joy a new baby can bring, and a focus on the emotional heart of a relationship.
8 stories per month.

Indulge in secrets and scandal, intense drama and plenty of sizzling hot action with powerful and passionate heroes who have it all: wealth, status, good looks…everything but the right woman.
6 stories per month.

HEROES

Experience all the excitement of a gripping thriller, with an intense romance at its heart. Resourceful, true-to-life women and strong, fearless men face danger and desire - a killer combination!
8 stories per month.

DARE

Sensual love stories featuring smart, sassy heroines you'd want as a best friend, and compelling intense heroes who are worthy of them.
4 stories per month.

To see which titles are coming soon, please visit
millsandboon.co.uk/nextmonth

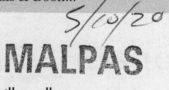